D1547888

Primary Intent

A Novel

Eric Gee

PublishAmerica
Baltimore

ISBN: 1-4241-6604-7
PUBLISHED BY PUBLISHAMERICA, LLLP
www.publishamerica.com
Baltimore

Printed in the United States of America

For my father.
Without your dreams this would never had been possible...

Doc,

I hope you enjoy this. I am very much looking forward to reading yours next.

Eric

Preface

Terrance Smith stared at the dirty ceiling of his small dingy two-room alley apartment just north of China Town. Sprawled out on the queen size bed, one arm folded under his head, the other held a cigarette. Beside him was the latest in a long line of whores he had used to satisfy his urgings. He had met her an hour ago. Convincing her that she was the most beautiful person he had ever met wasn't really all that hard. This one was actually the easiest one yet. It didn't even take half an hour and she was crawling on her hands and knees toward him naked and willing. He would treat a dog better than he did her.

She stirred awake, rolling over, facing him, sliding one hand up his body, resting it on his chest. Terrance didn't acknowledge the movement of the body next to him as he exhaled the smoke. She moaned and rolled over on top of him, kissing his neck. He pushed her aside, stood and pulled on his pants.

"Terrance, baby, that was awesome. You touched me in ways I have never felt before, you were so deep," the young girl sighed, out of breath.

"Get up, I have some things to take care of."

"Come back to bed, we have just started."

"Didn't you hear me, bitch, I said I have things to do."

Tears formed in the corners of the young girl's eyes as she pulled the top sheet off the bed to cover herself as she groped on the floor for her clothes. She felt like a cheap slut. Why was he treating her like this now after he screamed his love for her not fifteen minutes before?

Terrance grabbed her arm and pulled her away from the bed, dragging her through the narrow, dark living room. With a rage in his eyes he threw her out the door into the frigid night air. She was still wrapped in the sheet as she landed hard on the sidewalk. He tossed her clothes behind her so she could dress in the filthy street. He closed the door, locked it and walked the sidewalk away from her without once looking back over his shoulder.

"You are a bastard!" she shouted in his direction but he didn't even flinch. She threw a shoe at his back but it fell short and she slumped to the dirty sidewalk sobbing uncontrollably. She didn't know why she felt this way. This was not the first time she had done something stupid since leaving home a year ago. Standing cold and naked in the streets was almost a premonition in her mind, but still she allowed him between her legs in a vain attempt to find love.

"American women are too easy," Terrance whispered under his breath as he ignored the crying and rounded the corner. It was as if they didn't have the self-respect to stop themselves from becoming absolute whores. He wasn't complaining, he had no problems getting laid. He had seduced many within hours of meeting them, and he had to admit they were much more active in bed than the women back home.

The young girl, still sobbing, shamefully dressed on the sidewalk and walked in the opposite direction as the man she had just made love to. She was cursing him under her breath as the tears continued to flow from her reddened eyes. She wiped them away with her dirty hands, but still they flowed. She didn't know anything about him but that didn't matter; it wouldn't have changed what she had just done.

What she didn't know was that Terrance was not his real name. Yassad Mouhammad had slinked the streets of Washington D.C. for the past two years, looking and listening for information to send back home. His primary mission was to find promising targets for future operations. He spent most of his time taking pictures and writing notes on various security details for the locations that were specified by his contact. Yassad sent the information he had gathered to a generic e-mail address from several Internet cafes so that they couldn't be traced. Most days, however, he spent on street corners watching people.

When he returned later that evening, the girl was standing by his door. He looked at her dirty, tear-stained face and bloodshot eyes and felt a tinge of pitiful sorrow. He invited her in and within minutes they were intertwined on the soiled sheets. This one was a minx, she would be one to keep for a while, he thought as he neared his climax. Over the next six months he used her for whatever he wanted. He treated her as if she was a piece of property because that is what women were to him. Middle Eastern women were property with no human rights and very few freedoms. She didn't care, she had a roof over her head and food to eat.

She had kept the fact that she was pregnant from him for as long as she could. With her belly growing, it was obvious, and she had to tell him. She had convinced herself that he loved her enough to take care of her and the baby and was telling him tonight, but she was afraid. She was setting the table as he walked through the door. He had left the previous evening and had been gone all day, which was not uncommon anymore.

"Terrance, baby, I am pregnant with our child," she blurted as he pulled a chair out from the table.

"What did you say, whore?" he yelled, throwing the chair back under the table.

"I said I am going to have your baby."

Terrance stared into her eyes in disbelief. He had heard that American women did this to trap men into relationships. He had spent enough time on the streets to hear the stories.

"Bitch, why weren't you more careful?"

Tears quickly filled her eyes as she looked down at the floor. She heard his footsteps approach her from the front but she did not look up. Why did she think he would have been happy with the news?

Terrance could not have this. He could not leave any ties in this country. Anger rose in his blood as he raised his right hand across his body. He swung wildly, connecting the back of his hand with her temple. The impact threw her body across the small kitchen against the wall. She hit back first and her momentum caused her head to snap back against the wall with a dull thud. A spine-jarring pain flashed up her spine until it burst into a million stars in front of her eyes and then everything suddenly went black. Her body, now limp, slid slowly to the floor as Terrance rushed her once again. He pulled her up and punched her face, breaking her nose, splattering blood onto the floor and wall.

He had to kill her. He had to destroy all evidence that this ever existed. With a fury in his eye that would have made Allah proud, he wrapped both hands around the young girl's thin neck and squeezed the life out of her. The body once again fell lifeless to the floor and he checked the wrist for a pulse.

The rage ebbed from his body as relief set in. He opened the door and looked up and down the dimly lit street. It was dark but still early, and no cars traveled the street in this neighborhood when the sun went down. He immediately dragged her body out the door and deposited it on a corner under a discarded cardboard box and two bags of garbage. He walked away as if he didn't have a care in the world. Minutes later, two police cars and an ambulance screeched to a halt on the corner. Thankfully, an alert driver in a passing car had noticed the body and dialed 911 on his cell phone.

"What do we have?" the lead paramedic asked, pulling the large medical kit from the side door of the ambulance.

"It appears we have a white female, 15-20 years old with bruising on the left temple, a fractured septum, and skull trauma."

"Vital signs?"

"I don't have a pulse, but I do detect a faint breathing pattern."

"Bring out the cot, and we will get her to the emergency room. If she is breathing, she is stable enough to transport."

Minutes later the ambulance pulled under the overhanging entrance to the emergency room, at the Howard University Hospital. By the time they had arrived, the young girl had been revived.

"What is your name?" the paramedic asked her, trying to determine if she was suffering brain damage or memory loss.

"My baby, how is my baby?" she asked frantically.

"Everything will be just fine, we need to know your name."

"Tonya," she said groggily, trying to focus on the words.

"Where are you from, Tonya?" The paramedics continued the questions as he checked her pupil dilation.

"I live on the north side," she said, blinking through the brightness of the pen light.

The cot was pushed through the sliding doors and into trauma room. Nurses pushed open the curtains separating the beds and took over for the paramedics. The hand-over briefing was finished and Tonya was checked for additional injuries. The emergency room doctor bandaged her nose with a thin metal splint and left her to recover in silence, leaving a nurse to get the insurance information and schedule the MRI.

"Tonya, where do you live, sweetie?"

"I live on the north side of the city," Tonya said in a short answer.

"Do you have family that we can contact to let them know you are okay?"

"No!"

"Could you tell me how this happened?"

"I fell into the pile of trash after I tripped on the curb."

"How many months are you along?"

"I think I am six or seven months."

"Who is your OB doctor?" the nurse asked, hoping to get some information from her records.

"I haven't been to a doctor."

The nurse sat back and shook her head in amazement. She knew Tonya was hiding something, the terse answers were a dead giveaway. It was no surprise. Girls on the street often didn't talk because they were too afraid of the repercussions. The bruising around her throat could only indicate that whoever did this wanted to kill her and probably thought she was dead.

"If you want to talk, my name is Karen. Push the call button, and I will come right in. You know, there is a shelter for women just like you, offering support and guidance and it is close to the hospital where I could look in on you. I would love to take you there when you are released so you can begin to mend."

"That won't be necessary, I can—" Her voice trailed off as her eye lids started to close. The girl had been through so much the past twelve hours. She passed out more from exhaustion than the medication. Karen pulled the sheets over the girl and let her sleep.

Terrance knew that he had not killed the girl, and was angry at himself for being so careless. He didn't feel a pulse, so he just assumed she was dead. He watched the ambulance drop her off at the hospital and had kept close surveillance on the building for the next few days. Late in the afternoon on the fifth day, he saw a nurse push a wheel chair out of the main entrance to a car he did not recognize. He did, however, recognize the person in the wheel chair.

Karen helped Tonya into the passenger seat of her car. She had convinced the young girl to visit the shelter to see if she would feel comfortable. Karen had never gotten close to patients during her off duty, but Tonya was different. Tonya felt more like a daughter and she desperately needed help.

She glanced over at Tonya and saw her take a deep breath.

"It will be okay, I promise. I will be with you through this," Karen said, taking hold of the girl's hand, squeezing it tightly.

Tonya said nothing, flashing a guarded smile.

Terrance followed the car the four blocks to the shelter. He watched the two exit the car and walk inside. Perfect, now what was he going to do? He would surely be denied access to the girl until the baby was born.

For the next two months he watched the building daily. He had curtailed his normal scouting, spending the majority of his time outside the shelter. He saw Tonya walking outside one day enjoying the warmth of the sun. He noticed how large her belly had grown and also noticed a strange woman walking beside her. He wanted to find out what they were talking about. He sat on a bench near the sidewalk facing away from the road, but still within earshot, making sure Tonya did not see him. The two stopped close to the bench, unaware of the once familiar man.

"Please, honey, take this money. I want you to have enough to be comfortable. I know this heat makes it unbearable for you."

"No, really I don't need anything."

"I can't tell you, Tonya, how excited my husband and I are about the baby. We have the nursery ready and will give the baby all the love we have to give."

Terrance couldn't believe his ears. Tonya was going to give the baby away. There was something about the woman that was strangely familiar, he thought, as he walked away from the bench and circled back toward his apartment. The next day he returned with a camera. He wanted to capture the woman on film in hopes he could identify her. A few shots of her profile and five of her walking toward him and he was ready to have them developed.

What he found was almost too good to be true. The vice president's wife; it couldn't be. His son was going to be the adopted son of the vice president.

That night he stopped into an Internet café that he had never been to. His hands shook as he handled the disk with pictures on it that would soon be attached to the most important e-mail message he had ever made. His mentor, Nassir, would be proud of him today.

Chapter 1

How easy it is for the privacy of one's actions to conflict with the growth of the government, thought John Bastian as he walked down the long hallway exhausted from the sixteen-hour day he had just put in. His long white coat that hung down to just above his knees was now wrinkled, and it covered his pressed shirt and tie he wore every day on the floor. He normally had another freshly pressed coat in his office for days like this. He combed his long fingers, which had provided him with the skills of a successful physician, through his hair as he walked, amazed that he had made it through the night as he thought how quickly life was born and then died.

Although a little gray around his temples, the years had been kind to him. His age gave him a certain rugged masculinity that had been carried over from his athletic youth. John, at nearly seventy, was still very athletic, playing racquetball twice a week at the local gym and getting in a round of golf when he could fit it into his hectic schedule. However, his one true passion was sailing, and the position at Johns Hopkins was perfect for a sailor. Aside from being a premier hospital and a dream job, it was near the Baltimore Harbor and close to the water. The position required him to work sixty to seventy hours per week, but he could take three days off here and there to keep him sane.

John had spent almost his entire career in some aspect of labor and delivery in many hospitals throughout Maryland. He devoted his life to it and loved the work. When the director's position opened up at this hospital, he applied as an afterthought and never in his wildest imagination did he think he would get the job. He knew he had the qualifications but also knew that jobs like these were often filled with those having political connections to hospital administration.

He could remember the day he found out he was chosen for the position three years ago and the happiness that filled him as he told his wife, and they celebrated with a night out on the town. Throughout his long career he had received many promotions, but this one proved to be the most satisfying primarily because of the reputation of the hospital, but at sixty-seven he was long past his prime. He could not remember feeling so elated except for the births of their two children many years before. The new job required them to move, but they were used to moving, and this move they both wanted to make. Their kids lived near Baltimore, and they both wanted to be closer to them and their four young grandchildren.

Now, he was just thankful that he was strong enough to walk to his office to finish the shift reports and recap the day. He was used to the long hours and working dead on his feet, but he was getting too old to work many more of these double shifts. After forty years, he was ready to slow down.

He walked into the staff bathroom on the way back to his office to freshen himself up enough to write the tedious shift reports. He stepped up to the sink and carefully examined the image he saw in the mirror looking back at him. His skin, tanned very dark from the long hours he spent on the water, made him look twenty years younger. His dark hair had just started to fill in with gray, giving him a distinguished look, and his chin sported a few days of growth from not being at home much to shave. He cupped his hands under the faucet, filled them with cool water, and splashed it over his face, hoping it would provide him with enough energy to make it the rest of the shift. The water made him feel better for the moment, but he knew the feeling would not last long so he hastily dried off with a towel and continued on to his office.

His eyes burned a little when he entered his office as the morning sun hit him. His small office was plainly decorated with traditional hospital office furniture; he was never one to overindulge in expensive furniture. It was, however, large enough to accommodate a round conference table where he conducted staff and patient update meetings. The only personal decorations were three pictures of his wife and kids on his desk and a large picture of his sailboat, *Sailor's Dream*, on the wall opposite his desk, so he could look at it when the job became stressful. He remembered the day that picture was taken. The boat was heeling at thirty degrees with the mainsail, jib and colorful spinnaker full of wind making the boat silently slice through the water; oh, how he would love to be there right now.

Finishing a double shift, filling in for a colleague on vacation was simply exhausting. He was hit with three births and another two in hard labor just as his shift started. He enjoyed the work tremendously but was overly tired from the long night. He sat in his chair and rubbed his face, feeling how rough it was, and thought about the time away from his wife. He sighed deeply and began writing, but the exhaustion had not just hit his body, it had also taken its toll on his mind as it wandered far too much to focus on the paperwork. He had updated the individual patient records as he made his last rounds. These were his personal records of his shift activities and were difficult to write in his state.

It took the little energy he had left to start the first line, and even then he started thinking about the weekend and his plans of sailing out into the bay for two days and his upcoming retirement. He was happy about retiring and being able to spend more time with his family and doing the other things he loved, but he was also saddened over leaving something to which he had devoted almost his entire life. He pushed the paper away and sat back in his large executive style leather chair, staring at the picture on the wall. Exhausted and reminiscent, John rolled a pen between his fingers as his mind slipped deeper and deeper into aimless thoughts about his career and how it began.

BEEP...BEEP...BEEP...BEEP...BEEP

"Shit," John said under his breath as the beeper broke his thoughts. He looked at his watch and wondered how long he had been sitting there in his chair. Ten minutes—impossible. He rubbed the tired out of his eyes and scratched his head to get moving again. He looked at the LED on the beeper and saw the emergency digits. He stood quickly and rushed through his office door. He was practically running down the hallway to the delivery room, his long white coat chasing behind him. With his blood now pumping, and his mind fully alert, the immediate adrenaline rush he received when the emergency alarm went off gave him a familiar high.

"What is it, Nurse Thomas?" John asked as he rounded the corner to the ward.

"It's the young girl, she's having some difficulty, and we can't stop the contractions. It's the baby, sir, the heartbeat keeps dropping off."

"Shit, not this one. We can't lose this one. Please prep the mother for surgery, I'm not taking any chances on this. Let me know when she's ready. Also, get Dr. Austin on the phone. I want a spinal done; with the baby having difficulty, I don't want to run the risk of putting her under."

Dr. Tom "Painless" Austin was one of the best anesthesiologists at the hospital, probably even the States.

"Is she ready?"

"Yes she is; she won't feel a thing, I'll stake my reputation on it."

"Excellent, I'm glad you were in the hospital. It's early, I know how you like to keep banker's hours," John sarcastically said as he walked on to the operating room.

"How is the retirement planning going?" Tom asked, following behind the doctor.

"It's not. I have been so busy here that I have not had time to think about it," John said as he methodically picked up the scalpel.

"Ahh, I can see it now, you will have one of those 'honey-do' lists like all old timers have," Tom said, monitoring her vital signs closely.

"Shit, I would be happy to finally be able to do things around the house. I will watch the grandkids too."

"Ahh, yes, the happy babysitter," Tom said playfully, trying to get a rise out of him. "What are you going to do with your spare time?"

"I play racquetball from time to time."

"Well, you will have to find something more to keep you busy. I don't have to tell you how many people have not lived five years of their retirement."

"Don't worry about that, my dear friend, I have that covered."

"Well, at least you made a good choice for your replacement. I met her yesterday and she is a real looker, very easy on the eyes."

"Please stay away from her, Tom, she will have enough on her hands without having to dodge your endless string of bad pick-up lines," and with that the operation was finished.

*

Dr. John Bastian stood in the operating room admiring the very healthy baby boy crying on the metal table. The baby fussed as the nurse removed the fluid from his nose and throat, but the crying was always a good sign. The labor had been a difficult one for the mother, a young seventeen-year-old single girl from the city. She was alone, and he knew she was scared from the moment she arrived. The mother was crying uncontrollably as she looked at her son lying naked on the table, partly because of the life she had just given birth to, but mostly because she knew she had to give the baby up. She didn't want to be a mother at such a young age, but she waited too long to go through with an abortion. John knew that she had stayed at the women's shelter and that she probably had a tough time with her boyfriend after she became pregnant. But that was all he knew.

The nurse had finished cleaning and performing the normal battery of APGAR tests on the little boy, quickly wrapped him in a blanket, and took him from the room. The tears flowed even heavier down the girl's cheek as soon as she realized the repercussions of her decision.

John was busy doing his usual post birth checks on the mother as he had done hundreds of times before, realizing this would probably be one of the last.

He told the nurse to wheel the mother to her room as he walked to the nursery. He held the boy for a second, admiring the incredible gift of life, and then placed him in a covered hospital bassinet. John pushed the bassinet out of the nursery, down the empty hall, stopping at a solid wood door.

The placard on the wall next to the windowless door read post-delivery testing and John pulled his keys from his white coat pocket. The door was always locked and only the head of the floor was allowed inside, and in fact, possessed the only key to the room. Babies delivered in the hospital went through the same testing procedure, and John had performed each of them alone at this hospital since taking the job.

The room was sparsely decorated. A solitary stainless steel table stood in the middle of the room. A sterile foam pad held in place by a three-inch thin metal rim around the entire top was the only thing that could provide a clue as to what it was used for. An unpainted metal cabinet that looked as if it belonged more in a mechanics repair shop then a hospital maternity ward was pushed up against the far wall. The only light came from a single fluorescent fixture in the ceiling, illuminating the white floor, walls, and ceiling. Every hospital in the United States with a maternity ward had a similar room, set up exactly the same way, used for the same purpose.

He wheeled the bassinet next to the padded table and used his set of keys to open the dull metal cabinet. The inside of the cabinet had a shelf with a laptop computer and three drawers underneath it. Each one of them locked, requiring different keys. John opened the computer on the shelf, turned it on, and typed in his password, allowing it to boot into the operating system. He quickly double-clicked the NanoSoft icon located on the hard drive, starting the program. The new technology John didn't really understand, but he did know that the laptop was equipped with a satellite Internet connection linking it with the national registry of births located on a mainframe in the National Security Agency. The large database had a record of every birth in the United States for the past forty-five years. Locating the new birth menu, he typed in all of the necessary information, birth weight, mother's name, and other demographic data, methodically completing each field.

When all required fields were filled, John clicked on "new number," and the next available identification number appeared on the screen. Sliding the top drawer out, he removed a device that looked like a small handgun, but was nothing more than a digital transmitter. It had a trigger, an LCD screen on the top, and a barrel that housed the transmitter. He connected the transmitter to a port on the computer and moved the mouse on the computer to download the number. The process took less than five seconds, and the unique number, along with various other important data, was loaded into the gun. As the window popped up on the computer, indicating that the download was complete, he turned the laptop off and closed it. He pulled the second drawer out and removed a package containing a small syringe and a vial filled with what appeared to be water.

He noticed how low the supply was and wrote a quick note on his clipboard to remind himself to requisition more from the NSA as soon as he returned to his office. The NSA kept very tight security on these supplies and only gave hospitals a month's supply, but with the number of births in the hospital this month being more than usual, they were running short. He would get the next month's supply before his retirement so his replacement would not have to go through the dreadful paperwork process during her induction.

He carefully moved the transmitter gun close to the vial and pressed the trigger. An infrared light built into the transmitter barrel searched through the liquid in the vial until it found the small nano-probe, and within seconds all of the information was sent to the probe. The liquid was in fact not water, but a special fluid to facilitate the transmitting of the data to the probe suspended inside it, while at the same time harmless to the baby's body when injected. A message on the small LCD screen of the transmitter read finished when the download was complete, and John cleared the data by pressing the clear button on the transmitter and placed it into the cabinet. He slowly filled the syringe with the contents of the vial and placed it on the metal table. He removed the baby from the bassinet and laid him on the table and tore the top off an alcohol swab to prepare the baby's thigh for the tiny needle.

How many of these had he done? He thought back to all of the babies he had performed this procedure on in the past. He also thought about how this procedure had started many years ago in the Army test facility. He had been the one to pioneer the nano-probe, and it quickly became a mainstream part of the public health arena. The technology he was using now was considerably more advanced, but the underlying purpose had remained the same for four decades. It was top secret even today, and no one had known the full scope of the procedure except for a handful of scientists who had been part of the original team.

The official explanation for the procedure performed thousands of times each day was that it was an advanced system of fighting toxins in newborns. The body supposedly absorbed the probe within six months after the birth, leaving no trace that it ever existed. The fabricated lie seemed to work because the terrible diseases killing newborns had decreased tremendously over the past few decades, and astoundingly it was all attributed to this single procedure. John felt guilty, as if he had in some way contributed to this fallacy, and he also knew, somehow, that someday soon the secret would be known. Little did he know that the repercussions would shake the foundation of personal privacy forever.

John pricked the baby's skin and the baby immediately started to cry, but soon it was over. John could complete this entire process in less than five minutes. He wrapped the baby into the blanket, quieted him as best he could, and placed him back into the bassinet. The empty vial was placed back into the cabinet. All drawers and the metal doors were locked tight. With a tug, John made sure everything was secure, more out of habit than precaution. The syringe was tossed into the medical wastebasket, as it held no evidence of what was recently inside it. He rolled the bassinet through the door to the room, turned off the light and locked the door behind him.

The hospital staff was accustomed to the procedure and did not question or interfere with any of John's actions. He rolled the baby into the maternity nursery with the other newborns and turned his care over to the floor nurses. The baby had quieted and was sleeping peacefully as he walked out of the room. Ready to end his shift, he walked back down the long hallway to his office. John was more tired now than he could recently remember and was thinking about his bed and his few days off. He just needed to finish up the reports he had started earlier and head home.

Chapter 2

The last six months were but a mere blur. The inauguration seemed only yesterday and then it was one crisis after another. "What is going on?" the President whispered to himself as he sat at his desk staring at the NSA brief he had just opened. The covering on the document was marked *Presidential Top Secret,* as did most of the reports that landed on his desk, but the NSA report received the highest of security.

The daily brief gave the president a snapshot of events showing the hot spots around the world. The data for the report was provided to the NSA by the CIA using their multitude of intelligence sources and spooks. The NSA used their own filtering system to analyze the data and further break down the intelligence, sending it along to the appropriate governmental offices.

Tom always looked at the report before starting his day because he knew it was the most honest source of intelligence. He had found he could rely on the report to identify the situations requiring his personal attention because he trusted the intelligence staffers in the NSA. Their work was vital to the security of the United States.

He also was happy with his nominee for the National Intelligence Director to head the NSA. Tom considered the NID one of the most critical intelligence positions in the country, more so than the CIA and FBI directors combined. He knew the agency needed a strong leader, given its rocky past, and that is exactly what he found. A good NID needed to have a background in the "spook" trade, not in politics. His nominee, Manuel Cardoza, had thirty years experience, including five years as a deep cover contact in Cuba. He was not being overly confident, though, because Senate approvals were always a toss up. It was, however, a new position recommended by the Senate Intelligence oversight committee, of which Tom had been a junior member, in an attempt to make intelligence gathering functional again. So, the position would have the committee backing, but pushing his nomination through would be touchy.

He needed the NID in place before his planned dismantling of the Department of Homeland Security, which was an unmitigated disaster in all respects. Nothing of any importance had come out of the department since its inception. It had largely become an office to shuffle money, billions as a matter of record, rather than to do any real good. If things went according to Tom's plan, the Department of Homeland Security would cease to exist in the near future.

The former president had created the Department of Homeland Security to help quell the fears of U.S. citizens against further terrorist attacks following the tragic events of September 11, 2001. It was a bad idea from the start. One department tasked with coordinating all security agencies for investigative purposes was just a mistake waiting to happen. The bureaucracy of any governmental agency was bad, but this one was nightmarish. Breaking through it proved to be more difficult than expected. To date, the Homeland Security department had done very little to keep Americans safe.

It was for this reason that he voted against it when he was a Senator. But given the political climate at the time, the new cabinet level position and department was a forgone conclusion. However, filling it with a politician was the biggest mistake. What could a politician know about matters of security? Tom never understood that. His plan would fix this, but it would have to wait.

For now, the CIA director would arrive in forty-five minutes to give him an overview of the status of the nuclear stockpiles in the former Soviet Republics, and he wanted to scan through the latest information before he arrived.

Tom Lincoln, at forty-six years old, was a hard-line republican from New Hampshire and had won the presidential election last year by a landslide because of his vision on foreign policy and worldwide democracy. He also felt that having the last name of Lincoln didn't hurt much, even if the press had proven that he was in no way related to the beloved sixteenth president. The current political climate was perfect for a person strong in international affairs. The worldwide economic recession had sent the weakening U.S. markets into a decade-long slide. That, compounded with several governmental instabilities in the Middle East and Russia, had caused the longest bear market in recent history, and had the military spread dangerously thin.

With a doctorate in international relations from Harvard, President Lincoln's campaign promises could almost be considered child's play. He was regarded by many to be an expert in foreign policy. He understood, as few presidents before him, that the United States should not force democracy onto any nation. He knew one of the main problems with this country was arrogance. He felt he needed to provide countries ready and willing to change, assistance in developing their ideal political system. He truly hoped that a country wouldn't move back toward communism once they made a decision to become a democracy, because that would surely be political suicide for him. Sure, he knew that democracy was the strongest and most stable system because it allowed equal representation by every citizen; he also knew that democracy had its share of problems. He had learned that long before the disastrous democratic governmental restructuring attempt by the Russians. Experts in economics and politics were sent as consultants to help them, and millions of dollars were spent in aid, producing only moderate gains to date. Once again, the American arrogance was showing through. It was almost like fitting a round peg into a square hole. Even the experts knew democracy was not a good fit for the Russians.

He, in no uncertain terms, wanted to make one large worldwide democratic society. He only wanted to open a line of dialogue with as many governments as he could, and then keep the communications flowing if he had hopes of accomplishing any of his promises. He had learned early in his career that open communication provided a foundation for trust, and that in turn fostered change in many areas.

He carefully scanned over the daily brief, stopping at the heading, "Civil Unrest in Moscow," deciding that this section required a more thorough reading before the meeting. He knew that the fledgling democracy in Russia was shaky at best and was always a cause for concern, but civil unrest could present immediate problems.

SECRET--Civil Unrest in Moscow--SECRET
More than 4,500 residents of Moscow are standing outside the Kremlin demanding the resignation of President Stefanovich. Several members of the Red Liberty party are believed to be leading the rally and are recruiting more of the population to join the crowd. The president has not been seen since the beginning of the rally and no indication of military action has been noticed. Several members of the Duma have been seen trying to talk to the growing crowd, but have been denied access, and in some cases have been beaten or forced back into the Kremlin by rally members throwing stones and glass bottles. Moscow special police reported hearing small arms fire as they attempted to disperse the rioters, but they quickly retreated for safety.

After reading the article the president turned his television to CNN and pushed the intercom.

"Sally, could you get the vice president on the line and have him come to my office please?"

"Yes, sir. I will have him come in as soon as possible. Can I get you more coffee, sir?" she asked.

"No thank you, I am fine for now. Please send the vice president in as soon as he arrives."

"Very well."

The president had liked Sally from the moment he took office. She was in her early sixties and motherly. She had dark hair that had just recently started to turn salt and pepper gray. Her husband had died a year ago in a tragic car accident and now she devoted her life to her work. She was, without a doubt, the most efficient secretary he had ever had. She had, after all, worked for the last four presidents and probably knew more about politics in the White House than he did.

In many ways she reminded him of his mother, always smiling and knowing exactly what he needed when he needed it. There was one thing about her that oddly struck him though. She always seemed to be at her desk, greeting him in the morning and bidding him goodnight as he ended his day. He wondered if she actually went home, but never questioned it because he was becoming accustomed to being pampered.

He sat forward in his chair and rested his chin in the palm of his right hand. He had made a great choice in his vice president. David Arthur had served the previous four years as a senator from Louisiana. He was a republican from the Deep South and had endured endless harassment from the staunch Southern Democratic opposition.

He actually won his first senatorial campaign after the incumbent Democratic senator had been convicted of smuggling drugs out of New Orleans into New York City and Boston. That fiasco damaged the Democratic Party in Louisiana almost beyond repair, and David had been the right person at the right time. President Lincoln knew from the first time they had met on the Senate floor that David was destined for grandeur, and at forty-five he was young enough to do just about anything he set his mind to.

Tom was actually advised by his campaign manager to choose a running mate older and more experienced to work matters of the state and lead the Senate through the myriad of changes proposed in his campaign promises. However, the president knew that he wanted someone young and energetic to work with international governments and forge new relationships with them. He also wanted someone who was personable, and David was all of that rolled into one. Together, they formed the youngest political duo to ever win the presidential election.

The president was lost in thought as the door opened to his office, and David walked in briskly. He stopped in front of the president's desk and extended his hand as a gesture of their partnership.

"It's good to see you this morning, David."

"I was just getting some breakfast, sir. I got in late from the trip to Mexico City and slept in a little later than I would have liked."

"I am sorry to bother you then, but I have just reviewed the daily report and am concerned about the situation in Russia. The CIA director is coming in soon for the weekly briefing, but I would like you to look into the situation for me and report back tomorrow. Do me a favor, don't alert the CIA to your snooping. I don't need anything official. I know this is last minute, but I may have you take a little political tour of the region to help settle things. But only if you think it is a wise option."

"I will get on it immediately," David said and turned sharply and walked out the same door he had come in.

The president trusted David's skills of diplomacy as much as his own and could count on an honest and open report. He was not sure yet about the factual content in the CIA's reports because he had not put the information to the test. He was legitimately concerned because he just simply didn't trust the secrecy of the CIA. The information in the reports was undoubtedly factually true, for the most part, but he was sure it was being watered down to only necessary data so as not to portray a situation as grave as it really might be. This practice in particular, Tom felt, gave the CIA an edge to steer the government in whatever direction the CIA felt best.

The CIA was an organization that scared every president. It would be unwise to outwardly talk about his misgivings to anyone because the ramifications would surely be detrimental to his career. If he could prove this though, he would have the CIA director's balls in a vice for good. He would begin to build his case tomorrow after he talked to David.

Tom could have just as easily called the Russian President, Grigory Stefanovich, to find out what was going on, but quickly dismissed that idea. Internal conflict was always hidden from outside governments. After all, no one wanted to admit he was failing as a leader, especially to the President of the United States. He had known Grigory for the last ten years; not in a friendship capacity, by any stretch, mainly through visits to Russia during his doctoral program and the two had had actually met briefly early in Tom's political career. He personally liked Grigory for some reason. He didn't come over as a weak or vulnerable person.

"No, I will wait to call until after I am certain as to the severity of the situation," he said aloud to his empty office.

Sally's voice came over the intercom. "Sir, Mr. Palmer has arrived."

"Thank you, Sally, send him in please."

The door opened, and Ryan Palmer walked in with an unadorned black briefcase. The president motioned him over to the two chairs opposite the room and stepped from behind his desk to meet him with his copy of the report in his hands.

The smartly dressed CIA chief always impressed him. The gray Versace tailored suit and blue tie gave him a professional look in a flashier, debonair kind of way.

"Good morning, Ryan, how is the family?"

"Doing fine, sir, how is yours?" Ryan asked calmly.

"I don't spend nearly the time with them as I would like to."

"How is the golf going?" Ryan asked, trying to break the ice.

Tom played golf only because it was expected of the president. He would never consider what he played to be golf. It was as close to the "good ol' boys club" as he ever wanted to get. He didn't even like the game, but that was probably because he never devoted time for practice. His inexperience and terrible slice had become a legend in the White House and a good-natured joke among his cabinet members.

"Officially, I gave up on golf long ago. How is the state of the world, Mr. Palmer?" Tom asked, ending the small talk.

"Well, sir, we have some reports of a new terrorist training camp surfacing in Northern Afghanistan again, and one confirmed report that a possible member on our Palestinian terrorist list was inquiring about renting a car at a Toronto car rental agency. The rental manager alerted the FBI after he became suspicious of the documentation. Unfortunately, the report was also leaked to CNN and they have been flying with it. The FBI is working on that one as we speak under the direction of Homeland Security."

"This is very bad news, Ryan. Why wasn't I told immediately?" The president was almost irate at not being told, but calmly never let those feelings show in his voice. "Keep on the Homeland Security Department, I know they can be slow in responding."

"To be honest, Mr. President, reports like this surface daily, and I didn't want to alarm you if it were nothing. The CNN coverage is a problem. If this turns out to be Joe Arab on vacation with his wife and kids, the American people will soon become immune to the wild reports of CNN and take a complacent attitude to the newly initiated terror alerts."

"We both know what a joke those alerts are," Tom said sarcastically. "Keep me up to date on anything that you may find. I don't have to remind you of the recent Senate inquiry into the terrorism reports," the president said sternly, making sure Mr. Palmer understood the severity of his mistake of not telling the White House sooner.

"Now, Mr. Palmer, on to the Russian Republics."

"Sir, we have confirmed reports that a small uprising is causing some minor problems outside the Kremlin. President Stefanovich has used a military presence to secure the Kremlin and is posting walking guards on Moscow streets in hopes of heading off mass riots. From all appearances, it looks like these efforts are working, but it is only a matter of time until the people start a massive revolt."

"A small uprising for Christ's sake, have you seen CNN this morning? Ryan, what is causing these problems over there?"

"We have heard from our inside contact that the Red Liberty party is trying to overthrow the Russian democratic government because of their supporting efforts to unite all of the former Soviet republics."

"Would this be the same Red Liberty party that attempted to overthrow the Russian government twenty years ago? I thought they were eradicated soon after that attempt by the KGB."

"Well, we don't have much information on it to be honest, sir. Our contact is working on determining who is now leading the party and what their political goals are."

"Why are they trying to stop the unification efforts? My god, can't they see that unification is the only way NATO and the EEC will even consider admitting them? They need to keep moving forward or we will be facing an even bigger crisis than the cold war."

"Apparently, the members of the party feel that any unification efforts will bring back the old form of communist government and the individual countries will lose their voice." Ryan spoke the words, but it was really only an educated guess; he had nothing to factually back any of it up. His gut instincts were usually correct, but with so many variables this was different.

What he really needed was confirmation from the Russian contact. It had been days since he heard anything and then it was only a short encrypted message with the words: *Civil uprising against government, suspect Red Liberty party.* That was it! Their efforts to contact him to obtain more information have yet been unsuccessful and they did not want to risk exposing the contact by making obvious attempts.

A political shake-up in Russia was inevitable during his term. Next year is an election year for them and he knew many of the Russian citizens were unhappy. Going without food and the other necessities of life had a tendency to do that to people. He had known for a long time that a Russian democracy was an uncomfortable fit for the people. Russian people were followers. They were like a herd of sheep wandering in a pasture. They needed a strong leader. One thousand years of Russian political history was broken when communism fell, and they were in serious trouble. But he did not want to deal with a shake-up of the Russian political system now.

"How are the political parties matching up, Ryan? I want to know what and who we are dealing with should this 'small uprising' take Stefanovich out."

"The current party does not have an obvious answer to the worsening economy that has plagued Russian citizens since the fall of communism. Approximately sixty percent of the population lives in poverty while another fifteen percent are considered to be marginal. Petroleum stores are being monitored and rationed by the government, causing problems with heating and travel. It is a double-edged sword for the government; black market trade has taken much of the needed tax money away from the government, leaving them with very little money to assist with legislative actions or social programs. Russians need the black market to buy food and the government knows it. Stefanovich can't stop the market because his people would starve. At the end of the day, the Russian economy will not last another five years unless something major changes. To compound the problem, President, Grigory Stefanovich's power has weakened over the past few months in part for his lack of action to bolster the economy and inability to control the Duma."

"Tell me something new, Mr. Palmer. This is all information I could have received on the Internet or the evening news. I am looking for insight from you, and you give me old facts and useless bullshit," the president said as he threw the CIA report down on the small table between them and waited for a response. He needed to exert his power over the situation now so that the CIA director would know he meant business.

25

"Of course, sir, I am sorry," Ryan said, moving to the edge of his seat. He had never been talked to in this manner by anyone, especially the president, and was slightly offended by the insinuation. Ryan attempted to dig deeper. "According to our reports, the communist party is only expected to win ten of the two hundred open seats in the Duma. While not enough to impact legislative action, it may be a sign of things to come. President Stefanovich's position is in jeopardy, however, mainly because he is allowing the economy to suffer while he secretly builds the military back to cold war strength. He is not liked by Russian citizens and is considered weak by several members of his own party. The Red Liberty Party is, without a doubt, the most serious threat to Stefanovich. We have seen the rise of the more liberal RLP recently, but have no information on who will be their candidate. I do know that most of the break-away republics are supporting the RLP because they think it will help keep them autonomous."

"Something else must be going on over there, but what?" Tom mumbled to himself. "Mr. Palmer, is there anything we can do to help the elections along behind the scenes?"

"It is still early yet to start looking at helping them, Mr. President. We must wait until one party comes out as a clear frontrunner or we see a fundamental shift in the strength of the communist party to decide on who we will support."

"Mr. Palmer, could the Chechen situation that I have been reading in the reports for the past year have anything to do with the events in Moscow?"

"We don't think so at this time. The republics have been relatively quiet for the past few months. This is a Russian problem."

"Very well, Ryan. Keep me informed on the situation, and for your sake, please keep me up to date on those terrorists!" The president hoped he said this sternly enough to get Ryan's full attention.

"Of course, sir. When we have any information, I will personally deliver it immediately," Ryan said as he stood.

The handshake seemed genuine enough to Tom, but there was just something about Ryan that struck a chord. He walked back to his desk and pushed his intercom button.

"Sally, Mr. Palmer will be leaving through the side door."

"Yes, sir, I will let the guards know."

"What the hell does he want from me? I have been handcuffed by the Homeland Security Department for the past three years," Ryan said under his breath as he exited the office.

Ryan Palmer was visibly shaken from the meeting as he walked down the long hallway to the underground parking lot. He was thinking long past this meeting about the inside contact in the Russian government. The latest information was days old, what is going on over there?

He would have to address that as soon as he returned to his office. He walked through the security checkpoints to his car in the parking garage. The driver opened the back door and Ryan stepped inside without saying a word to him. As the car pulled away from the White House, Ryan stared out the passenger side window at the people walking down the sidewalk by the Washington monument, enjoying the warm day. "These people don't appreciate how hard it is to keep them safe at night," he quietly said to himself as the car sped through the busy streets toward Langley.

With the meeting over, Tom sat down in his chair unable to get the Russian situation out of his head. He knew that Chechnya had been a thorn in Russia's side for the past ten years. The Russian government has officially reported that nearly 11,000 Chechens have died since 1999, but Tom knew it was probably closer to three times that number.

Chechnya had won independence after inflicting heavy losses on Russian forces during two years of bloody conflict in the mid 1990s. But Russia, refusing to let it remain independent, mounted an offensive after Chechen terrorists bombed several sites in Moscow. Those bombings killed three hundred innocent Russian civilians and served only to strengthen the Russian resolve to eradicate the Chechen terrorists. From that point it had been one Russian invasion after another.

Tom knew the Russian military campaign in Chechnya had lasted far too long. The single biggest problem with the Russian military, he thought, was that they never accepted defeat. After all, the Russian occupation in Afghanistan went on for a decade and never accomplished anything. The president thought aloud, "The one bright side to my argument is that all through the Cold War the United States and Russia never met on a battlefield because the results would have been catastrophic for both sides."

Tom knew there had to be a link between the current uprising in Moscow and the Chechen situation, but what? He would wait until he heard from David to see what new information he would bring to help shed light on the problem. He did want to have more time to think about it now, but he was late for an appointment to talk to Israel's Ambassador to the U.N. about the possible growing resentment between the aid payments and PLO resistance to the U.S. involvement in the peace talks. Peace in the Middle East had been a political issue for thirty years, and Tom knew he would not be the one to bring them together during his term. However, if he chose to ignore the situation altogether, the press would eagerly tear him apart for not trying.

Chapter 3

Standing in front of the group of men, he felt strangely powerful. He was always a follower of sorts, never wanting to stand out in a crowd or draw attention. Living on the streets at the age of sixteen had scarred him both physically and emotionally, and in nearly every way, he was a product of this past. However, there was a deeper rooted passion that was always in Alexander's thoughts.

"Independence, my friends, will begin today!"

Alexander Poponov shouted to the group in front of him, holding a glass of vodka in the air.

"DA, Comrade!" the group echoed in unison.

He had known most in the group for fifteen years or more, having spent time with many of them on the streets of Grozny. Others he had stumbled out of local pubs with after drinking away their sorrows. They had been through so much together these past ten years and had learned the only way to survive was to fight for each other. Soon, they would be facing a fight bigger than themselves and bigger than they could fathom.

The Red Army was overrunning their country, and Alexander was determined to kill every Russian soldier for personal reasons more than independence. However, they knew it was impossible to fight the larger and better-equipped Russian military head on and expect to win—but there were other ways of winning.

"If you can't win fair, don't lose," his father would tell him and he would live by that statement over the next few months as they started their campaign.

Following the break-up of the Soviet Republics, Chechnya assembled a fledgling army to protect its borders. The ChRI soldiers were largely Russian trained men who came home when the Soviet Union broke apart. The Chechen Armed Forces, ChRI, had tried to take on the Red Army in 1999, and were beaten quickly by the tanks and aircraft Russia brought into their country in less than ten very bloody days. The ChRI forces were greatly outnumbered in both numbers of troops and weapons, but fought bravely for their new country, suffering tremendous losses at the hands of the Russians. Almost every member of Alexander's group had friends or family members killed during the initial battles, and they, like Alexander, were fighting for more than independence—they wanted revenge.

The men with Alexander had spent their lives scavenging for money or food, sneaking around the streets of the city, and he counted on these same skills to acquire supplies to help with his cause. They had obtained weapons any way they could. Most came from the highly illegal black market through the contacts he made while living on the streets. Alexander was careful about these purchases. He knew the prices were high and rumors spread like wildfire. The last thing he needed was a black-marketer with loose lips. Alexander had also used his position on the local base to his advantage, using his base identification badge to get into the armory. The Russians had very little security during those last months of the Soviet Union around their bases and even less accountability of their weapons inventory, and stealing was cheaper than purchases on the black market.

Alexander took advantage of the Russian ignorance to literally give his people a fighting chance. What they stole wouldn't be missed anyway, taking mostly small arms, pistols, AK-47s, RPGs, and an odd assortment of explosives. Those were the only items they could carry out of the nearly vacated base unnoticed and would draw the least attention during the sporadic weapons inventory checks. They had managed to conceal the small arsenal in an abandoned warehouse on the outskirts of town, but with the Russian Army declaring a police state in Grozny, they moved the weapons into Alexander's flat to avoid confiscation or worse.

The small group called themselves the Chechen Liberation Army, but was too small of a group to be anything more than a band of thugs. Their headquarters, at least that is what Alexander thought of it, was located in Alexander's small two-room flat on Sheripov Street just a few blocks from the central park in downtown Grozny. However, with the store of weapons they had amassed, it was becoming far too small to move around in, let alone do any real operations planning. As Alexander looked around the room at all the weapons and people cramped together, he realized that they would soon need to find a bigger place.

"We will win the fight for our fallen families and friends," Alexander said again with a toast of his vodka and a long stare in his eye. The thought of family and friends made him think of his own family.

Alexander was actually born in Tsotsin-Yurt, not Grozny, a medium-sized town 150 kilometers away. His father had worked his entire life in one of the oil production facilities for the government, and his mother stayed home to care for his younger brother who was born with meningitis, and she rarely left the house. They were not a rich family by any means. He lived in a modest row home made of brick at the end of a cobblestone street near the middle of town. They had money to eat and to live, just like everyone else. Communism may be a terrible thing for Westerners, but even as young as he was, he knew that no one person was better off than any other, unless, of course, you were one of the political elite.

Alexander was leisurely walking home from school with three friends, talking about Moreena. Moreena Svetlana, one of the most popular girls in their small school, had long black hair that nearly reached her waist. She could choose any boy in town, but she had her eye on Alexander. Moreena consumed his every thought, but he was too nervous to approach her. When he saw her at school his brain ceased to function and his words become a string of hodgepodge. He wanted to talk to her, but needed to increase his confidence if he had any chance of telling her how he felt.

The four teens were joking around when the first explosion rocked the ground. All eight eyes widened with horrified astonishment while they watched the smoke rise high above the trees, and with sickening terror in their faces, they watched the helicopters over their heads.

Alexander soon realized the thumping in his chest was not his thoughts of Moreena, but the pounding blades from five or six small helicopters darting around like large dragonflies. Air to ground missiles streaked through the sky from the Russian attack helicopters tearing through most of the buildings in the down town section, quickly setting them ablaze. The four boys, each panic-stricken and running for their lives in seeing the smoke, split apart in an attempt to reach the safety of their homes.

Alexander's chest burned with each deep breath of cool brisk air. Machine gun fire in the distance sounded like firecrackers he used to play with as a young boy. He stopped in the town park when the sound of gunfire erupted close to him. Exhausted from the run, he leaned against a large tree with his arms shielding his head until the gunfire stopped.

At sixteen he was a mature young man and well on his way to becoming an adult, but now he felt like a helpless boy. He cautiously started running again, passing Russian soldiers and tanks along the way as he made his way through the narrow back streets of town. None of the soldiers stopped him or even shouted to him as he sprinted toward home. When he rounded the corner of the cobblestone street in front of his home, he stopped dead. He had never cried before, but the image before him brought tears to his eyes immediately.

The entire block of small houses had taken several missile hits and was still smoldering. Tears rolled down his cheeks as he staggered forward, trying to determine if his family had managed to escape. His cloudy eyes searched neighboring yards and between homes frantically as he approached the front gate, kicking the bricks away so it could be opened. A Russian soldier grabbed his arm and dragged him away from the rubble, but Alexander was no longer the scared, helpless boy he was just a few moments before behind the tree. He fought with utter loathing to free himself from the soldier's grip. The burning tears that stung his cheeks gave him courage as he twisted and clawed to escape the soldier's tight grasp. A loud explosion off their right shoulder threw dust and debris into the air, forcing the soldier to release Alexander and shield his face. This chance elusion gave Alexander the time he needed to get away.

This time he didn't bother with the gate. He jumped the fence and stepped over the fallen bricks that blocked it. Unable to open the jammed front door, Alexander climbed through the broken front window carefully, avoiding the shards of glass, and climbed inside. The ceiling had collapsed and he could only envision the image of the second floor bedroom through the choking smoke. He dropped to his knees and crawled through the small room to the rear of the house toward the kitchen, where he was sure his mother would be. She was always in the kitchen when he arrived home after school with an offering of fresh bread or cake. The familiar smell of baked bread filling the house that gave him comfort, was now replaced with the stench of war.

On his hands and knees, he made his way through the tangled mess of steel and brick that was his home. When he reached the kitchen door, or what was left of it, time seemed to stand still. His mother, father, and brother were all huddled in the back corner of the room next to a gaping hole leading directly to the back yard where a rocket must have entered. Alexander attempted to deny the tears that welled in his eyes, but they overwhelmed him as he rubbed his eyes with his dirty palms.

The smell of burnt flesh and singed hair was etched into his brain. He wouldn't even have recognized them except for the tattered clothes they were wearing. His mother and father appeared to be huddled over his brother in a vain attempt to protect him from the explosions. They were dead, he was sure of that. Alexander fell onto his chest and began to sob uncontrollably.

When Alexander opened his eyes, he felt the rain hitting his face. He raised his hands to shield himself from the cool drops as he remained motionless in the ruble. The air was silent except for the rain. The smoke had long died away. As his eyes focused, he saw the house, the destruction and realized it had not been a dream. He was still lying on his living room floor, but the house had been so badly damaged, the rain was coming straight through the roof. He turned his head slowly to the kitchen with an aching sense of hope one last time that it was a dream, but the horror returned at the desperate sight.

Clearing the bricks away from the front door enough for it to open, Alexander remembered his mother's kiss that morning before he went off to school. Again, tears came to his swollen eyes as he opened it as he had hundreds of times before and left the house for the last time. He decided not to clear the front gate, but instead jumped over the fence onto the street. He walked away from his house, fighting the urge to turn around, leaving his past behind, never to feel the security of childhood again.

He found a car, a Russian-made Lada, parked down the street in front of another house with the keys still inside. Whoever had been driving this car made a hasty get away into the house, attempting to get to safety. It surely would not be needed if the owner had met the same fate of his family, and judging by the look of the smoking building, that was the case. He considered it borrowing anyway, even if he had no plans of ever returning it.

Alexander had never driven a car before, but this was the only way to get far away as fast as possible. He put the car in gear and released the clutch, making the car lurch forward in an awkward spin. Before he reached the outskirts of town he had the car under control, and was cruising down the narrow road toward nowhere.

When the rain started to beat harder against the windshield, he pulled the car to the side of the road, realizing that he needed to find a place to stop for the night. The cold, hard truth was that he had no money, food, or clothes and it hit him hard. Straining his eyes through the foggy windshield, he saw a sign for Grozny. He was sure to find a place to stay there. It was the closest city, only 100 kilometers from where he had stopped. He could decide what he was going to do when he got there. So, Alexander put the car back on the road and drove into the rain, following the signs to the city. He had been there many times with his family, but never alone.

Andre Asomovili found Alexander living on the filthy streets of Grozny, ragged, dirty and starving. Alexander had not bathed in weeks and his clothes had not been washed in months. Alexander was actually living under a bridge in the slums of the city. Andre felt sorry for the kid and took him into his small house he shared with his younger sister, and showed him how to survive in the city. Like Alexander, Andre had lost his parents years ago. However, his parents were not brutally murdered by the Russians, but rather died in an automobile accident while on a family vacation. Instead of going into the dreadful foster care homes, Andre took care of his younger sister in the family's home.

Alexander and Andre were actually about the same age and soon became tighter than brothers. Andre talked his employer into hiring Alexander on as an assistant in the cafeteria of the local Russian Army base. When Alexander had money, he moved into his own flat near Andre's. They would talk about girls and many other things young men talk about as they drank vodka and sang patriotic songs long into the night.

However, Alexander became obsessed with revenge against the Russian Army and started to hang out in clubs until the early morning hours. It wasn't hard to find others like him. He didn't intend to start the CLA, but rather it grew from his friendships. The group initially met in Alexander's flat twice a week to drink vodka. They would talk about the movements of the Russian Army and locations of their heavy armor. Alexander's interior decorator would have been disgusted. Maps of the country littered the walls of his small living room so that literally nothing else showed through except for the darkly stained white paint near the ceiling. They used the maps to pinpoint the locations of Russian troops.

He was the unofficial leader and none of the group, including Alexander, had seen any military action. But they had courage in their hearts and vodka in their veins, which would get them through some tough times over the next couple of weeks. Officially, there were fifty in the group, but less than half that were there today.

Fighting for revenge is always much deeper rooted and more powerful than patriotism, and Alexander would stop at nothing to exact his revenge on those Russian bastards. Even with his deep, vile hatred, the men saw Alexander as being smart enough to not allow the thoughts of revenge to make him do something stupid. No, he would be careful and systematic in his planning, and together their fight would end in success for both him and their cause. What they didn't know was that Alexander would stop at nothing, including risking the lives of those in his group, to get the revenge he sought.

Today the group was planning. They had marked on the topographical maps the new Russian Army positions. They were also fortunate to have intelligence on troop movements through sporadic reports by supporters in small towns and villages throughout the region. The only disadvantage to this type of fighting was that they had to rely on eye witness information, leaving little time for concrete planning. As word spread about the group, reports started flowing in daily.

A phone call that morning from a supporter in the small village of Guardemes, indicated that the Russians were mobilizing and moving toward the town. When reports like they just received came in, all planning and mobilizing had to be done on the fly.

"Shit, today is the day. We must hit them today," Alexander said with stone cold certainty.

They huddled around the maps while Alexander pointed out the strategic elements of the operation. He identified the movement of the Russian convoy, and the road they would likely take to enter the village. Andre had driven out to the village as soon as the call came in to survey the situation personally.

The plan was simple. Stop the motorized convoy as it started over the old stone bridge on the Terek River. The convoy would then have no other place to cross the river and would be forced to halt its advance and travel nearly 70 kilometers back to Chervlennaya to cross the river. Alexander knew the Russians had the resources to build a portable bridge, but they would not risk the exposure during the construction, and it was the largest river in the country. It would take hours to bring the bridge in and have it ready, and the effort was not worth the reward.

The Russians were arrogant, but not stupid. He knew that and counted on it. He also knew there would probably be infantry soldiers accompanying the convoy, protecting it from the potential threat of ChRi forces. Taking them out must be the first priority after blowing the bridge. Andre returned excitedly, carrying his camera and binoculars around his neck.

"Andre, what did you find, my brother?"

"As you suspected, there is only one road in and one out of the village. Hitting the bridge is our only option. I have pictures of the bridge at several angles and the surrounding fields and tree line."

"You have done well!" Alexander started. "The C-4 must be placed directly on the cross members of the east side of the bridge, here and here," he said, pointing to the picture. "We only want to disable the convoy, not demolish the bridge. Be careful with the size of the charges and choose the detonation time wisely. I will tell you when to detonate the first charge."

He really didn't want to destroy the bridge because it was vital to the citizens in the town, but he could damage it so that the heavy tanks could not cross. He chose two of the best members to place the charges and pointed out spots along the rock wall for the others to sit. The position, though Alexander didn't know if specifically, was a classic ambush position. The Russians would be moving right into the firing lines of Alexander's men. The two men with the explosives nodded in agreement and started out early to get set up.

Alexander told the rest of the men that if they were split off from the group to come directly back to his flat after the fighting. He did not want any of them to risk capture because they may talk and expose the group. If anyone man was captured, the agreement between them was to only say they were working on their own.

Alexander looked around the room into the faces of every man. He could see the nervousness of each of them and could sense that some were scared enough to start backing out. It was their first real attack on the Red Army and they had a right to be scared, Alexander knew that.

"This, dear comrades, will be the start of something bigger than anyone of us," Alexander said, holding his glass in the air one last time. The men slowly held their glasses high and each finished with a swallow.

"Some of you, my friends, will not be coming back to this place with me tonight. To you I say, you will never be forgotten. History books will forever be rewritten after this fight."

The planning was over. Alexander handed out the weapons and ammunition to each man as they exited the flat, concealing them under their long coats until they made it to their cars. Neighbors were overly suspicious of everything. Quietly, in twos, they walked out of the building into cars parked along the street. They drove off in different directions, meeting at the planned location, two kilometers from the bridge. From there, they would hike to their positions. The men were all silent during the ride through the country, each in his own way praying for his safety, intently focused on the mission.

Chapter 4

The sun crept through the curtains of his hotel room, waking Nassir from a fitful sleep. The air conditioner kicked on, trying to keep up with the heat, but that still didn't help. His room was already getting hot and sticky and the air conditioner was too loud for him to get any more sleep. He was not used to sleeping so late, but the night surveillance didn't give him the luxury to sleep any other time.

The heat didn't bother him. He had trained deep in the Afghan desert for the past three years. It was the heavy humidity that really took the energy out of his body. He sat on the end of the bed slowly dressing so as not to exert himself any more than possible before leaving the small dark room. The light-brown skin on his forehead quickly became covered with sweat as he walked down the sidewalk.

The heat of the day had just started to escalate when Nassir stepped through the door of the club on the main drag. The neon signs on the outside caught his attention the night he arrived and he had a few drinks each day inside the cool, dark strip club. It was the perfect place to keep hidden and relieve some stress. He had worked far too hard on this plan to watch it fail because of a poor choice or lack of discipline.

The moment he stepped through the solid, windowless slab door to the club, he immediately felt the cool dryness of the air-conditioning as his eyes adjusted to the darkness. The quick cool down actually made him shiver as he looked around the dim room to see if anyone acknowledged his entrance, and then walked up to the bar and ordered a whiskey. As he waited for the bartender he glanced toward the stage and watched the blonde dancer spin around a brass pole. He preferred dark haired women. They reminded him of the women back home. He picked up his drink and walked to a round table in a dark corner.

The table was away from the dance stage, but he had a good view. He took a long sip of the whiskey and reached into his shirt pocket for his pack of cigarettes. He loved to smoke when he drank, although western cigarettes were weaker and tasted stale, but that didn't matter. It helped him think and he needed to finalize his plans.

The flame off the lighter split the darkness as the tip of the unfiltered cigarette glowed with a deep drag. He exhaled and the smoke slowly rose, circling his head in the dead air. His eyes were on the dancer, but his thoughts were on his mission.

Nassir spent the last six months loosely planning with only the details coming in the past few weeks. It was actually after the e-mail from Yassad that he began to get serious. His goal was to catch the Americans off guard and vulnerable, to hit them where they would never expect.

He scouted the border to find a way across so he could get into the States without going through the border checks. He knew they reported all Middle Eastern travelers to the FBI, and he couldn't risk that. He secured three cars which was both difficult and expensive, but he had the backing of the PFLP so money was not a problem. The transportation was coming from the Palestinian supporters here in Canada. He had contacted them long before arriving and would rely on them to come through. The money they would make for supplying the cars would fund many political projects in each major Canadian city that housed a Palestinian neighborhood, and it was worth the risk to them.

The routes Nassir plotted were intentionally different once they successfully crossed the border. He decided after his scouting mission last night that it was best to cross at the same location over the course of a few hours. He watched the Canadian guards for the past week and took pictures of each one to memorize his individual routine. He knew this was going to be easy. The guards were so predictable. Each one had a specific routine. He targeted one guard who rarely stopped one car per shift at his station. It was a surprise to Nassir that Americans felt so safe.

The music stopped, snapping him back to the club and the dancer ending her routine. A few in the club clapped for the naked girl while others threw dollars onto the stage. She bent over to pick up the bills and walked off behind the curtain covering the back wall. Watching her walk away proved to him that, although he preferred brunettes, all women stirred his insides.

He watched the curtain flutter and the most gorgeous woman walked out on stage. She wore a leather cowboy hat, short vest and leather chaps with a holster around her waist that framed her tight ass. He couldn't take his eyes off her as she started to set up for her dance number. The music she danced to had a country theme and a fast tempo. She quickly started to seductively sway her body to the music. Nassir sat mesmerized as her hips moved in ways that drove him wild with desire. The vibrations from the loud music rattled him, and he wanted to move closer, but elected to sit back in the chair and watch the beauty in silence. He took another deep drag on his cigarette as he watched.

The door opened to the club, allowing the bright sunlight to spill into the room, interrupting Nassir's wanton thoughts. Glancing toward the door Nassir saw a familiar face searching the dark room. Only in extreme emergencies was he to be disturbed. He glanced once more at the dancer on the stage, hoping to burn that image into his memory, and then stood from the table. He swallowed the whisky with a wince and snubbed out his cigarette before standing to meet his friend, Ali, and then exited the club into the hot afternoon.

"Nassir, I am sorry I bothered you, but we may have a problem," Ali urgently said in Arabic before the club door even closed. "CNN is running a picture of Kahlid! He was spotted in Toronto inquiring about renting a car and asking for general information on the border crossings. Our plan is in grave danger now—the border security will be tightened for sure."

"How could Kahlid have been so careless?" Nassir sighed under his breath. "Six months of planning could be wasted." Mistakes like this could not be tolerated, and he would be sure to make an example of Kahlid. "We will proceed as planned except we all cross tomorrow together, God willing."

The Republican National Convention, where both the president and vice president were scheduled to present their support for the party, was in two days. Having them both in the same room at the same time off White House grounds was too good to pass up. Every security detail would be at the convention, leaving their target in Baltimore one ripe apple ready for the picking.

"They haven't learned one single thing," Nassir mumbled to himself. He knew if they waited, they would miss their chance.

"Ali, tell Kamal the plan will proceed tomorrow. The cars will be ready in the morning. Also, have Kamal meet you in the park at 6:30 and the two of you cross at the same time as I showed you. One more thing, tell Kahlid to meet me in my room tonight."

"Praise Allah," Ali said, bowing slightly to Nassir out of fear more than respect. "What about you, when will you cross?" He knew that his friend Kahlid was careless and that he would pay for that carelessness with his life. Each man then separated and spoke no more.

"I have something I must take care of that does not concern you. I will meet you as scheduled. Please do not be delayed."

Ali nodded as he looked into Nassir's tired eyes. He knew that this would be the last he would ever see his dear friend Kahlid as he walked directly away from the Nassir.

Nassir did not walk back into the bar. He turned his head toward the falls and walked off toward the park. It was filled with vacationers taking pictures of their families with the falls in the background and lovers on their honeymoons. The cars had not arrived, but he was not worried yet. As he followed the sidewalk through the park, his mind worked over the Kahlid problem. He sat for hours staring into the mist and thought over the new problem.

He had time, and excess energy, so he walked the mile or so back to his room to pack his clothes. As he stuffed his suitcase, he went over each step of the plan one last time, making sure he had everything finalized. He sat in the darkness of the room waiting for Kahlid to arrive, contemplating his next few steps. He so wanted to teach him a lesson. Arrogance could not be tolerated on this mission. Nassir was the leader, and he did not want to be remembered as the one who failed. He knew their success would shake the world more than the total destruction of the twin towers, and he wanted to be the new hero.

Nassir heard one barely audible knock on the door and he walked to open it before another could be made. Nassir slowly turned the knob, opening the door slightly, checking to see if it was Kahlid. When the familiar face met his gaze, he opened it enough to allow the tall man to enter. Kahlid was young, the youngest in his group. Nassir had objected to his being on the team, but Kahlid was the brother of Arkhim, Nassir's mentor and friend. Arkhim was also one of the most powerful and most prominent figures in the Population Front for the Liberation of Palestine, one of the largest Hamas-backed terrorist organizations in the world. Because of his family connection, Kahlid was arrogant and full of spirit, the kind of person you want on the team, but are afraid to admit it.

"Welcome, brother," Nassir said and offered his room by opening the door.

Kahlid bowed slightly before entering, acknowledging the offer and then embraced Nassir, kissing him on both cheeks in their formal greeting. Nassir pulled a chair out for Kahlid while he stood pacing the small room, which helped his mind to focus.

"Good evening, Kahlid. I trust the night finds you well," Nassir said, continuing to pace in front of the chair.

"It does, my friend, it certainly does," Kahlid said back.

Nassir walked directly in front of the chair and bent over, resting his hands on its padded back so that he could look the young man in the eyes. He wanted to make sure that the next thing he said was not only acknowledged, but more importantly, understood. Nassir could only be sure of this by looking directly into the man's eyes—the mirror to a weak man's soul.

"Kahlid, I have heard that your picture has been broadcast on CNN all around the world. Do you know what that means to our plans and to us, you foolish kid? How could you be so careless?" He looked deep into Kahlid's eyes, trying to get a sense of how he took the first barrage, pausing to give the younger man time to explain.

"I am sorry, Nassir, but I wanted to take some of the pressure off you by doing things on my own before I got here. I know this is the biggest action we have ever undertaken, and I thought this would help."

"Your help may have made it impossible for us to cross the border or worse, it may have caused the mission to fail," Nassir said as he straightened up. He could also feel the blood rush into his face as he continued to speak. "You need to listen to my orders and do exactly what I say. We do not have the luxury of being able to deviate from the plans your brother and I created."

"You really are the idiot my brother told me you were; he put me on this team because he was afraid you would become scared and weak and not follow through," Kahlid said with a stinging tone in his voice, knowing too late that those words should have never crossed his lips in anger.

The harsh words lashed Nassir's face and he stepped back away from the vulgar excuse of a man and started again to pace. Thoughts now raced through his head as he tried to match link the information he was just told to what he already knew about the plan. He needed to pick his words carefully now that he knew the truth.

"What has your brother told you about the plan?" Nassir hissed, trying not to sound defensive, but being unsuccessful.

"I know the entire plan once we get to the city. The only thing that was left out was the question of transportation and border crossing because those were to be scouted by you," Kahlid said indignantly, sounding more confident as the conversation continued. "If you think you can handle this on your own, you are sadly mistaken," Kahlid continued, adding to Nassir's growing embarrassment.

Nassir looked at Kahlid with a graven face. His mouth formed a grin as his eyes searched the face in front of him to make some sense of what was just said, but found none. He did see Kahlid looking at him with a smug smile. This incensed him, and he knew that something drastic would need to be done or the plan would surely fall apart. Nassir walked to the chair, laughed a loud, hearty laugh and slapped Kahlid on the shoulders. "My young friend, I am thankful and blessed you are with me today," Nassir said with the most sincerity he could muster.

Kahlid thought he had won the battle of words and laughed along with the older leader. Nassir walked over to the phone and called a cab. He slowly placed the phone back in the receiver, looking over his shoulder at Kahlid with graven darkness in his eyes. He picked up the worn suitcase from the unmade bed and offered his hand as an invitation to join him to the parking lot.

Once again the identification cards proved to be flawless as he checked out of the motel in less than five minutes. He stepped through the large lobby doors and walked slowly toward Kahlid in front of the building under the overhang, waiting for the cab. The humidity was still high, he thought, even this late at night. He looked to the sky and was glad that the moonless sky was deathly dark. As he walked, he pulled his 9mm Glock with a customized silencer from the front pouch of the suitcase and slid it into an inside coat pocket when Kahlid had turned his back to him.

"I will take you to pick up your car and then you can proceed to the first planned check point, my friend. That is, of course, if it meets your approval," Nassir said in a sarcastic tone.

"The sooner this is over the better. We will be victorious and heroes when we return," Kahlid stated in such an overtly confident tone that it turned Nassir's stomach.

The cab arrived before Nassir could formulate a comeback and he opened the door and waved his hand for Kahlid to enter first. Nassir threw his suitcase on the floor and stepped into the cab, telling the driver to take them to Niagara Park. The cars would surely be parked there now for them to pick up. The park's lot was always filled with vacationers visiting Goat Island until well after dark, which helped alleviate suspicion of the additional cars.

The short ride to the park was very quiet. Neither man spoke as he watched the neon signs pass by, advertising the men's clubs and bars on the main drag. When the cab pulled into the parking area, Nassir gave the driver a twenty, told him, "thank you," in his best English and exited with Kahlid. Nassir spotted the large white van and started to walk toward it with Kahlid following close behind. Kahlid wondered which car he would take, but didn't say a word until Nassir stopped behind the plain white van. The keys were exactly where they were supposed to be, and Nassir opened the back door, tossing in his bag among the supplies he requested. The empty parking lot was dark except for the dim lights illuminating the sidewalk.

"I would like to walk and go over the plan one last time," Nassir said in a directive tone.

"If you like. I have them memorized, exactly as you instructed," Kahlid said matter of factly.

The two walked through the lot into the park, which overlooked the falls. The thundering noise from the falls was deafening, making conversation difficult, but it proved to be a perfect setting. Nassir couldn't have planned this better if he tried. Kahlid walked slowly ahead, pausing at times to look back at Nassir to keep up.

Nassir began to go over the initial leg of the plan from Niagara Falls to Baltimore as he slowly pulled the pistol from his sport jacket pocket. Nassir knew this was the only way. Kahlid's confidence would ruin all they had worked for and Nassir didn't really like him anyway. He would tell Arkhim that he was killed saving his life, the highest honor one could receive, and that would surely make him a hero.

Nassir's tone reflected nothing of the plan he had just put into play. His words were fluid and his tone was flat as he slowly approached Kahlid. He looked around one last time to make sure no one was in the park as he firmly gripped the gun in the palm of his hand. The pistol produced virtually no sound with the silencer, but even an un-silenced shot would not have been heard above the falls.

Time seemed to stand still for that split second when Nassir leveled the pistol on the back of Kahlid's head. He had never ended another human life. He had planned, practiced, and even dreamt of it, but this was his first. He was amazed at how calm and indifferent he felt. What was the feeling he had at the very moment? He thought about the first time he had been with a woman. That was it! That was the last time he felt this way.

"Go in peace," Nassir whispered as he squeezed the trigger and the pistol recoiled slightly in his grip.

Kahlid didn't even realize what hit him as his numb body fell to the ground. He certainly would not have expected a 9mm caliber slug from behind. Nassir squeezed off two more rounds from the semi-automatic pistol into the lifeless body, only because he couldn't stop himself, and carefully picked up the spent cartridges, making sure nothing was left to be traced.

He was actually surprised how quickly the body dropped. Nassir's head spun as he looked at the limp body on the ground surrounded by a dark crimson pool of blood. He quickly glanced around again to see if anyone had witnessed what he had done, and was pleased that the park remained empty. He picked the body up and carried it over to the railing overlooking the falls and quickly dumped it into the turbulent, white, foamy water. No one would find Kahlid's body now; he was sure of it. The river current would drag the body back into the falls and he would be gone forever.

Just as he regained his composure, it started to rain, slowly at first and then large, heavy drops. Nassir walked back toward the van slowly, enjoying the rain because he knew that it would not only take the humidity out of the air, it would also wash away the blood from the grass. He opened the door to the van and sat in the driver's seat, staring straight ahead through the windshield as the sound of the drops hitting the thin metal roof echoed through the nearly empty van. The rain was a sign from above.

Chapter 5

Driving east on an Interstate in the middle of Wyoming was not a vacation that would put a smile on many faces. However, as the old jeep crested a small hill on the highway, the gray rock formation rose out of the ground in the distance like a pillar into the late afternoon sky—a large toothy smile erupted on Tony Hampton's face.

The closer he got, the more excited he became until he almost couldn't keep it inside. He had another couple of hours before it got dark and he just couldn't resist pulling into the Visitor's Center parking lot for one look. The view was mesmerizing. He stopped the old jeep alongside the road and stared unable to think of anything, but its natural beauty.

He had to get closer so he pulled into the Visitor's Center and he walked out toward the formation. From this vantage point, it appeared much more foreboding than it did in photographs. In the dying sunlight, the rock almost looked green, he thought to himself.

He looked at his watch and figured he had better get to the campsite before the sun went down.

Twenty thousand years ago the Cordilleran ice sheet covered most of the north-western part of the United States. At the same moment in time, the Laurentide ice sheet extended west from what is now New England, meeting in Montana with the larger Cordilleran. At points, the ice sheets were two miles thick or more. During the most recent ice age, ice covered most of the Northern Hemisphere.

Huge Mastodons, fierce saber-toothed cats and lumbering arctic short-nosed bears roamed the entire mid-western region from Missouri and Illinois to Washington State, feeding on snow-shoed rabbits and other small rodents. The barren landscape, cold climate and dangerous predators forced most human life south toward warmer, more hospitable lands.

Both the receding movement of the thick glaciers and the silt-rich glacial lakes created by the melting ice shaped the rugged landscape of this region. The predominate geologic theory behind the rock formations known as the black hills in Wyoming and South Dakota was that they were not created as the glaciers moved north as were the canyons and gorges in Arizona and New

Mexico. But rather by the thrusting of hot liquid magma through vents in the earths crust, cooling rapidly as it met the cool air and the ice cold water of a massive glacial lake. Regardless of how they were formed, the rugged crags of this region are some of the most unique and awe inspiring in the world.

Sometime around 10,000 years ago, a climatic warming killed off the predators and melted the large glaciers. As the ice sheets ebbed north, a shallow lake formed, covering an area from Wyoming to Arkansas. The silt left by the lake as it dried, was rich and thick. From the dry, fertile soil, tall grasses grew, providing food for large grazing animals like Buffalo and Elk.

Long before the pilgrims set foot on this continent, Native American Indians followed the migration of the Buffalo and Elk into the Midwest. The Lakota, Ute, and Pawnee all peacefully coexisted on the Great Plains, living off the fertile soil and bountiful wild game.

The Indians had a deep spiritual belief and respect for the land that gave them life. This respect was lost on the white man as settlers moved west past the Mississippi river toward the Rocky Mountains, ravaging the land and killing the game into near extinction.

An area in what is now Wyoming was especially sacred to the Native Americans. Just south of the Black Hills, a spire rose 1,267 feet into the air, appearing as if it were an alter to the gods. The Indians named the unusual formation *Bears Lodge* because of the ancient stories they told of how the unique rock was formed.

Around village fires, dressed in ceremonial skins, tribal elders would recount the sacred story told to them by their fathers and their father's fathers, acting it out as if it were a Broadway play.

The story starts silently with the chief elder, standing with his back to the fire, moving his arms in a wild manner mimicking the movements of children at play. His words are merely a whisper as he describes the children of a powerful chief and how they played in the waist tall grasses near the riverbank.

The flames of the large fire licked the cold night air as the elder's voice suddenly grew louder. Several of the junior elders joined him, dancing around the warm fire to the beat of a solitary drum as if they were frolicking in the weeds. The six sisters and one brother laughed and chased each other for hours, passing away a lazy, hot afternoon. The brother, overcome with a heat sickness fell into the tall grass nearly unconscious. The sisters became worried as they saw their brother fall and ran to the river to get him some cool water.

At this point in the story, one of the elders would come around from the back of the fire, wearing a bear skin on his back. The bear's head, with its small piercing eyes and mouth gaping open, exposing its unmistakable ivory colored teeth, was perched directly on the top of the elder's own head. The effect was dramatic, and the young ones around the fire all gasped, afraid of the bear as it came out of the darkness. The chief elder continues to tell how when the sisters returned with the water, their brother had been transformed, as if by magic, into a ferocious bear.

The drumbeat increased in tempo and the elders acting out the play started to dance faster, twisting and bending as the bear chased them around the fire. To increase the effect, one of the elders tossed mushroom dust into the flames, causing them to spike higher. The orange glow of the flames cast a large shadow of the bear on the ground as children sat spellbound, watching with wide eyes.

The drumbeat slowed once again and the elder continued the story. The sisters, terrified of their brother, ran screaming toward the hills, leading the gigantic bear away from their village. The girls ran as fast as the fastest antelope, but still the bear was upon their heels. Fearing for their lives, the girls jumped onto a large rock, which miraculously began rising out of the ground, out of the bear's reach. Mother spirit had heard the sisters' pleas for help and saved them. The rock continued to rise into the sky with a mighty rumble deep within the earth's crust. The bear, now wildly furious, began leaping, clawing at the rock, leaving large claw marks down the surface from the very top to the bottom. The striated marks on the rock face, supposedly created by the claws of the bear, are the most unique marking on any formation in the world.

As the bear tired, it walked away from the girls into the sunset, never to be seen again. Just before nightfall, a large golden eagle landed on the top of the rock and carried the sisters back to their village and to safety. The fire died down to embers as the elders finished the story. The drum silenced and the dance ended with the elders slipping into the darkness of the night. The younger members of the tribe would remember this story for generations, and retell it many times to their children and their children's children, keeping the spirit of the *Bear's Lodge* alive for an eternity.

Life could not be better, Tony Hampton thought as sweat dripped off his tanned chin onto his chest. He loved rock climbing and was standing at the foot of the Mecca for rock climbers, Devil's Tower. Rock climbers traveled around the world to climb this peak and Tony was on a week-long vacation, taking full advantage of every second. This was actually his first time at the tower and first vacation in several years. Secret Service agents travel to many exotic locations, but were always on the clock in an official capacity.

He wanted to come in June when the weather was cooler, but was forced to wait until July because the tower was closed to observe the sacred Indian rituals of the Sundance. Each year during the summer solstice, Native Americans from all over the United States made the pilgrimage to the *Bears Lodge* to celebrate life and recount the story of the six sisters.

Tony was strikingly handsome. His coal black hair was trimmed short and he had no facial hair. His body was lean and his chiseled features gave him the appearance of a Roman god. The strong jaw line and high cheekbones were perfectly proportioned to his wide shoulders and barrel chest. The six-pack abs that he had in college were fading, but he still maintained an athletic appearance. He watched what he ate, but didn't have much time to exercise in a way that he was accustomed. Rock climbing was his only real source of exercise, and he didn't have much time for that either.

The heat radiated off the brown dusty soil as he looked closely at the cracks in the giant slabs of stone creating the face of the mountain. He studied each one carefully as if he was preparing his mind mentally for an exam. He would not be taking an exam today, but his life would hang in the balance of how well he could translate the small cracks into a path to the top.

Satisfied that he had found a clear path, he secured a chalk bag to his waist. He climbed free of ropes and all the other safety gear that most climbers used here preferring to risk it all for the exhilaration. The chalk provided his fingertips with a sure grip on unbelievably small ledges that he used to skillfully pull his body up the smooth rock face.

With a deep breath, he inserted his strong fingers into a large crevice and began his ascent. The rubber-soled climbing shoes gripped the stone as if he wore suction cups. Within thirty minutes he was nearly half way to the top. Tony hung onto a small ledge with his left hand while his right wiped the sweat from his forehead. Now wet with sweat, he inserted his hand into the dirty canvas bag, coating it with the white chalk. He was nearly exhausted and his arms ached from the exertion. His body was out of shape, but he continued to push it to the limit.

The only problem with Wyoming in the summer was the heat, he thought, but continued up the rocky face of the mountain with a giant smile on his face. The salt in his sweat stung his eyes as it slowly made its way from his forehead to his chin. It wasn't the sting that bothered him the most, but the beads of sweat creeping their way slowly down the middle of his back that he couldn't reach that drove him crazy. He could barely feel a gentle cross breeze as he pulled himself higher up the rock face, which helped ease the heat—but not much.

As a special agent in the Secret Service, he was assigned to protect Eagle 2, the vice president, when he was away from the White House. Tony was used to challenges, and he loved his job and the excitement that went along with it, which is probably why he loved climbing. Death could come doing either activity if you didn't have your head screwed on tight. He was with Eagle 2 last week in Mexico and had taken a flight to Wyoming just after he safely escorted him onto Air Force One. That was yesterday and he wasted no time in setting up camp and relaxing.

He loved the travel, but it played hell on not just his vacations. His social life was nonexistent. What the hell? He was young and had plenty of time to settle down to live a boring life in the suburbs, and if he managed to get a vacation in once every couple of years, he was happy. Now, he just wanted to enjoy every experience he could manage to get himself in to.

Tony had an innate talent for knowing where the threats would be, and could look at an area, pinpoint the weak spots, and secure a site without ever having been there. He attributed this to his rock climbing experience. When climbing, if you aren't thinking one step ahead you would most certainly have a short climb and a long fall. A good climber could look at the rocks and set his path to the top before starting. He found many parallels to rock climbing in his job, and they all came in handy at different times.

The heat was almost too extreme for climbing. Knowing he had the rest of the week, he finished the short climb and returned back to the campsite tired, but content. There was no sense in getting completely exhausted the first full day. He could have used a nice hot shower or a nice relaxing hot tub, but had neither. City living had nearly turned him into a creampuff, he thought, as he washed off with a cold-water-soaked towel.

The sun was just starting to set, fading into a beautiful portrait of vivid red and orange streaks, running perpendicular to the clay-colored cliffs. Rays of sun brightly scattered through the cloudless sky into a scene that was almost surreal. Just as he watched the sun sink behind the horizon, the moon came up behind him. At one moment in time, both were visible in the evening sky.

The moon was as large as he had ever seen it. Even with the remaining light from the sun casting a red glow over its surface, he could see distinct recognizable features. The depressions on its surface were visibly darker, making the sea of tranquility stand out like a nose on a face. He had hated the astronomy class he took in college to get out of taking the much more dreaded Physics, but was now happily pointing out constellations, remembering how each had unique origins in mythical history.

He thought this might just be one of the most memorable times in his life as he thought back on it. At his young age, the highlight of his life was the day he was promoted to the team to protect Eagle 2. He earned the position, but was still happy for the opportunity. Many agents worked an entire career and never achieved this position. Protecting the president was the highest honor a Secret Service Special Agent could have, but this was close enough for now.

The only downside to the job was the lack of rock climbing opportunities on the East Coast, but he had found a local climbers club in the city that had set up some indoor climbing walls so he could maintain his skills. It was not climbing with the wind in your hair and the dust in your mouth, but it was as close as he was going to get.

Tony looked to the sky once again and smiled as he sat in silence.

Chapter 6

The meeting with the Israeli Ambassador went exactly as Tom knew it would. Peace in the Middle East would come at a price, a price to the American people. The Israeli Ambassador actually had the balls to say that his government could no longer afford to continue to protect its people from the PLO terrorists and greatly needed aid to support their military and provide training to their police force.

The request made Tom cringe as he thought about the money they had already spent in the name of Middle East peace. The PLO would, of course, resist all aid given to Israel, with blood. It wasn't just the threats that worried him. The PLO terrorists were ruthless savages. He would think heavily about this situation before making any promises that would endanger American citizens.

"Of course," Tom said to himself, thinking about the meeting, "we have already sent them God knows how many billions with the promise of peace, and now they want more." The PLO was against the aid to Israel from the beginning, actually publicly stating that if the U.S. didn't stop the aid payments that they would take action to ensure it stopped.

Rabin Abbas, the idolized leader of the PLO for the past thirty years, had died after an agonizing struggle with cancer three months earlier. For three decades he terrorized the west by uniting the Palestinians and empowering them to take action while secretly accepting aid from the U.S. At one point, Abbas arrogantly commented to the press that the money given to the PLO by the U.S. was a mere carrot, enticing them to agree to peace without the belief that peace was possible. But still the money continued to flow, along with the blood of innocent people, and Abbas condoned every death by secretly shunning the unification efforts.

Tom was always cautious around the PLO, but now more than ever. After the death of Abbas, a power struggle within the organization left Yassad Al-Bourth, the highest-ranking general of the Hamas, the most logical choice to succeed Abbas. Tom privately celebrated the death of Abbas, but soon found that Al-Bourth was even more ruthless. His popularity within the Hamas, the most radical side of the PLO, would mean that peace in that region would be virtually impossible.

The CIA reported the organization was trying to bring back more of a military power and would take drastic steps to see that the U.S. stayed out of their affairs. Al-Bourth had even gone as far as to declare the Oslo Accord, the 1993 secret peace agreement, null and void in a video tape secretly sent to CNN by his supporters. While the Oslo Accord, signed by Abbas, had not stopped the conflicts, it did lessen them considerably and was publicly supported by his predecessor. This act was tantamount to taking ten steps back after fifteen years of baby steps forward. The tension between Israel and the PLO was quickly reaching a desperate impasse, and Tom wasn't sure he wanted to get the U.S. in the middle of the conflict.

Al-Bourth did not hide the fact that he fully supported the Palestinian Front for the Liberation of Palestine, or PFLP. The vast majority of the top most-wanted terrorists on the American list were members of the PFLP, the most heartless organization in the Hamas. Although Tom could not prove it, he suspected the lion's share of the money the U.S. sent to the Palestines was directly funneled to the PFLP. He anticipated some level of resurgence in activity from the Hamas during his term, but had no idea what to expect.

It didn't take the president of the United States to know that Arabs, both Israeli and Palestinian, really didn't want peace. Anyone interested in Middle-Eastern affairs could see that. If peace ever did come to the Middle East, foreign aid would dry up and none of the Arab nations could afford that. If that should happen, sickness, famine and poverty would guide the decisions of every Arab ruler.

He sighed to himself as he sat at his desk. It was late and he needed to get some sleep. He had bigger things on his plate than the Palestinians. The hurricane looming off the coast of Texas and the Russian situation were heavy on his mind and he needed to have a clear head. As he walked to his office, Sally greeted him.

"Goodnight, sir," she said with a pleasant smile on her face.

"Goodnight, Sally," he said and continued walking past her desk.

"Will you need anything special for tomorrow?" she asked him as he passed.

"I know it is late, but could you please place a call to David for me? If possible, I would like him here first thing tomorrow with all of the information he could uncover about the Russian situation."

"Certainly, sir, right away," and she punched the vice president's private line on her phone.

Tom decided against going into the office and he walked slowly down the long hallway from the west wing into the living room of private living quarters. These were the rooms tourists never saw on the White House tour. He took off his suit coat in an effort to wind down from the day. He was not overly busy, but his stress level was through the roof. He had a bad feeling about the Russian situation and the report by Mr. Palmer. Hopefully he would find out tomorrow just how much information was left out of his earlier briefing. What would he do if he found the CIA was holding information from him? Vital information at that!

Tom walked into the bathroom, looked into the mirror and began loosening the tie around his neck. Was this the same person who took office less than a year ago? He looked so tired and weary all the time. He had felt so young and vibrant during his campaign, and now he knew how his namesake felt during the long years of slavery and the Civil War. It was no wonder there were no pictures of Abraham Lincoln smiling during his presidency, Tom thought to himself.

He removed the rest of his clothes and decided to take a shower before going to bed. He always did his best thinking in the shower and came out feeling refreshed both in body and mind. He turned the hot water on, filling the room with steam, and then adjusted the water temperature to lukewarm to lower his body temperature before sleeping. He stepped into the stream of water and immediately felt relaxed.

As he scoured his body with soap, he thought about President Stefanovich. He hadn't seen the man in over ten years, but could still picture his striking features as though they had met today for lunch. He knew that a decisive military move by the government would be seen as hostile action and would then be broadcast on every news channel from Beijing to New York City.

He also knew the moment the Russian army moved a couple T-90 tanks and a few BTR Armored Personnel Carriers around the crowd—it would get out of hand. The Russians wouldn't just stop at tanks though, they would arrogantly display their Hind helicopters equipped with air to surface missiles, for an extra show of strength. It was the Russian way. But this is exactly what Tom didn't want to happen. The press would have a field day with it, and innocent civilians would be killed, he was sure of that.

"Reporters were just war hungry scavengers looking for a story to fill a time slot," he mumbled through the warm steam. He knew they would exploit any action the Russian government would take and put a humanitarian spin on it so it looked as if the Russian government was preying on its citizens. He had seen it happen many times before and had no reason to believe it wouldn't happen again. CNN had reporters everywhere and would broadcast the entire event live as it unfolded to the world. He wished they would think about the consequences of their actions before leaking a story like this to the entire world, but each of the reporters was secretly thinking of winning the next Pulitzer. Oh well, he was not going to change the press. His only real hope was to stop the killing before it started.

The warm water cascaded over his body in sheets as he reached for the handles to stop the water. He knew what he had to do. *Regardless of the information David has, I am going to send him over to talk to Stefanovich in hopes of diffusing the problem.* David was good at resolving problems and was one heck of a salesman. Even if he couldn't talk directly to Grigory, the idea of a representative of the United States visiting, especially the vice president, would look good to both parties and even more importantly, the press.

He stepped out of the shower and grabbed a towel. As he dried himself, he thought at least the job came with nice towels. They were soft, like the ones people stole from very expensive hotels.

His wife was already sleeping, and he pulled on the silk pajamas that he wore religiously and slipped into bed. She stirred for a moment, and Tom thought she woke with the rustling, but she rolled over and he knew from her breathing that she was still deep asleep. She was used to his late night outings, enough to not wake when he came to bed. As his head hit the pillow, his mind raced over sending David into an unknown and potentially dangerous situation one last time, but he knew it was the only way to help. He drifted off to restless sleep with his mind wandering over many scenarios and he had more questions than answers.

His internal body clock woke him every morning at 5:30 without the benefit of an alarm, allowing his wife to sleep another hour. He slowly dressed in his workout clothes and stepped into the hallway. He was tired, but the exercise would get his blood pumping to start the day.

The secret service team assigned to him was already dressed and ready for the morning jog. Usually, the team members hated the fact that they were forced to jog at the president's pace, but it was all part of the job. This president was different than the others; he was younger and kept a healthy pace through the two-mile course, giving the agents a good workout.

Rarely did the president talk during his run and the team always kept a few paces behind to allow him breathing room and to dodge the myriad of reporters hoping to get a shot of the president in some compromising position. The veteran agents flipped quarters to decide who was going to ride in the Suburban that followed. The rookies knew they were just out of luck.

When he finished the brisk jog, Tom stretched out his aching muscles and headed to his shower while the agents showered and dressed in their tailored black suits for the remainder of the day. Steam filled his small bathroom as he washed the sweat from his body. He really wanted to wash the stress away with it, but that didn't happen, he was still exhausted. The run did allow him to focus on a solution to his immediate problem and knew what he needed to do.

Tom stepped out of the shower to find his smiling wife holding a towel. She knew he did not sleep well and wanted to show him that she knew he was feeling stressed, too. They had been married almost ten years and she saw the lines on his face getting deeper with each passing day. She handed him the towel and kissed him, hoping to make him feel better, but she could feel his lips tense.

"I love you, Tom Lincoln," she said to him. She was a sucker for dark-haired men.

"I love you too," he said directly back to her.

She looked into his eyes and turned to walk out of the room so he could dress. As he toweled himself, he wished he could tell her what was on his mind. He wanted to be able to talk to her about his day like they talked when they were first married. The thoughts he had swirling through his head she wouldn't understand; she couldn't understand the seriousness of the situation. He knew she was intelligent, that was one of the things that drew him to her, that and her sense of humor, but she didn't know the background and history of the Russian President. Of course, her gorgeous body didn't hurt either, he said to himself as he cracked open the door and looked out at her making the bed. Her sexy curves were outlined by the silk fabric of the long green gown, and her nipples hardened as the silk slid across her skin.

Tom dressed quickly and walked to the long mirror in the bedroom to make sure his tie was tightened and he looked like a president should. Satisfied that he at least looked the part, he walked out of the bedroom and up to his wife who was looking out the window at the bright rays of the sun shining off the buildings of the city.

"Oh, Tom, it all looks so peaceful in the morning."

"I know," he said, wrapping his arms around her.

"When this is all over, I want to move to a farm in the country and watch the sun rise over the trees without a care in the world," she said to him. "Can we do that, honey?"

"I promise, when this is over I will buy you that farm in the country," he said and kissed the back of her neck. He loved the smell of her skin. The presidency plays hell with a person's love life, he thought to himself as he took one last smell of her hair and stepped away before things got carried away.

Chapter 7

Bill Snyder, the president's chief of staff opened the door and Tom walked through, heading first toward his desk before greeting David. Tom picked up the daily brief before saying a word. He opened the sealed envelope and scanned the headings quickly. As he looked over the paper he told David to have a seat in the chair facing the desk.

"Good morning, David, I hope you got some rest last night," Tom said, still scanning the document. "How's the wife?"

"She's doing fine, and yes, sir, I am feeling more rested than I have in weeks, thank you for asking. Trips to countries in this part of the world take far less out of me than the damn trip to Africa I took last month," David said matter of factly. "I do have some good news. The hospital called an hour ago and told us the baby was born healthy and happy."

"Congratulations! You and Kathy must be thrilled," Tom said, smiling a large, genuine smile. "Being a father is one of the most precious gifts man can ever receive. I am so happy for you," he said as he finished shaking hands and patting him on the back. "No cigar for the well wishers?"

"Thank you, sir, and no cigars. Sorry, I didn't have time."

"It appears we have a nasty storm heading toward the Texas coast," Tom said, still scanning over the papers. "The latest National Weather Service forecast shows it hitting Texas in another twelve to fourteen hours. It's a nasty one. The wind speed is currently at 85 miles per hour, and the eye is nearly a mile wide. The warm weather this summer has raised the water temperature in the gulf, which doesn't help much. We could be facing a Category 5 storm in a hurry."

"Ah yes, the Mexican weather forecasters were following the storm across the Florida Keys when I was there. But, I thought that it was tracking more south."

"The gulf stream started to push it north early yesterday. It appears Mexico may not get anything from it."

"Sorry, I should be more up to speed on things, but I was swamped yesterday. I haven't even had a chance to watch the latest forecast," David said, picking up a newspaper sitting on the table.

"Well, I have the military bases on alert to provide security and whatever equipment they can manage. The governor and I spoke earlier this morning, and he hasn't mandated an evacuation order for Corpus Christi, but I think it is a matter of time. I have seen reports of traffic jams on I-37 and I-77 nearly ten miles long. People are getting out even without the order, but it is a real mess down there. The Red Cross and FEMA are already on-site, managing the preparation efforts. The last I spoke with Mr. Johanssen of the Red Cross, Padre Island is a ghost town. I have a feeling we will be dealing with a crisis this time tomorrow. Mother Nature sure has a way of throwing a knock out punch when we least expect it."

"How much help has the Homeland Security Department been with the preparation?"

"You know how I feel about Homeland Security. They are more worried about spending money than protecting Americans."

"I guess that means they have been no help."

"Hummpf, not even a phone call," Bill Snyder said coldly.

"I have been on the phone with the governor daily since Friday," the president said, looking at Snyder. We have done all we can—the rest is in God's hands," he finished, looking down at this desk. "Well, enough about my problems, what do you have on the riots?"

"To be honest, sir, the information about the riots in Moscow was very easy to get with it being so public," David said. The order to not contact the CIA put a wrench in his efforts, but he managed. Most of the information came from two very good staffers at the NSA. It didn't hurt that CNN was running a special report of the riots nearly around the clock, complete with interviews of people on the street outside the Kremlin.

"Give me the bottom line, David. I don't mean to be short, but I am afraid time is critical."

"Well, sir, it appears that the Russian government is in bad shape. One bad decision or move made in haste could launch the situation into a Civil War if it hasn't already. It is that critical. My opinion is the rioters are mostly angry Muscovites protesting against Russia's military involvement in neighboring countries. Over the past decade the Russian government has secretly diverted billions to the military. I am sure the majority of those in the crowd are cold, hungry citizens showing their displeasure about being ignored. However, anyone could be hidden in the masses including terrorists waiting for a chance at glory. If that happens, we both know how dangerous the situation is."

The president's eyes narrowed as he stared at David. Their friendship had grown over the past year into a highly productive team. He liked how the vice president was always straightforward. None of the functionary bullshit politicians have a flare for. This did present one problem. He would now have to rely on the CIA and Ryan Palmer, and he was positive he wouldn't like that much.

The government relied too heavily on the CIA before the Iraq invasion and the whole weapons of mass destruction debacle. The former president was forced into making a decision based on bad CIA intel, and it ended up biting him in the ass. Officially, the CIA was directly blamed for the way they handled the Weapons of Mass Destruction, but the president didn't come out unscathed. Tom just simply didn't trust them after that.

The Senate commission's inquiry had indicated the CIA needed an overhaul from the ground up, but nothing had been done to this point. Doing that would take some thought, and he didn't want to make the time.

"Is there any evidence of a Chechen involvement in the riots?"

"I could find no evidence of that, but the riot is growing by the hour. Anything could be possible."

"David, do you think a trip to Moscow would help?"

"I don't know, Tom. The whole city is a mess."

"I know, I have been watching CNN, too. We need to do something with this. I just can't let the situation get out of control."

"I think it's inevitable. I'm surprised Stefanovich has lasted this long."

"The press would absolutely destroy us if the Russian military started shooting," Snyder said. "If innocent civilians are killed, the Democrats will jump all over our foreign policy promises."

"Yes, that is the sort of thing we don't need. I still see pictures and news clips from the Chinese riots and that was twenty years ago," the president sighed.

"I have thought about that. From the reports it appears that the tanks and soldiers are already way too close to the situation. I saw one news clip late last night that showed the rioters close enough to an APC to toss rocks and bottles at it. It's a bad situation all the way around."

"You could meet with President Stefanovich to discuss a possible solution to his problems. You might try to suggest giving his people food as a good starting point," Tom said, appalled that a political leader would let his people starve. "As a side note, I would also like to see him move his troops out of Chechnya. If nothing, it will make the Chechens happy, but don't press it if you don't think it is a good idea. Don't worry about the convention—I'll cover for you. This Russian situation is much too important. I guess in short, I would really like you to go."

David stared at the papers in his lap, shaking his head because he knew what he was being asked. Of course, he could not refuse. *No one* refused the president. David nodded his head and said, "I will leave as soon as I am packed and the Air Force can get the plane prepped for the trip."

"Be careful, David," Tom said as he stood. He saw a look of disappointment on David's face, but figured it was just concern over how to handle the situation. He was confident David could diffuse it. Handling this type of situation was what he did best.

David stood tall and smiled back at the president. He put his best face on and turned toward the door.

"Oh, and one more thing, David, don't tell the CIA where you are going or why!" Tom said sternly. "I don't want this to get out. It is a personal request, you understand."

Chapter 8

A thousand things flew into his head the moment he walked out of the office, all of them telling him that he didn't need this trip in his life right now. As soon as he heard the door close to the Oval office, David felt an enormous weight on his shoulders.

"Shit," he mumbled under his breath. "Don't discuss this with the CIA! What the hell was he thinking going against protocol? How can I coordinate my security team without the CIA? Surely he didn't mean that! What am I going to tell my wife? She has been so patient."

He was trying to formulate a good reason to tell his wife why he had to go on this trip. He was sure she wouldn't understand, regardless of the reason, even though she would put a strong smile on her face and tell him she did. They had just received the call from the hospital that they could visit their son tomorrow and with the adoption papers signed they could bring him home in three days.

They had been trying for years to have a baby and couldn't. David had devoted his entire life since leaving home, to his career. Having kids was not on his hot list, but he was at the pinnacle of his career and getting older. It was now or never. They didn't want to take the traditional fertility treatments because of the higher risks associated with multiple births. Political careers are not a good mix with quintuplets or even triplets for that matter.

They went through the usual battery of tests and found that David was the reason. He tried everything the doctors prescribed, hot/cold treatments, reducing his caffeine intake, and even the special underwear didn't work for goodness sake. It is a wonder that never got out to the press! Nothing worked so they decided to adopt an infant to start their family.

After they made the decision, things started to fall into place. His wife's volunteer work at the battered woman's shelter just outside the city put her in touch with a young single girl who was recently beaten by her boyfriend for becoming pregnant.

His wife approached the girl about the possibility of adoption rather than abortion, something that women did when they had a bleak outlook and no health insurance. The girl quickly agreed because it meant that she would get health care and money for food, two things she desperately needed. The girl had no idea that the woman she was talking to was the vice president of the United States' wife. It would not have changed her mind anyway. She was tired, hungry and desperate.

That was two months ago and tomorrow they were going to be able to see the baby for the first time. They had picked a name and decorated the nursery in light blue as soon as they found out it was going to be a boy last month. His wife would be disappointed he was sure of it. She had been on a cloud for weeks.

He walked down the hallway of the west wing, his mind was racing over everything he had to do for the trip. The first thing was to alert Andrews Air Force Base to prep his plane for the trip and then call the security detail and have them assemble the teams. He wanted to have his best security detail because the possibility for things to get out of control was extremely high. As he entered his office, calling his wife was his top priority. Sitting in his large executive leather chair, he punched up his secretary on the intercom.

"Good morning, Jane," he said. "Please contact Andrews and have them have the plane ready for a trip to Moscow this evening. Contact Ben Lassiter and give him a heads up. Also, get my wife on the line."

"Certainly, sir," Jane said on the phone and he immediately heard the phone to his house ringing.

"Hello?" a sleepy voice said on the phone.

"Good morning, sweetheart, I am sorry to wake you. I have something that I need to tell you."

"Let me guess, you aren't going to be able to meet me at the hospital," she said with a sound of knowing disappointment.

"Tom wants me to fly to Moscow this afternoon and I need to prepare."

She knew he wouldn't miss this if he could help it. Since the election he had been traveling more than he had been home. She missed him when he wasn't around, but understood why he was gone. Knowing why didn't make it any easier though, and she knew that tomorrow was the biggest thing he had missed since they were married.

The silence on the other end of the phone proved that she was not happy. David thought for a minute what to tell her.

"I am sorry; this is a very important trip. You know I wouldn't miss seeing our baby if it wasn't."

"I know that," his wife said, but still couldn't mask her feelings. "I will take care of things until you get back. I always do."

"I love you," he added. "I promise, when I get back I will take a few days off."

"Oh—I love you too," she said unable to be mad at him. "I am just disappointed. I will hold you to that promise you know."

"I know! I am disappointed too. I will see you tonight."

"Okay, see you soon."

He decided to not say any more because she saw through him anyway, she always could. More words would just sound like excuses. He promised himself that when this trip was over he would take a break. He deserved it and with the new baby he needed it.

As he replaced the receiver the thought of a vacation brought a smile to his tired face until Jane buzzed him that the security unit had been notified.

"Jane, please get Lassiter on the phone for me. I need to talk to him personally about this."

"Certainly, sir."

As he studied the briefing he prepared earlier for the president, his mind wandered to the CIA comment. He would need the CIA to prepare for this trip, surely the president knew that. Other than the riots, he had no idea what he was getting into. He felt as if he would be flying blind. Even though he knew he could trust his security staff to keep him safe, David wanted all information the CIA could give him on the situation. One can never have too much information when entering a situation like the one he faced.

His phone beeped indicating that the security chief was on the other end. He picked it up slowly trying to formulate the words in his head before speaking. "Ben, have the security team prepped and ready for a trip to Moscow. We should be gone about four days and I want a team to leave now, if possible, to make sure the area is secure before we land. I want to leave tonight," David said in a voice that sounded more sure than he felt.

"With such short notice, I can only assemble two teams. I also won't have time to get the C-5 ready with the convoy vehicles," Lassiter said with a cringe. The normal compliment of three teams was what he felt comfortable with. He could then have two ride with one team in reserve should things go bad. He was having trouble with this already.

"Do you think two will be enough? I don't like going in without our normal security team," David said into the phone.

"I am not sure what we are going to run into over there. I have seen the reports on CNN, but I am in the dark with the rest. If the Russians give us the vehicles and drivers to get from the airport to the Kremlin we should be in relatively good shape without the convoy and the third team. I will do my best."

"We should be in and out within 48 hours with two travel days. Two teams should be able to button up tight enough to get us through," David said, trying to be confident into the phone.

"Yes, sir, I will advise you when we are ready," the voice on the other end of the phone said and then hung up.

Ben Lassiter looked the security part. His high and tight hair was turning gray, his ice-blue eyes seemed capable of staring through walls, and his large chest made his shirts appear a size too small.

At nearly sixty he was considered nearing retirement, but Lassiter had not even started to consider slowing down. He had come up through the ranks of the Army, seeing action in both Vietnam and the Gulf War. He was cautious and thorough—two qualities David had grown fond of. He had a gruff demeanor and tough exterior, but David trusted Lassiter with his life as had every vice president for the past fifteen years.

Chapter 9

Tony Hampton had just returned for lunch from a tiring climb in the most ungodly heat. His body was exhausted and his white teeth shown like pearls contrasted against his dust-covered face. He unzipped the door to his tent to get some water from his canteen to wash up before making something to eat over a campfire. He pulled off his sweat soaked t-shirt, bearing his tightly muscled, lightly tanned torso, tossing it over his shoulder. No sooner had he splashed water onto his face, his cell phone buzzed catching him off guard. He wiped his wet face on his dirty t-shirt and grabbed his phone from his pack. He looked at the number and recognized it right away. *Shit*, he thought as he thumbed the answer button.

"Yes, sir, this is Tony."

"Tony, I need you back here by 1600 today. You are going on a little trip for a week or so. No questions, just get back here ASAP."

"Yes, sir, I will leave right away. I will be cutting it close though."

"If you have any problems with flights let me know. I want your ass here."

"Will do, sir," Tony said as he disconnected the call.

The urgency in his voice was a concern. Tony knew the trip docket was empty because of the convention and he wasn't scheduled to work that. For his boss to offer help was odd, it must be an emergency.

He didn't waste any time clearing the campsite and packing his gear. He threw it all in the back of the rented jeep and drove the 27 miles to town just after eleven. He needed to drop the climbing supplies off at the sporting goods store first and then stop in at the gas station. He wasn't even sure if the town had a cab; Sundance wasn't a big town by any means. Rather than chance it, he would drive it to the airport. It was one they had repaired and the owner couldn't pay the bill, hopefully they wouldn't mind. It wasn't comfortable on the bumpy roads, but he didn't care as long as it got him back.

He pulled into town and made a call to the airport to see if he could change his flight and then decided to call rather than stop by the gas station and the sporting goods store. He didn't say exactly what happened only that an emergency came up at work and he needed to cut his vacation short. He was sure it would cost him extra money, tourist towns charged for everything.

However much it was would be cheaper than getting a cab out here. The man at the gas station promised to pick up the jeep and return the gear.

As the jeep's large tires hummed down the pavement toward the airport, his mind raced through a myriad of thoughts about the call from Lassiter. He tried to call a friend in the service to find out, but his cell phone battery was almost dead and the service was too intermittent to complete the call. This was very strange in deed.

He looked at his watch and quickly figured that if the plane departed on time from Wyoming, he would be in D.C. around 1500 with the layover and time change. He would stop by his apartment quickly unpack, shower, and repack and then report to the White House around 1600. This was as fast as he could possibly make it and he even felt lucky getting a flight out of this place last minute.

He pulled the jeep into the parking lot, locked it, and headed into the terminal. The only items he had with him were a carry on and the original ticket. He liked to travel light for just this reason. No bags to check made things very fast and convenient.

The agent behind the counter looked almost as tired as he felt.

"I called earlier about changing my flight."

"Ah, yes, sir, will you be checking any bags?"

"No," Tony said as he showed her his service badge."

"Very good, the plane will begin boarding any minute. Please wait for the announcement and thank you for flying Continental Express."

"Thank you," Tony said as he picked up his bag and headed through security.

Within a fifteen minutes, he was on a small plane bound for St. Louis and then a connecting flight to Dulles. The switch in tickets had cost him nearly $300, which he charged. *Thank god for plastic*, he thought.

The small Beechcraft 1900 held a maximum of 19 passengers, but was nearly empty on the trip to St. Louis. The plane's light weight caused it to bounce more with the turbulence than he was used to, but he took it in stride. With one seat on each side of the aisle, everyone had a window seat as he stared out into the clouds and thought about what could possibly be so urgent. He really wished that his boss had given him some idea about what to expect so he could at least prepare mentally before his arrival. Now he was walking in cold to a situation he knew literally nothing about.

What would he need? kept circling in his head as his eyes slowly closed surrendering to the time spent in the sun the last two days. The lone stewardess pulled a light blanket from the overhead storage and covered him up, letting him sleep the rest of the trip.

Chapter 10

Alexander glanced back at Andre as they moved towards the woods and deep cover. Neither said a word to the other as Andre followed quickly behind. Before entering the woods, Alexander looked toward the river and the large stone bridge to see if the other members were in place for the attack.

The large field sloped away from the tree line toward the river nearly five hundred meters from where he stood giving him an excellent vantage point to view the situation. The field was a mass of tall stalks of green grass topped with yellow and white flowers. A short stone fence barely waist high ran parallel to the river about thirty yards from its bank. Farmers built the wall when they cleared the field for pasturing and, like the bridge, it had been there for hundreds of years.

He could see his men running around placing the charges and finding suitable cover behind the short stonewall, just as planned. They would be ready when the convoy reached them. Alexander was not overly confident in the explosives. He was counting on the old mortar and the bridge's sheer weight to make the bridge unsafe, hoping the old stone bridge didn't get destroyed. That would cut off the townspeople from Grozny and make Alexander's group rather unpopular. However, if it came to it, he would not hesitate to bring it down. With some luck, they could stop the advance on the opposite side of the river and save the bridge.

Those closest to the river would have either light AK-47 machine guns or grenade launchers, allowing them to move quickly. Those responsible for setting the charges on the bridge carried only AK-47s along with the detonation device, while himself and Andre tasked with destroying the stalled convoy, carried launcher tubes with five armor piercing missiles each. Andre would be close to him through the day, which made Alexander feel better, but did little to alleviate the anxiety of the approaching tanks.

Alexander pressed the button on his radio. "Are the charges set and ready?"

"Da, we are ready for them," came the reply.

"Perfect. Wait for my order before setting them off; we don't want to give away our position too early."

With a deep breath, Alexander stepped into the tree line disappearing immediately into the thick growth. The branches of the short pine trees hung nearly to the ground making it difficult to move very far into the forest. The scent of the trees, the needles, and the pitch reminded him of walks he used to take with his father when he was younger. The picture etched into his memory of his father shielding his mother and brother in the corner of his kitchen immediately narrowed his focus as he found an opening with a view out over the pasture. The temperature dropped considerably in the shade and he was thankful that he remembered to wear a light camouflage jacket. The trees did, however, provide excellent cover from the convoy and the bright sun. From this distance, the sun would surely play a role in their ability to sight in the tanks with the missiles.

Alexander was sure the thick armored, tanks would require multiple hits and they would be vulnerable to counter attack during the reload. He looked up through the branches of the trees and knew that although they would help provide cover they wouldn't stop the 125mm tank shells. Alexander shuddered when he thought about the next few minutes of his life. It felt patriotic to plan attacks, but carrying them out took the kind of guts and determination that only came from a past like Alexander's.

Alexander could hear the metal tracks of the tanks screeching as they made their way down the road long before he saw their greenish-brown armored skin looming in the distance. He could swear he felt the ground rumble as they made their way toward the river. The road they were traveling, like all roads in the small country, was barely wide enough for two-lane traffic. The large tanks took nearly the entire width of the road forcing oncoming cars off to let them pass.

Alexander soon realized the narrow road was not even wide enough for the large tanks to turn around. The situation was actually better than hoped. If they could stop the first tank before crossing the bridge, they could stop the entire convoy and save the bridge. This couldn't be any more perfect. They would have them in the open and at a complete disadvantage.

Alexander grasped the binoculars hanging around his neck and scoped the advancing convoy. As he suspected, there was a fast moving armored personnel carrier leading the convoy followed by two large T-90 tanks and three smaller trucks filled with Russian troops. If they could wait until the personnel carrier was on the bridge to blow the charges they would only have to deal with the tanks and the troops in the trucks. The heavy armor would have no choice, but to remain on the other side of the river.

The rumbling grew increasingly more intense as the convoy approached the bridge. Alexander thumbed the switch of his radio and spoke in a whisper.

"Blow the charges when the APC is in the middle."

"Da, comrade," came the reply.

Andre glanced at Alexander and could see the tightness of his friend's face and knew he was as scared on the inside as he appeared on the outside. Alexander gave him the thumbs up trying to show a confident exterior, but his insides were also a jumble of nerves.

"Fire on the closest tank in the column as soon as the first explosive goes off; we can't give them a chance to fire those large guns. If we catch them off guard we stand a chance. I will follow with the second tank until they are destroyed."

Andre gave him a nod and then loaded the first missile as the convoy advanced arrogantly ahead.

Just as ordered, when the APC moved into the center of the old stone bridge, the first charge went off stopping the tanks and the trucks on the far side of the river. The bridge seemed to shake off the explosion as a cloud of dust and debris filled the air. He could see troops pour out of the APC in a stunned, frenzied race for survival. Four advanced toward the near side of the river while two others retreated to the safety behind the looming tanks.

The four advancing were the immediate threat. As soon as they crossed the bridge Alexander saw them spread out in traditional attack formation. Two groups of two crouched in single file covering each side of the narrow road before spreading out into the field. The four highly trained soldiers immediately spotted the one with the remaining detonation device and rounds burst all around him. Alexander, with the binoculars pressed tightly against his face, saw the rounds tear into his friend's body as the brave man's fingers clasped the detonation lever. Four, five, six times his body jerked from the bullets impacting his body and his shirt turned a dark crimson red. As Alexander watched his friend's body slump to the ground he thought it was too late, the bridge would not go down. Through the binoculars, he could see the others stare at their fallen comrade, as the second charge tore through the bridge.

The old bridge shook, but remained steady. For a split second Alexander thought the bridge was going to remain standing. Rocks and dust mushroomed into the air showering both sides of the riverbanks obscuring it from his view. With a sickening roar, the center of the bridge collapsed taking the APC and the two remaining troops into the river. The old stone gave in to its sheer weight, but large sections on both sides of the bank remained which would make rebuilding faster and easier.

Thank god, he thought as he prepared to take on the tanks.

A bright flash went off to Alexander's right and he knew it was Andre's first missile. He could hear the rattle of machine guns on the banks of the river as he lined up on the second tank. Unfamiliar with the launcher, Alexander lowered himself to one knee and placed the firing tube on his shoulder. Just as he squeezed the trigger he saw the muzzle flash of the tank's smooth bore gun firing toward them. The tank commander must have seen Andre's missile flash. They knew exactly where they were hiding. The launcher had relatively little recoil, he expected it to be more. He watched the track of the missile striking the tank just as its shell came crashing into the trees.

The sound was deafening which made his heart pound and his vision blurry. Splinters of shattered trees fell around them, but unfazed, Alexander still watched intently as the battle unfolded. The smell of burnt gunpowder overpowered his senses as he looked at Andre. He reloaded and smiled with as much confidence as he could muster. The second tank was now firing on the small group nearest the bridge. Smoke and dust filled the air as he watched his friends scramble for more cover. Andre fired a second missile at the tank and it was now starting to billow thick black smoke. In an instant, they both saw the deadly turret turning and lining them up. The two remained perfectly still, scared beyond comprehension. The muzzle flashed a second time and the two braced for the impact. This one came through the trees and hit ground twenty meters from them sending dirt, leaves, and branches into the air. They are getting too close Alexander thought as he reloaded for a second shot. Just as he was sighting the tank in, a third shell exploded to his right sending him to the cold ground. His ears were ringing and his fingers shook, still on the trigger. He lifted his head slowly off the ground and did a quick once over just to make sure everything was still attached. No blood, just badly shaken.

He then scanned the woods through the clearing smoke, but couldn't see a thing. "Andre," Alexander yelled. "Not you too Andre," Alexander cried out to the trees. He felt a rage build up in his blood as he returned to his knee to fire the second missile. It was as if the next few minutes passed in slow motion. With tears now forming in his eyes, he squeezed the trigger. The flare trail from the advancing missile streaked toward the tank as if it had a mind of its own. Every one of his movements seemed to him to be slow and deliberate as he took his eye off the tank to search for his friend. The ground still smoldered where the shell impacted the soft soil. "Andre," Alexander choked out again.

"Damn, it was going to miss," he sputtered as he turned to look at the tank. He needed to concentrate, but it was too hard. In an instant, the plan was falling apart. His comrades nearest the bridge were having no effect on the troops, partly because of the deadly tank rounds, and partly because of their inexperience with the weapons. The four trained Russian troops were bearing down on them quickly and would soon begin to overtake the stone wall.

Alexander had not accounted for the armor on the tanks being so difficult to penetrate. He immediately fired another missile at the tank that Andre had badly damaged. If this one could be destroyed it may give his comrades a chance. He took a deep breath to steady the launcher and closed his tear-filled eyes as he touched off the trigger. Within seconds, the tank exploded sending a shower of sparks twenty feet into the air. The Russian troops looked stunned as flames poured from the rear of the large pile of smoking, twisted metal.

The men hiding behind the wall heard the explosion. They excitedly fired their AK-47s in a wild, untrained fashion as grenades exploded on the partially demolished bridge near the dumbstruck Russian troops. The Russian soldiers remaining on the far side of the river expertly fired at the rebels. The unmistakable sound of the Russian rifles would be forever embedded in his head because it was those he heard the day he found his family. It was obvious his plan had all, but fallen apart and chaos was beginning to take over the action. If the second tank could be destroyed, they stood a chance to take the day. Moments wasted, and one thing was certain, all of his friends would die. He had already lost his best friend. He couldn't face losing the others.

Twenty meters to his right, Alexander saw a missile advance toward the remaining tank. Completely stunned, his head spun immediately toward where he thought it had come from—Andre, he was still alive. Alexander immediately felt his heart come back to life and he too fired his last missile within seconds of Andre's. Both impacted the tank in virtually the same location sending a large cloud of thick black smoke into the air. Alexander could see the top hatch of the tank open and troops scramble out of the burning mass.

The Russian tank crew ran toward the trailing transport vehicles and they all retreated back down the road. The acrid smell of smoke filled the air as he looked at the destruction in front of him. Through his binoculars, he could see Russian troops dead and dying on the far riverbank, but they needed to finish the plan before the Russians returned to counter this defeat.

He recklessly ran toward Andre through the thick cover and embraced him tightly. Neither man said a word as they looked at each other. The adrenaline of the past twenty minutes washed over them with each breath. It was now time to get to the car and head back to their flat. Quietly, they picked up their weapons and ran as fast as their shaky legs would take them. They threw everything they were carrying into the back seat of the small Lada and slumped down into the front seats, trying to restore their breathing back to normal.

Alexander turned the keys in the ignition and the small four-cylinder engine roared to life. As quickly as he heard the engine revving, he released the clutch and the front tires spun sending a shower of stones into the air. He jerked the wheel causing the car to fishtail as they raced off toward the city and the protection they knew they would have very soon.

The drive back was deathly quiet as the realization of what happened hit them like a brick wall. How many good friends were lost today? How would the Russians retaliate? What did they accomplish? What had they done?

Chapter 11

The small plane touched down at Dulles airport exactly at 1500. Tony walked down the narrow portable stairway onto the tarmac and was met by a fellow security team member. He was lucky enough to get some sleep on the last flight, but his head was still a little hazy.

"This must really be serious if they sent you for me," Tony said, smiling at his friend, Rodger Gentry. The normal transportation for a junior agent was a not so glamorous taxi while returning from vacation.

"We have got to get a move on! I have been waiting here for nearly an hour. The old man got the arrival times screwed up."

"I told him 1500," Tony said.

"I don't doubt that you did. Something has him pretty stressed out," Rodger said, opening the car door.

"Speaking of stress, what's the big emergency?" Tony asked as he tossed his bag into the back seat of the dark blue Ford and settled in the roomy front seat for the short drive back to the city. At mid-day the twenty miles back to the city didn't take long at all.

"I don't know any more about it than you do."

"Okay then, can we stop by my apartment quick so I can pick up a change or two of clothes?"

"Make it quick, we have a briefing at 1600 and Eagle 2 wants us in the air at 1730 at the very latest."

"15 minutes, I promise. I just need some clean underwear, shower, and a shave."

The car pulled up to his apartment building and Tony jumped out, pulling his bag with him. As he crossed the sidewalk the car sped off and he walked into the five-story building. He swung open the double glass doors and immediately was reminded of life in the city. The stale smell of the stairwell was unmistakably dank and the dark lobby was just another sobering reminder of not being on vacation and in the sun.

His feet hit every other step as he ran the two flights of stairs to apartment twenty-four and unlocked it with the set of keys in his bag. He tossed the bag with his dirty clothes into the corner behind the door and made a mad dash for his bedroom. He undressed in a flash, throwing his shorts and shirt onto the bed, and entered his small bathroom to clean up. He hadn't noticed how the dust had settled on his skin until he took his shorts off. The dust had coated his body everywhere his skin was exposed. It was the most unique color of red rock dust he had ever seen. He looked into the mirror while reaching for the electric razor he got from his mom last Christmas, wishing he was still hanging precariously by his fingers hundreds of feet off the ground instead of shaving the stubble from his face. With a satisfied last look, he jumped into the shower to rinse off the red dust and he was ready to dress in his traveling clothes.

He always wore the same outfit, dark blue suit coat, white shirt, paisley tie and dark gray slacks. He dressed in a flash and slipped his shoes on before throwing a change or two of clothes into an overnight bag and rushed out the door. One of the best things about being single was there was no one around to complain about leaving his dirty clothes on the floor.

Within thirty minutes Tony was sitting in the Secret Service offices at the White House. He really didn't have to rush. Lassiter had pushed the meeting back to 1630 to allow the others time to get there. Tony was just now starting to gather they were taking a trip to Russia. He could overhear the others talking around him and he soon began to comprehend the extent of the trip.

He was now grateful for the language classes he had back at the academy. Tony, having never been to Russia, finally would have a chance to practice his Russian skills on something other than translating intelligence reports. He had no reason to think it wouldn't be another routine visitation deployment like the one in Mexico City, only because he had not turned a television on in nearly a week. Besides, he thought, the advance team would have already taken care of securing the area and scouting for potential threats. Why was he called in for this one? There are others on the team with the same qualifications and he had this vacation planned for almost a year. "Oh well," he sighed under his breath as he glanced at his watch noticing it was still on Mountain time.

There was no shortage of clocks in this building. Every time zone in the world was represented with an individual clock with the zone names fixed in black lettering on the plastic faceplates. The largest clock in the middle showed the Greenwich Mean Time and was denoted with a large black Z representing its operational code name *"Zulu." Zulu* time was the standard that every government agency used to coordinate activities across time zones around the world. Regardless of the country or time zone, Zulu time remained a constant.

He pulled the knob on his Timex Expedition watch and spun the hands to the correct time, 1600 EST. Thirty more minutes and he would have a better idea of what was going on. He rocked the chair onto its back legs. Resting his head on the wall closing his eyes tightly, his mind drifted with exhaustion.

Tony was surfing the Internet one evening looking for information about a case on fraud he was assigned, and inadvertently came across the Secret Service web site. He loved the investigative nature of his job and, in reading the information provided on the site, it seemed to be the perfect match for him. He applied to the academy and was accepted in the first round of interviews. From there it took several months of tediously filling out a mountain of paperwork for the top secret clearance, lie detector tests, and then came the grueling personal interviews, but he was soon on his way to the Federal Law Enforcement Training Center in Georgia for ten weeks of investigative training. The Service hoped to weed most of the new recruits out in Georgia to save time and money in the advanced portions of training, so they made it tough in them. From there they moved to Beltsville, Maryland for the secret stuff, advanced weapons training and investigative techniques.

Tony had made it though the initial training top in his class and moved on with high marks through the James J. Rowley Training Center in Maryland. He was trained in the Russian language and soon became fluent enough to decipher Russian training documents and other political directives. Initially he was assigned menial duties of researching countries and terrorist groups in the new Russian Republics creating profiles of regions and political groups so agents would know what to expect when they arrived. He then moved into an *Advance Team* with responsibilities of surveying the actual site a dignitary was visiting and coordinating the visit with local police or military units. Tony learned a great deal from his work with the advanced teams. Within a year, he was promoted to his current position protecting Eagle 2.

Rodger kicked the chair leg Tony was sitting in startling him.

"The old man wants us in the briefing room," Rodger said with a grin.

"You, shit, I could have had a heart attack," Tony said, glancing at his watch.

Precisely at 1630, Ben Lassiter began the briefing by lowering the room lights. The brightness of the video projector hanging from the ceiling split the darkness as the most recent satellite picture of Moscow illuminated the screen. "Listen up, gentlemen. This will be a visitation trip to Moscow leaving at 1800 this afternoon. We will be escorting Eagle 2 to a meeting with President Stefanovich at the Kremlin."

All eyes in the room were focused on the screen, attempting to grasp how the rioting mass spread through the city. The picture was amazingly clear, having been taken during the last satellite run, and Tony could almost make out three pigeons perched on the Kremlin wall. The room was deathly quiet as Lassiter continued.

"I am sure by now you have seen the reports of riots in Red Square near the Kremlin. But as of thirty minutes ago rioters have yet to breach its walls. The latest intelligence indicates the crowd is growing and could contain some anti-Russian militant groups with small arms. The Russians have moved in some pretty heavy armor which, at the time of this reconnaissance photo, was placed in the corners here and here," Lassiter said, pointing the large tanks out with his red laser pointer. "St. Basil's Cathedral, over here," Lassiter circled the church with the pointer, "is being used by many civilians in the area for protection from the tanks and occasional helicopter flyover."

"Sir," a veteran agent spoke up, "how many rioters do you estimate are in the city?"

"That is not clear at this point because it changes by the hour; what is clear is that President Stefanovich has lost all control. President Lincoln wants to get a handle on how effectively the Russian President is handling the situation. He doesn't want this to turn ugly."

"Understood, sir," the veteran agent said, shaking his head.

Another slide was projected on the large white screen, showing a detailed map of the city. Lassiter continued to speak. "Eagle 2 will land at the airport, here," he said, pointing it out on the screen. "A convoy of three vehicles will proceed on this route," Lassiter followed the streets with his laser, "to the Grand Palace. With any luck, we will meet President Stefanovich at the front gate. Take note, we will not be taking the usual vehicles with us on this trip. With such short notice I could not get the C-5 in the air in time. We will be using Russian government transportation."

A new slide of the palace flashed with a circle around the elegantly decorated gated entrance they would be using. Lassiter used a laser pointer to show the exact location and positions he wanted each member of the team to be in as the president exited the vehicle.

Tony was running his assignment over in his head and thought that this was anything but ordinary—exit car one and stand ready as the second car with Eagle 2 pulled in behind. Fall in directly behind him into the palace. Hopefully the cars would be armored. They probably wouldn't need the armor, but with the situation as precarious as Lassiter has presented over there, anything could happen. One thing was certain, this trip would finally raise the excitement level—diplomatic trips were such a bore.

"One operational note," Lassiter said, shutting down the computer. "We did not have the resources or time to assemble our usual third team. Also, with such short notice it would have been a waste to send in the *Advance Team*. So, be careful. Copies of the slides with maps detailing the mission routes will be handed out at the door," Lassiter said, organizing his notes on the podium.

With the final words of the briefing over the lights came on and every member exited the briefing room discussing the trip quietly. In the parking garage, five dark blue Suburbans were waiting to take the team to Andrews Air Force Base where their bags were already being loaded along with the electronic equipment and weapons for the long trip.

The team settled into the large plane and the members sat quietly, the mission weighing heavily on their minds. Tony sat in a window seat, watching the airmen finalize the plane for takeoff. The presidential helicopter landed on the tarmac less than fifty yards from the aircraft as the jet's engines began their pre-flight test. Eagle 2 and several members of his staff exited the large blue helicopter and hurried up the steps into the plane. Within minutes, the VC-25A was taxing down the runway, cleared for the number one takeoff position. Of course they would be the number one position; only one person could trump that and he wasn't flying today.

With a tail number of 2900, the exterior of the large plane looked exactly like a Boeing 747-200B except for the painting scheme of a light blue nose, teal underbelly, and United States of America written in large lettering on both sides of the fuselage. It had the characteristic and unmistakable large hump along the top front of the plane, where in traditional 747s, first-class passengers would sit in large over-sized seats enjoying their wine and cheese.

But internally, this plane was vastly different. It carried state-of-the-art electronics, had a self-contained baggage loader, and could refuel in-flight, giving it an unlimited duty range. Meaning, it could fly anywhere in the world nonstop or remain in the air indefinitely, providing it could get to an in-flight refueling tanker. The seating layout was also vastly different.

The three levels and nearly four thousand square feet of floor space could easily seat one hundred passengers, including the crew. With that many passengers, the two galleys worked nonstop, preparing gourmet meals that were requested by the president. The food on Air Force was second to none. The chef was recruited from a five-star restaurant in New York City and stopped at nothing to ensure the food was five-star status, regardless of who was flying.

The president's separate living section was located in the nose of the plane complete with a bathroom with shower and workout room. While the crew, Secret Service personnel, and reporting staff sat in the rear out of sight behind the conference room. The upstairs, or first-class, section was an ultra-modern data center filled with electronics including a phone switch for the 90 telephones located throughout the plane. It also contained a medical facility staffed with a full-time doctor and was complete with a fully stocked pharmacy.

This unique aircraft was actually two of a kind. Tail numbers 2800 and 2900 were exactly alike, both housed at Andrews and lovingly cared for by the Presidential Airlift Group under the Air Mobility Command's 89th Airlift Wing. Each airman in the group was hand-selected by its commander from a pool of thousands of applicants. To say they were the Air Force elite would be an understatement.

Tony always loved the feeling just as the plane released its brakes and thrust forward under the weight of the four powerful General Electric jet engines. His back pressed into the seat and stomach jumped into his throat when the plane slowly lifted off the ground. Tony watched the long wing bow slightly from the air currents as the plane passed through the thick cloud cover. Nothing in the world besides rock climbing could compare to the feeling of sheer power at the precise moment of takeoff.

He loved flying on this airplane even more because of the space. Without the usual collection of reporters on this trip, the agents could stretch out in the cabin when they needed to get the blood flowing and when they needed some shut eye the seats practically folded flat. That was what Tony needed at this moment. The trip from Wyoming was starting to catch up with him and he wanted to be alert when they landed.

The plane leveled off at 33,000 feet and the cabin pressurized. Tony held his breath and his ears popped, adjusting to the pressure. Getting through the clouds was rougher than usual. Tony reclined the seat as far as it would go, hoping the rest of the trip was smooth as he unfolded a blanket to warm himself in the conditioned air of the cabin. His eye lids fluttered open each time the plane shook from turbulence, and then closed for the last time under the weight of being awake nearly two days straight.

At 5:35 in the afternoon, President Lincoln made the call to Moscow. He glanced at his watch and quickly calculated the eight-hour time difference. It was just after 1:30 in the morning, Moscow time; things should be quiet. He was sorry that he would be waking President Stefanovich, but this was not something that could wait. The phone rang twice before being picked up.

"DA," was the brief answer.

"President Stefanovich?"

"No, one minute," came the response in broken English.

Tom heard some muffled Russian in the background as a hand covered the receiver, and then heard his name. "Hello," came the more familiar voice on the other end of the phone. It was always amazing how crystal clear the phone lines were—5,000 miles and Stefanovich still sounded like he was sitting next door. Tom could hear the mass confusion in the background, sounding as if the governmental structure was crumbling from the inside rather than from the outside. "President, this is Tom Lincoln."

"Yes, how can I help you?" he asked in a heavy Russian accent.

"Well, sir, I have seen the reports on CNN about the riots and would like to know what is really going on."

"President Lincoln, with all due respect, I can't see where this is any of your concern."

"Human rights are the world's concern, President. If for one second you don't think these people are expressing their anger at the lack of support from your government, you are completely wrong. These people are hungry and frustrated. A starving dog will lash out at its owner simply as a means to survive, and these people are starving."

"This is a Russian problem and will be handled in the Russian way."

"Well, sir, I want to make sure your 'Russian way' doesn't harm innocent civilians on international television. Neither of us needs that right now!" Tom said, being strong with the president. "I have the vice president on a plane as we speak, to visit your country. I expect you to give him your attention and let him help you find a way out of this ugly situation. He will need transportation from the airport to your location. Please give him the highest level of security you have. I don't want to have to tell you that if something should happen to the vice president, my friend, while in your country, I will personally see an end to you." Tom hoped this was not over the edge, but he wanted to make sure the Russian understood the importance and necessity of this visit. He could not sit idly by and watch, like all Americans, a mass slaughter of innocent starving civilians. The effects of that will ripple through the U.S. for the next decade.

"I will see he is given the highest diplomatic security. But, as for the timing of his visit, I can only say I am disappointed in your lack of confidence."

"Let me make this clear, the vice president is coming regardless of how it makes you feel. Take the timing of his arrival as you wish."

The line clicked dead after that comment and Tom placed the receiver onto his desk, rubbing his forehead with both hands. He didn't feel nearly as strong as he sounded.

"Is this a mistake?"

Chapter 12

The white Lada pulled up in front of Alexander's flat, screeching to a halt. Their eyes searched the streets for signs of nosey onlookers before getting out of the car and gathering their equipment from the back seat wrapping them in the same long coats they used earlier.

Once inside the building, the two men could feel the walls embrace them in a warming comfort they had not known that day. Exposed in the tree line not an hour before, they had nothing but Mother Nature for protection, and now they were safe within the confines of brick and concrete. They quickly ascended the stairs and unlocked the door to the flat.

Alexander turned on the small black and white television to see if they had made the news. When his brothers and sisters of Chechnya heard about the heroic actions that took place today, more would join his group and they would soon have the numbers and confidence needed to fight the Russian Army out of their country.

He turned the knob quickly scanning through the channels, NTV, RTV, and even the smaller private stations.

"Nothing, unbelievable," Alexander mumbled under his breath.

Andre had stored the weapons and was in the kitchen pouring each of them a glass of Vodka to wash the dust from their teeth and the adrenaline from their muscles. He slammed back the first shot and topped his glass off before walking into the living room.

Alexander slumped down in the old threadbare recliner staring directly at the small TV. He purposely scanned the channels slower this time taking his time to see the images on the screen. Andre sprawled out on the old couch and handed the glass to Alexander.

"Andre, my friend, you are like a brother to me," Alexander said, holding his glass up.

"And you to me." Andre turned his gaze from the TV to Alexander, touching the glasses together with a clink.

"Let's hope the first loss is always the hardest," Andre said, referring to the man they both saw take several bullets to the chest in the field.

"I hope so, that was tough to watch. What are we going to do if today was wasted?"

"What do you mean wasted? Just because it has not made the news yet does not mean the day is wasted. We showed the Russians that Chechnya would fight their aggression."

Alexander pondered this for a second and sighed deeply. That would not be enough to be successful and he knew it. The Russians could easily sweep in and wipe out the entire city if they really wanted to. No, what they needed was a massive strike.

The two men stared at the images on the screen sipping the vodka and reliving the earlier action as footsteps came down the hall. The steps stopped at the door and each man waited for the signal that would signify a team member returning. One wrap then two in rapid succession and a third followed after five seconds, and both men released their breath.

Alexander stood, walked to the door and looked through the small peephole. He immediately recognized Shevard and hurriedly unlocked the door. The man looked exhausted and Alexander invited him in. Over the next few hours others began to straggle in.

Alexander shook each of their hands and gave them a hug. He couldn't begin to express his gratitude for what each of them did. He honestly didn't expect to see anyone return after the near failure of the mission, let alone all, but one. The one to die was the hero of the group that day. He had sacrificed himself to save the group by setting off the final charge. He surely had not expected this.

Throughout the remainder of the morning and well into the afternoon, they drank heavily and kept their eye on the television. Alexander was hoping for some news coverage on their actions today. RTV was airing a show uncovering the worsening conditions of nuclear power plants, a fact of Russian life that didn't even need reporting because it was obviously atrocious and NTV was covering the riots in Moscow.

Why was it not being aired, could the Russians have covered this up already? They had destroyed a bridge over one of the largest rivers in the country and had killed at least twenty Russian troops. The truth of the matter was that television stations, both public and private, in Russia still broadcasted under strict government censorship. Even after more than a decade of free speech, the murder two years ago of an executive in the largest public television station in the country by the KGB was still in the recent memory of every reporter.

"Comrades, we have been cheated today!" Alexander said loud enough for each of them to hear in a slurred speech.

"But, Alexander, we didn't do this for news coverage," Andre spoke up, walking out of the room. "We want to show the Russians that Chechnya will fight every attack on our country."

Alexander looked at Andre as he finished talking, and couldn't believe it was him speaking.

"Andre, you of all of us know it is only through the television that our liberation efforts will gain popularity with our people. With popularity comes membership and with membership comes the kind of strength we will need to push the Russians out of our country for good." Alexander eloquently spoke the words in a slow, almost deliberate tone allowing the meaning to sink in. This was not just what he wanted them all to believe—he needed them to believe. "We must strike another blow to the Russians fast and decisive. It is obvious that the blood spilled today on our soil was not enough to get the attention of the red bastards."

He looked around the room at the faces of each man to see their reaction to what he just said. Today was not simply a measure of their courage and willingness to fight—it was a test of their resolve. He was thankful for their loyalty and confidence in his leadership. Had today turned into a failure, the CLA would be destroyed forever and Alexander would have failed them.

Fueled by vodka and confidence, Alexander shot from the hip. "Comrades, I propose we travel to Moscow. It is time we faced our enemy on their ground. We need to take advantage of the chaos in the city and finally make the world see what the Russians are doing to our country."

Again, Alexander watched each of their faces to see how they would react to this revelation. It was not something that was planned in advance. This was an idea that had hit him after his fifth glass of vodka since he had returned from the woods. The vodka warmed his blood and his vengeance.

It was obvious to him. They would need to do something big to get the results they wanted.

Andre stood in the doorway listening to Alexander speak and couldn't believe what he was hearing. Is he actually proposing we travel to Moscow? What is going through his friend's mind? The fighting today had started as a statement of their defiance and ended in something entirely different.

Alexander had changed today. Andre didn't know what specifically was different, but it scared him. Alexander was obsessed with the Russians and thoughts of revenge were clouding his judgment.

Andre walked out the door to get some fresh air as he heard Alexander continue to speak. Alexander's voice did not sound as tired as they all felt. It had a spark to it that Andre was sure would start a fire. He only hoped that it didn't become a wild fire. The last thing this group needed was to do something stupid.

"What do you say, comrades, will you all be with me tomorrow as you were with me today?" Alexander shouted.

A collective "Da" came from the group as they all raised their glasses. Alexander had no idea what they would do. He had no plan at all and figured they would play it by ear as their trip unfolded. He would have time to think things through during the fourteen-hour trip. He did know they needed to take as many weapons as they could fit into their small cars. It was amazing how many options seemed to open up when guns were used.

As the group settled in, Alexander told them all to get some rest. Each of them needed a few hours of downtime after the long morning. He also knew some of them had families at home waiting and worrying. He did not expect them all to support him. He didn't need them all, the fewer the less obvious they would look. But he did need enough of a force to carry out his plans, whatever they may be.

"I do not expect you all to want to join me in Moscow. However, if you choose to go, I will personally be grateful."

The room was silent as Alexander started to speak one last time.

"Comrades, I can't tell you how proud I am of what you all did today. Tomorrow we will expose to the world Russia's treatment of our homeland."

Chapter 13

The nearly 5,000-mile flight felt shorter than Tony remembered. Of course, the hours he slept would make any flight seem short. The pilot's announcement of their arrival prompted those who could no longer sit on the plane to take their seats. The local temperature was 84 degrees, very hot even for Moscow this time of year. Tony knew that the hot weather, combined with the rioting mass of people, made for a tumultuous situation.

I hate this part of the flight, Tony thought as he watched the clouds pass by the window. The plane shuddered and the wing literally looked as if it would shake off the plane as it passed through pockets of dead air within the clouds. Tony could begin to see the ground approaching fast. He looked out the window and saw the tiny houses with their sparkling lights and could even make out the headlights of cars moving on the highway near the airport. He looked ahead and could see the bright lights of the runway approach. The world appeared so peaceful this high in the air at night.

Tony felt the landing gear move into place with an unmistakable bump. The change in airflow over the wing flaps as they were raised into position for landing was familiar, but unsettling. A moment later the tires touched down with the distinctive sound of rubber skidding on pavement and the engines roared to life slowing the large aircraft to a coast.

The night was very dark. The thick cloud cover didn't let any light from the full moon through. The plane taxied to the end of the runway and then turned right following the lead truck onto a taxiway that led toward a large hangar. The large building was difficult to see in the dark, but as the two massively large doors cracked open, Tony could just make out the red, white, and blue Russian Flag hanging down from the roof above the doors. As the plane approached, the doors slowly slid on their tracks, opening enough for the plane to enter.

Ben Lassiter stood and started the pre-operations briefing, going over the team assignments one last time before debarking the plane. The plane was still moving, but not fast enough to stop those on board from moving about the cabin, getting ready. Tony listened carefully while reviewing his pack of equipment. As always, he packed lightly with only a 9mm automatic pistol in a shoulder harness and like most of the other members, wore a light Kevlar jacket under his clothes as an extra layer of protection. He holstered the Smith and Wesson 9mm preferring it to the 9mm Glock's his teammates carried because he liked the feeling of cold steel in his grip rather than the high-impact plastic of the Glock. The pistol was the perfect size to fit into the shoulder holster without interfering with his range of motion. Tony also carried a small flight bag that contained extra ammunition and a Smith and Wessson, model 642, .38 caliber snub-nose revolver that he tossed into the pack for emergencies.

"Listen up, team. We have a change in plans," Lassiter said, standing in front of the team. "I have just received word that one of the vehicles we requested is out of commission. The team riding in the third vehicle will remain with the plane and provide security for our return. Those members riding in the first two cars will proceed as planned. We will have five fewer members than expected. Those riding keep a clear eye on the surroundings and your heads down. The closer we get the Kremlin, expect an increase in rioters so everyone keep a sharp eye. We may experience some hostility because the rioters might suspect us to be Russian politicians. Everyone keep the chatter to a minimum at all times."

"Sir, what is the latest Intel as to the numbers of rioters?" asked a member of the team riding with Tony in the first car.

"The riot numbers have nearly doubled in the last twelve hours. The last estimate I received from Intel just as we landed was 10,000, give or take a few hundred. As of the last report, we had no indications that the rioters were turning hostile. However, we all know that this could change. We are not here to stop the riots, people. We are here to escort Eagle 2 to the meeting and back again safely. I do not want to risk anything happening in the dark, so I have held off transportation until 0800. Traveling in any city is a problem, especially this city in the dark."

Tony glanced at his watch. "2300. Shit, what am I going to do for another seven hours?"

Fully awake after sleeping the entire trip Tony was thankful for bringing a book. He frequently passed the hours of boredom that accompanied these trips by reading. He had loved to read from the time he was in grade school. He was one of those unusual students who constantly read everything he could get his hands on. Scientific thrillers were his favorite and could read them for hours at a time, which he was thankful for because he had hours to spend waiting to move out.

The large plane pulled into the empty hangar and came to a sudden stop lurching forward on the tall landing gear struts. Interior lights were on now as a security team exited the plane and set up a guard around the hangar. When everything was in place, the interior lights dimmed and those remaining inside settled in for the night. Tony pulled the light blanket over his body as he reached above his head turning on the small light illuminating his seat so he could read. He was amazed at how bright the light was and that it didn't bother anyone else. The cabin was so quiet, a pin dropping would make an echo. It was so quiet, in fact, that when Tony turned the page, he was sure the sound would wake everyone. After two chapters, his eyes started getting heavy and he drifted off to sleep.

Chapter 14

Alexander slept fitful for a few hours. The morning had strained him beyond anything he could comprehend. Several members of the group had remained in his flat, which made Alexander happy. Most slept on the filthy floor with their shirts rolled up serving as makeshift pillows.

He walked sluggishly among the sleeping bodies on the floor on the way to the tiny bathroom. He had willed all his strength together to lead them in to action and even after the short rest he felt like he had nothing left to give them. Leadership did not come easy to Alexander. It took a considerable amount of time and effort on his part just to get the courage to stand in front of the men. He figured the riots in Moscow would present an opportunity at some point, but what? They didn't have the resources to spend much time there, but knew he had a very long trip to devise a plan.

The gravity of the attack that morning had not hit him yet. Had he killed a father, brother, son? When would the circle end? Would the Russians ever concede? Regardless of the answers, nothing could take away what he had done.

Alexander looked into the mirror above the small dirty sink. He didn't even recognize the face looking back at him. Weeks of stubble had grown into a scraggly beard, and his coal black hair was longer than it had ever been. The wrinkles drawn on his face from years on the street were deep, making him appear twenty years older than he actually was. Another day like today and he would surely feel twenty years older.

He could hear people starting to stir in the other room as he turned the faucet. Cold water filled the sink as he splashed some on his face. Quickly he readied himself and then walked out to wake the others.

"Come, my friends, it is time," Alexander said as he walked through the tangled mass of bodies.

Shevard rapped the signal on the door, and Alexander opened it slowly.

"It is good to see you," Alexander said, placing his hand on his friend's shoulder.

"I want to see this through and make our country proud," Shevard said, acknowledging Alexander's hand.

"And so we shall, so we shall." Alexander stared into Shevard's eyes in confidence.

Alexander looked into the stairwell to make sure no one was snooping, closed the door and walked into the kitchen.

Andre poured a cup of strong coffee as the two sat at the kitchen table alone in momentary silence. Andre had found a map of Moscow in the items taken from the military base and laid it on the table.

"What is the plan, Alexander?"

"I have no plan Andre," Alexander whispered. "Something will come up, I am sure of that. How can I plan for something that is so unknown and foreign? I only know this is something that we must do, and we must succeed."

Andre saw the same strange look in his friend's eyes that he saw in the woods. Andre was scared for his dear friend and for himself. The dark circles under his eyes and the deep stare was a look that Andre had not seen on Alexander's face since pulling him off the streets many years ago.

As the steam rolled off the top of his cup Andre felt a deep, gnawing feeling deep down in his soul that somehow this idiotic trip would kill them all and he was scared. The tank shell had nearly killed him and with it the realization that this was more than a game being played by kids in the street. It was real, and people died.

"What if we get there and we can do nothing? You have seen the reports on the news about the Army controlling the rioters," Andre said quietly, hoping the others wouldn't hear.

"Of course I have, my friend. If you do not wish to join us then stay. I will not force you to come nor will I think any less of you should you stay. I would hope that you choose to be at my side. You are my brother, and we gain strength from each other."

Andre said nothing, but continued to stare through the steam rising off his cup. He had just been offered an escape, a way to not take part in this and live. But sadly, he knew deep in his soul that he couldn't stay. He must go to show his support of their leader and his feelings of solidarity to the cause. Between the look in his friend's eyes and the reports on the news, he somehow instinctively knew that he would not live to make the return trip.

"What will it be, my brother?" Alexander asked as he stood to join the others."

"I will not leave you all the glory. Someone must protect you," Andre said in serious jest.

Alexander reached his hand out to grasp Andre's arm firmly to show his appreciation. For a second he doubted whether Andre would be at his side today. His face broke into a large smile and neither man said anything more to each other about it. Alexander stared at the map looking closely at the streets around the Kremlin. He circled in pen the spots where they would meet so that each man could see where they were going.

Alexander walked through the small room talking to the men waking them from whatever sleep each could muster. Some, he knew by looking at them had not slept at all. "Come, my friends, it is time for us to leave," Alexander whispered to each of them as they slowly stretched and yawned the tired out of their bodies.

Cigarette smoke immediately filled the dingy room as each man stumbled awake. The thick cloud of smoke contributed to the darkly stained walls and musty smell that permeated the room. Andre brought a fresh pot of coffee and poured a cup for each of them to clear the fog from their heads.

Alexander informed the group of his plans as he walked into the dining room which now resembled a small armory. "We must choose weapons that can be easily concealed. We do not want to raise alarm by carrying rifles into Red Square. Each of you carry three grenades and two pistols. I will carry the plastic explosives should we need to create a diversion."

"Hide the weapons in the trunks of your cars to avoid the searches of the Russian border guards. Carry the pistols and grenades in a backpack once we reach the city. You must conceal your actions from the security units until we are ready to strike. I don't have much intelligence on what we are going to see, only what has been broadcast on the news. The government has posted soldiers to secure the streets, so we must be careful," Alexander said to the group as they gathered outside the dining room.

Andre walked into the kitchen with the empty pot and set it on the table. As he headed to the bathroom to get himself ready, he overheard whispering around the corner and strained to listen. Two were discussing how crazed Alexander had become and they were scared. Completely unaware Andre was eavesdropping on their conversation, they continued. As soon as Andre stepped out into the dark hallway, the whispering stopped.

Andre looked into the faces of the men he had known since childhood. "The ideas we have talked about, the plans we have made, the sacrifices we have endured, have been just words until this morning. We struck hard and it didn't even faze them. We are nothing more than a nuisance to them, like a fly on a horse's ass. Can't you understand that Alexander is right? We must hit them where they can't help, but notice us. I have seen the look in his eyes since we returned from the bridge and I will tell you that, like you, I too fear the future especially making this trip. But, we must stick with him. He has led us to this point, let us now show him our support."

The words hung like a thick fog in the air after Andre finished speaking. They all knew that Alexander was their leader. It was easy to talk of liberation, to talk of freedom, but Alexander was making it happen.

Andre turned, leaving the two to finish their conversation. He walked down the hallway, skipping the bathroom, to see if Alexander needed help with the final preparations. He glanced at his watch and knew that they needed to get moving if they wanted to reach Moscow before day break.

"Alexander, it is time for us to leave," Andre said as he walked into the room.

"It looks as if we have nearly fifteen men joining us," Alexander told him in a surprised tone. He really didn't expect half that number after yesterday. He fully expected many would run scared after witnessing the death of a friend, a comrade in arms. He wouldn't have blamed any of them; Alexander was scared himself, but didn't show it. He couldn't show it, that was what was expected of a leader.

Chapter 15

Morning was just starting to break as Tony stared out of the dark cabin. Most of the men were just starting to ready themselves for the trip to the Presidential Palace. Tony slept for only a few hours. The rest of the time he spent reading, nearly finishing five chapters. He was getting to the most suspenseful part of the book, but he found his mind drifting toward the operation. An aching pit in his stomach about this trip troubled him from the moment they touched down. The change in plans bothered him and things always went wrong when plans changed.

He decided to get up and walk out into the hangar to stretch his muscles after sitting for nearly eight hours on the plane. The side door was open, and he walked through looking around to get a better view of where they were.

Sitting inside the hangar was another smaller jet that Tony guessed was the Russian Presidential plane. Aside from the plane and the two cars, the building was empty. It was easily one of the largest buildings he had ever been in. As his pupils adjusted to the dim lighting inside the hangar, he would have guessed that three football fields would have fit inside with plenty of room to spare. It was also quiet other than the faint footsteps of the perimeter security and Lassiter's distant voice.

A squad of Russian soldiers was permanently assigned here guarding the hangar. The presidential plane presented a sweet target should anyone want to take the president out in mid air. Guarding a plane was a boring job for trained killers, Tony thought to himself as he walked down the stairs to the hangar floor.

He thought about taking a brisk jog to get his blood pumping, like he did every morning before going to work, but dismissed that idea quickly. He didn't pack the clothes for exercise and it was almost time to make the final preparations. He decided instead to walk to the two cars to familiarize himself with the German built Mercedes having never actually seen the inside of one.

The General Motors Suburban used by the American government is much more functional because of its size and power, but it definitely lacked the class of these beautiful luxury cars, Tony observed as he approached the cars.

Lassiter stood next to a Russian officer at the rear of the car Eagle 2 would be riding in talking in broken English. He had spent enough time in this country to recognize a Russian General's insignia and knew from his work here that Russian Generals were always sent to greet foreign dignitaries. The conversation seemed very heated with hand gestures and head nodding filling in where words got lost in the translation.

At the last minute he decided to skip the Mercedes, he would see the inside soon enough anyway. His body was awake now and ready to start the mission or as close as it was ever going to be.

As he walked back up the stairs he could hear the movement and light murmur of the others as they started to wake. It wouldn't be long now. Behind him Lassiter started to climb the stairs to make some last minute detail changes to the already bastardized plan.

He reached his seat, picking up his flight bag as the new changes were being announced.

"Team 1 will now be comprised of five members plus the Russian driver in car 1. Team 2 will be comprised of three members plus Eagle 2 and the driver. We will be bare bones here, folks. Keep your head up and eyes clear. Reports are the rioters have gained in strength since we landed and have spread out over more of the city. We will be close to them during most of this drive. I have already expressed my desire to the Russians to avoid contact with everyone until we reach the drop off location. As of the last reports, the rioters were not in the location of the drop off, so we shouldn't have to worry about providing immediate cover during the debarking. It will be tough for five members to establish a walking perimeter, so I am sending out three members to set up in the crowd now to provide initial security so we will be ready when the vehicles come to a stop.

"Tony, you are being removed from Team 1 and will begin moving out in advance of our departure. As soon as you are ready a driver will take you to the square. Set up in the crowd and don't make yourself obvious. I have a change of clothes for you in the back of the plane so that you will blend in to the crowd. I have already sent two others out. Make your way through to the Kremlin gates as soon as possible. You will provide cover and protection as soon as the cars stop and coordinate with Team 1 to provide the moving shield for both Eagle 2 and the second team between the car and the palace."

"Sir, do we have an estimated number of Rioters yet?" Tony asked.

"According to the Russian military, the number is between ten and fifteen thousand spread out over twenty blocks. Until last evening, rioters were not overtly violent, but violent outbreaks were on the rise over night. Nothing drastic, rocks, bottles, and a few firecrackers thrown into the security force is all we have reported. It won't take much to set this thing off though so be careful. I think this is going to be a tough trip, fellows."

Tony nodded as he checked his gear for the fourth time and went to quickly change and move out. The car was already running as he took the last step off the boarding ladder. The large doors started to slide open with a loud creaking, startling him as he approached the car. He took the passenger seat and felt in his bag to make sure he had the .38, as they sped out the doors toward the center of the city.

Chapter 16

John Bastian stopped his turbocharged, midnight-blue Volvo s60 in the marina close to the slips to unload his supplies before parking it in the overnight spaces. His golden retriever, Maggie, followed him toward the water as he intently listened for the security beep when he depressed the lock button on the remote attached to his keychain.

Perfect, he thought, *an empty parking lot.*

As he walked out onto the dock of the marina with his hands full, he breathed in deeply, smiling from the reminiscent earthy scent of the salt water. Vacant boats tied securely in their slips on both sides of dock gently rocked with the waves as he walked toward slip 86. On the weekends, the docks were so full of people he could barely walk, but today it was deathly quiet. He always knew that when he needed seclusion he could come here on a weekday.

It wasn't that he didn't like the people. Boaters were the most outgoing people he had ever known. The marina on a Saturday night was more active than any nightclub and far more fun. He had made a number of friends here in the past few years and many even got together over the winter months to talk about sailing. But today it was a ghost town.

He pulled the dark green canvas cover off the cockpit of his 41-foot Hunter and did a quick inspection to make sure everything was in ship shape as Maggie sat waiting patiently for her chance to board. The Chesapeake Bay was no place to have problems, especially ones that he could prevent. Although he checked at home before he left, he turned on the marine radio at the helms station clicking the knob to channel two, listening to the latest weather broadcast. The weather had a way of changing fast. He wasn't worried in a boat this large, but sailing her single-handed was tricky even in good weather.

"Come on, Maggie girl, let's get ready to head out," John said, and the light golden colored dog wagged her tail and jumped onto the deck. Unofficially, she was the undisputed first mate of *Sailor's Dream* having logged more time on the boat than any other member of the family.

He stowed the food he carried aboard in the galley, making sure it was secure and the weight was distributed equally on each side so it wouldn't displace the boat. He tidied the cabin just to clear the cobwebs and went back up on deck for the final preparations. The sail cover needed to be removed, but he could do that after he got underway. He walked out onto the dock and untied the mooring lines, freeing the beautiful boat from captivity. Turning the key, he checked the battery and fluid levels and pushed the button at the helm starting the old inboard diesel. The engine idled and was quiet, but he couldn't wait to raise the sails, cut the engine and sail. John looked over the gauges, radar, GPS, and chart plotter to make sure everything was working and shifted into reverse pushing off from the dock with the catch pole. He was thankful he didn't have to contend with the weekend boat traffic, and he slowly made his way past the marina breaker toward the inlet.

John steered into the wind as the boat passed through the shallow inlet into the bay. He removed the canvas sail cover and slid the half-inch nylon line through the round starboard winch. His muscles came alive as his long fingers tightly gripped the handle turning it as fast as he could, pulling the mainsail slowly up the mast. Each ratcheting click inched the mainsail closer to the top of the 63-foot mast as the boom swung free searching for wind. He tightened the sail with a final tug securing the shiny stainless steel winch and cut the diesel. The boom moved enough to catch a gust of wind into the mainsail and with a surge, the sail filled with air and he was off. The brisk wind flowed over his face blowing his hair slightly. The only sound was water slapping against the fiberglass as the boat sliced through the choppy water. He secured the boom line into the clip adjusting it perfectly. The wind fully billowed the sail and John stared contentedly far into the horizon.

He had a particular destination in mind that would be perfect for three days of complete relaxation. He wanted time to reflect on his career and his future. Tonight his destination would be a quiet cove about thirty miles down the bay that was a favorite mooring spot because it was isolated from the bay. He calculated the distance and wind speed figuring he could make it by dark. The cove was just off the Talbot County point on the eastern shore across the bay from Baltimore. He wasn't towing the dinghy to go ashore on this trip because it was a hassle for one person to handle.

He was well underway as he unfurled the jib. He attached the jib line to a second winch forward of the centerline on the port-side and cranked it fast as he could. The smaller sail raised and fluttered in the wind. He made the subtle adjustments and the boat immediately surged ahead once again as it filled with wind, giving him another seven knots. The force of the wind in the sails was countered by nearly eight thousand pounds of lead ballast inside the keel located along the bottom of the boat. She was a heavy boat totaling just over twelve thousand pounds and still the wind force made the boat heel at almost fifteen degrees.

He plotted his position on the chart and set a course for the cove. With his bow low in the water and enough wind in the sails, he was alone with his thoughts. The spray from the waves washed over the cockpit just enough to keep him and Maggie cool in the late morning sun.

A young lieutenant stationed at Bethesda Medical Hospital on the outskirts of Washington D.C. seemed like such a long time ago. He performed his residency under one of the Army's best doctors. Which, at the time, he innocently thought was one of the most stressful times in his young life. He was an immature and very naive resident, working 80 hours a week with very little time for a social life.

John was the youngest of three sons from a very poor, but hardworking and proud family in a small town in Northern, New York. He played on the football team in high school and instead of following in his father's shoes as his older brothers did after graduation of working long hours in deplorable conditions at the large paper mill in town, he decided to attend college. His talents on the football field were noticed by scouts from as far away as Ohio, but he ultimately decided to stay close to home accepting a football scholarship to Syracuse University. Being the first and only college graduate made his parents proud.

During his time at Syracuse, John became increasingly interested in science. Biology and Physiology were his favorite subjects and he loaded his schedule with as many science classes that his advisor would allow him to take. After football season, he volunteered in the science labs tutoring students and assisting his professors' research projects. The professors took advantage of John's knack for conducting the tedious research they detested leaving them time to analyze the complex data he uncovered.

John was particularly interested in a project his physiology professor, Tom Greely, had started a decade ago. It was Professor Greeley who actually convinced John to change his major to pre-med during John's sophomore year. John had inadvertently found out that Greeley was researching the feasibility of bio-electronic nano-microbes when he was looking for information for another professor.

John found a stack of hand-written notes stored in a thick dog-eared notebook written in Greeley's own hand. He was instantly both intrigued and unsure about what to do with his findings on the unfinished project. John read the entire notebook finding at the end the project was dropped after only a few years because Professor Greeley could not match the available technology with the physical requirements of the nano-microbes.

Professor Tom Greeley was the head of the world-renowned Syracuse University Science Department and the most recognized scientist on the Syracuse staff. He was most known for his work in human cloning and early genomic theory he proposed two decades earlier and was thought to be a pioneer in the research for advanced microbe technology by colleagues around the country. Greeley was constantly writing articles and being interviewed by reporters from every major scientific review in the states.

John couldn't get the project out of his head. It was the last thing he thought about before drifting off to sleep and the first as he dressed for class. He somehow knew that this failed project would greatly impact his future, but couldn't yet grasp the magnitude in which his entire life would change in finding it.

A week after finding the notebook, John approached Professor Greely in his office to inquire why the project was halted.

"Good morning, Professor," John stammered, mostly in awe of the professor's reputation, but also nervous about bringing up the notes.

"Good morning, John, what brings you into my office so early?" the professor asked, never once taking his eyes off the exam papers he was grading.

"Well, sir," John said, continuing to have problems finding the correct words to roll off his tongue, "I was conducting research for Professor Simmons last week and I came across your notes on a nano-microbe project."

The professor continued to stare over the stack of exams he had on his messy desk without saying a word. "Go on," the professor finally said in a very flat tone, giving John the green light to ask more about the project.

"I have been reading the notes I found," John said, almost ashamed for intruding. "And, well, sir, I am very curious as to why the research was stopped," John pressed the professor.

Greeley was now facing a situation he hoped would never happen. He needed to answer John's question, but how? He knew he had to give an answer because John's curiosity would continue unabated until he had the answer he was looking for.

Many things ran through his head as he fought for words to say. He knew exactly why he stopped the research. It was a project he worked on alone in his spare time. The original purpose was to produce a microbe small enough to be implanted into the bloodstream to fight cancers and the many other advanced diseases that plagued the human body for thousands of years. He came up with the original idea during his work on genome, but after years of work he came to a profound realization. The design of the probe was amazingly simple. However, developing the ability to control the microbe once it was inside a body, directing it to the disease was nearly impossible.

Designing a transmitter and receiver for the microbe was difficult, but he had done it. It took years and hundreds of thousands of dollars working through failure after failure to find the solution. He had to personally design every complex piece from scratch in the dark hours of night in the University's science lab. He had perfected the control of the nano-microbe using radio waves, carefully testing it in test tubes and then finally in one of the lab animals. He had done what no one else had done. He was sure this would win him the Nobel Prize for scientific achievement. It was only during the solitary celebration that his elation soon turned to horror as the gravity of the project hit him.

With a transmitter implanted into the human body, the nano-microbe could do more than fight disease. It could be used to control human development and God only knows what other things it could do. *My God, what have I created?* he thought to himself. He felt like a modern-day Dr. Frankenstein after waking the monster for the first time. His technology in the hands of a greedy capitalist or corrupt government could do more harm than good. Well after midnight in his dark office he sank back into his chair with that thought.

Greely knew that his achievement would eventually be used for human exploitation. Growth rates, thinking patterns, behaviors, all of these things could be monitored and controlled through the probe he invented. How could he live with himself if it was used to collect this kind of data or worse, control human interaction? He was lucky he had managed to keep the project a secret and hide his notes so no one would find out what he already knew.

"The project was stopped because technology will never be adequate enough to make the development of a microbe feasible," the professor finally said, hoping that would be enough.

It didn't work, however. John was still curious. He had many questions to ask, but knew by the professor's response that he would not learn anything more by asking. He also knew that this explanation was not enough.

"But—" John didn't even get it out.

"John, what I meant by that was that the project was a failure," knowing in his mind that was not true and trying to hide the lie with his eyes.

"If you ever decide to pick up the project where you left off, I would like to be a part of it," John finally said, but he somehow had a feeling that would never happen.

"I will keep you in mind, if or when technology becomes available to continue the research." The professor ended his side of the conversation.

"Thank you for your time," John said, exiting the professor's office.

John graduated six months after his conversation with Professor Greely, but could never get the project out of his head. His interest and aptitude in science, in particular medical science, gave him the confidence to apply for medical school in New York City. His football scholarship provided him with four years of free undergraduate education that he knew his family could not afford, but he was unsure of how to pay for the more expensive medical school tuition.

The letter of acceptance arrived at his home four weeks after he graduated, but he still had no idea how he or his family could afford it until he saw a U.S. Army commercial on television. The next day he drove thirty miles into Utica to visit the Army recruiter.

He sat in his car in the parking lot of the recruiting center struggling to summon the courage to go in. The last time he could remember being this nervous was playing his first home game in the Orange Dome back in Syracuse with all those people in one place to watch him play. He knew the acceptance to medical school was going to change his life, but not as much as the Army would. He also knew there was no other opportunity to get to school but to join. He slowly reached for the door handle, opened it and stepped out of the car. As he took his first step toward the building the butterflies in his stomach almost convinced him to turn back and find another way, but he continued on with the same conviction that helped him during that first football game.

With his head high and with as much courage as he could muster, he pushed the large glass doors to the recruiting offices open and stepped inside. He walked slowly up to the receptionist sitting in front of four office doors.

"Hello, my name is John Bastian and I would like to talk to the Army Recruiter," John told the receptionist.

"Do you have an appointment?" the receptionist asked.

John immediately knew that he should have called first, but he was so excited about the possibility of being able to pay for medical school that he could not sleep that night and left as soon as he could in the morning.

"No."

"The recruiter is with someone right now, but if you have a seat, he will see you shortly."

"Thank you," John answered and turned to find a seat.

The large waiting room was empty so he chose a seat next to the front windows. As he sat, he looked at all of the recruiting posters hanging on the walls. He saw posters for the Navy, Marines, and Army. The picture of Uncle Sam pointing with the words "I want you" glared at him as he sat nervously. He noticed brochures lying on a table opposite the room where he sat and he stood from his chair to pick one up. He chose one that had the word Army in big bold green letters and returned to his seat near the windows. The brochure he had chosen focused on the benefits a career in the Army would bring to a young soldier. He read the cover and opened it. The brochure was primarily focused on training, and medical care, but a paragraph toward the end gave a little information for those wanting to get money to attend college. The Army policy was that college tuition would be given to those who serve for one four-year term. However, as he turned the brochure to the back page, he noticed several other opportunities for education the Army offers. The one that caught his attention was a program for doctors. As he read the words explaining the program, John would glance out the large windows trying to picture himself as a soldier. What was he thinking? He heard a door click open to one of the offices and a young, bright-eyed, long-haired kid exited with the Army recruiter following him.

"Thank you for stopping by, I will schedule the testing for next week and call you," the recruiter said as he reached out his hand.

"Great," the kid said and walked out the door.

The recruiter said something to the receptionist that John could not hear and then looked toward the waiting room. John felt a nervous twinge in his stomach when their eyes met, but stood and walked toward the very professional looking Army sergeant.

"Good morning, I am Sergeant Noviello." He reached his hand out to shake with John.

John returned the greeting, grasping the large man's hand. The first thing he noticed was the firm strong handshake of the sergeant. John was impressed already by the professionalism in the greeting and his nervous feeling seemed to disappear instantly.

"Please come into my office and make yourself comfortable," Noviello said as he extended his arm toward the open door.

John took a seat in front of the desk as he watched the Army recruiter walk to his chair. John looked around the office and was again impressed by the extreme neatness. He had really only been in his professor's offices which were cluttered with notebooks and texts that comes after years of teaching. Some of his professor's offices he could not even walk into because of the immense amount of clutter. This office was different, much different.

"What can I help you with today?" the sergeant asked as he made himself comfortable in his chair.

John felt the nervousness return, first to his stomach then move up to his chest. His mouth suddenly went dry as he nervously came up with the words to answer.

"Well, sir, I have recently graduated from Syracuse University and have been accepted into medical school, and I would like to talk about entering the Army to help pay the tuition."

The recruiter reclined his chair as he looked over his desk. He did not get many college graduates in his office and surely had never had any who had been accepted into medical school.

"When were you hoping to start medical school?"

"I wanted to start this fall."

"I see. Well we have a couple of programs for you to consider that may help, but for you to start in the fall we must move fast," the sergeant said quickly. "Let me show you some options."

The meeting lasted well over an hour and John left the recruiter feeling very good about his chances of actually being able to proceed to school in September. He would need to accept a full commission into the regular Army attending school full time during the school year and working in an Army hospital during the summers.

He completed the six weeks of Officers Candidate School in August and proceeded to medical school in September. Three years later, John graduated with honors and as a first lieutenant was transferred to Bethesda Medical Center. He was hoping to finish his internship and then move to a smaller base closer to home.

He met his future wife, Georgia, while stationed at Bethesda where she worked as a young attorney in a large firm. Neither of them had much free time for dating, but they seemed to find enough time to get together and talk about their future. Surprisingly they found they had much more in common than just living in the same city. She was from a small town in northern Pennsylvania and they would talk for hours about growing up in close-knit communities.

During his residency at the hospital, the Korean War had started to take many field surgeons, but he was assigned to the hospital to support the wounded coming in from overseas. He would like the experience of tactical medicine, but was content with the work he was doing for the moment.

On his second year anniversary at the hospital, the chief doctor, Dr. Jim Rogers, called John into his office. John assumed it was the routine evaluation sessions he received on his performance in the hospital. He was accustomed to them and even looked forward to them. However, John soon realized this one was very different.

Dr. Rogers had joined the Army during World War II. He was a combat surgeon in France during the Battle of the Bulge where he saw his share of triage and medical procedures under fire. He was an excellent doctor, one of the best, but his demeanor was like a prickly pear, rough on the outside, but caring and honest to his patients. As a mentor, he was tough and demanding, but always fair in his assessments of John. He walked into the office fully expecting to receive his annual feedback report.

"John, come in and have a seat. I have been very impressed by your work. You have a unique ability to look at a patient, breakdown the symptoms, and prescribe an accurate diagnosis every time, an unusual quality for someone so young."

"Thank you, sir," John said as his face started to turn a little red with the unexpected compliment. "I like the challenge and the connection with the patients. If you look at the entire person instead of just the symptoms the diagnosis tends to be easier. There is a close relationship to the scientific approach I learned during my undergraduate schooling at Syracuse. I did a considerable number of research projects for professors there," John added.

"Well, John, that is what I would like to talk to you about today."

"I have just received orders that the Army wants you to move to their medical research center at Aberdeen," the doctor told him. "I have been working with the folks in the Pentagon on the design and scope of a facility for research on new combat medical procedures and with your background, knew you would perfect for the job so I took the liberty of submitting your name as a potential candidate. Of course," he added, "the position is entirely voluntary because it will take you away from the hospital and your patients."

John was flattered that Dr. Rogers had even considered him for the position. He knew that he was capable of doing the research and was very interested in designing new procedures that could change the way all doctors in the Army would treat patients. But, there had to be hundreds of more qualified doctors in the Army who would love to have this assignment.

"Well, sir, to be honest I would like to think about this position before giving you my answer."

"I would like your answer within the next few days; the research center has already been equipped and is looking to quickly fill the five positions," Rogers said with a matter of fact tone. "John, I don't have to tell you that this is a chance of a lifetime opportunity. The Army has hundreds of doctors, like yourself, dying to have this chance. The future is looking very bright for you, son."

John knew this, but still he had so many things to think about. Thoughts of his budding relationship with Georgia, his medical practice at the hospital, and moving to a new place ran through his head all at one time. He wasn't overly fond of Washington D.C. anyway, he thought; too damn many people.

"Thank you, sir, I will give you an answer in two days," John said as he stood from his chair.

"Choose wisely, son," Dr. Rogers said as he reached out his hand in a friendly gesture.

This one act struck John rather odd. In his two years working under Rogers, he had never once shook his hand. John had thought it was because of the mentor/trainee relationship and that the doctor had not considered him anything more than an underling. With this simple gesture, he felt like his mentor's colleague.

John's hand clasped the doctor's hand at the same time their eyes met. John saw the years of experience in Roger's eyes and knew right then what he had to do.

"I will get back to my rounds, sir," John said as he released his grasp. John exited the office as Rogers sat back down in his large leather chair looking at the orders on his desk. He hoped the young doctor would fill the position. The army needed someone with his abilities in the new facility. When his shift was over, John called Georgia in her office.

"Georgia, you will never guess what I was offered today," John quickly told her on the phone as soon as she said, "Hello."

Georgia could sense the excited tone in his voice and wondered what he was going to say next.

"Georgia, can we go out for dinner tonight so I can share with you my news?"

"Yes, John, I will finish around 5:00 and should be ready by 6:00." Georgia was now curious about the news, but also knew that she would have to wait until tonight to find out what it was. She placed the phone onto the receiver and tried to resume her work, but her thoughts quickly turned to John and his urgent news. John hung up the hospital phone and immediately started to look up the number to their favorite restaurant to make reservations for 6:30. He quickly finished his patient rounds and left the hospital thirty minutes later. John arrived at his apartment spending just enough time to get changed because he had to make one extra stop on his way. As he drove to Georgia's apartment, he thought about the best way to break the news. He decided that he would wait until the time seemed right, when he could sense her relaxing.

At the restaurant, they ordered their food and Georgia could not wait any longer. The anticipation was killing her and she finally asked John to tell her now. John looked over the table and reached out both hands as an offer for her to do the same. She placed her hands in his as they looked deeply into each other's eyes.

"Baby, you know that one drawback of being an officer in the Army is moving where they need me. We have talked about this possibility, but only as a passing thought." John started reaching out for her hands.

"Yes, I know that, John," she said with thoughts flying around in her head of him being assigned to Korea. She knew he badly wanted to go because of the action and experience.

"Well, I have been asked to fill a position at a newly formed medical research facility in Aberdeen," John quickly blurted out almost unable to keep it inside any longer.

Georgia sat back in her chair and thought about what was just said. So many thoughts ran through her head that she could not formulate a feeling. Her relationship with John was just starting to grow closer, and now this. She wasn't sure she knew what this meant for them. However, she knew by the tone in his voice that he was excited and she didn't want to spoil his mood. She forced a smile on her face and squeezed his hands with hers.

"That is wonderful, John," she said weakly.

"Georgia, it means that I must move to the new facility and away from you," John said, stating what she already knew.

"It is a great opportunity for you. I know how feel about this type of work. I am happy that you will be doing something that you love." Georgia forced the words from her lips.

"It is a great opportunity at the wrong time," John told her, hoping to belay some of her fear he saw on her face.

The arrival of their food seemed to end the conversation on the current topic for the moment. They ate, mundanely talking about their day's work trying desperately to take their thoughts away from the prior conversation. John was too excited to eat and Georgia moved her poached salmon around on her plate, never once taking a bite.

As they finished the meal, John kept looking at Georgia, trying to see on her face how she was taking the news. She was beautiful, but stone serious. He decided that he would continue on with his plan even if he couldn't tell how she was feeling inside.

He stood, helped Georgia away from the table and held her coat so she could easily slide her arms inside. As they walked through the door of the restaurant, John could not hold it in him any longer.

"Georgia, I have one more thing I would like to talk to you about. Let's not go home right away, I would like to walk to the park."

"If this is about the new position, I think it is a decision you must make on your own," Georgia said, hoping that would be enough to get him from talking about it any longer tonight.

"No, actually it is something bigger than the new position. Please walk with me for just a moment," John said, coaxing her into walking.

He put his arm around her shoulder and led her down the sidewalk toward the park. He had chosen this restaurant not just because it was their favorite, but also because of the close proximity to the park. The moon was full providing enough light to see, as they walked through the arched brick entrance. He wanted this night to be as perfect as his day had been and he drew her even closer into him.

He hoped the park would be empty this time of night and it was a very romantic place to say what he wanted to say. He stopped in front of a bench to enjoy the quiet tranquility and they both stared at the moon for a moment. Getting up the courage, he turned, took her hand and looked deep into her eyes. He could see the moon reflecting in them and thought he could see tears welling as he started to talk.

"We have grown so close to each other over the past year and I don't want that to end because of my new position," John said softly. "After I found out about the position, I could only think of you—of us. I love you, Georgia."

Georgia had a feeling what was coming next. She knew there would be a "but" and the relationship would be over and she braced herself for the inevitable words. John fumbled in his pocket for the package he had purchased just before he picked her up at the apartment. His fingers nervously grasped the small box and he stood, again taking her hands in his as he stood.

He looked into her eyes and could almost see tears forming in her eyes as he romantically kneeled on one knee opened the small box and in the most confident voice he could muster.

"Georgia, will you marry me?"

She was speechless. Tears rolled down her cheeks now out of happiness and disbelief over the words. She was sure he was going to call off their relationship and instead he had proposed.

John knew he could feel the time moving slowly now as he waited for her response. He looked deeply into her tear soaked eyes and could not get a clear sense of what she was thinking.

"Yes, John, I will marry you," Georgia yelled. She threw her arms around his neck and kissed him as she had never kissed him before. She even thought she heard a sigh of relief escape his lungs as she squeezed him tightly.

John slid the ring onto her finger and they talked about their future differently than they had before. However, John knew that she was giving up her career to spend it with him and he loved her even more because of it. With her head on his shoulder, he now knew today was the best day of his life.

John couldn't sleep that night. He was marrying the girl of his dreams and getting the job opportunity of a lifetime. He didn't wait the two days Dr. Rogers had given him to make the decision. The first thing he did upon arriving for his shift that morning was stop by Dr. Roger's office and tell him that he would accept the position. Dr. Roger's was very pleased at the news and told him that he would be expected in Aberdeen in three weeks. Wow, John thought, this is even sooner than he expected and left to begin his rounds.

The following year passed in the blink of an eye. John loved the work, but detested the governmental bullshit. He worried constantly over the project, but could tell no one.

Secrets, everyone had secrets. His secret was one that could never be told. If the details of his past were ever revealed, every United States citizen would be thrown into a panic. The worst part about this special project was that John couldn't control it. Once his research had found a solution to the problems Professor Greeley had run up against, the project grew beyond his control. The Army had a way of doing that with projects.

They compartmentalized everything so that one person had no idea what was really happening in the bigger picture. John saw it though. He knew what was happening and understood the effects his project would have on society and voiced his concerns. His superiors were government bureaucrats, not physicians. They saw only what they wanted to see and stifled any opposition. John was seen as a loose cannon to the project.

A loose cannon?

It was because of him that the project was a project at all. He had found the initial research, worked countless hours over ten years away from his growing family, and performed hundreds of test experiments before he got it right. The work was grueling, but he felt like a pioneer. He was sure that his work would qualify him for the Nobel prize as it would have Professor Greely. He would have given most of the credit to the professor anyway. Without his historical research John would have never been able to finish the project as quickly.

In the last year, John had even developed a mobile receiver-decoding device to read the data transmitted by the nano-probe. This was the breakthrough he had been working hard on. Developing the nanotechnology was half of the project. Having a transmitter inside the human body was useless if nothing could read the transmissions being sent.

After this, John was expendable inside the scope of the project. After speaking out about the potential abuses of the nano-technology he was quietly dismissed not only from the project team, but also discharged from the army. He wasn't complaining about that at all. A doctor in the private sector made much more than the army could pay and he was ready to begin a new career anyway. It was the way it happened that left a bad taste in his mouth.

The debriefings, the endless promises, and the vow of secrecy he had to swear to was almost overwhelming to him. He could never speak of what he had done to anyone, forever. That was definitive to him. He guessed the Nobel Prize would be awarded to another fortunate researcher less deserving than himself.

The change forced him into his current career path and he was happy about that. He had delivered many babies into the world and still smiled and felt happiness in his heart the moment each of them was born. This was the only career he truly enjoyed.

Now he was retiring, where did the time go? It just wasn't fathomable to him that he was retiring. He would pass the torch onto a younger doctor and that was the way it was supposed to work.

The thought of it made him feel suddenly inadequate. Almost as if he was being led out to some pasture where retirees spent the remainder of their days; no, he couldn't let that happen. He still wanted to be in the thick of things, to make a difference. He had to find a way to do that.

The sun was beginning to set and he was still miles from where he wanted to be. "I need to get my head back to sailing or we are going to get stuck out here, Maggie," John said, releasing a little line tension on the jib, allowing more wind to billow the sail. The wind increased his speed an additional two knots.

Keeping one eye on the compass and the other on the water, standing behind the large wheel, he let the boat sail itself into the sunset. He loved to sail after dark. The lights of the homes on the shoreline twinkled like stars and the moonlight reflected off the mirror-like surface of the water allowed him to see well after the sun went down.

Chapter 17

Thousands of vehicles passed through the border security checkpoint at Niagara Falls daily. The vast majority of those were filled with commuters working on one or the other side of the border, but in the summer the numbers grew exponentially with travelers on vacation. The approval of NAFTA, the tariff free sale of goods to Canada and Mexico, had also increased the flow of delivery vehicles, which were difficult to inspect.

The white, windowless van inched closer to the border as Nassir waited for his turn to cross. The swing-shift guard was tired and ready to end his shift in another fifteen minutes. Nassir's timing could not have been more perfect and he pulled slowly up to the window. The shack was just big enough to hold a chair and shelf for a computer monitor.

Nassir knew by now that one camera had taken his picture while another scanned his license plate number, immediately displaying the data on a monitor in the guard shack. The Americans would not have his face in any database; he was confident of that and the license plates were perfect forgeries of a real floral delivery van.

The digital pictures were stored on a server inside the main building while the two video cameras mounted on the roof of the tiny shack fed a VCR that could store days of footage on a single blank tape. The new digital systems could store a week or more of footage on a large computerized hard-drive, but they were expensive and were just now being piloted in a few stations. The new digital cameras had extremely high resolution and could instantaneously provide real-time data to the guards. Nassir had no way of knowing, but he had lucked out and had picked a lane with the older system.

"Perfect," Nassir mumbled under his breath as he looked calmly at the tired guard.

"Nationality and purpose for travel," the guard said flatly. "U.S., flower delivery," Nassir said, trying to hide is accent handing the guard a forged sales receipt.

"What state and city are you from, sir?"

"I am from Buffalo, New York." Nassir hoped that the business advertisement on the side of the van would support his story.

"How long have you been in Canada?"

"Eight hours," Nassir answered coolly.

"Purpose of travel?"

"I delivered flowers to a wedding party."

"It's a bit late for a flower delivery, isn't it?" the guard asked, looking closely at the van.

"Don't get me started. The wedding was supposed to be next week, but they rescheduled it for tomorrow. We have been working for the past eight hours in the reception hall. I am looking forward to getting home," Nassir answered.

"I know how you feel, passport please."

Nassir handed the guard the fake U.S. passport and stared ahead through the windshield.

"Proceed to the next guard, please," the guard said, handing back the passport. Nassir pulled slowly ahead and took a deep breath. The tough part was over. The planning he had done had paid off.

"Americans are weak," Nassir mumbled under his breath as he passed the American border guard without incident.

He followed the signs for the Turnpike and sped out of the city. The others would make it through. If they followed the instructions, each would pass through with no problems. But people always made mistakes and situations changed; he knew that. Kahlid had made the mistake of pissing him off and Nassir had made sure that would never happen again.

In less than an hour he was turning south on Interstate 390. According to the map he would take this nearly all the way to the Pennsylvania border. Nassir looked at his watch and knew that he didn't have time to poke around. He needed to get to the city with enough time to get set up. However, one thing he didn't need was to be pulled over for speeding, and the van didn't have cruise control so he watched the speedometer with a close eye.

The whine of the tires on the dry pavement was hypnotic. He caught himself daydreaming about days long ago within a few miles after turning south. Nassir's glory days of his past were happy and care free. The images made him smile outwardly. He would not be smiling if he knew what was transpiring back at the falls.

*

Jim and Nancy Jacobs were on their honeymoon. They had spent the last three days watching the *Maid of the Mist* traveling up the river directly into the falls, or at least as close as it could come. Jim was not overly fond of boats, especially one that he considered to be on an insane trip. They were leaving tomorrow and they had a great time walking under the falls, visiting museums in town, and enjoying the romantic atmosphere, but Nancy couldn't get Jim to board the large boat. They had even had lunch in the Skylon Tower. The view of the massive falls at that height was breathtakingly awesome and the food was out of this world, even if it was a bit pricey for Jim's liking.

Finally, after watching the boats for three days and listening to her incessant begging, he finally relented to make her happy. Boarding the bobbing boat, Jim could feel a knot of anxiety build in his stomach as he put the heavy yellow raincoat on and found a place along the starboard rail. He figured he would feel more secure if he could actually grab onto something, and he had watched enough to know that this was the side that was away from the falls.

The guide started talking as soon as everyone was on board. Everyone listened intently as the monotone voice spoke over the crackling, weathered speakers about the history of the falls, providing inane geologic facts about the river as the boat closed in on the powerful falls.

He could already feel the mist on his face and it covered his glasses. He wiped them with his shirt under the raincoat and decided it was useless to put them on again, so he folded them and put them in his shirt pocket. As big as the falls were, he was sure he wouldn't need them anyway.

He looked at Nancy and saw the biggest smile he had ever seen on her face. The look of excitement was hard to hide, and at that moment he was so happy that he decided to take the plunge; he only hoped it wasn't going to be literally.

As the tour guide continued to speak of the how far the falls had receded through the valley over the last millennia, he felt Nancy's hand grasp his arm. He thought she was getting scared and he turned to look at her. She was staring down into the water and pointing, unable to speak. Her eyes were wide with horror as a blood curdling scream rose from deep within her soul, passing her lips seconds after it started. He quickly reached under the coat for his glasses as others stood staring in the white foamed water.

With his glasses in place he saw what the others had already seen. A lifeless body floated in the turbulent water, tossed around like a rag doll. The screaming on board muted to a dull chatter as they watched the body intently.

It was generally assumed the person had jumped into the falls, choosing suicide over life. The museums in town were full of stories of people committing suicide by jumping off the cliffs into the falls. Amazingly, he had read that the sudden impact with the water surface didn't normally kill. According to what he read, it was the back current of water created by the falls that killed. In fact, most jumpers were never found; they became caught in the turbulent water never to be seen again.

It was still very surreal seeing the dead body. Some were sobbing while others just stared in curiosity. The captain had already spotted the body and radioed the authorities. He wanted his crew to pull the body from the water, but was told to leave it for the police recovery team. They would be arriving soon, so the Maid turned around and headed back to its mooring, wisely ending their trip into the falls prematurely. No one on board, including the captain, wanted to continue.

On the way back to the dock, the *Maid of the Mist* met the recovery team speeding by them. Everyone onboard was now watching excitedly as the professionals approached the floating body. They would find out what happened, soon enough, Jim was sure of that. These things were always in the papers. It would no doubt be another statistic on the museum walls within the month.

Corporal Schuman of the Canadian Mounted Police stood at the bow of the boat looking through a pair of large marine binoculars. The 19' Boston Whaler's white fiberglass gleamed in the sunlight as it sliced through the water. The boat was a favorite for fisherman because of the open deck and small center console for the pilot. The flat deck and low sides made it ideal for pulling on large fish and made it rock steady in any water condition.

Schuman pulled on large rubber swim fins and pressed the clear plastic swim mask over his eyes. The one air tank was strapped to his back, connected to the regulator that he fit securely in his mouth by a long black hose. Schuman had done this hundreds of times, but the cold water always gave him a jolt. He was grateful for the dry suit he purchased the past spring. He sat with his back to the water and slipped over the edge of the boat as the pilot feathered the throttle of the powerful 225 HP Mercury outboard against the current, keeping the boat nearly stationary in the water.

Schuman swam gracefully to the body. Even in the terrible condition that he immediately determined, it had probably been in the water less than 24 hours. Any more time and the force of the turbulent water would have torn the body apart. The water had literally pounded the body like a boxer after a bad fight. He was lucky it was still in one piece. As it was, the body was twice the original size and the skin had turned the darkest black Schuman had ever seen. He had only encountered this once before when a hiker fell after heavy flooding washed out one of the main hiking trails on the bank of the Niagara River. His men searched for that body for three days and it was almost unrecognizable when he found it twelve miles down stream.

They always practiced water rescues with living people who could help themselves get back into the boat. He had never actually pulled a dead, water-logged body from the water. It was heavier than he expected and he needed help actually getting it on board. Schuman pushed up while the others on board lifted, and finally the body sprawled out on the open deck.

Schuman held out his arms for the crew to lift him out, and he immediately took off his diving gear. It didn't take long once on board for him to realize this was not a suicide. He spotted the hole where the forehead used to be. Even with the severe bloating and discoloration, the wound was obvious. Schuman felt along the back of the head for an entry hole, and sure enough, just at the base of the skull, he felt three large diameter holes.

"My God, what happened here?" Schuman said.

The small boat roared toward the dock as Schuman preliminarily searched the body for additional evidence. Unfortunately, the force of the water near the falls had left the body in bad shape. Most of the clothes had been ripped from the body; most of the fingernail and toenails were gone and one eye had been torn out. That, he thought, was more from bullet wound than the water. What was left was virtually useless for evidence. We will have to wait to get the body dried to begin the investigation.

The pilot edged the boat parallel to the dock and reversed the engines, abruptly stopping it on a dime. Even before the boat was tied off, Shuman was on the dock, grabbing his gear and shouting orders.

Chapter 18

The inner-city of Moscow was a dirty, grimy place from the lack of attention and complete disregard by the government. It was once a beautiful city on the threshold of Europe for hundreds of years and was now woefully falling apart. The once proud Russian crown jewel was crumbling from the inside out.

The small Lada pulled onto an empty side street close to the square and the two men inside organized their gear. Neither of them said a word as they stepped onto the street and locked the car doors leaving the packs hidden in the back seat for the time being. Before departing from home, Alexander had given them a meeting point so they could coordinate their actions. He had hoped that through a good deal of luck the others would make it here. Alexander couldn't worry about it, everything would work out.

Andre walked ahead of Alexander to the corner of Tverskoy Boulevard. The meeting point was just two blocks ahead.

"Andre, have we made a mistake coming here?"

"No, are you thinking of backing out now?"

"No, but the realization of what we are about to do just hit me."

"You cannot back out of this now, Alexander. You brought us here, now finish it."

None of his men had ever seen this many people—angry people. The sound was almost deafening as the crowd spilled out over an area of the city as far as the eye could see. Alexander looked around and could see armored personnel carriers on the fringes of the crowd, attempting to control the horde. The low thumping of helicopter blades splitting the air overhead made their eardrums vibrate. It was obvious that it wouldn't take much to spark this riot into one mass of destructive power.

He quickly glanced at his watch, 7:45, they had made good time.

"Did you have a pleasant trip, Shevard?" Andre asked as he first approached the man.

"Very good, I am anxious about this day."

"Ah, my friend, so am I."

"Did Alexander give you any indications of his thoughts on the way here?"

"None, the trip was deathly silent, unbearable."

"I will ask. We have the right to know what he expects of us."

Shevard walked past Andre toward Alexander, who was attempting to see over the crowd.

"Good morning, Alexander," Shevard said with a hearty smile on his face.

"It is good to see you, Shevard," Alexander said, reaching out both arms to the large man in a pleasant greeting. Shevard reminded him of an overgrown teddy bear.

"What is the plan, Alexander? The men are tired."

"Give me a chance to survey the situation, Shevard. I am sure something will present itself."

"I have trusted you this far. I have no reason to doubt you, yet." Shevard let the last word sink in, but instead it seemed to hang in mid air. He turned and started walking back toward the other men on the corner stopping briefly to light a cigarette. He exhaled the first drag as a slight breeze sent it swirling above his head into the morning sky.

Alexander walked away from Shevard and the group, looking at the mass of people in front of him. The sheer volume was momentarily overwhelming to him and he felt lost for a second. He needed to be able to see over the people to get a handle on how big the riot was. He looked around and saw a five-story apartment building with the entrance door wide open.

"Wait here, I am going to survey the situation. That door is open," Alexander said, pointing the apartment building. "If I can get high enough, I will see over them."

Alexander walked toward the building, stepping over people either drunk or sleeping and in many cases both.

He glanced up at the building one last time before entering through the wide-open wooden doors. The foul smell hit his nostrils like a brick wall as he stepped over the threshold. The dark stairwell smelled like a sewer. He looked around the small entryway finding human feces and figured the rioters were using the open building as a toilet. Russians were nothing more than low-life, filthy pigs, he thought as his feet hit every other step quickly ascending the stairs to get away from the stench. He covered his face with his shirt to mask the smell just before his stomach turned and he threw up.

He didn't uncover his face until he reached the second floor. The higher he walked the less strong the odor became, but it wasn't until the top floor that he didn't smell it altogether. Searching through the six doors on each side of the narrow hallway, Alexander tried opening the three at the front side of the building, but they were locked. Alexander looked down the empty hallway, putting his ear to each door to see if he could determine if any were occupied. Choosing the one in the middle, he backed across the narrow hall and lunged into it with his shoulder. The door cracked at the latch, but still held. A sharp pain immediately shot from his wrist to his shoulder from the collision, but he ignored it. Backing up one last time, Alexander gave it all he had and the door flung open with a crash sending Alexander to the floor with the excess momentum.

Still sitting on the floor and rubbing his bruised shoulder, he looked around the front room finding it empty. He slowly stood and walked up to the window as his jaw dropped seemingly to his chest. He couldn't believe the sea of people that lay in front of him. It appeared to be endless. He quickly glanced to the corner at his men who looked lost in the throng. Frantically, he searched for a way to get closer to the Kremlin. There, he saw it! The crowd thinned two blocks to the east. They could move their cars closer and enter the crowd near the palace gates. Their cars would be close enough to the palace entrance so that if anything went down they would be near their enough to make a quick get away.

Before he could make his way back down the hallway, an ugly, old woman approached him from one of the apartments next door. She pointed wildly both at the broken door and at him, screaming about the damage and that he was not wanted there. Her words were more of a slur, and he suddenly realized that she was drunk. He held his hands open for her to see that he had not taken a thing from inside and pushed her out of his way as she continued to rant about leaving money for the repairs.

Pulling his shirt back over his face he hurried down the dark stairs. The smell was still overpowering as he burst through the front door onto the street. He let out a gasp of breath and shook his head violently to clear his nostrils as he walked toward the corner, glancing again at his watch.

"I have found a way to get closer to the Kremlin without having to fight through the rioters. We must move our cars two blocks to the east and then three blocks north. We will be a block away from the palace residence. It is 7:55 now, we will meet near the palace at 8:10."

The men all nodded in agreement and walked back to the cars they arrived in. At least they were still safe.

"What did you see, Alexander?" Andre asked as they opened the door of the old Lada. "The rioters are all over the city, but it thins out near the Kremlin. If anything is going to happen, that is where it will be and we should get there soon."

Chapter 19

Tony had made his way through the rioters in good time. The crowd seemed to open up when he walked through, and he fleetingly suspected that he might not quite blend in as well as he would have liked. He stopped to survey the situation and envision the plan again in his mind. He was still six blocks away from the end zone and it was getting close to kickoff. He carefully looked at the street map he taped to the inside of his coat getting his bearings. He looked around one last time at the street names and headed in the direction of the palace at a pace that would not appear out of place within the mass of people.

He could feel the sun creeping between the buildings as daybreak hit. The heat had not kicked in, but he knew it was not far away. The forecast was near 90 today. That heat mixed with this many people only spelled disaster. Russians were not big on deodorant. and these people had not bathed in days. The smell would be tremendous, Tony was sure of that.

The radio in his ear was silent, and he began to wonder if the mission had been scrapped. He was sure he would at least hear Lassiter giving the three spotters in the crowd updates as soon as the two-car convoy left the airport. He glanced at his watch, 0800. He needed to step it up if he was going to make it.

Weaving through the crowd, he made his way closer to the palace. It was getting tougher with people coming in waves as the day broke. Earlier there were only the diehards who camped out on the street. Daylight brought out those who lived close and went home to sleep in their own beds. He heard the low chants get louder as the rioters raised their fists in anger, led by a person on a loud speaker in the center of the square.

Tony could almost make out the tall walls surrounding the Kremlin over the heads of the masses and he knew he was getting close.

"0810. Shit, I am not going to make it on time," Tony said under his breath. "If only they wouldn't have dropped me so far away."

He wondered if the others were having as much problem. He had no way of knowing the others were actually in worse shape. One was still a full seven blocks from the palace and the other was closer behind him, but still in no position to make it on time.

Tony heard Lassiter's voice in his ear bud, but it was filled with static.
"The Eagle has taken flight."

"Shit, what happened, they were supposed to leave ten minutes ago. Oh well, that gives me more time to get in place."

"Estimated time for the Eagle's flight is..." and the static overpowered the remainder of the transmission.

Tony glanced at his watch. Fifteen minutes meant that the car would arrive at 0825.

"Eagle base, this is Hawk 3, do you copy? Please repeat the last transmission," Tony said into his radio. He heard nothing, but static in response.

He felt his pack making sure everything was in place. He felt the .38 and the extra ammunition clips still inside, but he felt better with the 9mm safely in his shoulder harness hidden under his coat. Weapons that close to his body always made him feel safer for some reason. He really wished he had a way to communicate with the command post to advise them of his position. It would also have been nice to know where the other two spotters were. It was Lassiter at the last minute equipping them with the ear buds. These are the bad things that happened when operations fail.

*

Andre parked the car a block from the palace entrance. They both saw guards on the sidewalk outside the large, ornately decorated door and didn't want to appear overtly arrogant alerting them. The crowd had just started to creep its way to the palace providing them with cover. Alexander slowly got out of the car watching to see if there were other guards or security posted along the street. He didn't see any, but that didn't mean none were there.

Andre opened the trunk letting the lid slowly open up. He pulled out bags of clothes and food placing them on the sidewalk as if he was here on vacation. The Lada's trunk, while very small, proved to have great hiding places. Andre pulled up the fake cardboard floorboard covering the trunk floor and snatched out two packs. One had several small arms, mainly pistols and the other held explosives. They had made it through two border checks with no questions. One guard even made Andre remove the bags of clothing. Stupid Russian scum.

The others walked toward him having purposely parked on different streets. It was 8:10 and they were all on time, fifteen members ready, and waiting, for a sign from Alexander. They were all tired and hungry and growing more and more impatient.

Andre spotted it first between the buildings on the next block. Two large, black Mercedes Benz S-Class automobiles moving slowly down the street toward the palace. He alerted Alexander to the movement as they watched the large automobiles approach. At the same moment, the crowd also spotted the government vehicles.

Far below the ornamental tops of the Kremlin spires on the ancient cobblestone street, a tidal wave of rioters rushed the cars as they turned the last block to the palace. The two cars stopped because they could do nothing else. An angry mob surrounded the cars beating them with fists and wooden sticks. Among the mob was a group rebels looking for a chance.

Alexander gathered his men around him as the mob viciously attacked the cars. It seemed that a thousand plans ran through his head, but it all came down to which one would be the easiest.

"This is our chance. The cars are carrying Russian politicians. We need to capture and hold them until their government leaves our country."

Andre spoke first. "You are insane. We don't know who is in those cars."

"Andre is right, Alexander. Even if they are Russian, you can't be sure that the people in those cars are even important enough for the government to care about," Shevard followed.

"True, but this is all we have."

The men looked at their leader with fading confidence. Alexander was looking at the cars and the people surrounding them with a glimmer of hope.

"Listen to me, this will work. If you trust me today, we will succeed. If we assume that they are following traditional governmental tactics, an assault team will be riding in the first car to provide security to the occupants of the second car, politician or not. If we can destroy the first car the rest will be a walk in the park."

"How do you propose we do it with the streets filled with people?" Shevard asked.

"The idea is very simple. I will break through the people surrounding the first car and place an explosive under the front passenger door. When it goes off, we will attack the second car."

"Are you fucking insane?" Andre blurted. "The explosion will kill hundreds of innocent people."

"A small price to pay for removing the Russians from our soil, don't you think? Can't you see this is perfect? Back-up security will not be able to move in because of the massive amount of people."

"What do we do after we have taken prisoners, huh? We are not prepared for this," Shevard said.

"I will drive the car to the outskirts of the city and meet Andre with the Lada. Then we will slip back across the border."

The men all knew this was an insane plan. Most of them stood astonished that Alexander had thought it through this far, this fast.

"We need to move now while the two cars are still stopped in the street. If the helicopters fly over, or the troops move in, we are in trouble."

"No, Alexander, this is suicide. We agreed to come here with you, but not for this; it is crazy."

"You still don't see the brilliance of the plan. The empty warehouse we once used for weapons storage is a perfect place to hold our prisoners. The building is large enough to hold our cars and still has electric and water for an extended stay. To an outsider, it will continue to look abandoned. That will serve as our new headquarters until the Russian government pays us dearly for the return of their politician."

"There are tanks and personnel carriers surrounding the riots. Getting out of town will be nearly impossible," Andre said, still trying to talk his dear friend out of this.

"From the window, I found a path that is clear. This will work, Andre. I promise you we will do this. Andre, go to the Lada and be ready to follow me. Shevard, Leonid, and Stephan will eliminate whatever security comes out of the second car. Make sure you are very careful to not harm the VIP. It may be difficult to tell, but do your best. If we kill them, all we have ruined our chance. The rest of you will eliminate the guards at the palace door and any others lurking around the crowd. When we have the car secure, Shevard and I will take it out of town. Andre, make sure you stay close behind me in the Lada. Once I am clear, head for your cars and get out of here. We will meet at the warehouse."

The men all nodded their heads in agreement and walked to their assigned location.

An alert security guard would have noticed the fifteen men huddled in a circle on the fringe of the rioting attack thirty meters from the cars. The suspicious nature of the group could have been seen by even the most naïve. As it was, Tony was still three blocks from the palace entrance and in a difficult situation. The narrow street leading to the palace was acting like a funnel for the thousands of people wanting a piece of the action. Tony was in the wrong place to take advantage of the thrust through the center. People rushed by him pushing him further to the outside. He would need to force himself into the middle to have any chance of getting through.

Alexander pushed his way to the center of the crowd one layer at a time. His plan was simple enough in his head, but these people were crazed. He had to exert his force weaving through the shouts and cries of injustice until he could almost touch the shiny black car. He could see the occupants inside were frantically radioing for help and looking for a break in the attack to extricate themselves from the car. The once stately Mercedes was battered and broken. The windshield looked like a spider web of cracks and the rear window was completely missing. Three men were standing on the large black roof holding bats above their heads shouting words of encouragement spurring the crowd on. He took the backpack off his shoulder and hid the small plastic explosive device in his jacket. Looking around the car for an opportunity to get closer he decided the only chance he would have was to crawl the last few meters.

The hard, uneven cobblestone road scraped his knees as he avoided the stones being thrown from within the crowd. From this vantage point, the crowd looked like a forest of legs that spread out for hundreds of acres. Slowly he closed in on the passenger side of the car. A fat man with a wooden cane was directly in front of him beating the car wildly. The man's legs looked like barrels as they thrashed about giving leverage to his swing. Alexander was almost there when the overweight man's left foot trampled Alexander's fingers on his right hand against the hard stone street. The excruciating pain rippled through his body to his brain as his face winced, screwing his eyes shut. The foot seemed to Alexander to be nailed to the street as he tried to free himself. The man swung his cane once more as his twisted on Alexander's outstretched fingers, snapping the bone of his middle finger.

Alexander felt nauseated when he felt the cracking of the bone. The sharp pain didn't register with his brain immediately. Instinctively, he shoved the fat leg off his hand afraid to look at it. He wrapped the hand tightly in his jacket, which nearly brought tears to his eyes. The quick shove was all that was needed to move the obese, angry man enough for Alexander to move next to the car. The pain was now just a heavy throb from the tip of his finger through his arm to the shoulder.

Dirty Russian bastards, Alexander thought as he pulled the plastic explosive from his jacket pocket with his left hand. Still on his knees, he felt under the car for a place to secure it that would hold until he could back away far enough to be safe. Crawling under the car, he placed it between the boxed frame and the heavy metal body. The men inside had no way of knowing this would be their last minutes on earth.

Satisfied it would remain in place, he slid from underneath the carriage and stood at the front of the crowd. Though he had never seen the ocean, he imagined the crowd resembled it as it moved toward him, beating the surf. He followed the fat man who was sweating profusely from the exertion. The crowed opened allowing the two of them out to the frenzy. His only regret was that the explosion would not kill the fat Russian who had stepped on his hand.

His hand, still throbbing from the pain was buried in his jacket. The rush of adrenaline of the mission, however, quickly replaced the pain and he looked toward the car. He couldn't see the others now, but was sure they would do what needed to be done. As sweat poured form his forehead, he gripped the detonator with his left hand. He didn't know exactly how large the explosion was going to be. He wasn't an expert on plastic explosive devices. He only hoped that it would destroy the car and everyone inside. Alexander's pupils narrowed as his long fingers squeezed the trigger.

In less than a second, the car rose off the ancient street as if pulled by the heavens. Those closest to the car vanished instantly. The sound came a second later as a fireball erupted toward the sky. The deafening boom from the explosion shattered windows in buildings on each side of the street. A thick black cloud of smoke formed above the car as it returned back to the street bent and twisted. The result was exactly as he had hoped. The car was utterly destroyed. Most of those closest to the car were killed instantly by shards of metal coming from its exterior. Panic erupted through the crowd as he stared in astonishment.

Flames engulfed the hood, but did little in actual damage the car. Alexander took advantage of the panic and walked as fast as he could through the people to the second car. The occupants inside were stunned at the destruction of the first car. As he neared, Shevard and Stephan were in perfect position to assault the second car. As the front passenger door opened, Shevard fired at the exiting man. Blood splattered the driver's side window as the man slumped back in his seat. Stephan pulled the drivers door handle and smashed the driver's forehead with the butt of his rifle. He pulled the arm of the limp body into the street emptying the clip of his automatic into the man's chest.

The explosion had caused the desired effect on the guards, too. The two guards near the palace stood shocked, like stone statues on guard, fixated on the burning fire. They were completely unaware of the men approaching them from the sides as they stared at the flames reflecting in their eyes. Large slugs entered their temples at virtually the exact instant, closing their eyes as they fell lifelessly to the ground.

Terrifying screams of women and children made the scene feel more like a massacre than a planned attack. The rioters assumed this an action against them by the Russian government and immediately rushed the palace entrance, leaving the street void of people. Nothing could stop the mob of rioters from breaking into the palace now, not even the entire Russian Army.

Alexander approached the second car and could still see two people in the back seat. He motioned to Shevard into the passenger seat with his rifle, as he settled in behind the wheel. This was easier than he thought. Now all they needed was to get out of the city. Alexander hoped Andre was ready.

Tony heard the explosion ahead and saw the small mushroomed-shape cloud of black smoke rise above the buildings. "Shit, something has happened," he said as he started running toward the smoke. He literally had to shove his way through the mob to make any headway at all. Muscling his way onto the cobblestone street to the palace, he saw the beautiful black Mercedes he was admiring earlier this morning. It seemed like a lifetime ago that he was gazing at the classic lines of the heavy automobile in the hangar. It looked to him as if two large hands had taken the car and bent it in half. Rows of bodies and charred flesh surrounded the burning car, their blood staining the street a dark crimson red.

His eyes burned with terror as he searched the crowd for members of his team who were inside the car. Only the unfamiliar faces of Russians met his gaze. Turning back to the carnage, he saw the second car start to move down a side street. Were they attempting to escape? He again pushed his way toward the side street away from the crowd just as Lassiter's voice erupted in his ear bud.

"We have lost Eagle 2. I repeat, Eagle 2 has been fumbled."

Tony's entire world seemed to collapse at that instant. He wasn't even sure he had heard the words correctly. *My God, there is nothing we can do to stop it,* Tony thought as he ran ahead, determined to follow the route the car was taking. As he rounded the corner next to a large century old stone building, he saw the unmistakable black Mercedes he had admired in the hangar, stopped two blocks ahead.

Acting on the sound of the explosion was the second nearest spotter, Rodger Gentry. From the moment he heard the unmistakable sound of the bomb he ran toward it as the rioters ran away. All he needed to do was follow the smoke rising like a serpent between the buildings to find it. Like Tony, Gentry stopped dead in the street when he saw the twisted metal of the Mercedes. He had heard Lassiter in his ear just a second ago with the message, but still could not believe the destruction on the street. He looked around to see if others were near and found Tony standing on a corner a block away.

"Tony, did you see what happened?" Gentry said frantically.

"No, I arrived a minute too late. Have you seen Kevin?" Tony said, referring to the third spotter.

"No, not since he left the car this morning. Have you been able to get in touch with Eagle base?" Rodger asked, indicating that his radios were out.

"No, I lost the last transmission and have not heard a word since," Tony said, tapping his ear bud.

"Damn, we are worthless here like this," Rodger said, feeling his heart thumping against his chest.

"I know, the second car just turned left two blocks north of our current location. Let's split up and canvas the area. They can't get far with this many people in the streets in that car," Tony said, trying to gain some control over the futile situation.

"Agreed, but don't lose sight of me. We should stop every block to make sure we are together. We won't be any good in this crowd alone," Gentry said, happy that Tony was taking the lead.

"You take this street. I will go north to the next block and follow it east," Tony said, pointing down the empty street.

The two men split from each other. They would continue east until they ran out of space or found the car. After three blocks the crowd thinned. They could easily see each other as block after block passed. When they had reached seven full blocks the crowed was almost nonexistent. They were on the edge of the city and quickly running out of room. At the next block, Rodger motioned for Tony to wait.

"Have you heard anything from Lassiter since we split?" Gentry asked.

"Not a word," Tony said with a growing defeated tone.

"Keep trying. The closer we get to the airport the better the reception will get."

Tony looked around to get his bearings and come up with another search plan when he spotted the Black Mercedes two blocks to the north on the same street. The front driver's side door was the only open door and it was open as wide as it could go. The two tires on the passenger side were up on the curb indicating the driver made a quick get away.

"Rodger, there ahead, is that the car?"

"It is. I recognize the Russian flags on the fender."

"Come on, let's go," Tony said, running toward it.

As they approached the car, they feared the worst. They could see the blood covering the passenger front window and the broken windshield. When they were within 20 yards of the car they slowed to check for anyone left behind. Gentry scanned the area with his pistol drawn while Tony focused on the car.

"I think it's empty," Tony said, panting.

"Be careful, it could be rigged with explosives. Maybe we should wait until the team arrives."

Tony knew Gentry was right, but had no idea when that would occur.

"I just want to make sure there is no sign of Eagle 2 in the back seat before we move on. Cover me, I am going to check the back."

"I got your back. Be careful."

Tony walked guardedly up to the car with his pistol in both hands. His palms were sweaty, but his eyes were widely scanning over the car. As he neared, he saw a body slumped in the back seat. "Shit, we got one here," he said, flipping the rear door handle. He fearfully looked in the back, turning the body over.

"Rodger, get over here."

"Who is it?"

"Rick Shaeffer," Tony said, looking at the bloodstains on his arms and chest. "Damn—Damn—Damn—Damn!" Tony said, looking at the dead man.

"Shit, what the hell happened?" Rodger asked, cautiously looking around, his eyes scanning the area for someone to blame this on.

"I don't know. Calm down, man. Eagle 2 is not here, which is a good thing for now," Tony said, willing his mind to think. He was frantically searching to find an explanation to all of this, but the sight of his dead friend overpowered his rational thoughts. "Listen to me. I think we're going to have to hike back to the hangar to inform Lassiter where the car is. They will never think to find it here."

"Shit, the airport is miles from here. What are we going to do about Shaeffer?" Gentry said in a tired tone.

"I know, we had better get a move on before it starts to get hot out here. I will carry Rick. He deserves more than to be left here."

Tony glanced quickly at his watch before starting out, realizing it was nearly 1130. It seemed like a lifetime, but they had been searching the streets for nearly three hours. He quickly calculated it would take another couple hours to hike back to the airport, and by then the trail would be cold.

"Let's get a move on," Tony said, hoisting the weight of his dead friend onto his shoulder.

Chapter 20

Corporal Schuman watched with anticipation as the body he just pulled out of the Niagara River was carefully strapped to the long, wooden body board. The two men draped a large white sheet over the entire board and carried it into his small detachment office. The excitement on his face was masked by a solemn look of respect for the dead man.

Schuman couldn't know it, but this was going to be the single biggest case he had personally ever handled. The highlight of the past year was the armed robbery of the Cantina Bar down on the main drag by a couple of two bit thieves. That investigation took less than a week. They might as well have left a trail of breadcrumbs. They were obviously amateurs and the loose talk of one of them after too many beers raised the eyebrows of a local bartender, which ultimately sealed their fate. The bartender called the Mounties with the tip, and within a day the two men were behind bars.

The small detachment office was certainly not set up to handle a murder investigation. Schuman sealed off the crew briefing room moving out rows of hard metal folding chairs, making way for the very large gurney they kept in the cell area for drunks. He pulled out a dusty leather encased examiners kit from the back of his closet as the body was placed gently on the gurney. His hands shook as he pulled out a large magnifying glass, forceps, tweezers, and several evidence bags.

"Trooper James, get the digital camera to take pictures of the body. They may prove to be useful in the identification. I don't know if anyone will recognize him, but it is a start," Schuman ordered. James was his most experienced and trusted of his young staff.

James left the room to retrieve the camera as Schuman neatly arranged the tools on a desk next to the cold, pale body. Schuman slid a pair of thick latex gloves over his trembling fingers and took a deep breath.

The trooper had returned and was snapping pictures as Schuman turned the palm of the man's right hand into the light. The flash from the digital camera created a strobe effect in the enclosed room as picture after picture was stored on the small camera. He was not surprised that the fingers did not show any visible fingerprints. He picked up the magnifying glass and began the slow, methodical search for anything that could possibly be used for identification.

In less than an hour, Schuman had gleaned everything he was going to get from the victim. His training had not gone into anything remotely close to this level of forensic research. He stood up straight after bending over the table for nearly fifty minutes and his back ached a bit with the sudden change in posture.

"Trooper James, load those pictures into the computer database and let's see if we can't get a positive ID on the John Doe. I found absolutely nothing," Schuman said.

"Yes, sir, I'm on it."

Schuman left the makeshift autopsy room and walked across the hallway to his office. For the first time in nearly three hours he sat in his chair behind his small metal desk. He stared at the papers on his desk for several seconds before the phone buzzed. "Sir, I think I might have something," the voice on the intercom said dryly.

"I'm on my way," Schuman said into the speaker, already nearly to his door.

James met him at the computer terminal as the pictures of the John Doe were displayed clearly next to a picture from the terrorist database. "It looks close. The two have the same hair color and facial structure," Schuman said as he sat in the armless office chair directly in front of the monitor.

"Yes, that was why I stopped at this one. Look closely at the right cheek. Do you see the scarring?" James asked.

"I do. Nice work, James," Schuman said excitedly. "Print that picture, and get the FBI on the phone. I need to talk to them ASAP."

"Will do, sir," the trooper said as he left the room. Schuman stared intently at the two pictures, convinced they were a match.

"Sir, I have Agent Metcalf on the line."

"Very good, patch him through."

"Agent Metcalf, I took a little fishing trip today."

"Corporal Schuman, it is Corporal isn't it? I don't have time to listen to your hobby report. The Trooper mentioned something about a body you dragged out of the river."

Schuman could tell the agent was not in the mood for a cat and mouse game. Ever since the Homeland Security department started sniffing around the FBI, the agents always seemed on edge. Oh well, he thought what he was about to report was going to make their day.

"Yes, Agent Metcalf, it is Corporal, and I have something that you need to see right away. I have in my ready room the nearly naked body of a male of Middle Eastern origin. He has what appears to be three 9mm or .38 caliber entrance holes in the back of the head and one exit hole that blew off nearly half of the bastard's forehead. He was most likely dumped into the river over night with the hope of it disappearing forever. It very likely could have had it not been for the tourists on the *Maid of the Mist*. I can tell you it was most difficult to identify what is left, but it appears to be the man identified in recent news reports inquiring about rental cars in Toronto a few days ago."

The line was silent for another second as the Agent tried to comprehend what was just said.

"How can you be certain that you have a positive ID?"

"As I said, it was difficult. We ran the picture through the database of all identified terrorists, and there was something about the facial hair that struck me as odd. This one had a scar on his right cheek that prevented the hair to grow in symmetry. I would stake my professional career to say that this dead guy is Kahlid Marqhem."

Again the line was silent.

"My God, do you realize what you are saying? It really was him in Toronto then. We suspected the CNN report was a mistake. Kahlid Marqhem is the brother of Arkhim Marqhem, one of the highest-level terrorists we have on our terrorist list. I will be in your office in thirty minutes. Don't touch the body," Metcalf said with a hurried tone. "I want it analyzed by our team of crime investigators to confirm your findings."

"With pleasure," Schuman said with obvious relief. "This is one I will be happy to turn over to you. I need my ready room back before the next shift change."

It was actually more like twenty minutes when the black Mercury Grand Marquis pulled up to the detachment office. Three men in black suits exited the car and slammed the door. Schuman watched out the window of his office as the men approached the front entrance between the fluttering Canadian flags. They are nothing if not efficient, Schuman thought as he stood and walked into the lobby to greet them.

"Agent Metcalf I presume," Schuman said with a smirk as he extended his hand to the man in front.

"And you would be Corporal Schuman."

"Correct. If you gentlemen would like to follow me, I will take you to the body."

The three followed behind the Corporal to the ready room. They were not nearly as impressed with the improvisation as Schuman had been. Agent Metcalf circled the body amazed at the condition. He had never seen a body this battered by water.

"The condition of the body is unbelievable."

"Yes, it is amazing what turbulent water can do to a body," Schuman said in a rather unusual matter of fact tone.

"Show us why you believe this is Marqhem."

"Well, I didn't pick it out at first. The facial hair had fallen out of the water-logged pores. It was then that I realized the scar on the cheek. Luckily, we have pictures of Marqhem taken before and after the moustache and beard. See how the water-softened skin lightens the areas around the scar? If you look closely at the picture, you can see the scar in the same location and pattern. The man is approximately the same height, weight, and eye color as the body. I would say without conclusive DNA or dental evidence, we have a 90 percent chance of a match."

Agent Metcalf was duly impressed. From the condition of the body and the circumstances surrounding the retrieval, he would not have guessed the Mounties would have been this thorough. His curiosity was now fully aroused as his eyes shifted from the body, to the grainy picture, and then to Schuman. His brain was trying to make some connection between the report of the rental car and the dead body and why here in Niagara Falls.

"A van is on the way to pick up the body. Please see that everything you have goes with it," Metcalf said as he walked out of the room. "Corporal, you have done an excellent job given the circumstances. The United States is definitely in the Mounties' debt on this one."

"Thank you. You know the saying, we always get our man," Schuman said with a smile on his face.

Schuman felt a flash of pride spread across his face as he watched the other two men turn and exit the building.

"Trooper James, please see the FBI has everything we recovered from the scene when they come to pick up the body. I will be in my office making out a report if you should need me."

"Yes, sir."

Agent Metcalf stared through the windshield of the large Mercury still trying to piece together what had happened. He could not make sense of it all. Something within him was telling him to send this up the chain because it didn't feel right. The brother of one of the most powerful men in the PFLP, was found floating in the Niagara River after being shot in the back of the head. Clearly something was going on, but Metcalf couldn't put a finger on it.

Punching the buttons on his cell phone before leaving the parking lot of the Mounted Police officers, the call went out to Washington D.C.

"Sir, this is Agent Metcalf of the Buffalo office."

"Right, your office has been investigating the rental agency reports."

"Yes, sir, that is correct. I think we have found our man," Metcalf said in a solemn voice.

"Really, how did you find him this fast?"

"Well, sir, he was found floating in the Niagara River this morning. I don't have a 100 percent match on the body yet, but all the evidence is pointing in that direction. Our preliminary data indicates the body is Kahlim Marqhem, a confirmed terror suspect and member of the PFLP organization who was last seen in Toronto."

"Have you been able to find anything else—maps—plans, anything?"

"No, sir, the body was damaged beyond anything I have ever seen before."

"Very well. I will pass this report on. Nice work, Agent Metcalf. Do keep me informed if anything new comes along."

"Of course, sir," and the line went dead.

Agent Metcalf closed the phone and returned it to the breast pocket of his coat.

"Let's play a little Sherlock Holmes and visit the border guards to look at the video of crossings over the past few days. Schuman had said the body was dropped last night. If my hunch is correct, whomever murdered our friend Kahlid hightailed it across the border soon after. That gives us an approximate time frame of twelve hours to wade through. I hope you boys don't have any plans for the evening," Metcalf said to the junior agents, who just stared out the car windows, well accustomed to the long hours.

In ten minutes, the Mercury pulled into the parking lot of the main border guard offices. Metcalf entered first and was greeted by a short, heavyset man who was sweating profusely in the air-conditioned office.

"Hi, Sam," Metcalf said as he shook the man's clammy hand.

"Well, Agent Metcalf, to what do I owe this unexpected surprise?"

"We would like copies and access to the database of all crossings over the past twelve hours."

"Do you know how many cross every hour?"

"I do, Sam. I have all intentions of this being an all-nighter, and you know I wouldn't ask if it weren't a matter of the utmost security."

"I know, I know. I will get on it immediately. Can I have someone drop it by your office in two hours?"

"Two hours, surely you can do better than that."

"Come on, Metcalf. It's summer, and I have people on vacation. My guards are stretched as thin as I can possibly stretch them without compromising security. You will be lucky that it will *ONLY* take two hours."

Metcalf knew the man was telling the truth. Sam Jefferson was the head of the U.S. side of the border security who never played games and always kept a deadline. From the tired look on his face, it was obvious that a few shifts in a guard shack were in his recent past. Metcalf liked the man immensely, and they had become good working friends over the past few years.

The next hour seemed to drag into forever. With nothing to do, but speculate on the reasons behind the death he decided to take some time and grab a bite to eat. They couldn't do anything more without the video anyway. He released the two junior agents to take the next hour off, and he left, opting to walk in the stifling air.

Two blocks from the large Federal Building, where the FBI office was located in a basement, was a little diner. The diner looked like an old train car and was a popular hangout for the working stiffs in the downtown section of Buffalo. The place was always crowded during lunch, but was nearly empty at this hour in the afternoon. He took a seat next to a window and ordered a cup of coffee and a ham sandwich.

The coffee was black and bitter, just as he liked it, but he still stirred it with the spoon. He watched the swirling black liquid trying hard to link the murder with a theory he was mulling in his brain. Could it have been a plan that went wrong? He knew Marqhem had to have a reason to be in Canada because he surely wouldn't be here on vacation. *There must be something else, something I am missing.* The waitress brought him the daily paper to read as he waited for the sandwich. The front-page article was about the Republican Convention tomorrow. He scanned the article, but he knew more specifics about it than the reporters could ever know. A memo was sent to all regional offices for volunteers to help provide security to the delegates was made nearly a month ago. He considered going, but decided against it at the last minute—Too many people for his taste.

His brain started to link something together just as the waitress arrived with the plate. The plate was filled with potato chips and a large slab of pickle along with the sandwich. The convention would make a prime target for any terrorist group, of course. That had to be where Marqhem was headed before he met the wrong person. He ate quickly so he could get back to his office. The more time he had with the videos the better. If he could identify additional terrorists entering the country, the stronger his case would be to his supervisor. If he played his cards right, he might get that promotion that had eluded him for the past decade. Buffalo was not really that exciting, and he hated the winters.

The FBI office in Buffalo occupied the entire basement level of the Federal building. Metcalf liked the location because it was the only office in the building with a back door directly to the parking lot. Visitors to the building rarely noticed the Federal Bureau of Investigation lettering on the building directory in the lobby. The office was actually a suite of many offices interconnected by a reception area. Only three agents worked out of this branch location mostly supporting the border security and conducting background checks on new Federal employees.

Metcalf had just renovated the offices putting in new carpet and updating the furniture. It had been twenty years, and the carpet was too ragged to repair. He had enough money left over after the renovation to install a state of the art digital lab, complete with a new video system.

The new equipment could digitize analog videotapes and then compare the digital images with the FBI database in Washington D.C. instantly. The only problem was that the system was not yet working. They didn't have the equipment to digitize the video. Metcalf walked through the office peeking into the dark room filled with equipment that would have come in handy tonight.

Just as Sam promised, the videos arrived in exactly two hours. Metcalf had the old equipment ready to review the play back by the time they were delivered. This was the boring part. Watching an endless number of faces pass through the border check ranked up there in popularity with all-night stakeouts. The only positive was that he could sit in his chair with his feet propped up on his desk. There were three playback machines rolling at once. No sound came from the tapes, just passing faces requiring constant attention.

Well into the third hour, Metcalf felt the coffee starting to put pressure on his bladder as he stretched his tired legs. He decided that five minutes away from the tapes wouldn't matter as he made his way to the small bathroom down the hall.

"Do you two need anything while I am up?"

"Not unless you can piss for me. My back teeth are floating," Agent Joe Davis said bluntly.

"I know how you feel. I will be done in a second and then you can take a break. Do you mind pulling double duty while I am up? I haven't seen anything interesting except for a car full of sorority girls taking a summer vacation."

"Damn, how do you get all the luck? I haven't seen anything but wrinkled old ladies," Joe said, sitting back in the chair.

"Just keep watching, you never know what you may see."

"Yeah, yeah...Just hurry it up, I gotta go."

Metcalf walked to the bathroom with an obvious limp. His legs had gone to sleep having been propped up on the desk for so long. Each step was torture as the pain of hundreds of needles shot from his ankle to his knee. It took until the trip back to his desk for the pain to subside.

"See anything interesting while I was gone?"

"Nothing but three overweight fisherman and an uptight businessman who was obviously late for something very important. I wish we had sound to go along with the pictures. It didn't take much imagination to figure out the words that guy had for the guard after holding him up to ask the usual questions. The guard even had the balls to ask him for his passport."

"How do you know that? Are you a lip reader now?" Pete Simpson said with hazy red eyes from watching the screen for hours.

"That's right, I am the amazing Kreskin," Joe said over his shoulder. "Now I am going to disappear or you are gonna need a mop. Will one of you watch my screen while I am gone?"

"It is the least I could do for the amazing Kreskin," Metcalf said.

Joe had not even made his way to the bathroom when a suspicious looking van pulled up to the guard on his monitor.

"I think we may have something. I'm going to pause this frame and print out the picture. Run it through our database and see if we can find a match when you are finished," Metcalf said loud enough to be heard down the hall while Pete had moved over to check it out.

"Once again luck is on your side," Joe said as he whistled his way to the bathroom and closed the door.

Metcalf was sure he was on to something. The picture was run through the database and came back almost immediately with a positive match.

"Nassir Al Zarim is the man in the picture. It lists him as being a lieutenant under Arkhim Marqhem. He is, without a doubt, armed and dangerous."

"What the hell is he doing with a van full of flowers?"

"Maybe he has decided he has more of a green thumb," the younger agent said, growing more and more tired.

"From this point on, keep a closer eye on everyone who crosses. He probably crossed first and he can't be alone. If my hunch is correct, more will cross in the next few hours of tape."

Just as he predicted. two more listed terrorists crossed through the same guard station.

"None of them were stopped or even questioned. "What was that guard thinking for Christ's sake?" the other junior agent stated.

"We can't worry about that now. We have three known terrorists making their way to Washington. At this point, they are probably already there. I have to get in touch with the Secret Service and make them aware of the potential threat. I will call Sam in the morning and make sure that guard is taken off the line."

Within minutes, Agent Metcalf was making the call to his supervisor.

"Sir, we have reviewed every inch of tape over the past day and have verified that three identified PFLP terrorists have made it across the border."

"My God, I can't believe it."

"Sir, I have double checked the pictures personally, and there is no mistake. My hunch is that they are headed for the convention."

"Agent Metcalf, you have done an outstanding job. Asking for those tapes was an act of genius. I will make sure to note that on my report."

"Thank you, sir. If I can be of any help, don't hesitate to call."

"Just keep an eye on the border and make sure no more cross. I don't like surprises."

"I have already thought of that, sir. I will personally visit Sam in the morning and have them be doubly careful at who they let cross."

"Very good, Metcalf, I will take it from here," and the line went dead.

"Well, fellows, it looks like we earned our pay today. Nice job! Now go home and get some rest."

They didn't have to be told twice. The two agents were already headed out the door. The last thing Metcalf did before leaving the office was fax the photos of the men to Sam Jefferson with the words, "If these men try to cross back over the border, contact me immediately," hand written across the bottom. As the fax machine ended the transmission, he shut down the equipment and turned out the lights to the office.

Chapter 21

Nassir was dead tired after the long trip. The past 500 miles had taken its toll on his body. He was sure he just needed a quick nap and a bite to eat and he would feel better. The drive through southern New York and Pennsylvania had been the worst. The endless mountains and leafy green trees were torturous. As he crossed over the Pennsylvania/Maryland border, Interstate 83 turned into the *Jones Falls Expressway* and he knew he was getting close.

Once off the main highway he planned to look for a place to eat. It was very early morning and still dreadfully hot. The airflow from the open windows didn't cut down on the humidity. His body felt sticky and wet from the nearly eight hours in the seat. The dimly lit sign over the highway showed the *Fayette Street* exit was two miles ahead. Nassir was glad for that. He pushed the button on his cheap digital Timex illuminating the face—it was just after 2:00 am. He had four hours before the others would start to arrive.

He would need to find the hospital parking garage, but that could wait. For now he just wanted a place to pick up something to eat. After turning left off the exit toward the city, he spotted a 24-hour convenience store. He could fill the van with gas and get something quick to eat. An olive and goat cheese sandwich would be perfect on an empty stomach, but he would have to settle for tuna on wheat. He topped off the tank and paid the cashier with a one hundred dollar bill. Foreigners in this part of the city with that much money were literally a dime a dozen. The cashier didn't even bat an eye when he returned sixty-seven dollars in change to the Arab for the gas and food. He also used the stop to remove the magnetic floral company signs on both sides the sides of the van and replaced them with two new signs.

The medical supply company, MedSafe, he chose was not a real company, but no one would notice. They looked professional and parked in the garage of the large hospital—the van would go completely unnoticed. He rolled the old signs up and tossed them in the metal garbage can next to the pumps. He wouldn't need them for the return trip. Only a fool would tempt fate twice. No, his exit was not going to be back across the border in the van.

Nassir decided that he would find the parking garage before settling in to eat and nap. He turned right onto *Fayette Street* making a left onto *Broadway* and a quick right onto *Monument*. A huge sign at the second light pointed him right onto *Wolfe Street* taking him directly in front of the hospital. With a final right onto *Jefferson*, he could see the large parking garage lit with a thousand lights casting a yellow hue against the thin fog surrounding the building. He slowly pulled up to the ticket machine stopping only long enough to grab the ticket. The arm automatically raised and he proceeded slowly winding his way higher into the garage. He had failed to notice the small camera mounted in the ticket machine taking a picture of everyone coming in. The scouting of the building had only noted the cameras mounted at various locations on each level in the garage, not the ones at the gate.

Nassir pulled into one of the few parking spots in a coverage blind spot on the third level. This was their agreed upon meeting place, so he would just wait here until the others arrived. He had all of the equipment for the operation in the van, and he was feeling confident, with good reason.

The hospital security guard was bored to death this early in the morning. He had nothing to do and there was so little going on tonight that he had tuned in the late movie on the small black and white television in the guard shack. His eyelids felt as though they had bricks on them as he turned the volume to maximum to help him stay awake. The volume on the tiny set was so loud that he didn't hear the van entering the garage. Hundreds of cars entered and left the garage every day, but few if any came this early. Visiting hours didn't start for another eight hours and doctors didn't start seeing patients for another six. As it was, he continued to fight off the sleep that was closing in on him in a losing the battle.

The alarm on Nassir's Timex went off at 5:30 and his body felt completely revived. He would have loved a cup of the strong coffee from home, but settled for a swig of water from the bottle he purchased earlier in the morning. He was thankful the van did not have side windows as he dressed in a blue jump suit with the company logo on the left chest just above the breast pocket. Hidden inside the jumpsuit was the 9mm pistol with the silencer that he had used yesterday to kill Kahlid. He had replaced the three bullets in the clip that went into the younger man's head before he left the falls.

At the bottom of a large box labeled, *Surgical Gloves,* two automatic pistols exactly like the one Nassir used to kill Arkhim, complete with the hand-made silencer, were hidden from view. Nassir thought of them as insurance policies just in case they needed to fight their way past the hospital security. A second empty box would be stacked on top of the hand cart to carry their prize out of the hospital. If things went as planned, they would be in and out without anyone getting hurt. As he checked his equipment for the third time, he noticed headlights shining on the front wall of the garage a few spots down from where he was parked.

Cautiously he peeked out the passenger side front window to see who had pulled in. His eyes met his dear friend Ali, and he smiled. The man walked up to the sliding door of the van just as Nassir slid it open. Each kissed the other on the cheek happy that he made it.

"It is good to see you, my brother," Nassir said with a smile.

"I had no problems getting across the border, but I did get turned around trying to find the garage."

"No worries, my friend, we are nearly there. Come, get into the van and get yourself ready."

Nassir glanced around the empty garage as he slid the door closed, slowly trying not to make a noise. Two sets of hospital scrubs were laid out across the boxes. Nassir was still amazed that an operation of this importance could be carried out with so few people. They had originally planned on four, but they could make do with three without jeopardizing its success.

The fewer involved, the higher probability of success, Nassir thought. Even the best-made plans went bad if too many people had to be relied on. He had learned that you couldn't count on anyone but yourself if you wanted ultimate success. As it was, he had chosen the finest team he could get his hands on. These men would give their lives, if necessary, to ensure a successful operation. Arkhim assigned Kahlid to the operation at the last minute and Nassir argued his participation from the moment he was told. There was no arguing with Arkhim and he knew that. It didn't matter anyway. Kahlid was gone forever. He had no fear about what they were about to do, but was worried about telling his mentor about the death of his only brother. He would have to put that out of his head for now and deal with it later.

He looked at his watch; 6:30.

"Something has happened to Kamal. He should have been here thirty minutes ago."

"Don't worry, Nassir, he will be here. Traffic starts to get bad in the city at this hour."

"I know, that is why the plan was to meet early enough to avoid it."

"He left Canada just after I did. He will be along."

Before he had finished talking, a second pair of lights reflected off the dull cement walls of the garage. The two men inside the van crouched low in the front seats and peeked out each window being careful not to be seen. The headlights belonged to a blue BMW, and it passed the van without even giving it a second glance.

"The signs on the side of the van were a nice touch, Nassir," Ali said as he stepped between the seats to put on the scrubs.

"I know—no one will suspect us parked here all day. Quiet, do you hear footsteps?"

"I do. It is probably the driver of that BMW. I think it stopped just around the corner."

"Keep quiet. If we are found now, we are dead in the water."

Nassir looked out the driver's side window, making sure his head would not be seen. The footsteps were not from the driver of the BMW, but from a large black security guard making his morning rounds.

"Shhh—keep hidden behind those boxes. We have a guard approaching the van," Nassir whispered as he slowly moved behind the driver's seat. The sound of the footsteps echoed inside the thin bare walls of the van as each man held his breath. The guard circled once satisfied that it was empty and continued on checking out the other floors before the garage filled with cars carrying patients for whatever doctor appointments they had that day.

When the sound of the footsteps grew fainter, the two men let out their breath.

"That was close. Stay quiet. The guard may return after his walk-through."

No response except for a silent nod was given. During the close call, neither man had noticed the red Chevrolet Cavalier park in the spot between the vehicles. They heard a door close and a faint rap on the thin metal sliding door. Once again, each held his breath as Nassir looked through the passenger side window.

It was Kamal! He had made it! Nassir slid open the door quickly this time and literally pulled the man inside in fear the guard would return any moment. Once safely in, they exchanged greetings. Nassir was now feeling as confident as any man could feel.

"I was fearful that you didn't make it through the border."

"I had no problems at the border. The guard let me pass through without even a question."

"When the Americans find out how easy it is to get into their country they will feel stupid."

"What do we care? Americans are fools to think they can keep us out," Nassir said arrogantly. If it happened in his country the guard responsible would be publicly shamed and then beheaded in the town square as an example of failure. Americans and their civil rights were still a bit of a mystery to Middle Easterners. Actually, in most Arab nations, the liberal American court and penal system were more of a joke than a deterrent to crime. To think that murders and rapists sat in comfortable jail cells for years was unconscionable to him.

Kamal had finished putting on the matching scrubs and clipped the hospital identification card on the breast pocket. They were now ready to complete the plan. Nassir went over the remaining steps as the two stared at him intently listening, visualizing each step in their heads.

"When we return to the garage, we will all leave in the van. The cars will remain behind. I don't want to risk the three of us being stopped individually. The cars cannot be traced to us even if the guards run the plates. By then we will be safe where no one will think of looking. Do either of you have any questions?"

Both nodded, ready to get moving. Nassir checked the traffic in the garage and opened the two rear doors when he was satisfied no one was approaching.

"The guard must have taken the elevator from the top floor when he had finished the round. Another lucky break! Let us hope the day is filled with them."

The two men stepped out from the rear of the van and wrestled the two-wheeled hand truck out that would carry the boxes. Nassir loaded the boxes and secured them with a bungee cord. With a last check to see if they looked official enough to pass as hospital employees, they headed for the elevator.

Chapter 22

Tony Hampton was bathed in sweat as he double-timed through the streets back to the airport. He and Rodger had kept a fast pace through the hottest part of the day, but had to retrace their steps a few times after getting lost in the old city. It was a good thing Tony had the city map tucked into his shirt that he had long since shoved into a side pocket of his pack opting to wear only his thin t-shirt. Tony had kept track of the time, but it had taken longer than he expected, carrying the weight of their dead teammate as they stopped briefly to catch their breath and let the sweat lessen just a bit before heading out again.

"I can't believe the helicopters couldn't find the car," Tony said as his breath started to return to a normal rate.

"I can't either. For Christ's sake, it was right out on the street in the open. I didn't even see anyone chasing after it."

"That's no surprise. Did you see the mob of people outside the palace? Stefanovich is probably fighting for his life as we speak. He has some very angry people knocking on his door," Tony said coldly.

"I wouldn't want to be in his shoes right now," Rodger observed. "When I came past the palace entrance, the crowd had all but crashed through the large steel gates and three CNN reporters were right in the middle of it all."

"Speaking of shoes, my feet are killing me," Tony said as he looked ahead at the route they were going to take, completely ignoring the CNN comment. If the press found out who was really in those cars, they would have a field day.

"My guess is that President Stefanovich has more on his mind than our vice president," Rodger said, glancing down at the badly cracked pavement.

"That's true. I doubt we'll be getting much help from the Russian government on this. I just hope they allow us to conduct a rescue operation on their soil without having to go through the usual red tape."

"We won't have long to wait to find out," Rodger said tiredly. "We'd better get a move on. It's already 1230 and we probably have another two miles to go."

"I know, I know. Don't remind me."

Before they had a chance to walk another block, a small black car pulled up behind them next to the curb. Tony didn't recognize the make of the car, but knew it was an obvious Russian make from the size and shape. The passenger side window rolled down, and the passenger started talking to them in English.

"Jesus, what the hell happened?" Kevin asked the sweaty men.

"Kevin! My God, are you a sight for sore eyes, back and feet," Tony said.

Tony and Rodger didn't waste time getting the dead man into the back and then piling in on the other side of the small car. They were cramped, but it didn't matter. They were at least riding. Before the doors were even shut, the car sped off toward the airport.

"It is good to see you guys. Is that Steve Shaeffer?" Kevin asked.

"I am afraid so. He was the only body we found," Tony said breathlessly.

"Yeah, well, what the hell happened back there?" Rodger asked, hoping Kevin had some answers.

"I don't know. I was slowed up more than expected through the crowd. When I heard the explosion I had not yet passed through the square. After that, it was no picnic getting to the palace. The people started to go wild and attack the soldiers stationed on the corners. I saw one get overwhelmed by at least fifty people. The poor bastard didn't even know what hit him. When I did get to the palace, the gates had been pushed open and people were pouring in like a dam break. I saw the mess of a Mercedes, but I didn't know which car it was at first. I tried searching for the two of you, figuring you would be near the site, but was picked up by the Russian driver Lassiter sent for us."

"Have you been back to the airport?" Tony asked.

"Yes, and Lassiter is fit to be tied. He has not been able to get through to Stefanovich or the military. They are too busy trying to protect that slime of a president."

"I can only imagine," Tony said with a hint of disappointment in his voice. "He will definitely be happy with our news. We found Rick in Eagle 2's car."

"You what? You found the car?"

"Yes, it's marked on my map," Tony said proudly.

Kevin was afraid to ask the next obvious question. "Did you find—?"

"Other than Steve, the car was empty," Tony said, cutting him off before he had a chance to finish.

"Thank God! He will be happy to hear that bit of good news. I think Lassiter expected to find Eagle 2 with a bullet in his head."

The car entered the back gate to the airport and sped to the hangar. The large sliding door was open, and Tony could see Lassiter standing with the telephone in his hand. The three men walked up to their boss and reported in.

"Sir, I have some news that you will want to hear," Tony said before anything else, hoping it would take some of the stress out of the situation.

"It is good to see you," Lassiter said despairingly. "I have no idea what is going on and trying to get through to the Russian military is like pulling teeth. I might as well be using tin cans on a string. They aren't answering our calls for help nor are they even acknowledging that an incident has occurred. Things are quickly going to hell in a hand basket."

"Yes, sir, I would imagine that is putting it lightly," Tony said as he pulled the map out. "Rodger and I found the car."

Lassiter stared at him as if he just fell out of the sky. "Did you find—?"

"No," Tony said quickly. "But we found Steve. We didn't try to search for evidence to give us information on who was behind or what exactly happened. We just wanted to look for bodies."

"Thanks, and nice work, by the way. Without a body, we still have hope. I want you to take Kevin to the car immediately," Lassiter said as he took the map and placed it on the table. "I don't have much left as far as personnel goes to start much of a rescue mission, but you can bet your ass we will find him if I have to search this whole damn country myself. I'll take care of Steve—you guys bring back that car."

"Sir, you can count us in," Tony said as he started to show the tiredness in his muscles.

"I already have," Lassiter said as he turned away. "You three get rested up. We have a long day ahead of us, and I need to update the president."

The three men walked to the plane to change out of their clothes and get cleaned up. Before walking up the stairs, Tony glanced around the deserted hangar. The team members and friends lost today were still fresh in his mind, but he couldn't spend time thinking about that yet. Lassiter stood behind a large table shouting into a telephone at God knows who—Tony was just glad it wasn't him. The large black cars were gone, and the car they arrived in was just pulling out, leaving only the two planes remaining in the building. It was ghostly quiet, making Lassiter's booming voice echo in the large building.

Lassiter finally sat wearily down at his chair behind the table that was covered with communications equipment. He punched the numbers into his satellite phone and waited for the call to go through.

"Yes, sir," the female voice said.

"This is Mr. Ben Lassiter. I need to speak to the president."

"I am sorry, Mr. Lassiter, he is on his morning jog."

"I don't care where he is. I need to speak to him NOW, damn you!"

"Just a moment, sir. I will patch you through to the security attachment."

"Hello, Ben, how are things in Moscow?" the familiar voice said on the phone.

"Gerry, I need to speak to the president right away."

"What is it, Ben? Can't it wait until he is done jogging? It is dreadfully hot here, and he is not in the mood for a chat, I can tell you that."

Gerry Simons was the team leader of the president's security detail. He was Ben's counterpart and friend. Gerry had been a marine, and the two would entertain the young rookies with an endless number of old war stories each trying to outdo the other.

"Jesus, Gerry, you had better get the president on the phone in the next ten seconds, or the president will have you sweeping the sidewalk outside the Washington Monument."

Gerry recognized from the tone that something was wrong. Lassiter was never this short on the phone. "Hold on a second. I will get him."

Ben heard the muffled voice on the phone tell the driver of the Suburban to stop and its heavy door open and close. Within five seconds he was talking to the president.

"Mr. President, sir, Eagle 2 is out of the nest." Lassiter spoke in a calm and slow manner to allow time for the satellite delay to reach the president.

"My God, Ben, how did this happen?" he asked, looking back at the Chevy Suburban.

"It is a long story, sir. I will have the details typed and on your desk before you return. We are working a long-shot lead as we speak, but have yet to get any assistance from our Russian friends."

Tom Lincoln looked around and saw the press following him as they did every morning. He always detested them following him during the run, but it seemed the attention came with the position. He knew the parabolic listening devices they used could eavesdrop on conversations a hundred yards away, and the last thing he needed was for this to get to the press.

"I am getting in the car now and will be in my office within fifteen minutes. I want an update then and every hour until he is found. Do you understand me? I will do what I can to see you get help from the Russian government."

"Yes, sir, I will call in fifteen minutes," and the line went dead.

The dreaded call was over, and now he could get back to finding Eagle 2. "Jesus Christ, how can I launch a rescue mission with four men and nothing to go on? I hope we get something from the car," Lassiter said to himself.

Tony, Rodger, and Kevin emerged from the plane cleaned up and changed. They walked down the narrow stairs and saw several Russian soldiers prepping the presidential plane. They were working frantically on their pre-flight checks, and Lassiter was screaming at them in English every step of the way. Lassiter had finished typing the email report moments ago, sending it over the SIPRNET top-secret network system to the president.

"Sir, we are ready to do whatever you need," Tony said as he walked up to him.

"I will be with you in a minute—I have to call the president and give him a detailed update."

The president had changed into his suit, complete with a dark blue power tie, as the phone on his desk rang exactly fifteen minutes after the initial call.

"Ben, do you have any news?" Tom said, belaying the normal greetings. Time was of the essence, and they both new it.

"No, sir, I am afraid not. We have found the car, and I have sent a team to retrieve it. We know Eagle 2 was not inside when it was found, so it is safe to assume he was kidnapped. I won't know more until the car returns in approximately half an hour."

"What the hell went wrong?"

"Well, sir, the Russians did not greet us with open arms. They sent two cars for our transport instead of the three we requested, which limited the number of team members we could send in support. I sent three members ahead as spotters, but the estimated figure we were using as far as the number of rioters outside the Kremlin was optimistic. The crowd was far larger than we expected."

"I don't want excuses, Ben—I want to know what the hell happened," Tom said sternly.

"Specifically, I can't answer that yet. But they blew the cars up, sir. All my men are dead except for the four I sent out early," Lassiter said solemnly.

"Jesus, have the Russians provided any assistance?"

"Not exactly, sir. I have not received any assistance from them."

"I have tried to contact President Stefanovich, but have gotten nowhere," the president said.

"I can only imagine. They are prepping his plane as we speak. I suspect he is going to try a hasty getaway."

"Call me in one hour with an update. I will keep working things on my end to help."

"Yes, sir, sixty minutes," and the line went dead again.

Tom Lincoln sat completely numb. He was responsible for this and would never be able to forgive himself if anything happened to David. He punched the intercom button on his phone as he thought over what he needed to do.

"Sally, have Ryan come to my office ASAP. It is imperative that I see him as soon as he arrives."

"Yes, sir, right away."

Lassiter looked pale as he stared at Rodger. "Let's hope that car gets here soon. The president wants another update in an hour," Lassiter said, expecting more than he knew he would receive.

"We will go over the car with a fine tooth comb. If there is anything there to find we will," Rodger said with confidence.

"We had better. We need something more to go on. I simply can't believe this was a random operation by the rioters. The explosives, the surgical elimination of the guards—it all spells professionals."

"Let's hope that is not the case," Tony said, already knowing the answer. If it were true, they were professionals with a purpose and powerful weapons. Two ingredients that did not go well together.

Lassiter fell back into the chair. What could the president work on? He was too far away from the situation to do any good. He wasn't going to be able to stiff-arm the Russians into helping. He couldn't order a Special Forces team to the area. That would spell political suicide, and there would be no way of hiding that from the press. In short, Lassiter was on his own, or so he thought.

*

Ryan Palmer walked through the door to the Oval office at 8:30. The president was on the phone, but Sally rushed him in anyway. Bill Snyder, the president's Chief of Staff, was sitting in a chair by the fireplace talking on his cell phone.

"I can assure you, Governor, I will put every resource at my disposal in your state to assist."

He was talking to the governor of Texas who was frantically trying to get his state ready for Hurricane Jasmine. Just yesterday it had devastated the islands of Tahiti and Puerto Rico. The storm lost much of its power after making landfall, but would certainly pick up all it lost and more once it reached the gulf waters. The latest *National Severe Storm Center* radar loop put the large storm hitting Texas between Brownsville and Corpus Christi. The large storm was forecasted to pick up over the warm water of the gulf because it was moving so slowly. The president motioned for him to sit as he finished the call.

"I have given the Secretary of Defense the authority to have every base in your state on alert, and I have the FEMA Director and Red Cross already in place. You have to understand that we just discovered the storm was going to hit Texas. We are doing everything we can to help. Let me know if you need anything. We have another couple of days to get ready," the president said, hanging up the phone.

"Ryan, it is good to see you again."

"Yes, sir," Ryan said coldly as the sting from the comments earlier in the week was still on his mind.

"Ryan, as you know, I have the convention speech tonight and am quite satisfied that the security is in place to protect all the attendees."

"Yes, sir, I would hope so. An attack on the convention would be tantamount to committing suicide," Ryan said with no emotion in his voice. "I don't understand, sir, what does that have to do with me? You know I had nothing to do with the security planning for the convention, that was Homeland Security."

"Yes, I know that, Ryan. I just wanted you to be aware of the status."

"Very good, now what can I help you with, sir?" Ryan asked in a short tone.

"This is very difficult for me to talk about. The other day we discussed the riots in Moscow."

"Yes, we did. They have grown tremendously since we last spoke. I am attempting to ascertain what exactly is happening over there, but it seems that it changes every second. The latest is that Stefanovich has been driven from the palace and is being escorted through the city. My guess is that he is heading to the airport and to his plane."

"Your guess is absolutely correct. I have reports that the president's plane is in fact being prepped for an unscheduled trip," Tom said, looking over the report Lassiter had sent to him ten minutes before. It was tough reading, but it was all there in black and white. Lassiter was positive David was still alive, and his estimation was hours before we received the initial communication from the terrorists. In most cases, the demands came within 24 hours after the abduction, and that is what both Lassiter and Tom were hoping for. If they only knew who was behind the attack, it may provide some clue as to where David was.

"But how could you know that? We have not heard from our mole for nearly four hours. What reports are you referring to? I must tell you that I am a bit confused."

"I sent David over in an attempt to help Stefanovich work out his problems," Tom said, getting it out.

"You what? How could you do that without me knowing?" Ryan's voice raised in anger.

"It was to be a routine visitation. Just to see how things were going and to show our support."

"Sir, you know all trips outside the country should be run by my office as a matter of protocol."

"I know that, Ryan. You don't have to remind me of protocol for Christ's sake."

"I am sorry, sir, I didn't mean to imply anything. I am still trying to make some sense of all—My God, something has happened, hasn't it?"

"I am afraid so. Ben Lassiter called ninety minutes ago with the news. He is standing by in the Russian Presidential hangar to mount a search operation. At this point, he has very little to go on. The Russian government, or what is left of it I should say, is too concerned about their own problems to help us."

"A search operation? What the hell happened over there?" Ryan asked, shifting his weight forward in the chair.

Tom handed Ryan Lassiter's report detailing the incident. It was tough reading, and Ryan was silent as Tom continued to speak.

"Ben's men have found the car David was in and are gathering evidence in an attempt to find some clue as to who is behind the abduction. I am afraid that is all I have to this point."

Ryan was dumbfounded. He didn't know what to say or how to respond.

"So far, the number of people aware of the situation is limited. I don't have to tell you that if this leaks to the press I will have the person's head. Ben Lassiter, his team, Mr. Snyder, and now you. See that you tell only those with the need-to-know, with the understanding that this gets the highest security."

"When will Lassiter be calling again?"

"I would expect his call in approximately thirty minutes for an update on what they found in the car," Tom said, looking at his watch.

"Please call me after that, sir. I would like to have the latest information."

"I will do that. From you, Mr. Palmer, I would like whatever you can scare up about the riots, terrorist groups, the shake-up of the Russian government, anything you feel is important enough to investigate. I am relying on you here. We are flying blind on this one."

"I will do what I can—I promise you," Ryan said, thinking how ironic it was that three days ago he was the president's whipping boy, and today he was the saving grace. Oh, how the winds of change blow, he thought.

Chapter 23

John Bastian was putting the green canvas sun cover over the long aluminum boom, that held his mainsail in place, to shield him and Maggie from the hot sun. The two had a glorious night out in the bay, sleeping soundly in the peace and quiet as the boat rocked gently on the rolling waves. He prepared a light breakfast of eggs and toast in the galley, sharing most of it with Maggie. By 9:00, he pulled the anchor with the electric windlass and he lazily sailed south.

By mid-day, the sun had become unbearable in the cockpit, so he programmed the autopilot and went below to retrieve the canvas cover out of the aft-cabin storage compartment. Putting it up was no big deal, and in no time they were relaxing in the shade. It was still ghastly hot on the water, but the cover helped tremendously.

The sleek boat skimmed over the water's surface with its large sails filled with wind. With the wind out of the north, he planned on heading south for a few hours and then circling back to spend the night in the cove, but if he didn't make it, he didn't make it. Today was a day of no deadlines or commitments, and he didn't want to push it if he didn't think he could make it back before dark.

The water was absolutely perfect as his wake widened out behind him until it disappeared from view. The smile on his tanned face was unmistakable. No beeper or cell phones to distract his relaxation was exactly what the doctor ordered. If an emergency came up, his replacement could handle it. She started last week and was coming along nicely.

The fact that she was in place decreased his stress level to the point where he could enjoy his time off. He had not done that in years. Sure, he had taken vacations and long weekends with his family, but he had the inevitable feeling in the back of his mind that he was going to be called in.

He selected the new director after pouring over nearly one hundred applications and resumes. The process took months, and Dr. Sherrie Robard had come out on top. They interviewed five candidates, and she was without a doubt as impressive in person as her credentials were on paper, and she had the experience to back it up. He was positive and confident he was leaving the department in good hands and would bow out gracefully.

*

Ryan walked into his office after the puzzling conversation with the president. He sat at his desk and stared at nothing for five minutes. The ride back had been productive as his mind mulled over the situation which he refused to think of as impossible. "How can I possibly find him?" he thought out loud. Idea after idea was quickly dismissed as soon as they popped into his head. One in particular kept coming back to him and he couldn't get it out of his brain.

"Sharon, please get the agents handling the Moscow riots in here."

"Right away, sir," Sharon said. She was his new secretary, but she was not new to the political atmosphere. She had come from Senator Chamberlain's office as a highly regarded employee, and she was working out better than Ryan ever dreamed.

"Also, could you pull the files on a special project entitled *Project Chandler*? You should be able to locate it in the electronic database, but if not, the hard copy will be in the project vault in the basement."

"Yes, sir, I will get right on it."

"Thank you," and he pushed the release button. As a rookie agent he heard rumors about a secret project started during the Korean War that may just be the solution. However, it was a long shot for sure. If he was wrong about this, precious hours would be wasted and he was positive that his career would be over.

The project was actually named after a battle hardened American Lieutenant who commanded troops near Taejon, a city in Central South Korea. The city was in American hands until a detachment of Korean tanks bombarded the city forcing the American troops to retreat. During the retreat, Lieutenant Chandler stayed behind and helped guide American B-17 bombers to the enemy tanks. During one late night spotting mission, he was separated from his men, and for nearly a month he attempted to make it back to the American lines, only to be captured by a squad of North Koreans and held for nearly three years as a prisoner of war before being safely released. He was awarded the Medal of Honor for his heroic actions in Taejon and has been an symbol of courage for all soldiers for the past fifty years. However, it was not his heroic actions which put his name on the project. It was his missing in action status that prompted the special project to bear his name.

Ryan would know all this as soon as he had a chance to review the project documents. For now he would just have to wait and think about the other less promising alternatives should this one be a dead-end. Sharon stepped into his office to announce the arrival of the agents.

"Thank you, Sharon. Did you find anything on that special project?"

"I couldn't find anything in our computer database. I am headed to the basement to see if I can dig up anything. I will be out for a bit."

"Very good. Close the door on your way out," he said as she turned, letting the door close on its own.

Two men sat at the large conference table on the wall opposite Ryan's desk near a window that overlooked the parking lot. They each carried a folder with the familiar red top-secret markings in their hand and placed them squarely on the table in front of them. Ryan walked over to the chair at the head of the table and sat down acknowledging them with a smile and a nod.

"Gentlemen, thank you for coming up on such short notice."

"It is our pleasure, sir."

"Give me an update on what you see happening in Moscow with the riots."

"Well, sir, communications between the Kremlin and the KGB have been flying over unencrypted lines for the past twenty-four hours. I don't know if they are not aware they are broadcasting information in the clear or just don't care because of the situation. Whatever the reason, things are easier for us. It appears that Stefanovich has made it to the airport, but a mass of people has blocked the runway, stopping the plane from taking off. We have yet to get confirmation, but our guess is that at this point he has taken off for an unknown location. We have also coordinated with Signal Intelligence over at the NSA. They are listening to all communications and will let us know if they hear anything important."

Signal Intelligence, better known by the acronym, SIGINT, was the eavesdropping spy department under the NSA umbrella. Its only mission was to listen to conversations around the world with a network of super-secret equipment. They could literally tap thousands of personal phone lines within seconds and record individual conversations for weeks at a time, including cell phones. This was in fact, their single point of failure. The American public didn't trust the NSA simply because of their eavesdropping ability. The electronic resources they had at their disposal were unbelievable and incomprehensible to the average person. Their one-story brick building on the NSA complex had hundreds of antennas of all shapes and sizes including three eight-foot diameter satellite receivers mounted on cement platforms pointing toward the horizon and at least six white domes that looked more like large golf balls than antennas. To an outsider the building appeared to have a metal forest on its roof.

"Interesting, what else?"

"Our mole inside the palace has yet to be compromised. He will remain within the Kremlin until forced to leave."

"Good idea. It is always best to know your enemies. Security should be looser than normal over the next few days as the KGB scrambles to pick up the pieces of the government. Maybe this time it will be destroyed forever," Ryan said, resting his tired head in the palm of his hand.

"I would sincerely doubt that, sir. The KGB lost much of its power after the Soviet break-up ten years ago, but don't let that fool you. It will take more than a government takeover to kill the KGB."

"I need to know what is going on as soon as it happens. I don't care if a dog shits on a sidewalk outside the palace, I want to know. I can call our boys over at the NGA's Satellite Imagery lab and have a bird diverted over the area to gather intelligence if that would help."

SIMINT, or Satellite Imagery Intelligence, was nothing new. In fact, the United States used data gathered from aerial reconnaissance from as far back as the Civil War. In those early days the military used balloons to survey battlefields. In the 1950s the government replaced balloons with the highly covert U-2 jets to fly over key areas taking pictures, providing real-time data to military planners. However, the newest edition to the military's "Looking Glass" satellite collection was absolutely amazing. It had a ground resolution of six inches from an altitude of fifty miles and could produce a nearly perfect three-dimensional image of the surface of the earth using an enhanced electro-optical mirror mounted to a solar charged satellite.

The picture Ryan liked to paint when he explained the satellite's ability was that he could not only see the horse in the pasture, but the distance each fly was from the horses back as its long tail splashed over its ass. Two-dimensional imagery was great when that was all there was, but this new technology was incredible. It was a good thing the cost of the project was buried under layers of bureaucratic bullshit, hiding the nearly $200 billion price tag or the satellite project would have been scrapped for sure.

The National Geospatial-Intelligence Agency, NGA for short, had the control of every satellite in orbit. Ryan liked to say that they had the ability to look into the heart and soul of every human being on the face of the earth. The sad thing was that he was probably right. The NGA controlled SIMINT, but worked closely with the CIA and NSA on many projects requiring a closer look or special handling.

"I think it is too premature at this point to start talking satellite imagery. The area in question is simply to large to get with one pass. It would take days to realign it to make a second pass, and in that time we may miss a target."

"Good point, you two follow up every lead regardless of where it takes you. When you need Looking Glass, I will coordinate it for you. I want every resource in the Special Operations Center to be focused on this region," Ryan said as he stood.

If the CIA was considered the lifeblood of the secret spy service, then the Special Operations Center could be considered the pulse. Every CIA field agent kept in direct contact with the SOC for updates, both sending and receiving top secret data via the most modern of communications equipment. From the SOC, agents could literally tune in any television or radio station anywhere in the world, receive piped in real-time satellite images, and listen to phone conversations much like the NSA. The technology inside this dark room would make even Bill Gates smile. For the most part, the CIA monitored general local chatter in identified key countries. But when all resources were focused in one location, it was amazing what they could find out in a short period of time. If the terrorists were communicating, the SOC would find them.

"Understood," the two men said as they pushed their chairs away from the table.

"Good luck and remember, anything happens, I want to know."

Both men nodded as they opened the door to leave, and Sharon walked through right after them. She was carrying a dusty box that had seen better days.

"Sir, here is the information I could find on 'Project Chandler.'"

"Thank you, Sharon—hopefully it will come in handy. I will look it over before I leave for the day."

She huffed a bit and walked back out in the hallway and pushed in a cart filled with boxes. "Here are more, and there are another two carts still in the elevator."

"Shit! There goes my night by the looks of it. Thank you again, Sharon. Have a good night. Before you leave, could you please call my wife and tell her I will be late again tonight?"

"She won't be happy—this is the third time this week," she said, bringing in the remaining two carts.

"I know—that is why I want *you* to call," he said with a smirk.

"Goodnight, sir," she said as she closed the door with the knowledge that he would be right where she left him tomorrow morning, except there would be piles of papers surrounding him like a moat surrounds a castle.

Ryan took the musty top off the first cardboard box and picked up a notebook that was badly dog-eared from use. The name Dr. Greeley was written in black ink on the inside cover, which Ryan didn't immediately recognize, but flipped through the first few pages anyway. Page after page of scribbled notes of formulas, and pencil drawn pictures filled the notebook. Ryan still didn't understand the project, so he set the notebook aside and pulled out the next set of documents.

As hour after hour passed by, Ryan sat terrified at what he had discovered. *My God, I can't believe this project ever existed and even more, was kept secret for over fifty years. If the details should ever be known about it, the government would never be trusted again,* Ryan thought to himself.

He found the Army had first quietly recruited a team of top-notch research physicians to research the feasibility of tracking soldiers on the battlefield. They began by resurrecting the project first developed by Professor Greeley in the 1950s. However, the effects of the project went far beyond locating soldiers.

It appeared from what he had read so far that a young Lieutenant Bastian was the team leader for the project. His work spanned nearly a decade and in that time, he and his team had developed a revolutionary nano-probe that could be injected into a human body without a trace. The probe was, in fact, a miniature electronic transmitter that could be programmed with information, which could then be transmitted to a special receiver. During the early years, the distance the probe could transmit was limited to a few miles, but advances in technology during the sixties increased the transmit radius to over a hundred miles.

Early on, researchers had also found that the probe could track human movements and be programmed to not only transmit stored information, but also body patterns such as heart beat, breathing rate, and body temperature. The Army had tested the probe on small animals and volunteer soldiers during the Korean War, but by 1960 the probe was considered ready for normal use and was secretly approved by the NSA and FDA to be injected into all newborns in test beds around the country.

"Bingo. I think I am on to something," Ryan said out loud to the walls in his office. He stood for the first time in nearly five hours and looked at his watch. It was after midnight as he shook his legs to get the blood pumping. His mind raced over the project as he paced, staring at the cherry paneling that covered the walls of his plush office. He headed to the bathroom attached to his office to release the two pots of coffee he had consumed during the reading and take a little breather.

Ryan assembled all the documents that related to the employees who worked the project during the early years and placed them in a neat stack on his desk. He would have Sharon run bios on them in the morning in an attempt to find them. From what he could gather, there were five researchers on the initial team recruited from the Army, who should be easy enough to track down. The record keeping within the military is meticulously accurate.

Sometime between midnight and six o'clock, he stumbled onto a notebook containing the sites for the initial public tests. St. Augustine Children's Hospital outside of Atlanta was one of the first to get a supply of the probes, and according to the records, injections started on July 7th, 1960. Amazingly, he turned the page to find a roster of the babies who received the first generation of probes. The list was in four columns with the name, probe number, and locator ID. The fourth column was blank under the heading, *Programmed Information*. He scanned down the list quickly, but didn't immediately recognize any of the names.

He was amazed the project had actually been approved and piloted in such a short period of time—three years from the looks of it. Today, projects of this magnitude take decades to be approved with all of the protesting from the bleeding-heart liberals.

The decade of the 1950s was a period of technological exploration. Governmental scientists and engineers were developing equipment that would place men on the moon, make planes fly faster, and make weapons more powerful. It was a time of vast expansion evidently, Ryan surmised, because it overshadowed the secret implementation of the largest cover-up he had ever seen.

His finger again moved down the yellowed sheet of paper and back up to the top where it stopped, and he literally fell back into his chair as his knees gave way. The name on the top of the list—the very first baby to receive the probe—David J. Arthur.

He stared incredulously at the name for over a minute. It was too early in the morning, and his mind was in a dense fog. He rubbed the sleep out of his eyes and looked again at the name on the paper as he fired up his computer. As the computer started, he paced again to get his body and mind moving. He glanced at his watch and with a frown noticed it was nearly time for Sharon to arrive. He was tired, but sometime around 4:00 he got a second wind, and now his adrenaline was working overtime. He could easily access the NSA database to gather the data he needed. He just needed to confirm the birthplace and date of the vice president to prove his hunch.

His eyes were sore and dark red, but you wouldn't know it based on how focused he was staring at the computer screen. He was accessing the NSA's personnel database, running a demographic search on the vice president. The database contained all of the available data on every employee who had ever worked for the United States Government. The volume of data stored in this single database was so immense that it took nearly fifty terabytes of disk space to hold it all. The complexity of the technology was well beyond Ryan's expertise. He relied heavily on the agency's technology department to handle the tedious, but critical task of maintaining the connectivity to the various databases the CIA had developed over the last decade. *Without a doubt, the invention of computers had to rank among the top innovations in the past century*, Ryan thought as he typed David's name into the search field.

Within seconds, the information on the vice president was on his screen. On the first page was the vital data—birth date, place, and parents names were all at his fingertips. He quickly printed off what he needed, but just glancing at the screen he knew it was a match. He rubbed his eyes as the printer on the small table next to his desk came alive and began spitting out the results of his tireless research.

"My God, how am I ever going to explain this to the president?" he whispered to himself. He was sure that no one knew about nor could anyone fully comprehend the far-reaching effects the project would have on public trust should it ever get out.

"Good morning, sir," Sharon said as she poked her head into his office realizing that he had not made it home that night.

"Is it morning already?" he asked sarcastically.

"Yes, and I see you put in another all-nighter. Your wife is going to kill you if you do this too many more times."

"I know. She has an understanding and forgiving soul, but I must agree with you. I will call her later."

"Can I get you a fresh cup of coffee?"

"That would be great, but could you make copies of these papers first?" he asked, handing a large stack of loose notebook papers along with some other official looking documents to Sharon.

"I will get right on it as soon as I get you that coffee," she said, realizing that he needed the coffee more than he needed the copies. "Your eyes look terrible, and you need a shave."

"Trust me, I feel worse than I look if that's possible," he said as she closed the door. Ryan stood from his chair and walked into his bathroom. He looked in the mirror and couldn't believe what he saw.

"My God, you do look terrible," he said to the man staring back at him in the mirror. He kept a full supply of toiletries just for nights like these. He couldn't visit the president looking like this. He pulled out another designer suit from the small closet to the left of the sink and started to unbutton his wrinkled shirt. Having a bathroom complete with a shower in his office was definitely a nice perk of the director's position. He had requested it soon after he was selected for the position. The Agency's maintenance personnel had grumbled when they got the order, but it was installed within weeks. *Another perk*, he thought to himself as he stared into the mirror. Directors can cut through the normal red tape when it comes to work requests.

The hot shower did wonders for his mental state, but did very little to revive him physically. He dried off, wrapping the towel around his waist as the sink filled with steaming water. He lathered his face with the shaving cream and quickly removed the stubble from his chin and cheeks. His wife had bought him an electric razor for father's day last year, but he refused to use it. He preferred the closer shave of the razor he deftly held in his fingers and after thirty years, he could shave just as fast.

He wiped the remaining shaving cream from under his ears with the towel and dressed. He tried to tell himself that he felt better, but one passing glance in the mirror as he left the small bathroom still showed that he looked like hell. "Oh well, this is the best I can do," Ryan muttered.

A steaming cup of coffee was waiting for him on his desk in the empty office. Sharon was making the requested copies as he picked up his phone and dialed in the number for the president.

"Good morning, Sally," he said to the cheery voice answering the phone.

"Ah, and a good morning to you, sir. What can I help you with?"

"Is the president in yet?"

"Yes, he skipped his normal routine to get here early. He has been in his office for the past couple of hours. I will warn you—he looks like he is under a lot of stress today."

"I have some information that may just make his day. Could you please put me through to him?"

"I can, but he is meeting with the Chief of Staff at the moment behind closed doors. Would you like me to interrupt the meeting?"

"Yes, this is important. Both of them should hear what I have to say."

"Very well, I will put you through immediately," she said as Ryan heard the phone click as the transfer went through.

"Good morning, Ryan, how are things at the CIA?" the president inquired, putting the call on the speakerphone.

"Quiet today. I have been here all night looking through some paperwork that I think you should see."

"What do you have, Ryan?"

"I would prefer to talk to you in person. I don't trust the phone lines even if they are supposed to be secure. The Russians are very creative when it comes to surveillance."

"Okay, come right over with what you have and we can talk about it. Lassiter should be calling any minute with the latest on the situation in Moscow."

"I am waiting for copies to be made, and I will be right over. I should be there in sixty minutes depending on morning traffic."

"Sixty minutes—I will see you then," the president confirmed as the phone line clicked dead.

Ryan walked over to the window to watch the sun rise. He already knew that the president didn't trust the CIA, and that feeling didn't stop at the president. Ryan had his time on the damn hot seat during the Senate inquiries after Operation Desert Freedom. They were trying to pin the government's inability to find weapons of mass destruction on the CIA. The endless barrage of questions from the Senate panel had taken its toll on him and the organization. The former president tried to make the CIA the scapegoat, and Ryan didn't like it.

This, however, could bring the CIA back in good standing for the first time in over a decade.

It didn't take much imagination, though, to see it had every potential to unravel the very fabric of society. Ryan also knew this president was not stupid. He would immediately know the implications this project would have.

He knew the only way to present it was to simply lay it all out on the table. The hard part was that he had the facts of the project, but not the understanding. To get that, he needed to find the people who had worked on the project. After fifty years, that might pose a bit of a problem. The original team members would have to be in their 70s, if they were still alive to find.

Ryan walked through the door to his office and into the copier room where Sharon was neatly arranging the copied documents into organized packets. He thumbed through the stack of originals, stopping at one that listed the original project team stationed at Aberdeen.

"Sally, could you please run a search on these names and see what you come up with? I want addresses, telephone numbers, anything you can get. You may want to start in the military database. All five of them are veterans, and if we are lucky, retirees. You have fifteen minutes. I'm leaving for the White house, and I would like to be able to take the list of names and anything you can dig up with me."

"Certainly, I should be able to have something for you to take. I will get right on it," she said, taking the list from Ryan's hands.

"Also, could you put these copies in a *Top Secret* folder, so I can hand-carry them. I will be in my office should you need me," Ryan said as he walked past her desk.

Ryan walked back into his office, still trying to collect his thoughts. He was positive he was on to something, but he wasn't quite sure yet how it would all come together. He paced his office again, now staring at the floor instead of out the window.

The phone on his desk beeped. "Sir, I have some preliminary findings, but this may take longer than what you have time for."

"What do you have for me so far?"

"Well, sir, out of the original five members on the list, three retired from the Army and two of the three are deceased. Those were the easy ones. The third was last located in the Florida Keys, or that is where his retirement checks are being sent anyway."

Ryan's hopes were quickly being dashed away. He knew this was a long shot, but it was the only way to find out about this project.

"Okay, what about the fifth?"

"Well, he left the military and entered the private sector. I took the liberty of running the name of John Bastian through the NSA database and amazingly he is still among us and is a doctor at Johns Hopkins. I have a home address and phone number for Dr. Bastian. I knew you would want it."

Ryan's eyes lit up with an obvious spark of hope. "Now we are getting somewhere. Great work, Sally. Give me what you have found so far and keep working on the remaining one in Florida. I'm going to send someone out to the address you have listed for this Dr. Bastian. He, so far, is the best bet to help shed some light on this project."

"Would you like me to call the Baltimore office and have them send a car to pick him up?"

"That would be great, tell them it is under my direct orders that Dr. Bastian gets here as soon as possible. I don't care if he is in the middle of surgery."

"Yes, sir, and I will call the car for you."

"Thank you, Sharon, you are a sweetheart. What would I do without you?"

"You would be late to see the president, that is what you would do," she said as she hung up the phone

Ryan pulled the freshly dry-cleaned designer sport coat off the hanger and straightened his tie before picking up the three folders marked *Top Secret*. He took a deep breath and left his office door pausing to talk to Sharon.

"Well, how do I look?"

"You look like shit, if I can be blunt. That is what spending the night in your office does to you," she said with a grin.

"Thanks for the vote of confidence."

"You had to ask."

"You know that isn't the way to get a head with the boss," Ryan said with a huge smile on his face and turned to walk toward the elevator.

"Oh right, you look like a 'million bucks,'" she added sarcastically. "Good luck," she yelled as the door to the elevator slowly closed.

The rush hour traffic died away as the large car made its way across town. Ryan glanced at his watch and thought that he should have given himself more time. The sixty minutes was just about up as the car stopped at the security gate outside the White House. The Marine guard talked to the driver as Ryan opened his window to show his ID. Even the president's wife didn't get through the gate without showing ID—personal recognition was a thing of the past. Security had tightened almost too much in the past five years. The Marine looked at Ryan's CIA badge and did a cursory inspection of the car before motioning to the second guard to raise the gate.

The car slowly made its way to the parking garage and Ryan already could feel the butterflies in his stomach. The president was stressed and didn't need the repercussions of this to deal with, too. The only thing that could make this any easier was that it could be the only way to find the vice president. With that knowledge and fifty years of silence, Ryan couldn't keep this project hidden any longer.

Chapter 24

The two junior agents parked their car in the concrete driveway of the beautiful Victorian two-story home in Roland Park, one of the wealthiest suburbs on the north side of center-city Baltimore. Several large, stately oak and maple trees lined both sides of the wide street framing the dark-green lawns giving the neighborhood more of a country like setting than a city suburb.

They double checked the address one last time and walked up the sidewalk past the ornately manicured lawn and meticulously landscaped flowerbeds to a beautiful wraparound porch. The first agent to reach the large oak door rang the doorbell and waited. Within minutes, Mrs. Bastian made her way to the door and opened it slowly. She was impeccably dressed in a gray blazer and skirt, ready to leave for work, looking impatiently at the two as she made it obvious they were interrupting her morning routine.

"Good morning, ma'am. I am Agent Rafferty, and this is Agent Markus. We are from the Baltimore office of the CIA," Rafferty said as he fumbled in his coat pocket for his badge. "We are looking for a Dr. Jonathan Bastian. He wouldn't happen to be at home, would he? We have some questions for him."

The lawyer in Georgia Bastian made her look closely at the man's credentials. "Please come in," she said, "my husband is not at home, but if you tell me what you are looking for maybe I can help you."

"No, ma'am, we are looking for Dr. Bastian. I am afraid we can't tell you why. We are not even sure. I can only tell you that my partner and I were told to escort him to the CIA building in Langley."

"Well, in that case you two had better be sailors or swimmers because my husband is on our boat somewhere in the bay," she said, still looking closely at the two men with just a hint of sarcasm in her voice.

"Is there any way we can get in touch with him, ma'am?"

"He carries a cell phone and pager with him religiously."

"Could you please give us those numbers? It is important that we speak with him as soon as possible."

Georgia eyed the two men closely. "Why don't I try to call him?"

"Ma'am, we really need to contact him. You can try to call him, but we will need those numbers."

Georgia walked into the living room to retrieve the cordless phone and pushed speed dial "1," and the line rang directly into voice mail. "That is strange—he always answers his phone. It is attached to his body like a third hand." She dialed the number this time without pressing the speed dial and still reached his voice mail. "Hmmm, let's try the beeper. He always calls within minutes of getting the page, and it has a much better range."

The three waited for the return call while Georgia resigned herself to being late for work. "Would either of you like a cup of coffee?"

"No thank you, ma'am. If we don't get in touch with him we will have to be going. Could you possibly give us a description of the boat—name, marina, and slip number?"

"I don't understand what all of the rush is about. He will be back in a few days—can't this wait for goodness' sake? He is taking a well deserved break from work."

"No, it can't. Please, ma'am, we can get the information from you or from the Maryland Boating Commission's database, but we would prefer it from you. It would save us a boat load of time, pardon the pun."

"Alright, it is a Hunter 41-foot sail boat, white with a blue stripe at the waterline. The sail number is 06819 and has the name *Sailor's Dream* written across the back. We keep it at Jack's Marina in the Inner Harbor, slip 86. But I promise you that you won't find him there. He left early yesterday with Maggie. They could be anywhere by now."

"Maggie?"

"Yes, she is our Golden Retriever. They go everywhere together when he is off. I swear that she sees him more than I do."

The two men smiled, but did not lose their professional demeanor. "I am afraid that he is not going to answer the page either."

"It is not like him to not answer the calls. He knows that it could be the hospital. No, I am worried that something has gone wrong. He has sailed alone many times in the past, but has always called to let me know he was safe."

"I assure you, Mrs. Bastian, when we find him we will have him call home."

"That is if you find him. It would be like looking for a needle in a haystack. John knows that bay like the back of his hand."

"We will find him, ma'am," Rafferty said confidently. "Thank you for your hospitality. We are sorry to have bothered you so early in the morning," Rafferty added and turned to walk out the door.

"Are you sure you can't tell me what all the fuss is over my husband?"

"Like we said, we were only sent to escort him to CIA headquarters."

"Very well. Good luck and goodbye."

"Goodbye and thank you again," the two said as they closed the door and walked back out to their car.

Before they left the driveway the information on the boat was radioed back to their office, and a second car was dispatched to the marina. Slip 86 was empty. Only the mooring lines were left to indicate that a boat was there. The two new agents walked the docks of the marina looking at the names on the boats to see if any were the *Sailor's Dream*. Satisfied that it was not there, they stopped by the Marina's office.

"Excuse me, sir, have you seen Dr. Jonathan Bastian within the past few days?" the agent asked the teenager behind the desk, flashing his badge.

"Ummmm—no, sir," the scared kid said to the two men. "This is my first day back. I only work Mondays and Tuesdays. Let me get the Marina manager. He is out looking at an old sloop that was brought in last week for repair," the kid said as he stumbled out the door.

Within minutes, an old sea dog of a man entered the office looking like he would have been more comfortable on a lobster boat than shored up on land. His short legs looked even shorter in his darkly stained, blue-jean overalls. The white t-shirt underneath appeared to have more holes than a slice of swiss cheese.

"Can I help you gentlemen?" the man asked, wiping his pudgy fingers on an oil stained rag he pulled from his back pocket. He replaced the rag, wiped his right hand one last time on his overalls and held it out. "The name is Earl, Earl Jones."

The two shook hands with the old man, each flashing their badge. "We are looking for Dr. Jonathan Bastian. His wife said his boat is docked here in slip 86, but it is empty."

"Dr. Bastian...Dr. Bastian..." the old man said, stroking his scraggly beard stalling for time, pretending he was thinking on the name.

"Come now, Mr. Jones, we don't have time for your failing memory," the agent closest to him said firmly.

"Jonathan Bastian, ah yes, he left out of here yesterday. Alone as I recall. Just him and his dog Maggie," he said as if suddenly remembering the name.

"Did he leave a float plan or give you any idea where he might have been heading?"

"No, sir, we don't require our customers to file a plan. Many come in here looking for some peace and quiet. They don't want to be found."

"Did he tell you when he might be returning?"

"No, as I recall he parked his car over there," pointing to the blue Volvo. "He didn't even stop in the office. That is not unusual—it was a quiet day."

"Very well, and thank you for your time," the two men said, turning to leave the office.

"Is Dr. Bastian in some sort of trouble?" the old man asked curiously. "Rumors spread like wildfire around the marina, and two CIA agents looking for one of their community members would surely make its rounds."

"No, sir, no trouble. We think he could help us shed some light on something. We just want to ask him some questions."

"I see," the old man said, removing his oil-stained cap, revealing a nearly bald head.

"Again, we want to thank you for your time," they said and quickly left the office.

The two agents returned to their car and radioed in to their supervisor what they had found.

"Sir, the boat is not in the slip. We questioned the marina manager who indicated that the boat had left yesterday. Where would you like us to proceed?"

"Just sit tight. Is there an open area to land a helicopter?"

"There is a parking lot just north of the marina that is empty. Bring the bird in there."

"Perfect, I want you two canvassing the bay until you find him. Do you understand? I don't want you back here unless you have Dr. Bastian with you."

"Yes, sir, we copy and will be awaiting the new transportation."

The two agents looked at each other as soon as the radio link had been closed.

"What the hell could be so special about this guy?" Jackson asked.

"Beats me, but they are pulling out all the big guns to find him," Flaherty answered.

"Right, like I didn't have anything better to do than stare through binoculars for hours at the water. It is going to be damned near impossible to find a sailboat in the bay. Christ, it could be anywhere," he said, staring out at the vast expanse of water.

In fifteen minutes the sound of helicopter blades split the air. The two men exited the car and waited on the edge of the dirt parking lot. It stopped fifty feet off the ground in a graceful hover and started to descend, sending a shower of dust over the two agents. When the bird touched down, the agents stooped low enough to avoid the spinning blades and approached the door. Just as they were getting in, Earl Jones came running out of the office with a map flapping in the turbulent air.

Jackson turned to stop him as he approached.

"Sir, it is too dangerous for you to come any closer," Jackson yelled over the whine of the engines.

"I thought this might help," as he handed the agent a map of the bay with an area circled in red. "Start the search here. It is a popular spot for sailors to moor overnight," Earl Jones yelled.

"Thank you, sir. The CIA appreciates your help."

Earl waved and ran back into the office before putting back on his dirty cap. He watched the helicopter take off with all the grace that it landed and it sped off over the water in a southeastern direction. Damn, this is going to make quite a story tonight. It wasn't often that he had this much excitement in one day.

The two agents had large fifty-power marine binoculars glued to their eyes from the moment they went "feet wet." They wanted to find the boat in a bad way and get home.

They were lucky that the weekend boating action was over on the bay. By late afternoon on Saturday the water would be filled with thousands of happy-go-lucky boaters enjoying the hot sun on the water. When that happened, it would be near impossible to find their man. They first searched the area that the old man had circled and came up empty.

"Shit, nothing," the agent in the front seat said into the microphone to both the pilot and his partner in the backseat.

"We have two—maybe two and a half—more hours of flight time before we have to land and refuel," the pilot said into the radio. "With the thirty minutes it took to get here, we had better start heading back in another hour or so."

"Okay, we'll head south from here before heading back," the lead agent said.

"You're the boss," the pilot said and pushed the stick forward making the nose of the large copter dip and speed off in a straight line south.

For the next hour they passed over eleven boats. Only one even remotely looked like the Hunter and they circled it twice slowly before continuing their search. Then the lead agent spotted a white sailboat with all sails flying heading north toward them.

"I think we have him," the agent said as he pointed in the direction just west of their flight path.

The pilot eased the collective and the foot pedals causing the helicopter to veer to the right as they set a course to meet the boat head on. Satisfied it was the boat they were searching for, the pilot settled in to a hover directly above the boat high enough to not let the down wash interfere with the sails.

The agent in the front seat picked up the marine radio on board and tuned it to channel 16.

"*Sailor's Dream*, this is the CIA helicopter, do you copy?" Jackson said into the radio.

The airwaves were silent for a moment and then they heard a response.

"This is the *Sailor's Dream*, I copy."

"Dr. Bastian?" the agent spoke into the radio.

"Copy, this is Dr. Bastian. What is wrong that you are bothering me?"

Maggie went below as soon as she heard the loud noise. She was too afraid to remain on deck.

"Sir, I am Agent Jackson of the CIA, and I would like to ask you some questions. Could you please bring your sails in and hove to?"

"The CIA? I don't believe it. Leave me alone—I'm trying to enjoy a few days off," John scoffed.

"Sir, I assure you it is true. Did you participate in a Project Chandler?" the voice asked.

Project Chandler—how could they know that? He had not heard those words in a very long time. As a matter of fact, he was told to carry any knowledge of his work on that project to his grave.

"Yes, I was the project lead. But…how could you know that?"

"Please, sir, we just want to talk."

"Fine, give me a minute to furl the sails," John said as he dropped the radio and started to winch in the spinnaker. In five minutes he had downed the sails and was weighing anchor with the electric windlass.

"Okay, now talk," John said breathlessly into the radio.

"I am coming aboard," Jackson said, dropping a line onto the deck.

"What, are you insane? You can't repel onto a boat in the middle of the bay."

"I am on my way, please secure me when I get close," the voice said, dropping off as John saw a body being slowly lowered from the sliding door.

I must be on Candid Camera or an episode of the Twilight Zone, John thought, as the man lowered closer to his boat. How could they know about Project Chandler and better yet, how did they find him out here? The man was close enough to reach out to, but John had been around long enough to know not to touch him directly without grounding himself. The static electricity generated by the downdraft could kill both of them if they weren't careful.

John hooked the dangling rope with his long mooring pole and pulled it in while the man still on the helicopter let more slack in the line. The boat pitched with the waves almost knocking him overboard as he pulled the rope toward him. It felt like he had hooked a dead fish with the weight of the man dangling precariously over the water.

"Quick, reach out your hand," John yelled at the agent over the sound of the rotors. The man twisted on the end of the rope, attempting to comply with John's request.

"I am going to cut myself from the line, fish me out of the water," the agent said, realizing that getting wet was going to be inevitable. He looked at his tailored suit and wished he'd worn something more appropriate for this.

It wasn't long before John was staring into the face of the dripping young agent in disbelief.

"Hold on, I have a towel stowed below," John said.

Jackson gave the thumbs up to the pilot and the aircraft moved out of the graceful hover.

John returned with the towel, handing it to the drenched man sitting on the padded starboard bench.

"Now, would you mind explaining to me how you know about Project Chandler?" John asked as the man attempted in vane to dry himself.

"I am afraid I don't know anything about it specifically, just the name. I was sent to find you and bring you to the CIA headquarters," Jackson said, pulling out his dripping badge.

"Are you crazy? I have no intention of leaving this boat in the middle of the bay just because you have some hair-brained orders."

"I can assure you, sir, that it is a matter of national security that you meet with the director immediately."

"Bullshit! I have seen a lot of things in my life time, sonny, and this may just trump all of them combined, but I am not going. How in the hell did you find me anyway?"

"A team was dispatched to your house this morning in hopes of catching you at home. They talked with your wife who gave us your general whereabouts. My partner and I were sent to the marina and now here. The government has gone to a lot of trouble to find you, sir."

"I can see that," John said, looking out over the water, formulating more questions in his head than he knew he would get answers to from the agent who was literally still wet behind the ears. "National security you say? What the hell would I have to do with national security?"

"I don't have a clue, Dr. Bastian. I only know that we went to a lot of trouble to find you and taking you in are my orders." With the sound of the helicopter now circling in the distance, Maggie came up on deck to see what was going on.

"I sure hope you know how to sail because I am not leaving *Sailor's Dream* adrift. It would take me two days to get her back in to the marina," John said, looking over his boat.

"My partner and I can sail her, sir. You will find her safe and sound in slip 86 when you return."

"Slip 86?" John asked incredulously. "So you really have been to the marina."

"Yes, sir," the agent said, draping the wet towel over the back of the seat. "A man named Earl told us we might find you out here."

"Earl," John said, laughing, "the old sea dog sold me out. The rumors will be flying around that place this weekend, especially if you come sailing in on my boat."

"You can trust us, sir, if you would just get on that helicopter."

"And, Maggie, will you take her home for me?" John asked, scratching the top of her head.

"We will do that. We will also assure your wife you are okay. The agents who visited your house said she tried to call you, but when she didn't get an answer she started to get worried."

"I left my cell in the car, purely by accident you understand," John said sarcastically.

"If you don't mind, sir, I would like to radio my partner and have him drop down so we can get going."

"Alright, I don't know how my old body will take dangling thirty feet in the air, but you have convinced me to go."

"The radio if you don't mind, sir."

"Right, it is up next to the radar screen," John said, pointing to the large dash.

"Thank you," the agent said as he spoke into the transmitter, requesting his partner follow him down the rope.

The trip up the rope was actually quite exhilarating. John had not had this much excitement since playing college football. He had almost forgotten what it felt like to be both scared out of his mind and excited beyond belief in the same instance. Unbelievably, he was safely aboard the helicopter within minutes as the nose dropped sharply, and it quickly accelerated on a westerly direction toward Washington. The prop wash from the large blades sent water cascading over the men on the sailboat soaking them as the boat bobbed and wove on the foamy water. As the helicopter pulled out of sight, John looked back one last time just as the sails were being unfurled. "It surely is a beautiful boat," John whispered into the radio attached to the headphones he fitted to his head.

"Don't worry about her, Dr. Bastian. Those two have been sailing for years. You may not know it to look at them, but they are partners on a 25-foot racing sloop that won last year's Baltimore Sailing Club Regatta."

"I sure hope so. That boat is my retirement plan."

Chapter 25

The three men looked harmlessly inconspicuous as they entered the empty elevator of the parking garage. The directory on the wall to the left of the door above the floor buttons gave the locations of each ward. Nassir reached out and pressed the one for the lobby, and the elevator moved slowly up to the hospital entrance.

"From this point, we will split up until we reach the ward. We must each arrive separately to avoid suspicion. Do you both know the plan from here?" The men nodded without a sound. "If we should get separated, head toward the van. I will not leave without either of you," Nassir said, lying through his teeth. "With luck we will be long gone before they realize what has happened."

The elevator door opened and they individually walked out as if they were complete strangers. The butterflies in Nassir's stomach started as soon as he crossed the threshold of the large sliding glass hospital entrance with Maternity and Birthing Center in large letters over it. He pulled the two-wheeled cart behind him, past the receptionist sitting at the welcome desk in the middle of the waiting area. She didn't even look up from the book she was reading to notice the man. She wouldn't have stopped him even if she had noticed him. The outfit he was wearing was convincing. He was even carrying a written work order, which was fabricated, to perform maintenance on the infant incubators in the nursery, should he be questioned.

Nassir whistled a nonsensical tune as he waited patiently for the elevator to arrive. He wondered briefly how Ali and Kamal were doing as the door opened with an arriving "bing."

Again the department locations were listed on the elevator wall, and he found the maternity ward with no trouble. He was now crossing the point of no return. Once he stepped into the hallway of the ward, there would be no turning back even if he had wanted to, which he had no intention of doing.

With a fast jerk the elevator quickly rose to the floor. He took a deep breath as the door opened excruciatingly slow. He exited pulling his cart behind him. He looked around the hallway and noticed Ali coming out of the stairwell at the far end. The nod they exchanged would not even have been recognized by even the most perceptible. The morning sun reflected brightly off the highly polished light tan tile floor. In the middle of the reception area stood a beautiful seven foot tall bronze statue of a pregnant woman holding her naked belly in the palms of her hands staring thoughtfully down, which he passed by briskly heading for the far hallway.

Nassir turned left and walked around the corner right into the busy nurse's station. The flurry of reports of those on mid-shift were just finishing as the day shift was arriving. He had timed it perfectly.

"Excuse me," Nassir said to the nurse sitting at the desk.

She looked at the man talking to her and to the MedSafe patch on his left chest pocket. "Can I help you?" she asked.

"Yes," he said, showing her his fake MedSafe ID badge. "I am here to check on the incubator that was called in yesterday."

"Incubator? I am not aware of any problems with our equipment. Are you sure you have the right hospital?"

"I am positive," he said, feigning surprise at the response. "I was given the work order this morning," he said, handing her the work order.

She looked it over and then checked the shift logs from the day before. "I don't see any mention of anything being called out."

"I don't know what to tell you, ma'am. I was only told to be here ASAP this morning. This hospital is our best customer, and we do our best to keep our best customers happy."

"Right, well wait right here. I will check this out with the Charge Nurse."

"No problem. My next job is just two floors up so take your time," he said as she walked away from him.

Two minutes later she returned. "The Charge is not aware of any problems either, but she wants you to check them anyway just to make sure. We have so many babies in the Neo-natal ICU that we need all of them running in top condition."

"Well, I can assure you that when I leave they will be as good as new."

The nurse walked him to the room across from the nursery and opened it for him holding the door so he could pull his cart in without it getting stuck. "Here they are. Check them and report back to me before you leave," she said as she turned to leave, noticing one portable unit in the nursery. "Oh, and there is one across the hall in the nursery you might as well check, too."

"Sure thing, Nurse, um—" Nassir squinted a bit, looking down at her badge.

"Snyder, Nurse Snyder," she said, finishing his words. "Like I said, just don't forget to check back with me with what you find. I want to make sure I update the shift logs," she said as she walked out, leaving the door to close on its own.

This couldn't have gone better. The operation was going perfectly. He moved the incubators slightly to give the appearance that he had taken them apart and waited nearly fifteen minutes to give his work even more credibility. He opened the door to the room and moved his cart out before walking across the hall to the nursery, Ali and Kamal where not in sight. He glanced over to the nurse's station, and it was empty.

He opened the door to the nursery and made a beeline for the incubator. The room had a large window the entire length of the wall facing the nurse's station. He glanced around at all of the babies in the room carefully, with no obvious intention. He pulled the portable unit into the middle of the floor and began unpacking his cart. The empty box was on top and he opened it like he was opening a toolbox. He walked the rows of bassinets stopping in front of the one with the name Tonya Richardson, Room M22 written in large black lettering on the paper fixed to the front.

With a cautious glance around the room and the hallway he picked the sleeping boy up and placed him in the box. The baby barely even stirred as Nassir gently placed him in the bottom of the box lined with blankets. Nassir placed a tray of tools on four tabs inside the rim of the top of the box so that it wouldn't touch the baby, but would appear to anyone opening it as an ordinary maintenance toolbox. He slowly closed the box and strapped it back onto the cart.

He pulled a pen from the inside of his suit writing notes on the work order using the incubator to write on. Finished with the details, he walked out of the nursery, calmly forgetting about the incubator he had pulled out from the wall.

Nurse Snyder was not at the desk so he left the work order on top of the stack of papers and proceeded to the elevator. He pushed the down arrow, whistling the same meaningless tune as he waited. Time seemed to stand still and the baby didn't make a sound. As the door opened, the Nurse yelled at him to stop.

"Excuse me, but did you find anything with the incubators?"

Nassir's heart stopped for just a second and he thought quickly. "You were not at the station when I finished, so I put the work order and my notes on the desk so you would know what I did," as the elevator arrived and the door opened.

"Okay, I will file it in the daily report. You didn't find anything did you?"

"The temperature sensor in unit four needed a slight adjustment is all, nothing serious," Nassir said, thinking quickly on his feet. He held the elevator door open so he could make a quick get away.

"Thank you for coming over so quickly," the nurse said, turning her back to him.

"Like I said, we like to keep our customers happy," he said as he stepped into the elevator, treating his cart a bit more gently than he did when he arrived.

He quickly pushed the lobby button and the elevator fell.

The nurse walked past the nursery noticing the incubator and spun around on her toes. She pushed it once again back against the wall where it belonged and decided to walk the rows of bassinets. She made a mental note of the babies out and walked the hallway to the mother's rooms to make sure the babies were being taken care of. Mothers frequently came into the nursery to take their babies for their morning feeding. It was unusual for a bassinet to remain empty, but it happened, and Tonya's was empty. She decided to stop by room M22 just to check in on things.

"Good morning, Tonya, honey. How are you and the baby this morning?"

Tonya was just waking up and the nurse quickly realized the baby was not with her. Without causing alarm she pulled the curtain around the bed.

"I am sorry to wake you. I thought I saw you out in the hallway earlier. Get your rest, dear, and I will check in on you later."

Tonya sat up in bed, yawning, feeling a bit of discomfort when her stitches pulled her skin tight as she moved.

Nurse Snyder made a beeline for the nursery just to recheck the bassinets to make sure the baby was not misplaced and then made a frantic call to security. The security guard rushed through the stairway door onto the floor within minutes.

"One of the babies is missing," Nurse Snyder yelled frantically to the burly security guard rushing toward her.

"When was the last time you saw the baby?" the guard asked.

"At shift change, no more than thirty minutes ago."

The security guard didn't move, but spoke rapidly into the radio attached to a clip on his shoulder to the security office supervisor. "We have a situation, sir," the nurse overheard him talking. "An infant is apparently missing from the maternity ward. We need to lock down the access doors now! With any hope, we will seal the baby inside," the security guard spoke again into the radio. The reply was garbled a bit from the nurse's ears, but she could tell by the tone that it was more urgent than the normal radio banter.

The three men had exited the elevator in the parking garage and were walking together toward the van. They had accomplished the impossible without a shot being fired or a suspicious eyebrow raised. All of Nassir's planning had proved flawless as he unlocked the door to the van unloaded the boxes from the cart and gently placed them in the rear of the van. As they took their place in the front seats, security guards began a sweeping patrol of the floor just below them, carefully looking at cars as they passed through the gate.

"Ali, you and Kamal walk out of the garage. I will pick you up on the side street behind the garage. It will look suspicious for you two to be in the van with me should we be searched by security."

"We will do what you ask—just don't leave us here," Ali said to him in a barely audible whisper.

"We are in this together. We will all be heroes when we get home. I will not leave you, trust me, brother."

The two men, dressed in hospital scrubs, got out of the white van and walked around to the walking entrance. The security guard didn't even bother to walk over and question the men walking empty handed talking together. If the guard had a dime for each pair of doctors passing through his gate, he would be a wealthy man. Nassir watched them exit successfully and his nervous, but steady fingers turned the ignition to start the van. He slowly rounded the concrete barrier placing the van at the rear of the line of cars that was now forming at the gate. He saw two guards searching each car carefully before letting them leave. He was thankful the baby had yet to cry out for its mother. He was not a person familiar with babies, but knew he was on borrowed time, the baby would begin screaming to eat any minute. His hope was that it wasn't in the next ten minutes. Finally his time came at the gate.

"What were you doing in the hospital, sir?"

"I was dropping off surgical supplies on the same-day surgery floor, they go through them like a hot knife through butter."

"Do you mind if I look in the back of the van?"

"Not at all. I will need to unlock it for you. The company requires us to secure our equipment all the time," Nassir said as he opened the driver's door. He left the van running and walked around the front to unlock the sliding side door. The guard looked inside at the boxes opening each one looking at the tools and supplies.

"It is going to be another hot one today," Nassir said, trying to make small talk as the sweat began to bead on his forehead. He removed a handkerchief from his back pocket dabbing at the perspiration before it gave the guard any more reason to be suspicious.

"It sure is. This is not my idea of a good time. I could be inside the air conditioned guard shack with a big glass of sweetened tea, watching CNN."

"What's all this about? This is the first time I have had to go through this," Nassir asked, trying to find out if the maternity ward had reported the baby missing.

"I don't know. Something came over the radio from the maternity ward."

"It never ends does it?"

The guard, satisfied the van was clear, backed out of the sliding door. "It sure doesn't. I look at it as job security. Lock her up. You are clear to get back to work."

"Yeah, thanks for reminding me," Nassir said as he fumbled with the keys, locking the door. He rushed around to the driver's side door as the guard lifted the gate. He put the van in gear and slowly passed the guard, waving to him and smiling as he put on his right turn signal and left the garage. Nassir took the first right past the garage and another right down the alley behind the east wing of the hospital.

Ali and Kamal were waiting for him just as he told them on the next block near a bus stop sign. He stopped the van only long enough for them to jump in and then sped off, retracing his route north out of the city. They stopped at a strip mall on *Fayette Street* to change their clothes and take the magnetic MedSafe sign off both sides of the van. Ready to proceed, they took the *Jones Falls* expressway to Interstate 83 north. It was only after they passed the last exit sign for the city that they started to feel safe. Ali walked to the rear of the van and opened the box carrying the baby. The two-day-old infant was crying loudly, now hungry and afraid because he could not smell the only familiar smell he knew in his short life, his mother.

Ali took a bottle out of the bottom of another box and coaxed the baby to eat. It was not easy as the infant stirred and fussed, not used to the plastic nipple. He cradled the baby in his arms supporting its head in the elbow joint. Ali was in no way a father; at twenty-five he had never even been with a woman. He was the least of the three even remotely qualified for this task, but he was doing it for now.

The gentle rocking of the van as it traveled the highway seemed to sooth the baby just enough to eat. It seemed to Ali they had packed enough powered baby formula and diapers to last them for three months. Without interruption their trip would take nearly a week. At least the baby can't talk back, Ali thought as he watched the baby suckle the nipple with enough force to get the formula through the pin-sized hole.

"How is he doing?" Nassir yelled from the front.

"He is finally eating, but I would not want to try to get the bottle away now. He is attacking it like a rabid dog. He was a hungry little guy," Ali said, proud of himself.

"Excellent, six more hours until we start the second leg. I can't wait to ditch this van. It feels like a giant target traveling these roads. By now even the stupid Americans must be on to us. We did well today. Allah was smiling down upon us," Nassir said proudly.

Chapter 26

Safely outside Moscow, the three men started to breathe again. Shevard had gagged the helpless captive in the back seat before the man could say a word. Neither of the three knew the man, but they didn't let him know that. Actually, they were just as scared as he was and avoided looking at him the entire trip.

This was not the sort of thing Andre and Shevard had signed on to do. They wanted to fight to get the Russians out of their country, not kidnap politicians. Kidnapping was not the sort of thing heroes did. They knew the Russian government never gave into ransom demands even if they had Stefanovich himself in the back seat, and they knew enough to know the person they had was not him. Plus, with the government in a shambles, they had no idea if the Russians would even want the person back.

They also knew that the KGB would stop at nothing to find and kill them all. That is what happened to terrorists. They were not given trials. They were simply executed. They had all watched the television in rapt fascination two years earlier when a handful of Georgian terrorists took over an elementary school holding students hostage. Andre wanted the Russians out of his country too. But he never wanted to hurt innocent civilians; he was not a terrorist. The special terrorism unit of the KGB shot every one of the Georgian terrorists. Even those who made it out of the building were hunted down and executed in their homes. As far as Andre was concerned, the terrorists got what they deserved. Andre was not ready for this and he trembled a bit as he thought about the next few hours and days.

They had long since tied the man's hands to his belt and blindfolded him so that he could neither get away nor see where they were taking him. Amazingly, they even had enough room in the trunk to hide the man from the border guards. Luckily when they passed through the border, the guards had their attention focused elsewhere. The small single speaker FM radio blared with the voice of a frazzled reporter describing the events in Moscow. The guards also had their hands full with the thousands of refugees getting out of the country fearful of what the new government might do. When Andre pulled up to the gate, the scared young soldier just waved him through.

Andre pulled the Lada off the road in front of the abandoned warehouse. They were only two miles from the outskirts of Grozny on a small country road. The haze of the city could be seen from this distance as they relaxed just a bit after the long, stressful trip.

Grass and weeds had started to grow through the cracks in the old pavement in front of the large door. Around the building, the grass was nearly waist deep from years of neglect. In its day, the building was kept neat and clean by the soldiers assigned there. The Russian military had once used it as a maintenance and storage facility for a tank battalion, but had left nearly ten years ago. The proud, old warehouse once held nearly twenty tanks and support vehicles, but after the Soviet Union fell, it was left empty.

The inside was void of anything that would give a clue as to what it was intended to be. An open balcony that overlooked the cracked, stained concrete floor circled the large office section on the second floor. The commander of the battalion probably used the balcony to oversee the operations and to shout orders to the men below. The office was suspended in the middle of the building and the interior lights could not be seen outside. The large sheet metal walls were nearly twenty feet tall, constructed of corrugated sheet metal. In many places, holes as big as a fist were punched through allowing the sunlight to penetrate through from outside.

Alexander had stumbled on this place when he lived on the streets. He called the building home during many a cold and damp night. It was also where Alexander hid the weapons he confiscated from the base nearby.

"It looks as if we are the first to arrive," Andre said in surprise.

"Let's hope we are not the only ones to carry this through," Shevard said solemnly, trying to convince himself Alexander's crazy idea had not scared them all off. Before opening the large sliding door, they looked around to see if anyone had followed them or was watching them enter the building.

"Open the door just enough to pull the car through and then shut it tight. We need to make it look as if no one is home," Andre said to Shevard as the car door quickly opened.

Just as Andre had suspected, they were the first to arrive. Andre drove the car to the opposite wall and backed it in so that the front of the car faced the large door, just in case they needed to make a hasty getaway. The small four-cylinder car could scarcely outrun a bicycle, let alone the American Army. However, they might just be able to capitalize on an element of surprise and give themselves enough of a head start to get away.

The trip went better than any of them had envisioned, even after being cramped in the tiny car for the past several hours. Shevard walked around the car as Andre and Alexander both exited at the same time. They all stood and stretched their cramped legs and rubbed the tension out of their eyes.

All three looked around the empty building trying to find that comfortable feeling they had when the group used it as their armory and meeting place, but nothing could bring that feeling back. What little light that came through the small row of windows at the top of the building, cast long shadows and a dingy hue on the floor inside. Every movement caused tiny particles of dust to rise into the air and they seemed to be suspended in the rays of light like tiny balloons as they drifted back to the concrete floor. Every exposed surface was covered with a thick layer of dust including the oil-stained floor.

The inside was deafeningly quiet as none of the men dared to speak first.

"I will go up to the office and look things over," Alexander said, breaking the silence. "You and Shevard get the man out of the car, but leave his hands tied and the blindfold on until I get a place to keep him secure. Remove the gag if you want, and find out who he is," Alexander said to Andre as he looked up at the old office. He needed a place to be alone to collect his thoughts and think his way through this.

"What are we going to do with him?" Andre asked him before moving an inch.

"I don't know yet, but be assured that the hard part is over."

Andre was convinced that his friend was wrong as the television images of the school gymnasium came flooding back into his memory. "We will not make it out of this alive! You know that don't you, Alexander?"

"Stop talking like that, my dear friend. We will not only make it out alive, but we will be heroes to our countrymen."

Shevard stood behind Andre, taking a deep drag on a cigarette, listening to the conversation, trying hard to ignore it. He knew there was no chance they would succeed. They had just sealed their own fate and only he and Andre knew it. He also knew that Alexander had gone completely mad with vengeance. His only hope was that more fighters would show up so he wouldn't have to deal with Alexander alone. Andre would do whatever Alexander wanted, Shevard was sure of that, leaving him to be the only rational voice when things started to go wrong.

Andre opened the back door of the Lada, grabbing the arm of the man pulling him out of the cramped rear seat. The man was wearing an expensive tailored suit, which was now badly wrinkled and stained black at the knees from his time in the trunk. His dark black hair was soaked with sweat and his shoulders sagged under the strain of the ropes. Andre stood next to the bound man who was taller than him by a good five inches, wondering who it was.

"I am going to remove the gag—just don't say a word," Andre told the man. The blinded man nodded his head in understanding as Andre pulled the knotted rag from his mouth.

"Just relax, we will get you something to eat and drink in a minute. We will not hurt you. I can promise you that."

"I am David Arthur, the Vice President of the United States," David said as soon as the gag was pulled from his mouth.

Both Andre and Shevard looked at the helpless man and their jaws dropped. The man had the resemblance of the vice president, but they had only seen him on the television. It couldn't be! They wanted a Russian, not an American.

Andre looked nervously at Shevard who just shrugged his shoulders. He motioned with his head for Shevard to follow as they walked away to the other side of the building silently.

"What have we done, Shevard? Could he be telling the truth?" Andre whispered frantically.

"I have only seen the man on television, but he does look like him—a bit heavier and taller, but I think he is telling the truth. If he is, even God won't be able to help us out of this one. The Americans will stop at nothing to get him back," Shevard said as he pulled another cigarette out of his pack nervously lighting it.

"Alexander must know about this immediately. Wait here and keep an eye on the American while I go up and tell him. I will also see if I can't scare up something to eat. I am starving."

Just as Andre reached the metal stairs, a car pulled up to the warehouse. Shevard walked slowly to the large doors and peeked out a small crack between the door and the thin metal skin of the building.

He recognized the car immediately and started to slowly open the door allowing the small car to enter. Leonid rolled his window down as he passed by Shevard and the two grinned at each other. Shevard looked around outside to make sure they were not followed and quickly closed the door.

Andre ran to the car to greet Leonid and Stephan.

"It is good to see you two. We were beginning to think something had gone terribly wrong," Andre said as the four shook hands and hugged each other.

"The crowd went crazy after the explosion. We were caught in the middle and just barely made it to our car before the gates were crashed to the Palace," Stephan said as he looked at the long faces of Shevard and Andre. "Why are you not happy, my friends?"

"I must talk to Alexander," Andre said flatly as he turned away. "It truly is great to see you safe. Did you see any others behind you?"

"No, it was all we could do to make it out," Stephan said as Andre walked away.

"What has happened, Shevard, my friend?" Leonid asked in a panic.

Shevard glanced at the man tied up and blindfolded and then at the two near him. He turned his back to the captive and started to speak in a whisper. "It appears that we have made a grave mistake today. The man we captured is not Russian."

"What are you saying, Shevard, not Russian?" Stephan asked.

"His name is David Arthur, the Vice President of the United States."

The statement took the breath out of the two men as they both leaned back against the car, unable to stand on their feet. "But, the cars were flying the Russian flag. How could it be?"

"I don't know, but if it is true, we will all be dead before night fall," Shevard said without flinching.

"My God, what have we done?" Leonid asked the rhetorical question not expecting an answer.

"Alexander will get us out of this just as he led us to victory against the tanks," Stephan said.

"Alexander? Alexander has gone completely mad. You are a fool if you think Alexander will get us out of this. Andre is up there now telling him who the man is. The only hope we have for survival is to let the man go now," Shevard stated as he watched Andre walking the stairs.

Andre slowly walked the stairs, each step more labored than the one before, to the second floor. His stomach was in knots as he tried to come up with something to say to his friend. He fully expected to look into Alexander's eyes and find a renewed confidence. However, when he opened the door to the office, he found Alexander sitting in the only chair staring at the far wall. As he neared, he noticed Alexander smiling, watching a spider capture a fly in a very large web.

"Alexander, we have made a terrible mistake. The man we have is not Russian—he is American," Andre said in an almost frantic state, waving his hands wildly as he spoke.

"Andre, calm down. I heard him," Alexander said, holding his broken hand gently.

"So, you know the man downstairs is David Arthur, the American vice president."

"You saw the cars. They were flying the Russian flag—an American wouldn't have been in those cars. It is of little consequence. We are not going to back out of this now. They will hunt us down whether we walk away or carry this through."

"I did see them, Alexander, but I can only tell you that we are all scared. What the hell are we going to do? The Russian government is no longer in power, leaving us no political leverage. We can't even call anyone who would care. I say we leave him downstairs and walk away from this. No one knows who we are now. I beg you to walk away. We could leave the man tied up and blindfolded here in the building."

"No, we must continue with our plan. We will be successful if we carry this through."

Andre shook his head in disgust at his friend. "Leonid and Stephan have arrived, but didn't see any other members make it from the city. The five of us can't hold this building if the Americans track us here. When they do find us, we will be no better off than that fly," Andre said in a breathless tone.

"That is my worry, Andre. I am responsible for this operation, not you."

"I know that, Alexander, you are our leader, but I must tell you that we are all frightened of what you have us involved in. The men are tired and hungry. We must find something to eat and get some rest."

"I know, I can see that. Have Leonid drive into town and pick up enough food for a few days. Let me alone here to think this through. You are positive the man we have is American?"

"Yes, I am positive," Andre said as he walked out the office door toward the stairs.

The heat was becoming almost unbearable inside the large metal building. The sun beat down on the sheet metal roof turning the inside into an oven. The smell of sweat and cigarette smoke filled the stagnant air with an odor of pure fear. Andre walked up to the three men who were talking quietly, but he stared intently at the floor, unable to look at their faces.

"How did it go, Andre?" Shevard asked.

"Not well, Alexander's mind is slipping. He will not admit that we made a mistake. He wants Leonid to drive into town and pick up enough food for a couple of days," he said, looking up into Leonid's eyes. "Bring back as much as you can carry without looking suspicious or obvious. Please keep your movements to a minimum and hurry back, please."

"Why me? I don't want to leave and risk being noticed."

"Either you go or we stay here hungry."

"Okay, I will go, but you had better convince Alexander to walk away from this before I get back, or I may just drop the supplies off and drive away."

"I will do what I can."

"Shit," Shevard said as he kicked the tire of the old Lada. "Why the hell don't we all just walk out of here?"

"Stop that, Shevard. We will get through this. I will talk to Alexander again."

Chapter 27

The helicopter touched down expertly on the landing pad atop the CIA building in Langley, Virginia. Before the blades stopped turning, CIA director Ryan Palmer stepped onto the roof, shielding his eyes from the dust particles swirling around his head from the down draft of the blades. He ran ahead bent over at the waist to avoid the turning blades and approached the helicopter door John was now exiting.

"Welcome to the headquarters of the CIA, Dr. Bastian," Ryan said loudly over the whine of the large turbo charged engines.

"If you don't mind, could you tell me what was so important to pluck me from the middle of the bay?"

"Not here, sir. Let's get to my office," Ryan said, his voice returning to a normal tone as they walked toward the stairwell.

John followed Ryan down the stairs to the floor below and into the plush office. Ryan offered him a chair as he walked behind his desk.

"Can I offer you something to drink, sir?"

"No, thank you. But I would like an explanation before we proceed any further."

"Of course, but first I must ask you to call home. We tried to get you at home earlier this morning, but your wife told us you left yesterday. She tried to get in contact with you, but got worried when you didn't respond to the cell call or page. I am sure she would like to know you are safe."

"May I use your phone? I left mine in the car back at the marina."

"Of course, I will leave you alone. Please come to the door when you are finished," Ryan said, turning the phone around handing him the receiver.

"Could I tell her what I am doing here or how long I will be?"

"I would appreciate it if you didn't mention anything about this. Tell her you will call later with more news."

John shook his head still confused as to why exactly he was there. "Fine, I will play your secret spy games for now. Let me be perfectly clear though, I don't think I can be of any help in whatever you are looking for."

"Let's worry about that later. Just call your wife—she will be happy to know you are okay," Ryan said as he walked out the door.

John punched the digits and the phone rang in his ear. After five rings the answering machine picked up and his wife's cheery voice stated that the Bastian's were not home. He glanced at his watch and noticed that at 3:30 she would still be at work. "Shit, 3:30. Where did the time go?" John mumbled as he clicked the receiver to hang up and punched in the numbers of her office line.

On the second ring her voice caught his ear.

"Hello. This is Georgia Bastian, can I help you?"

"Hi, sweetie."

"John!" she nearly screamed into the phone.

"Hi, baby, I am safe."

"But the agents came to the house this morning. I tried to call you, but you didn't answer, and I started to get worried."

"Yes, I know. They found me and brought me to Washington. What did you tell them?"

"I told them nothing. They caught me getting ready for work and wouldn't tell me a thing. They only wanted to get in contact with you."

"I don't know how long I will be here nor do I know what they want me for, but I will be home soon, I promise."

"Oh, John, what on earth could they want you for? What have you done?"

John could sense a bit of concern in her voice as he groped for an answer. "I don't have any idea, but I will find out soon. Please call the hospital for me. I don't think I will be at work tomorrow."

"Okay, I will, but hurry home."

"I love you, sweetie," John said.

"I love you too—see you soon," and the line clicked dead.

John replaced the receiver and spun the phone back around on the desk. His eyes searched the papers on the desk for a clue as to why he was there. Just as he was standing to walk to the door, his eyes focused on the words, *Project Chandler* typed in bold at the top of a yellowed sheet of paper.

My God, the agent was right. They want to know about the project. But he was sworn to secrecy. He was even threatened by the government if he should ever speak of the project, John thought. What could they possibly want to know about a project that ended four decades ago?

He slowly stood from the plush leather chair and walked to the door. Ryan was sitting on the edge of the desk talking to his secretary. Ryan heard the door open and glanced at John emerging from his office.

"Well, John, did you contact your wife?"

"I did. She was relieved."

"Very good, now we can get down to business," Ryan said as he went back into his office and closed the door.

Ryan walked behind his large cherry desk, but did not sit. He put his palms flat on the desk surface, stared straight down and started to speak.

"John, what we are going to talk about is highly classified. In other words, you are not to talk about it to anyone ever again outside this office. Is that understood?"

"Yes, sir, I understand that, but I still fail to understand why me. What could you possibly want to know about a project that I worked on forty years ago?"

"Forty-five to be exact, John. You were the lead scientist on *Project Chandler* is that correct?"

"I was the lead, but there were others on the team."

"Yes, we know about the others. Most of them are either dead or can't be reached."

"Dead?" John thought back into his memory for their faces. "Has it been that long?"

"John, once again, the security of the nation is in grave danger, and I must implore that this conversation be kept entirely between us."

"That is fine. I have kept my work on the project a secret until now. Do you doubt my integrity?"

"No, Dr. Bastian, that is another reason you are here."

"Another?" John said flatly. "So let's get down to it. I am on vacation," John said, growing more impatient.

"Very well. I sent the vice president to Moscow in an attempt to quell the fears of a government massacre and its effects on society. One only needs to think back to Kent State to understand what I am talking about. We think he was abducted on his way to the Kremlin yesterday morning. We have no idea as to the identity of the abductors nor have they attempted to make contact. In short, we know very little." As he finished talking, the intercom buzzed breaking his concentration. Annoyed at the interruption, he shortly spoke into the speaker. "Yes, what is it?"

"Sir, the Director of Homeland Security is on the phone for you. He said it is urgent."

"Thank you, patch him through."

Ryan picked up the phone and listened to the voice on the other end speak John noticed the color of Ryan's face go pale as he slumped into his oversized Italian leather chair.

"I see. Has the FBI arrived? Very good. I will send a team out to the hospital immediately to assist should this have international ramifications," and Ryan hung up. Like the president, he was not fond of the newly created department either. It added one more layer and many more problems to a system that was already mired in bureaucracy. He rose from the desk and raced out the door.

"Sharon, get the head of the Baltimore office on the line and have him personally go to the maternity ward at the Johns Hopkins hospital with his best unit. There has been a kidnapping, and I want a response as soon as he finds something. Let them know they will be coordinating the investigation with the FBI."

"Yes, sir, right away."

Ryan reentered his office slower now and with deliberate steps feeling as if the schoolhouse bully had just punched him in the chest.

"Did I hear you say the maternity ward at Johns Hopkins?" John asked impatiently.

"Yes, it appears that a baby was taken this morning from the ward."

"What did you say?"

"I have agents en route to verify the claim, but it appears that the vice president and his wife's newly adopted baby was taken from the ward sometime around 0800 this morning."

John sat stunned by the words. He had delivered that baby just two days ago. It was his last delivery before leaving on his boat. He had heard that a government official was adopting the infant, but not the vice president. "Holy shit," he said under his breath. "Could there be a connection between the two?"

"I don't know yet. If a connection exists, we are dealing with more than what we thought," Ryan said, slowly sitting back into his chair, taking comfort.

"How could my work on *Project Chandler* possibly help you?"

"Right, *Chandler*. Last night I read most of the documentation written on the project. This is a long shot, but I think your work may be able to assist us in locating the vice president and now the infant."

"Are you sure you have the right project?" John asked.

"I believe I do. Project Chandler was named after a Korean War hero, a POW of the war the army could not find. You led a top-secret project to find soldiers through the injection of a nano-probe that transmitted certain, how should I say, key information. If I am correct, the probe may be our only hope."

John was impressed by what the CIA director both knew and surmised about his work. He had not thought about the project in a very long time. "Yes, I did work on that project, and yes, theoretically the probe could be tracked."

"The project continued long after you were let go by the government. It progressed over time taking advantage of newer technology and advances in nano-engineering. After the U.S. involvement in Vietnam, the project lost government funding and was disbanded. However, the practice of injecting probes into newborns continues simply as a method of accurately tracking births, but the primary intent of the probe has long been forgotten."

"I still don't understand," John said dryly.

"The probes injected are programmed with a unique number that is stored in a database on an NSA mainframe. The probe transmits that number constantly over the lifetime of the individual."

"Theoretically that is also true. But after this many years, we have no idea if the power of the probe is still strong enough to transmit over long distances. Our last breakthrough in technology put the usable power at no more than twenty years. We were looking for soldiers in war not civilians after four decades. Maybe you didn't read the part where we could never find a way to receive a signal over fifty miles because of the power limitations in the small nano-probe."

"You are forgetting the subsequent innovations after you left. It appears from the notes that they found a method of self-regenerating the probe's power within the body."

John shook his head. They had investigated that possibility, but could never find a way of making a stable power cell small enough to fit the probe. It was possible, John knew, but highly unlikely.

"I see the look of disbelief on your face. It is true, I can assure you. I have the notes from the scientist's own hand."

"I believe you. I still fail to see why you need me if you have all this information."

"After the project was disbanded, all of the equipment was destroyed because of the secrecy of the project. The government felt it best to see that this project never became public. You can understand that the view of the government following Vietnam and Watergate was less than trusting. Public opinion on a project that could track human movements would forever damage the government of the United States."

"I am beginning to understand."

"John, we need you to design a receiver that can track the probe's transmissions. If you can do that, we can find them."

John thought back to the birth two days ago and the procedure he had methodically performed as he had hundreds of times. Never did he dream it would actually be used for the purpose John had invented it to be used for. "It would be nearly impossible to design the equipment after this long."

"I have all of your notes and a team of engineers, scientists, and programmers waiting in our labs to assist you. I wouldn't have brought you here if I thought it was impossible. Oh by the way, I have already briefed the president about the project. I hope that doesn't add to your pressure."

"If what you say is true, I will do my best. I delivered that baby myself," John said.

"Thank you! I knew you would help. May I also offer the thanks of the president. I will be briefing him personally with an update within the hour. I would love nothing more than to tell him you are willing to help."

"I guess I should get to work. Could you point me in the right direction?"

"I can do better than that," Ryan said as he rose and walked toward the door after John. "I will take you down myself."

The two entered the elevator and Ryan hit the third floor button. The elevator dropped quickly, and the doors opened within seconds. John followed Ryan out the door down the long narrow hallway. Rows of windows stretched the walls of the hallway, reminding John of the maternity floor of the hospital. The only difference was that inside the rooms, men and women were wearing white suits that covered their entire body from head to toe.

Ryan walked up to a door on the right side of the hallway and pressed his hand to a blank silver plate on the wall. A green light flashed above the plate and the door buzzed open. He held the door for John as the two walked into a small room where several white suits hung on hooks on the wall. After putting the thin suit over their clothes and the booties made from the same material over their shoes, a momentary wash of air from both sides of the wall blew any loose dirt and dust particles away that may have settled on the suits. Once again, Ryan placed his palm on the wall plate and the inner door buzzed open.

Inside, John saw the boxes of notes and the old notebook that he took from Professor Greeley. "My goodness, I thought that notebook was gone forever. I never expected to see it ever again."

"This is the government, Dr. Bastian—we throw nothing away."

"But how did you ever find it? I have not seen that in forty years."

"Tucked in a box in the basement of this building a person might find Jimmy Hoffa," Ryan said with a hint of a smile.

John reached for the old notebook and immediately remembered the day he had found it and the conversation that ensued with his old friend and mentor. Would the professor be proud of him now he wondered?

"Dr. Bastian, this is the lab," Ryan said, looking around the large room. "You should find everything you will need, but if you do need anything, don't hesitate to ask. You have an open checkbook on this project. In other words, failure is not an option. I will introduce you to the team and leave you to your work."

"First, if I am going to be working here, call me John. Second, I will do my best and that is all I can promise."

"Let's hope for the entire nation your best is good enough," Ryan said as he made the introductions and left.

Chapter 28

The Finger Lakes region in upstate New York State, as it is known, was named because it appeared to the early settlers that the hand of God had reached from the heavens and touched the ground. The impressions of the fingers filled with water forming some of the most beautiful lakes on earth. The area is steeped in history. For centuries, American Indians used the land as their lifeblood. Seneca's, Mohawks, and Iroquois used the interconnecting system of lakes and rivers as a means of transportation, food, and religion. They knew the value of the area long before the white man came. During the first two decades of the Eighteenth Century, settlers began migrating south from Canada then north from Southern Pennsylvania exploiting the fertile soil, forcing the Indians out.

In the nineteenth century, vineyards sprang up on the steep shores of the lakes. Vineyards brought wineries and sometime around 1860 the first winery started producing a rich grape wine entirely made from grapes grown on its own ground on the shores of Cayuga Lake, the largest of the five lakes. Today, literally hundreds of wineries now grace the shores of the Finger Lakes.

Mixed in with the numerous wineries along the shores of the lakes are cottages of all shapes and sizes. The wine region, as it is called, is a favorite vacation spot for people all along the East Coast. Some come to enjoy the rich fishing, some for the fabulous wine tasting and all come just simply enjoy relaxing to the sound of the water lashing the shore.

Nassir pulled the van into the empty parking lot of the Seneca Harbor Marina well after dark. He planned to arrive nearly three hours earlier, but with traffic, road construction, and a stop for additional supplies along the way, they were behind schedule. The marina was closed now, and all activity on the canal had stopped.

"Looks like we will have to spend the night in the van," Nassir said as he turned the van off.

"What are we going to do with the baby?" Kamal asked.

"We have enough supplies to last us for the next couple of weeks. Just do your best to keep him quiet so we can get some sleep," Nassir said.

"What is the plan, Nassir? What are we doing here?" Ali asked.

"Crossing the border will be nearly impossible in this van. The Americans will have the border tied up tighter than a virgin by now. Traveling north by boat will be the last thing they expect, and it is exactly what we are going to do."

"What are we going to do with the van?" Ali asked. "If they find it parked here it won't take them long to find us."

"We will have to take our chances. It will take the Americans days to track our movements even if they have determined it was us who took the baby."

"How far are we from Canada, Nassir?" Kamal asked.

"I think we are about 70 miles from the border. We will need to cross Lake Ontario and head up the Saint Lawrence River before meeting up with our Canadian supporters."

"How long will that take?" Ali asked.

"It shouldn't take more than three days to get through the canal into the Thousand Islands. From there it is just a matter of hours to our meeting point."

Both Ali and Kamal looked at each other incredulously. They surely did not expect to be doing this to get home.

"Why couldn't we just cross at another point?" Ali asked.

"Because you fool, the Americans will stop at nothing to get this baby back. He was just adopted by the vice president."

"Are you crazy?" Kamal asked in astonishment. "We don't know anything about boats."

"Relax, my friend. I have everything taken care of. Arkhim and I came up with this plan because it was the last thing the Americans would expect. We are guaranteed success if you follow me. Plus, I have a surprise."

"You have not even given us a choice, Nassir. What is this surprise you are talking about?" Kamal asked as he slumped back into the passenger seat for a long, uncomfortable night.

"Let's all get some sleep. You will find out soon enough," Nassir said as he turned off the inside lights and reclined the driver's seat as far as it would go, feeling very confident.

Ali did his best to quiet the infant. He was restless and Ali could not seem to do anything to stop the crying. He could hear both Nassir and Kamal snoring loudly, as he held the infant in his arms. The tiny boy snuggled into Ali's chest as he laid out on the floor of the van. It seemed to Ali that, for an instant, their breathing was in unison.

The sun rose on a beautiful day. The rays of sun reflected brightly off the surface of the water as boats filled with vacationers moved slowly in the narrow canal. Nassir paid for the rental and walked back out to the van.

"Get up. We need to load the boat and get moving. Make sure you hide the baby. We need to make this look like we are on vacation. There are many eyes upon us. We don't want to make a mistake this close to the finish," Nassir said as he opened the back door of the van.

Ali and Kamal both stirred awake nearly exhausted from a lack of sleep. The baby had kept Ali awake nearly all night and Kamal, being a light sleeper was stirred awake on more than one occasion. It wasn't until the sun started to rise that the van had become silent. None of them had planned on this hardship.

"What is this surprise, Nassir?" Kamal asked. "I don't like secrets or surprises."

"Kamal, you will find out soon. Ali, put the baby back into the box. We will carry him on board in the box to avoid suspicion. Kamal, you take the rest of the supplies and meet me on the dock. Make sure you get all of the supplies. We will not be stopping until we get to Canada."

The two were silent as they worked packing their gear. Neither of them believed they were actually going to make it back to their homeland, but they didn't want to voice their concern. Each of them knew what happened to their friend back at the falls.

Ali gently placed the infant in the padded bottom of the plastic box. To an outsider, he would appear to be carrying a box of clothes. The only thing that would give away the precious cargo he was actually carrying would be the cargo itself. Sweat formed on his forehead as he stepped out of the van and walked the long dock to the moored boat. Once again, Allah was watching down on them as Ali made the fifty yards without a stir.

An old Ford pickup truck pulled into the nearly deserted parking lot. The tires crunched the gravel as it slowed to a stop next to the white van. A strange man opened the door and exited the rusty truck. Ali looked back briefly at the man, but continued on to the boat.

Nassir and Kamal walked around the 38' Carver Sport Cruiser, marveling at its beauty as they heard the truck pull in.

"Praise God! He made it," Nassir said out loud.

"Who made it?" Kamal asked.

"The surprise," Nassir said as he walked the dock to meet the man.

Nassir smiled wide as he approached. When he was face-to-face, he embraced him, kissing him on both cheeks.

"I was beginning to lose faith. I have filled out the paperwork, and we are ready to get moving."

"I didn't think I would make it over the border. The Americans have really zipped the security up tight."

"The old truck is a nice touch," Nassir said, looking over the man's shoulder to the truck.

Kamal had arrived behind Nassir. His curiosity of the new addition had gotten the better of him and he decided to be nosey.

"Kamal, this is Sharal Al-Zahowie—our surprise," Nassir said, formally introducing the two men.

The two men exchanged greetings, both sizing the other up.

"Kamal, Sharal will get us to Canada. He is a member of the PFLP, but has lived in Canada his entire life. His family owns a fleet of fishing boats on the northern shore of Lake Ontario. He will get us through the next leg of our journey."

With the introductions finished, Nassir walked with them both to the boat thinking that Sharal was the best $30,000 he had ever spent.

The large boat was beautiful. The physical length of the boat was actually just over 40 feet, including the swim platform with a wide 12-foot beam. The sparkling new white fiberglass gleamed in the morning sun as they untied the half-inch lines securing the boat to the floating dock. Sharal boarded the boat and climbed up the stairs to the fly-bridge that towered over the boat. From this position, he would pilot the boat through the canal locks with relative ease. He felt completely at home on the tall bridge, taking a minute to familiarize himself with the position of the equipment. With a turn of the key, the massive diesel engines roared to life.

The engines generated a respectable six hundred horsepower. At full throttle the boat could slice through calm waters at close to thirty-five knots. However, this boat was not built for speed. It was strictly a cruiser with two large staterooms, a large galley with full sized refrigerator, a main salon with a 32-inch flat screen TV, and air-conditioning throughout the entire living space. With a name of *Serenity* emblazoned in glittery gold lettering on her aft panel, this boat was built purely for pleasure.

Kamal explored the inside in disbelief. This was the most beautiful thing he had ever seen. Nassir yelled below for both men come topside and help cast them off. Sharal expertly engaged the drive units, and slowly the boat inched away from the long wood dock. Once inside the canal, Kamal, Nassir, and Ali could relax and get some sleep.

"We can catch up on the lost sleep in shifts. One will sleep while the other two watch for boat traffic and tend to the baby. The hard part is over my friends. We are on the last leg of our mission," Nassir said with a giant toothy smile.

The fly bridge's floor was actually the roof of the main salon cabin. In really bad conditions, the boat could be captained from the pilot's station inside the cabin. However, the view from inside was very limited because of the sheer size of the boat. On the fly bridge, there were three large captains' chairs on swiveling pedestals and a long couch-like seat that could be laid flat. Six adults could comfortably sit and enjoy the scenery as it leisurely passed.

The middle of the pedestal seats was reserved for the captain. The large steering wheel was nearly 16" in diameter, mounted vertically in the middle of the long dashboard. Two sets of levers were mounted on both the left and right of the steering wheel. The left set of two levers controlled the two inboard props, and the right two controlled the engine throttle. Nassir looked at the line of gauges across the teak dash as Sharal synchronized the engines by adjusting the throttle levers. Sharal didn't need the gauges to let him know when the engines were properly synched. He could tell by their sound.

Sharal turned on the marine radio, listening for boat traffic and adjusted the twelve-inch screen of the Lowrance chart plotter to show the route north through the canal. He touched the screen of the large plotter at the small town of Geneva to indicate the starting point, and the screen flickered a few times before calculating the trip distance and projecting the route within seconds.

Geneva was on the northern most shore of Seneca Lake. It was a quaint, small town surrounded by orchards and vineyards, but they were not here to sight see. They only briefly noted the town as the bow of the boat pointed north and the marina slipped out of view.

The southern part of the canal was less than thirty feet wide with homes and cottages lining both shores. Many people spent their days watching and waving to the boats as they passed. It was quiet and peaceful this early in the morning with a few small boats floating idly with fisherman trying their luck on the large lake trout.

"Ali, before you go below to rest, I need you to check the fenders on both sides of the boat. The first lock is about five miles ahead, and I want everything to be in place. For the first lock, I want us all to be ready to give a hand."

Ali was confused by the order. He had never been on a boat before. His home was in the desert. He had not seen the sea until he left home and had never dreamed he would ever be on a boat. "I will do my best, Nassir, but you will have to explain to me what you want."

"The locks lift and lower the boat in the water to compensate for the difference in elevation. One hundred years ago, this river had many sections of rapids, which were replaced by the locks so that boats could make their way to the ocean. You will see what I mean when we go through the first one. I have read about the history of the canal, but I have never been through locks quite this large. We will be fine. Trust me, Sharal has done this hundreds of times."

Both Kamal and Ali were impressed with the knowledge their leader had on the locks. They looked at each other in disbelief, but the confidence Nassir was displaying helped calm them for the moment. Kamal walked the deck on the bow and checked the lines, holding four of the large blue fenders as Ali checked the two astern. Each fender was nearly two foot long and ten inches in diameter. They were made of soft plastic and filled with air to protect the side of the boat as it rested against the wall of the locks.

The entire length of the canal was officially a no-wake-zone, meaning the speed of the boat needed to be kept at a meandering ten miles-an-hour or less. At this speed, walking to Canada would be faster, Kamal thought as he waved at two kids onshore, skipping rocks across the surface of the water.

For the next hour, Ali slept below in relative peace. The baby was sleeping softly over the hum of the engines after being fed and changed for the second time today, and it was only 8:30 in the morning. One of the staterooms was dedicated to the baby simply because most of the supplies they had on board were for the baby. Nassir had bought cases of formula, diapers, and water, which sat on the floor, bed, and closet of the small room.

Nassir watched the plotter intently while keeping an eye out for oncoming boat traffic. The sun beat down on the water without anything to block it in the cloudless sky. Kamal still did not yet have his sea legs, but was enjoying the relative peace and quiet watching the scenery pass by slowly. One mile before the first lock at Waterloo, Sharal picked up the handset of the radio.

"Waterloo—lock four, this is *Serenity* traveling East bound. We have one to pass through at one mile out."

"Copy, *Serenity*, we currently have one in now. It will be about fifteen minutes. Proceed to the west wall when you see the green light."

"Copy, lock four, thank you, *Serenity* out."

"Kamal, wake Ali up, it will take all of us when we enter the lock."

Kamal opened the sliding door and entered the upper cabin. To him this looked quite plush complete with a full size leather sleeper sofa. Stepping down three stairs, he entered the galley and then the larger of the two staterooms.

"Ali, wake up, my friend. We are approaching the first lock and Nassir wants us both to help."

Ali stirred, but did not wake. Kamal approached the bed and tapped his friend on the toes. He hated to wake him after the last few days. They all needed the sleep, but this was more important.

"Ali, come on, we need your help."

Ali's dark eyes opened slowly. "How long have I been asleep?"

"Thirty minutes."

"My God, it feels like a lifetime. Tell Nassir I will be up shortly, let me refresh myself and look in on the baby." Ali didn't want to admit it, but he was growing fond of the tiny baby.

"Okay, but make it quick. Nassir wants to go over what is going to happen before we get there. He does not want us to stand out to the lock crew. Nassir said the lock masters would probably have radios that can be used to contact the local Sheriff if they should get suspicious," Kamal said as he walked back up the stairs to the sliding doors.

Ali sat up, rubbing his tired eyes. It had been months since he had seen his home and now he was in a run for his life thinking he may never see it again. He slowly stood forgetting for a minute he was on a boat and nearly fell over sideways as the boat rocked after hitting the wake of an oncoming boat. He looked around the room one last time pausing to check his reflection out in one of the mirrors and walked through the galley to the second stateroom. He quietly opened the door a crack to check on the infant and then shut it tightly and headed topside.

"You look terrible, old friend," Nassir said, laughing out loud.

Ali looked at up at him shielding his eyes from the sun with the palm of his hand. "I look worse than I feel. I had the displeasure of catching a glimpse in one of the mirrors. Did anyone notice the number of mirrors down there?"

"No, you fool, it is an illusion to make small spaces feel bigger," Nassir said, still laughing at Ali. "Listen up," Nassir said, getting serious. "We are approaching the first of twelve locks during this trip. Sharal is going to go over the procedure."

"Each of the locks will lower the water level until we reach Lake Ontario," Sharal began. "Each side of the lock will have ropes or wires attached to the top and bottom of the lock walls to secure the boat. I will bring the boat in slowly parallel to the wall and Kamal will grab the first line at the bow. Ali, I want you to stand on the stern swim platform and be ready to grab the line closest to you. Keep hold of those lines until the water lowers and the outer doors open. Keep the boat tight against the sides at all times, this is a big boat so be on your toes. The fenders will protect the fiberglass."

Ali was still unsure of himself as he slumped in the large bench seat across the entire back of the boat. He could easily spread out and nap here until they reach the lock, but decided against that. Nassir was not fond of slackers and screwing up this close to the end was not in his best interest.

On the bow, Kamal shouted that the lock was straight ahead. The boat passing west met them and the light glowed green signaling the go ahead to enter. The look of concentration on Sharal's face was evident in the lines across his forehead and the beads of sweat dripping off his bare chin.

"Does everyone know what to do?"

"Yes," came the reply from both ends of the boat.

"Here we go, nice and easy," Nassir announced not loud enough for the other two to hear.

Slowly the boat slid between the large blue metal doors. Sharal pulled the two drive levers into reverse and the boat gently kissed the west side wall. Kamal grabbed the large rope pulling the bow into the wall as the fenders strained against the weight of the boat and the wall. Ali used a long pole with a hook on the end to grab the rope closest to him and gently pulled it toward him. Satisfied that the boat was secure, Sharal shut the engines down and waited for the doors they just came through to close.

The lockmaster waited until the boat was settled safely against the wall to start the lock mechanism. Once started it could not be stopped until all of the water was pumped out. He pressed the buttons and the door started to close with a distinct sound of metal rubbing against metal. He walked out of the small operator's booth and up to the boat. Standard operating procedure dictated that all boats coming through the locks must have a current registration and lock pass.

"Captain on board the *Serenity*, do you have your registration?" the lockmaster yelled down to Sharal.

"Yes, it is NY 90996 FT," Sharal answered him and the lockmaster noted the number on his clipboard.

The water started to become turbulent inside the doors as the water lowered, causing the boat move slightly along the wall.

"That is one beautiful boat," the lockmaster said, whistling. "Where are you headed?"

"We are going up to Lake Ontario to fish for Salmon," Sharal told him, trying not to provide any more information than necessary.

Ali stood on the back platform watching a dead fish floating in the water as the boat slowly moved down nearly fifteen feet. He was in awe of the entire process as more of the wall came into view. The lock sides were made of large slabs of concrete covered with a thick skin of metal in six-foot square blocks and as more of the wall came into view, Ali noticed they were covered with a layer of barnacles. The large metal doors were eight inches thick and painted a royal blue. The thick ropes hanging from the gold railing running the length of the lock were covered with slimy green algae from being covered with water and the slime coated Ali's hands. He made a quick note to get a pair of gloves from the maintenance kit before the next lock.

"Have a safe trip," the lockmaster yelled down to them as his voice echoed in the empty chamber.

All four men waved to him and yelled, "Thank you."

The large front doors opened slowly and the green light appeared on the top of the lock signaling the time to exit as Sharal turned the engines on. Both Kamal and Ali released the dirty ropes and the boat slowly pulled out leaving the first lock behind.

Nassir took a deep breath as they made their way on through to the next lock.

"We passed that one," Nassir said as he looked around the boat.

"I never thought we could have pulled it off," Ali mumbled from down below.

"This is out of our hands, Ali, it is up to Allah to bring us home now," Nassir said in a matter of fact tone.

Waterloo passed out of sight as they headed east. The next two locks were just passed Seneca Falls about twenty minutes away. Locks two and three dropped them nearly fifty feet in two stages. Combined, the two locks emptied five million gallons of water into the canal each time the locks were used. Over the course of the trip to Lake Ontario, they would pass through 13 locks using the same procedure each time.

Chapter 29

Kevin had driven the large black Mercedes back to the hangar hours ago, followed closely by Tony in the small, black Lada. None of them wanted near the Mercedes. Tony hesitantly opened all four doors of the luxury car as wide as they would go and walked slowly around the car. The blood inside the car was almost nauseating as he thought of what had happened to its occupants. All of those inside the car were his friends. This was obviously a set-up. The car had driven into an ambush, and the feelings of revenge rose in him to the point in which he could focus on nothing else. "God help those who did this because I will kill them all when we do find them," Tony said under his breath.

Tony was the only one of the five team members experienced in crime scene investigation. Each of the members had been trained on gathering evidence during their service schooling, but only Tony had real life experience. His time with the Colorado Springs Police Department had come in handy as he scoured the car looking for anything that could help pinpoint who or what was behind the abduction. He didn't have much to work with as far as tools. Lassiter had found a small maintenance kit on board the plane, which helped, but with only one set of everything they needed, dismantling the car took longer than they planned. He directed the removal of the seats so he could search the carpet covered floor, but came up with nothing. A single strand of hair would at least give them hope. So far the team was batting zero in an exhausting search.

Tony searched every inch of the seats and floor for hair samples and fingerprints, but found nothing. He directed the others, even putting Ben Lassiter to work removing the carpets from the floorboards until he was satisfied nothing was to be found in them. After three hours in the hot hangar finding nothing, Tony sat down on the concrete floor and wiped the sweat from his forehead.

"Well, how many opportunities do you get to tear apart a Mercedes?" Lassiter asked, lightening the mood just a bit.

"After today, I will be content if I never see another one," Tony said as he stood and walked over to the car.

"Even if we could lift a print, we would have no way of getting it into the FBI database," Lassiter said solemnly.

"That is true. If only they had left a calling card or directions to wherever they went, we would be in business," Rodger said as he slumped down in the rear seat that was now out of the car on the hangar floor.

"We have found no evidence that we can use, if only we could identify the blood samples to know who was killed. We have no way of knowing if Eagle 2 is alive or dead," Tony said in an exasperated voice.

He felt completely helpless in the empty hangar. The lack of communication from Washington over the past six hours made the time pass excruciatingly slow. Rodger had taken to pacing the inside perimeter of the hangar and Ben Lassiter had only left the makeshift desk to help dismantle the car.

"I will inform Washington that the car was a dead end. Let's hope they found more than we did," Lassiter said as he picked up the secure phone.

"Mr. President, the car did not give us any leads as to who or what is behind this. We took the car apart to the floorboards and found nothing useful."

"I see—yes—we will standby. Lassiter out."

Ben Lassiter replaced the small black receiver in the cradle and looked at the weary team members who were in front of him hanging on his every word during the conversation with president. They had high hopes of finding something that they could use to give them hope. Sitting here was killing them. Anything was better than sitting on their thumbs, and that is what they were doing.

"Mr. Ryan Palmer is scheduled to brief the president in thirty minutes. He has brought in some expert in locating hostages to help in finding Eagle 2. He wants us to standby until the next phone call."

The five men were now standing with sagging shoulders and a defeated look. The realization had started to set in that they had failed in their mission and could do nothing about it. Lassiter himself looked ragged; the ever-existent confident look in his eyes was replaced by utter defeat. This was his responsibility, and he had blown it. He felt the weight of the world on his shoulders, and his hands were tied.

"Look, I want to find him as much as each of you. But, we will not do any good leaving here without any direction. We must remain close to the phone for now. Trust me, Eagle 2 is alive, and we will find him or die trying, I promise you that much. Now, we have all had a long day. Get some sleep, so you are fresh when the time comes," Lassiter said, fully aware that none of them would actually sleep until it was over.

"Rodger, before we get some downtime I want to get this car out of here. I can't look at it anymore," Tony said as he started to toss the carpets and seats back inside.

"I know what you mean. We could have been in that car. I don't want to think about it."

The phone rang, making Tony jump.

"Yes, sir, this is Lassiter," Ben said, sitting stiff in the chair. "Of course, sir, we have the man power. All we need is a location. No, sir, the Russians have not been in contact. I think it would be safe to say that they will stay out of our hair. I will have two of my team do some reconnaissance work to find out. I will give you a full brief on your next call. Yes, sir, and thank you. Lassiter out," Ben said as he hung up the phone.

"Tony, I want you and Rodger to take a car and head back out to the square. He wants a first hand account of what is going on in the Kremlin. I know you have been trained in Russian and can interact with the locals. Talk with them and find out what the hell is going on. I want you back at 2100 with an update. That gives you a little over three hours to get there and back."

"Yes, sir, we will be back at 2100," Tony said, relieved to be doing something to take his mind off the car.

Rodger changed his clothes back to what he had on that morning and started the small car, waiting for Tony to change. They didn't want to give the appearance of outsiders or they would get nowhere. Plus, the presence of an outsider might just set the rioters off one more time, and that they didn't need. Tony jumped into the passenger seat while Kevin slid open the large hangar door.

"Keep your heads down, you two!" Lassiter said in a gruff, but caring voice. "The bad guys may still be out there waiting for you. I will need you both when the call comes," Lassiter added before the two set off.

Tony nodded in understanding, and Rodger pressed the accelerator to the floor screeching the front tires of the small four-cylinder car.

Inside fifteen minutes, the two men were standing at the very spot they walked through that morning outside the Kremlin gate. The ancient cobblestone street was virtually empty—except for the mangled Mercedes. Tony walked around the car looking for bodies, alive or dead. The car was empty, but the sight of blood inside the charred, black car and on the dark, cobblestone made the stomachs of both men turn sour. Tony wondered how many men, women, and children had died at this exact location over the past five hundred years unnecessarily spilling their blood in the name of history.

"There could be no way anyone lived through that. Look at all that blood," Tony said, holding his hands over his mouth.

"I agree, but where are the bodies?"

"I don't know, but my guess is that they were taken into the Kremlin to be hanged in the square along with the other political prisoners," Tony answered, wishing he didn't have to be here to be a witness to it.

"Let's get to the mission. We only have a little over two hours to finish up before we have to get back," Rodger said, looking at his watch.

"Right, any idea on where to start? Something tells me that knocking on the gate won't get us too far."

"Let's move out to the square. We should be able to find someone there willing to talk."

"It is as good a place as any, let's get to it. If we get separated, meet at the car at 2040."

"Copy that, 2040," Rodger answered, moving out toward the square.

Walking toward the center of the square was easier now than it was a few hours earlier. Tony did notice, however, an increase in military personnel spread out in a perimeter around the square. Nothing was happening at the moment aside from a few dissenters on top of vehicles shouting to those last remaining diehards who had no home and would listen to anyone.

The two men stayed away from the soldiers as they looked around to determine the best course of action. Neither of them could get a handle on what was really going on.

"Let's take a side street. We need to get away from the prying eyes of the soldiers. No one will talk to us if they are watching," Tony said, nodding his head in the direction he wanted to go.

"Sounds good to me," Rodger said. "This place feels like a tomb."

The two walked down the center of the street because the sidewalks were littered with trash and God knows what else after days of being filled with people. All of the small shops lining both sides of the street were closed. Most had broken windows and empty shelves from the looting of hungry people. Neither could believe that just hours ago this street was packed with people so thick that it would have been impossible to walk. Something monumental had happened this morning, and Tony's best guess was that the government did indeed fall. The sun was starting to set now, and they both knew that time was of the essence. They picked up the pace and searched for someone, anyone to talk to.

Two young men walked out of a stairwell across the street from where Tony stood. He doubted that he would be able to get information from them, as they appeared quite drunk from the way they were holding each other up. An elderly gentleman walked out of an old row home just ahead of them.

In his best Russian, Tony asked the man why the street was so empty, but the man waved his arms motioning him away. Tony asked him about the riots and the explosion, but again the man just waved him away.

"Shit, this is going nowhere. Let's get out of here," Tony said to Rodger as he turned his back to the old man.

"Copy that, I have a bad feeling about this place."

"I agree, let's get back to the car before it gets dark."

Just as the sun disappeared, Tony and Rodger were heading back to the airport in the small car.

"I can't believe the entire square was empty. Not more than twelve hours ago we couldn't even get through it," Rodger said.

"I know. I think if nothing else, we can report the riots are over for the time being. I didn't see anything out of the ordinary inside the Kremlin walls. The new government, if there is a new government, must be keeping a low profile."

"My guess is that the rioters are stunned at being successful and need to plan what to do. They, no doubt, didn't expect to get this far and will need some time to regroup."

"I know that the sooner we get out of this damn country the better," Tony admitted.

"I'm with you on that thought. I would hate to spend any more time here than we have to," Rodger said, looking at his friend.

"The only good part about this whole situation is that with no one in charge we can feel free to conduct a rescue mission without getting permission," Tony said, trying to put a positive spin on it.

"I agree. That is, of course, if we can get some idea as to where."

"We will, I am confident of that. I only hope it's not too late," Tony said, trying not to think about the consequences should that happen.

Chapter 30

John Bastian had spent the last twenty-four hours of his life reliving a past that he had long forgotten. He had nearly exhausted every idea that was brought to the table. They had analyzed every aspect of the notes and had so far come up dry. John was not ready to give up and as a last ditch effort, he had assembled every available scientist assigned to the project for a brainstorming session. John looked into their tired faces and saw the look of utter defeat. Their white suits where now well wrinkled from working tirelessly for the last twenty-four hours. Most volunteered to remain on the job, catching short naps in a quiet back closet in shifts, and they needed a good ole' locker room pep talk.

"Listen up, team," John said, drawing on his old football days. "I know we are all exhausted, but we need to continue. Failure is simply not an option I want to explore. I don't know what you have heard about this project and the importance placed on it, but I can assure you that we are not working here in vain."

"We have heard nothing about this," a young, ruddy-faced engineer said with bloodshot eyes. "It may make our work easier if we knew why this project is so urgent."

"I don't think Mr. Palmer will mind if we take a well deserved break. From the look on your faces, you not only deserve one—you need one. However, what I am about to tell you never leaves this room. Does everyone understand? I could be in serious trouble telling you what I am about to say."

John looked around the room at the nodding heads and decided to proceed. For four decades he had kept his promise of secrecy, but today he was going to talk. He was going to tell them about the project, to hell with the consequences. These people had the right to know why they were pulled from their daily routine to work on a project that had no meaning to them. Even more, they deserved to know.

"During the Korean War, I was assigned to lead a team of scientists, much like yourselves, to develop a way of tracking soldiers on the battlefield," John began his story. "The project was designed to find prisoners of war, but we knew it could have easily been adapted to a variety of conventional uses.

When the project was completed, I was asked to leave the team by a pencil-pushing government bureaucrat and was told to never speak of it again. The order, in effect, was to erase the ten years I spent working on my invention, from my memories. I say my invention, because as a young college student, I found notes—the very notes you are using today, squirreled away in a back office at the university I attended. The project was not my idea, but I made it work. I invented the original receiver that was used later by the military," John explained.

The scientists all stood in awe. Those who were working, now were gathered around listening to the story in rapt attention. No one spoke a word as John continued.

"As you all know by now, the original receiver had a very short range, but it was an incredible breakthrough for its time. We had done exactly what we had set out to do, but it was too late to really be used to any large degree during the Korean War. It was tested, but that was it."

"Why were you asked to leave the project after achieving such a huge success?" a voice asked from the back of the group.

"It became clear to me as we progressed, as my mentor had no doubt surmised, that the underlying impact of the probe could devastate the basic principle of individual privacy. As a medical doctor, I voiced my concern over the ethical ramifications of the nano-probe to my superiors, and it was then that I was asked to leave the project. I was young and naïve at the time, and while I didn't like someone else getting credit for the work I had done, I left and started a life in the civilian sector."

"But what does all of this have to do with what we are doing today?" the same engineer asked.

"I am getting to that, son," John said, feeling the weight lift off his body as he told his secrets. It was the first break most of them had in nearly twelve hours, and while the story had gone longer than he planned, he noticed the tension in the room slacken as he continued his story.

"The probes I developed continued to be injected into babies and that practice continues today. As a matter of fact, I delivered a baby just three days ago, and I injected the infant with the probe."

"What is the significance of the probe now after so many years?" a rather stunning design engineer asked with the deepest green eyes he had ever seen.

"Well, that is a good question. Without a receiver capable of reading the transmissions, the significance is literally zero. To be honest, I have done the same procedure on thousands of babies and have yet to understand why I am still doing it. I actually feel guilty at times because if the real reason were to get out, too many terrible things could happen by unscrupulous people. That is why I left the project forty years ago."

"I don't understand. What kind of terrible things are you talking about?" she asked.

"Well, after all of the research, it became clear that with the right receiver, the probe could be used to track human movements, and theoretically, it would also allow the government, or anyone for that matter, to control the receivers to gather data on many human daily functions."

"Wow, all that from such a little probe?" the design technician asked.

"Yes, all that and more," John continued. "Each probe has an unlimited life span. I invented a way to regenerate the probe's power as it traveled through the blood stream, but was released before I could make it work. My idea provided a way to recharge the probe using the power in red blood cells as they attach themselves to its surface. It is perfectly harmless to the body and while it has never been proven, may actually fight off certain diseases."

"The probe fights off diseases. So why exactly are we here?" the ruddy-faced engineer pressed.

"The best part is yet to come. Each probe is also programmed with a unique number generated by the NSA. The number is stored both in the probe and on a mainframe computer in Ft. Meade, Maryland, which if you can imagine, has millions of recorded births since 1960. Each birth record contains the birth date, weight, height, mother's and father's name and address, plus a few other data points. It is this unique number that we are trying to track with this project. That is the background. Now, why are we here today? This is the part that is the most difficult. Believe it or not, I was on my sailboat in the middle of the bay just yesterday when I was snatched by the CIA and brought here. Yes, I know what you are thinking—this is crazy."

John glanced at the large black clock on the wall and knew they had to get back to work, but it felt good to actually be able to tell someone. He could tell that the group was enthralled and even he had to admit that he felt somewhat important with the attention he was getting.

"I don't need to remind you that what I am about to tell you is top secret. It never, and I mean never, leaves this room," John said as he looked around the room to see if everyone understood his statement. John looked at the floor before he began to speak again. "Two days ago, the vice president was abducted while on a trip in Moscow. The government has no clues as to where he is or who was behind the abduction. Also, on the same day, a baby boy was taken from the Johns Hopkins maternity ward. The baby was to be adopted by the vice president and his wife."

A gasp echoed in the large room as he finished speaking.

"Why didn't anyone tell us this when we started?" an older gentleman said, waving his hands and speaking loudly.

"You know the government. If this got out, the press would have a field day. I am assuming the more people who knew about it the greater the possibility existed for leaks. I am sure I was not told the entire story, but trust me, you now know everything I was told."

"What about the little baby?" the woman asked.

"I know very little about it, really. A call came in to Mr. Palmer when he was telling me about the vice president, and he sent an investigation team to the hospital."

"So you have no way of knowing if the same group was behind both abductions?" the same older man asked.

"No, I don't know, but don't you think it is uncanny how they both happened simultaneously? It is our responsibility to build a device that can receive the probe's transmissions so we can find them both. We need to buckle down and start to come up with something within the next twelve hours. Every minute we waste allows the abductors to get away."

When he finished speaking, no one said a word. The group of scientists could not believe what they were just told. The vice president, abducted with no idea as to where he was, was almost unthinkable. As if on cue, the inner door clicked open, and Mr. Palmer walked in for an update. John looked at him and wondered how he always looked impeccably dressed in his designer suits when he knew he had not gone home in days.

"How is it going, Dr. Bastian?" Ryan asked him.

"Well, sir, we were just finishing a brainstorming session," John answered as the group broke up and started back to work with a renewed strength and purpose.

"Have you come up with anything?"

"Not yet. Everything we have thought of does not have the power to read the transmission over any distance. We are back to where I left the project forty years ago."

"Hmmm, that is disappointing. I was hoping to take some good news to the president. I brief him in just over an hour."

"We are working as hard as we can I assure you. I told you from the beginning this was not going to be easy. What we are attempting goes beyond normal engineering."

"Yes, I know all of that. But you know what is on the line should you fail."

"You don't have to remind me. We will not fail."

"I will tell the president you are still working, but are getting close to a breakthrough."

"Tell him what you like, Mr. Palmer. I will let you know as soon as something looks promising."

"I guess that is all I can ask for. Good luck to you all," Ryan said as he turned and walked through the inner door and took off in his white suit.

"Okay, team, this is for the vice president. I want to see and hear any idea, no matter how crazy or unorthodox it may seem. We are looking for something that breaks the mold, and I am relying on you to come up with it."

Chapter 31

Agent Metcalf was cutting the thick slice of ham on his plate as his cell phone rang.

"Metcalf speaking," he said, clearing his throat.

"Metcalf, this is the Baltimore bureau. We have a situation down here that we hope you may be able to help us with."

"Can it wait? I am right in the middle of breakfast."

"No, sir, this can't wait. A baby was taken from the maternity ward at Johns Hopkins yesterday. We don't have much to go on except for a sketch based on eyewitness descriptions. The Charge Nurse on the floor also reported an unscheduled repairman arriving at the time of the abduction. We have also reviewed the tapes at the hospital parking entrance from the security system and have found a man similar to the eyewitness description, driving a white Ford van. The van is relatively standard. White with no side windows. Do you think you could try to match the sketch with the man in the van you reported passing through the border a few days ago?"

"I can try. Can you fax them to my office? The van sounds as if it matches the description of the one that passed through."

"They are on the way as we speak. Call me ASAP with whatever you find."

"Will do. Metcalf out."

Metcalf threw a five on the table and gulped down the black coffee to get his mind rolling. He was not a morning person by any stretch. The diner he ate breakfast at every morning was close to his office, so he slipped out the door and walked at a healthy pace to retrieve the sketches.

The smell of fresh coffee filled the small, bureau office suite as the pot finished gurgling.

The coffee pot in his office was always full and he poured himself another fresh cup just as the fax machine finished printing the pictures.

"Joe, come over here. I need your opinion on this sketch," Metcalf said to one of his junior agents, glancing at it briefly over his steaming cup.

"The fax is pretty poor, but it appears to be Nassir, the one we tagged two days ago. But I have a hard time telling the difference. They all look the same to me," Joe said, confirming Metcalf's suspicion.

"Right, get Sam Jefferson on the phone. See if they spotted the van trying to get back across."

"What's going on, sir? Anything we should know about?" the junior agent asked, puzzled by the sketch.

"Not just yet. When we have confirmation on the ID, I will let you in on the situation."

Metcalf walked into his office with both the sketch and the photo from the hospital faxed earlier and the photo taken from the video at the border. He put them flat on his desk and sat upright in his chair, sipping his coffee and staring at the two trying to place the connection. It was tough, but Metcalf was positive this was the same person. The phone rang as he was lost in thought.

"Sam, this is Agent Metcalf. Did you spot the van trying to get back across yet?"

"No, sir, I had the pictures you sent posted in every guard shack from Maine to Washington state, and the guards have been briefed on what to do should any of them attempt to cross back into Canada. To this point, we have neither seen nor heard a thing."

"I see. Keep me posted on any changes. This has become your number one priority."

"Understood!"

Metcalf replaced the receiver, continuing to stare at the two pictures, thinking out loud.

"This has to be the same person."

Metcalf picked up the receiver and dialed the number to the Baltimore office.

"This is Agent Metcalf of the Buffalo office. Can I get in contact with the senior agent please?"

"This is Agent Simms, sir. What did you find?"

"I am positive the sketch is of Nassir Al-Zarim. He crossed the border in a white van three days ago along with two other suspects in different automobiles. I have had the border guards on alert since we ID'd the bastard."

"Has he crossed back over the border?"

"Not at the Falls, and Sam Jefferson has alerted all other crossings points and provided them with the pictures, so I think it is safe to say he is still here and probably heading back north. I will put out an APB to the New York State Police with the make and model of the van. Our goal right now is to catch him in transit while still in New York," Metcalf told Simms.

"Very good. I will report to my superior that you are picking up the ball. We will continue to investigate the scene, and if we find anything useful I will pass it along personally."

"Sounds good," Metcalf said as he hung up.

"Joe, Pete, come into my office—we have a situation," Metcalf yelled out to the two junior agents.

"What's up, sir? I haven't even had a chance to get a cup of coffee," Pete said as he yawned.

"I was just on the line with our Baltimore office. They are investigating a kidnapping at Johns Hopkins. It appears that our friend Nassir has surfaced in the Baltimore area. The sly bastard had the balls to take a baby from the maternity ward of one of the most prestigious hospitals in the country."

"Jesus, what do we have to do with that?" Joe asked.

"Well, take a look at these," Metcalf said, handing them the fax of the sketch and the photo taken from the parking garage security video. "It does look like Nassir. He must have made a mad dash for Baltimore after slipping over the border."

"The sketch is pretty weak, but the van is the same. I would say they are the same person," Pete said in confidence.

"So would I, which is exactly what I told Agent Simms in Baltimore. Joe, I want a bulletin sent out to all police agencies immediately with both pictures, a make and model of the van and a notice that there may be two others with him. All three may be armed and dangerous, so tell them to take all precautions. Also, please tell them to be careful. They will most likely have an infant with them."

"I am on it, sir."

"Pete, I want you to drive over to meet with Sam Jefferson and have him stop all vans meeting the description."

"Yes, sir, I will be back ASAP."

"Oh, and Joe, one last thing. I want to be notified by the police should they find these bad guys. I don't want the local authorities to do anything stupid. I want to be there when they are taken down."

"Yes, sir, I will put that on the alert."

"Very good! Finally something we can sink our teeth into. I was getting bored," Metcalf said with the hint of a smile on his face. This was going to be a good day, he could tell already.

Metcalf's next call was to his supervisor in Washington.

"Sir, the van I reported two days ago has resurfaced. It wasn't heading to the convention as I originally suspected. The man driving is a suspect in the kidnapping of an infant from the maternity ward at Johns Hopkins."

"Yes, I've heard. What are you working on now?" the voice on the other end of the line asked.

"My bet is they will be heading back north. We are sending an alert out to all police agencies, including the State Police—in an effort to catch them on the way back through. I have also asked Sam Jefferson to tighten up the border security until they are caught."

"Excellent. Will you need additional manpower to handle this?"

"No, sir. For the time being we have everything covered, but I will remember that offer."

"Good. Keep me up to date."

"Yes, sir, I will do that," Metcalf said into the phone as the other end went dead.

"Hot damn! We got ourselves a real situation here and we are right in the center of it!" Metcalf yelled out loud, slapping his hands together.

Chapter 32

Ben Lassiter was losing patience waiting for news from Washington. He was also losing confidence in ever finding Eagle 2, but he would never let his team know. It had been nearly twelve hours since the last communication with the White House, and each passing hour made his shoulders sag an inch lower. He didn't have to tell the others that each day that passed decreased Eagle 2's life span by 25 percent—that's if he was still alive.

He was surprised that the terrorists had not attempted to communicate. He told himself that with the political situation, the terrorists didn't know who to call, but in the back of his mind he wondered if they had not yet called because they had killed Eagle 2. He shook that thought out of his head and reassured himself that they were probably trying, but couldn't get through.

While sitting idle, each man had replayed the mission over in his head a hundred times. Tony had found a map of the region in one of the back offices of the hangar. He thought if nothing else, it would give them a frame of reference, should they need it.

The only excitement they had was when President Stefanovich arrived six hours ago with his entourage and attempted to leave the airport in the state-owned jet. A large mass of people blocked the runway for nearly two hours not allowing the plane to leave. Lassiter couldn't believe the rioters were actually willing to put themselves in this position. The black pavement had to be hotter than hell and most were sitting square in the middle of it chanting something in unison that Lassiter couldn't quite make out. Lassiter actually felt sorry for them because he knew what an ass Stefanovich really was.

The soldiers stationed at the airport finally moved them out of the way by hosing them down with high-pressure water from the three-inch hoses on the airport fire trucks. It was all rather comical to watch the people rush the trucks only to be harmlessly propelled backward. The water jetting out of the hose literally knocked them off their feet, sending them hurtling across the steaming pavement. The water, in some twisted manner, actually took the heat off the situation in more than just the obvious way.

Lassiter tried to talk to the presidential security, but was pushed aside. He was trying to find out what was going on inside Stefanovich's inner circle, but was given the cold shoulder. He doubted they knew Stefanovich's planned destination. The plane could fly anywhere on the continent without refueling, but it was most likely heading for a military base outside the city where he could regroup and develop a plan to retake his seat in the Kremlin. Stefanovich was a shrewd politician. He didn't have to be told the longer he waited, the harder it would be to reclaim his position. Timing was everything in the political arena.

Lassiter was now growing weary and desperately needed some rest. "Tony, come over hear and sit by the phone. I need to get some rest; I have not had a chance to sleep since we arrived," Lassiter said, looking more distraught as each hour passed.

"Go up to the plane, sir—it is quiet in there. We can handle things here," Tony told him.

"Okay, you sold me. If the phone rings come get me ASAP."

"Yes, sir."

Lassiter left the four men and walked to the plane. His eyes hurt and his tired muscles ached from stress. He wasn't sure if rest would make him feel better, but he would be no good to his small team exhausted. A quick nap would clear his head from the fog that it had been in for hours.

Rodger walked up to Tony who was sitting at the desk, looking into his face searching for some of the confidence that he usually found, but received none.

"I hope something happens soon. We won't have much of a rescue mission if we don't get started," Rodger said as he sat next to his friend.

"I know. I have thought of nothing else since we came back from the city," Tony answered him in a low voice, so the others wouldn't hear his worries.

"What do you think our chances are for finding Eagle 2 alive?"

"I don't know, but if he is out there we will find him," Tony said with the old spark coming back into his voice.

"But how in the hell are we going to do that? It would seem as if the kidnappers would have called by now with whatever sick demands they had if they wanted to return him alive. The others think Eagle 2 is already dead because we haven't heard anything."

"Don't lose hope, Rodger. He is still alive—I can feel it."

"I hope you are right. I don't want to be the one who finds him dead."

"Not only will we find him alive," Tony added, "I am going to rip the hearts out of the bastards who took him myself."

"I will be right behind you every step of the way, my friend," Rodger told him as he stood and put his hand on Tony's shoulder. "I am going to get some rest, too. I haven't closed my eyes since we returned from the square."

"I will wake you as soon as we get news."

"Very good, and if you need to rest, wake me and I will take over manning the phone."

"Thank you, I will do that. Now go and rest up, you will need all the energy you can muster very soon."

"I hope you are right," Rodger said, walking away picking his backpack up off the floor. He dusted it off with one hand pulling his coat out with the other. He balled the coat up and threw it into the corner to use as a pillow and lowered himself slowly down on the hard concrete floor of the hangar. Within minutes he was dead asleep, dreaming of his wife and new baby.

Tony was left alone to think. He thought about the Russian citizens and the way they were reacting during the riots. Although the rioters were loud and unruly, they didn't strike him as callous terrorists. They were poor and hungry and this was the only way they could express themselves to get noticed.

No, something was not right. The explosion had killed a dozen or more of the rioters. Surely they wouldn't have wanted to kill their own. The ones responsible were hardened, cold-blooded killers not hungry peasants. With that thought Tony sat upright in his chair, scratching his chin trying to continue his thoughts.

If those responsible were not Russian, who were they? All this time they were trying to locate where the kidnappers would be hiding in the city. But, what if they weren't in the city. What if they weren't even in the country? Tony was now lost in thought as he tried to develop a sound theory.

"My God, that is it. They are not Russians at all. We have been focusing our attention in the wrong direction," Tony said out loud, throwing both his hands in the air.

Rodger stirred awake as he heard Tony talking, figuring that he was on the phone.

"What is it, Tony? Who are you talking to?" Rodger said sleepily.

"Rodger, what if those responsible are not Russians?"

"What are you talking about? You saw the riots—who else could it have been if not the Russians?"

"I don't know. But listen to this," Tony started explaining his idea.

Rodger sat on the floor, listening to the explanation, finally understanding Tony's thought process.

"It makes sense. But we are still no further ahead if we don't know who they are. I prefer to think it is the Russians. At least it gives me a direction to focus my anger."

"Think about it though. They wouldn't do something like this on their own soil to their own people."

"That is true, but like I said, we are still left with nothing."

"We can narrow down a list of suspect countries to three or four. We both know the small countries bordering Russia have as much to gain by pulling something like this off than anyone."

"So now we have to start looking at other countries? My God, Tony, do you honestly think Lassiter will buy this?"

"If we can determine the country, we can start doing something on our own instead of waiting for the phone call that may never come."

"Before we do anything you had better talk to the old man," which is what they called Lassiter behind his back. "Explain it to him the same way you did to me which may prove to be a much tougher sell, trust me."

"I know. I will wait until he wakes up on his own. I don't want to bother him with any wild ideas until I can think it through."

"I think we could put the Georgia Republic high on the list. I don't have to remind you of the hand grenade incident last year during the presidential visit. They have proven their dislike toward the United States time and again. That would be the most obvious choice to start looking," Rodger said, now thinking out loud, trying to help his friend come up with more evidence to convince Lassiter.

"I thought about them, and you are right, that would be the most obvious choice. They would be at the top of the list, for sure. But Chechnya also has good reason to do something like this. They have wanted the Russians out of their country since the break-up. Excellent, keep thinking and we may just get somewhere on our own. We already have two and we just started."

"Even if we don't get anywhere, I feel better trying," Rodger said, standing up from the hard floor, walking around to get the blood flowing.

After three hours of deep sleep, Lassiter came stumbling down the stairway. He looked like death warmed over and probably felt the same way.

"Damn, could I go for a large latte from Dunkin' Donuts right now," he said as he reached Tony.

"I don't know if I can get that for you, sir, but I can send Kevin out for some coffee."

"Yes, that would be great. I haven't had an ounce of caffeine in nearly two days."

Tony got up from Lassiter's chair and walked over, talking to Kevin. In minutes, Kevin was out the door.

"I take it the phone didn't ring," Lassiter said, yawning the last part into incoherent babble.

"No, sir, it has been quiet," Tony answered, wishing he could say that Washington had called.

"Jesus, what do you think they are doing over there?"

"I don't know, sir. But Rodger and I were brainstorming some ideas that I would like to run past you."

"Ideas on what?"

"Ideas on where Eagle 2 might be."

"Oh, and what did the two of you come up with?"

"Well, hear me out before you make any comments. We were just trying to make sense of what happened."

"No promises. If I this starts going down some fantasy highway, I may just cut you off. I am not in the mood," Lassiter said in his rough, but groggy voice.

"I understand fully. We aren't either. There is something about this entire situation that doesn't add up. We don't think the Russians were behind the kidnapping. It just doesn't make sense that they would risk something like this on their own soil."

"So how do you explain it with the riots?"

"You know as well as I, those people were just tired and hungry."

"Go on, you haven't lost me yet," Lassiter said, sitting back in his chair, interlocking his fingers behind his head.

"The explosion killed many Russians along with members of our team. Russians would not do something like that to their own people. It is just, well, out of character for them."

"So if the Russians aren't behind this, who do you propose is?"

"Well, sir, that is tough to determine with what we have to go on. Many of the breakaway republics have cause to pull something like this off," Tony said, thinking as he went. "The Republic of Georgia is the most likely candidate given their past, but this is too over the top for even them. Our guess is that whoever did this thought they were getting a Russian. Think about it— the cars were Russian and they were even flying a Russian flag on the fender. I am betting that the terrorists are shitting a brick right about now because they know the person they have is American."

Lassiter's eyebrows raised in thought and Tony went on with his speculation.

"Chechnya is also a possibility. The tension between the two governments has reached a head and this is just the gutless thing Chechan's would stoop to just to shake the Russian government to the core. If I were a betting man, and I'm not, but if I were, I would put my money on Chechen rebels," Tony said, ending his thought.

Lassiter sat up and looked at the young agent. "But, how do you explain the border crossings. If the terrorists aren't Russian how did they get past the border guards, especially with Eagle 2 riding shotgun? I don't know son, this seems a bit far-fetched."

"Think about it, sir. On the way in, they had nothing, but maybe a few weapons and explosives. They could easily have been hidden in the trunk. The return trip was after the government takeover. The border guards were swamped with people trying to get out. God only knows what they let slip through."

"Tony, I think you just might be on to something," Lassiter said, scratching his head. "The only problem is we have nothing concrete to go on, and if what you say is true, we are in for quite a search."

"Rodger and I were just tossing some ideas around is all, trying to take our minds off the situation and be more productive."

"Well, I will report your ideas to the White House to see if they can come up with something for us to go on. At this point, even a wild goose chase sounds like a good idea. Nice work son," Lassiter said as he patted Tony on the back.

"Sir, we are ready to go at a moment's notice when you get the word. Nothing could stop us from finding Eagle 2." Tony didn't add dead or alive to the statement even though those three words were on the tip of his tongue.

"I know, son, I know."

Chapter 33

Andre watched Alexander's actions like a hawk. For the past few hours Alexander's mood had changed dramatically for the worse. Shevard was also watching and growing more and more impatient with each passing minute. Alexander had not attempted to contact the Russians with their demands to return the captive, and the atmosphere in the warehouse was so thick with desperation you could cut it with a knife.

"What in the hell are we doing here, Andre? It is obvious that Alexander has lost all sense of reality. If he thinks for a minute we are going to get out of this alive, he has lost his mind," Shevard said with a tiredness in his voice that came from the stress of the situation.

"I can't answer that, Shevard. I don't know what is going on in his head. I have tried to talk to him, but he just sits in that office and says nothing. We have enough food with what Leonid brought back to last over a week. We will be fine."

"We will be fine until the Americans come looking for their vice president, and you're right, Andre, we won't be hungry, we'll be dead," Shevard said coldly.

"We will get through this. I am worried, though, that this plan will not bring the results Alexander wants. When our countrymen learn that we kidnapped the vice president of the United States, they will turn against us. Mark my words. When this gets out, we will be outcasts in our own country. Even if we make it out alive, we will never be able to go home," Andre said solemnly.

"Exactly, this is what I was telling Alexander when he first came up with this idiotic plan. We should have walked away in Moscow, but it is not too late Andre, don't you see that?"

"Let's just wait and see what Alexander is going to do. He may surprise us."

"I doubt that. He's just crazy enough to see this through to the end. We need to walk away."

"I may just have to agree with you on that," Andre said with a nod, giving Shevard the first indication he may go against Alexander. "I will go back up and try to get something out of him."

"Good luck, my friend. I will come with you if you think it would help," Shevard added.

"That may not be a bad idea. Maybe the two of us can talk some sense into him," Andre said, slapping his friend on the back.

"If we can't talk to him, I say we leave him here with his captive and we get out while we still can. No one knows who we are. Thank God we left the blindfold on the vice president. He can't identify us, and I can go home to my wife and kids."

"We still have time. The Americans can't be on to us yet. They are probably still trying to figure out who was responsible. With so many possibilities, it may take them a week or more to even find a starting point. Let's just go up and talk to him and go from there."

"Okay, but if time starts running short and he still won't listen to reason, I will kill him before it is too late to save ourselves," Shevard said, staring Andre in the eyes, looking for a hint of emotion to the comment but finding none.

"If that time comes, I will be with you," Andre said, walking toward the stairs.

Shevard followed, glancing back to make sure their captive was still sitting on the cement floor with the blindfold in place. As long as he was blind, they would have a chance. If their identification was ever known, they would forever be hunted.

Shevard felt the beads of sweat on his brow as he crested the top of the stairs. Even as crazy as Alexander appeared, he was still afraid of him. He didn't like the tension between them. After all, they had been friends for nearly ten years. With a pit in his stomach, he thought about his earlier comment, wondering if he really could kill his friend.

Andre turned to Shevard just before entering the office. "I will talk, you just listen. I don't want Alexander to hear the dissension in your voice.

Andre turned the knob and pushed the door open. Alexander still sat in the exact position he had been when Andre came earlier.

"Alexander, Shevard and I came to talk with you."

Alexander turned to face the two men, but never really focused on them. His eyes were staring over them at some undetermined point on the ceiling.

"Alexander, did you hear me?"

"I heard you. Why are you not downstairs looking after our captive?"

"He is not going anywhere. Leonid has returned with additional supplies. We should be in good shape for a few more days," Andre said in a whisper.

"Ah, that is excellent news. How are you, my dear friend, Shevard?"

Shevard looked nervously at Andre, afraid to speak.

"I am well, Alexander. *How are you?* is the more important question."

"I am fine. My hand is throbbing from the broken fingers, but that is to be expected."

"You should have that looked after by a doctor."

"It will be fine. I don't suspect you two have come to inquire about my well being."

"We have been worried about you and about the situation. What are you planning?" Andre stammered.

Alexander looked at his friend briefly and then back to the ceiling. "We wait here until the Americans come looking for their leader and then we kill them all. We have the element of surprise. They have no idea where he is nor who we are. We wait until they are in our web and then we suck the life out of them."

Both Shevard and Andre stared at Alexander unable to speak. Their suspicions were gone about him. It was obvious that he was absolutely mad. They couldn't kill Americans—their fight was with Russia.

"Alexander, are you saying you want us to stay and fight the Americans? They have done nothing to us. Admit it, this was just a mistake. If we walk away now, we can still fight another day. Who knows? Maybe the new political system will be more willing to talk to us," Shevard said firmly.

"Shevard is right, Alexander. We cannot stay here and fight them. They are innocent. We should regroup back at your flat and plan for another day. There is no shame in that, I can assure you," Andre said nervously, looking at Shevard.

Alexander sat quietly unaffected by the words. He made no movement or gesture acknowledging the two had even spoke.

"Alexander, did you hear us? We don't want to do this," Andre said, raising his voice toward his friend for the first time in months.

Alexander turned in his chair, staring at the two with the same thousand-mile stare as before.

"Gentlemen, we are not doing this for each other, we do it for freedom. Shevard, what of those nights we sat and talked into the morning hours about our plans? Are they so easily forgotten? Now, if you have lost confidence in me, then I will consider you traitors to our cause. You are scared and can't see past your own selfish reasons to walk away. If either of you attempt to leave, I will kill you before you get through the door."

Shevard could feel his skin redden as he listened to Alexander talk. He couldn't believe his friend was this crazy. He threw his hands in the air and shook his head in disgust as he turned around and slammed the door to the office behind him. "Kill me?" he mumbled. "We will see who kills who."

Andre approached Alexander, pulling a chair up to the desk to look into his friend's eyes.

"Alexander, can't you see this is a no win situation? We can get out of this alive if we leave the man tied up downstairs and go home. You have been closer to me than a brother, but I have to disagree with you on this. Please, won't you come to your senses long enough to hear what I am telling you?"

"Andre, I have heard you, but it is you who is not hearing me. This is our chance to be heroes. Every news station from here to China will be focused on our victory and our cause. We will show the world what the Russian bastards have done to our country. The Americans will bend over for us because they want their politician back and then we will have the world by the balls," Alexander said with a visible smile, cupping his hands as if he held the ball sack of the world already.

"But, Alexander, this is not a game we are playing. People are going to get killed. We are going to get killed," Andre said vehemently.

"It is a small price to pay, my brother—a small price indeed to achieve the attention we deserve."

"Jesus, Alexander, don't you see that if we are all dead our cause dies with it?"

"My parents died and the cause still survived," Alexander said without a pause. "No, Andre, you are wrong. If we die, more will pick up the fight. The Russians will be stopped, and our country will be free of those filthy rats."

Andre had run out of words. He could no longer reason with his friend. "You have gone mad. If you think kidnapping an American politician will make us heroes, you are the one who is dead wrong," Andre said in such exasperation that he mostly spit the words out of his mouth.

"We shall see who prevails. History will indeed be rewritten after this."

Andre sat back at those words. *My God, that is the second time he has alluded to history books. That is all he wants. He doesn't care about us.* "You selfish bastard. You have gotten us into this with no intention of getting us out alive. You are no longer a brother to me," he said as he threw the chair under the dust-covered table and walked out of the room, leaving Alexander alone once more with his thoughts.

Shevard was downstairs talking to Leonid as Andre descended the long metal stairs. The look on his friend's face could only mean that he didn't talk Alexander out of this.

"I am sorry, Andre, I couldn't just stand there and say nothing," Shevard said before giving Andre a chance to speak. "That man insulted us and I couldn't just take it. How dare he threaten to kill anyone of us after all we have done for him?"

"Don't let it worry you. We have other things to worry about right now."

"What did you two talk about after I walked out?" Shevard asked.

"I was just trying to convince him that he had made a mistake and that it was not too late to regroup and pick up the fight another time."

"Let me guess, he thinks we are going to prevail."

Andre looked at the two men and then at the floor. "He does, and he will not back away."

"Damn, why is he being like this?" Leonid asked.

"I don't know, but there is no changing his mind. I have tried three times to talk to him and each time he becomes more distant. It is as if he is in his own world up there in that office."

"Well, I think it is time we put an end to this, so we can cut ourselves loose," Shevard said.

Chapter 34

The trip from Langley to the White House took more time than Ryan expected as he hurriedly walked into the Oval office with an update. Bill Snyder, the president's chief of staff, was near the fireplace ranting with his back to the president, on his cell phone. Ryan's sheer distaste for the man ran deep. He was just under six feet tall and deathly skinny. He wore a terrible toupee that was always neatly parted down one side and then combed over. His long pointy nose, pasty white skin, and closely set eyes even made him look like the weasel Ryan thought he was. The battle-hardened Gerry Simmons, the president's security chief, was sitting in a wing back chair leafing through a six-inch-thick file folder.

"What do you have for us, Ryan?" the president asked, standing to shake his hand.

"Well, sir, Dr. Bastian and his team are working frantically on a solution to the reception of the probe's transmissions. They are getting close, but have yet to come up with anything useable."

The president's face grew long, and the stress of the situation showed greatly in the deepening wrinkles on his forehead. "I see, but they are close as you say?" the president asked in an obvious skeptical tone.

"I just left the lab, and the team was brainstorming ideas on boosting the power of the receiver. The engineers estimate the device will need a sensitivity level capable of receiving the probe's signal within a 500 mile radius and then be able to track the signal to fifty feet of the probe's exact location. Given the search area, that should put us in the ball park."

"Even if Dr. Bastian succeeds, Lassiter only has a team of four men in country. Surely they can't launch an attack against a force of God knows how many," Snyder said, covering the mouthpiece of his phone with his palm.

"Those men are specially trained for this sort of mission. Two of them I trained myself," Gerry said, joining in on the conversation.

"Gerry, what is the possibility of getting more men on the ground over there?" the president asked.

"Slim to none. I have been in contact with Lassiter, and he advised that the new government has shut the airport down. All planes are restricted from entering or leaving the city. I think they want to try to keep Stefanovich out as long as possible while they build internal support."

"Would it do any good for me to place a call to the Kremlin? I could see about landing in another city. I need to do something to help," Tom said.

"I will attempt to answer that one," Ryan spoke up. "We have been constantly monitoring the communications within the Kremlin. If chaos could be a situational form of government, Russia is in it right now. No one has stepped up to take charge of the country within the last forty-eight hours. I fully expect the Duma to convene within the next twenty-four hours to plead with the rioters to let Stefanovich return. It is in their best interest to do that, given the communist party does not have the strength to take control for good yet. They need time to get their ducks in a row before making a move to control the government. Getting Stefanovich back will provide them the necessary time."

"Shit, who do we have over there?" Tom asked.

"We have Tony Hampton, a solid agent who has Russian language skills, and Rodger Gentry, an ex-Seal who led a team during the Panama invasion, if I recall correctly. The others I only know by name—Kevin Deal and Steve Thurmond. They have been with the security detail for quite some time. I am not nearly as concerned about the numbers as I am about their equipment. They didn't take the kind of firepower with them they are going to need," Gerry answered.

"If the Russians have shut down the airport, how in the hell will we get Dr. Bastian's receiver to them?"

"I am working on that, sir," Ryan said.

"Well, if we can get the receiver through why can't we get more weapons to our boys?" Tom asked.

"To be honest, sir, getting the receiver in will be a piece of cake. From what I have seen, it isn't very big. We can hide it in a bag, or coat pocket if we have to. Getting weapons in will take some doing. If I could make a suggestion, I say we wait for the receiver and then start the operational planning. We could even have the team scope the situation out after they find David's location, and then let them make the call," Ryan said, trying to take one step at a time.

"I agree," Gerry said. "We may be putting the cart before the horse."

"Okay, we wait," the president said in an exasperated voice, not willing to wait any longer than necessary. "Can I assume the terrorists from the hospital are being tracked?"

Ryan fielded this question as best he could. "Sir, the FBI is handling that investigation with the resources of the Homeland Security Department until we can establish a connection between this and the Russian incident."

"Ahhh yes, the Homeland Security Department," the president said loudly, rolling his eyes. "Ryan, if you don't mind, I want you to take over that investigation immediately. I think it is a fair assumption that the two are related at this point. If they aren't, I will take responsibility for it."

"Understood, sir. I will get myself up to speed as soon as I get back to the office."

"I don't have to tell you that I feel responsible for this," the president said, sitting back in his chair. "I should have never sent David into this."

"With all due respect, sir, it wasn't that you sent him into this," Ryan said forcefully, seizing the opportunity to inform the president of his possible grave mistake in not following protocol. "It was that you sent him into this without the knowledge and resources of the CIA," Ryan added, hoping the president realized his error.

Tom looked at Ryan with a sharp eye. "I fully understand what I mean when I say I feel responsible. I don't need you to provide me with additional commentary."

Ryan felt the tongue lashing strike his face and he glanced at Bill who was now off the phone. The chief of staff had a smug smirk on his face after the short exchange of words, but said nothing. Ryan and Bill never did get along. Bill seemed, to Ryan, to be the consummate "yes" man who had kissed more ass in his career than a downtown hooker.

"The damn press is starting to snoop around asking questions about the kidnapping at the hospital. They are requesting a press conference, but I have held them at bay until I have more information. Bill has fielded their questions for the time being, but if we don't come up with something soon, I will have to go public with this. My hope is that we can keep the Moscow situation under wraps. Does everyone understand? The four of us are the only ones who know anything about this besides Lassiter and his men."

Everyone in the room shook their heads in affirmation. "Ryan, I want something from you in the next twenty-four hours. Please let me know as soon as Dr. Bastian and his team come up with something," the president said.

"You will be the first to know," Ryan said as he gathered his paperwork and walked out the door with Gerry following him.

"Ryan, could we speak for a minute?" Gerry asked as they headed down the hallway.

"Sure, Gerry, what's on your mind?"

"Come down to my office. We need to talk about some things, but I don't want to do it out in the open."

"If this is about my comment concerning not getting the CIA involved sooner, you can save your breath. I have expressed my feelings and it's over."

"To hell with that. I honestly think that was Snyder's idea and the president is covering for him. That freaking weasel has his head so far up the president's ass it is tough to determine where one ends and the other begins."

Ryan laughed about that comment because he thought the same thing. "Sure, Gerry, I have time. Let's talk."

The two men walked in silence to Gerry's office. It was sparsely decorated with a few service plaques on the wall and a picture of his family on his desk. Not all that impressive for the head of the presidential security detail.

"Have a seat, Ryan. Can I get you anything—coffee, soda?"

"No thanks, I have had my share of coffee the past two days to keep me jittery for the next month."

"Understood, you have put in your share of overtime on this. I would like to say that bringing the project out of mothballs was a sheer act of genius. Where did you come up with that idea?"

"I vaguely remembered the project being whispered about as a rookie. I had no idea what it was about until I found the research tucked away in the basement. It will only be an act of genius if it works. I have my fingers crossed on that, but I have been impressed with this Dr. Bastian. If anyone can make it work, he can."

"Well, it was good thinking on your part, nonetheless."

"What's on your mind, Gerry?" Ryan asked, briefly looking at his watch.

Gerry leaned forward in his chair and interlaced his fingers on the desk in front of him. "I just wanted to fill you in on some troubling comments being thrown around the office before you arrived this morning. Bill Snyder is trying to sell you out on this. If this leaks to the press before we find Eagle 2, you will be the fall guy. I am not sure what he has up his sleeve, but don't be surprised if the blame is placed directly on your shoulders. That bastard Snyder has been looking for a reason to ruin the CIA since the Iraq fiasco in not finding the weapons of mass destruction."

Ryan was floored by what was said. He couldn't believe that this was going to be pinned on him and the CIA. He was actually speechless. Were it not for him, the vice president would have no hope of being found alive.

"Snyder even has the press release ready when it happens. I have no idea what it says, but the two were talking about it as I walked in. They hushed up as soon as I arrived. I could lose my job in telling you this, but I couldn't let them blindside you. You deserve better and job or no job, I will never let Snyder win as long as I am here."

"Thanks, Gerry, I know you are sticking your neck out for me. Let's hope Bastian hits a homerun—I have a feeling I am going to need it soon. The longer this goes, the odds are that someone will talk. I am actually surprised this hasn't been leaked already."

"Use the information however you like, but you must understand that I will deny this conversation."

"I won't say a word. You know I am not like that."

"Good luck. I'm pulling for your man, Bastian."

Ryan stood up and looked his old friend in the eyes. He held out his hand in a show of understanding, which was met by the larger, more calloused hand of the security chief.

"Thank you, again," Ryan said and walked out of the small office.

If the stress level Ryan was under wasn't enough ten minutes ago, it just kicked up a notch. He said nothing as he entered the back seat of his car for the trip back to his office. For the first time in many years, he was worried. He was grateful for the tip, but it may have been better not to know.

Ryan was a career CIA agent following in his father's footsteps. He graduated from the University of Maryland with a degree in Accounting in 1967. His father helped him get a position in the agency and over the last thirty nine years he had given everything he had to give to his work. He earned a masters degree in Political Science from Georgetown in 1978 after years of night school. He moved up through the organization after his father retired, to the position of Deputy Director. He was a natural leader and thrived on the responsibility. He was happy and would have been content to retire at that level. He thought about becoming the director and at times dreamed about it, but he was content with being second in command.

He didn't like playing the political games the director had to play. As the deputy he could do what he did best and fly just under the political radar. However, when his boss was pressured to step down, he accepted the position with honor. He felt compelled to give it his all and wanted to leave his mark on the agency. His goal was to improve the reputation of the organization which was severely damaged after the Gulf War. Ryan soon found out that goal would be very difficult, if not impossible, to reach.

He soon realized, as had his predecessors, that the CIA was the easy scapegoat because of its required secrecy. He reorganized the entire agency and even hired a public relations consultant to rebuild credibility with the American public. He took a considerable hit from within the agency because he was seen as bowing to political pressures. He didn't let the rumors bother him. He knew that the CIA had to change or it would suffer a very ugly political death. He stared out the car window suddenly feeling very alone.

The first thing he would do when he got back would be to pay a visit to the lab. He didn't want to put any more pressure on Bastian and his team, but he had to know how things were going. Then he had to contact the FBI and let them know he would be leading the investigation on the kidnapping from Johns Hopkins. That would make the FBI furious, he was sure.

The traffic was light this late in the morning. It never occurred to him that today was Saturday. In forty minutes he was standing in the lab listening to the conversation taking place between the team. Instead of bothering them, he walked out and headed to his office. The call he was about to make, he dreaded more than anything he had ever done. No one liked another agency stepping on toes, and this went beyond. The kidnapping was clearly an FBI operation and usurping that would definitely put Ryan on the FBI black list.

"Sharon, get me the FBI headquarters on the phone. I want the person in charge of the hospital kidnapping."

"Yes, sir," she said into the speakerphone. She knew her boss was under an enormous amount of stress. She wondered what happened at the White House this morning because he said nothing to her as he walked past her desk. That was just not like him, but she could tell he was deep in thought and didn't bother him.

Ryan used the time to take his double-breasted jacket off and hang it back in his closet. He didn't like to wear it around the office because it wasn't comfortable.

It wasn't long before the phone buzzed.

"Sir, I have Agent Simms on the phone."

"Thank you. Please don't interrupt us for anything."

"Agent Simms, I understand you are leading the investigation of the kidnapping at Johns Hopkins."

"Yes, that is correct, Mr. Palmer. How can I help you?"

"How is the investigation proceeding?"

"We are working on some leads. I have an agent out of the Buffalo office leading the ground work."

"I see. I am going to be taking over that investigation," Ryan said without beating around the bush. "I can't tell you why right now, but we think this might be connected to an investigation we are working."

"Jesus, Palmer, you guys think you can strong arm anyone don't you?"

"You don't have a clue how much I dreaded this call. This was on presidential orders—I had no choice."

"I don't care if God himself ordered you to make this call—it isn't right."

Ryan let the agent blow off steam. He knew he would be just as pissed if he were in Simms' shoes. "Keep me up to date on the progress and please understand that I don't want to make things difficult for you."

"How can you avoid making things more difficult, you just added another level of bureaucracy to my world, Mr. Palmer."

"We have all had investigations taken from us. I can assure you that as soon as it is determined to not be connected, you will have it back."

"What is this connection you have referred to? The least you can do is fill me in, now that you just took the wind out of our sails."

"I am sorry, you know I would if I could, but it is too early to give you any details. Tell your agent in Buffalo that I will be sending a team to assist him."

"This is bullshit, Palmer. I am going to officially file a complaint as soon as this conversation is over."

"File your complaint. This conversation is over," Ryan said as he hung up. He didn't like to be that way, but he had no choice. A presidential order wasn't something a person could refuse. He really wanted to tell the agent why he had to take over the investigation. That way it would have been easier to take. It was done, and that was all he cared about right now. He stood and walked out of his office to talk with Sharon rather than pick up the intercom.

"Sharon, who were the agents who fished Dr. Bastian out of the bay today?"

"I am not sure who went. I can find out in a jiffy, though."

"Perfect. When you do, please tell them I need to see them ASAP. I don't care if they are home. I need them here today."

"I will find out and contact them personally."

"Thank you very much. Oh, and one more thing—you have been a tremendous help with all of this. I just wanted you to know that I appreciate everything you have done. I know I am a demanding and tough man to live with, so my wife points out, but you put up with it pretty well."

Sally blushed a bit with the unexpected compliment. "Thank you, sir, and since you think so highly of me right now, let me be the first to tell you that you need to go home. You haven't left this building except to go to the White House in four days. I love to see you, but not this much."

"Thank you for your concern, but I have just heard some very troubling news. I don't think I will be getting much sleep until this is all behind us."

"I knew something was bothering you. I could tell from the minute you walked off the elevator."

"I wish I could tell you what is going on, but I am afraid it is going to have to wait."

"Well, I am going to find those agents and then head home. It is Saturday after all," Sharon said, feigning she was offended by the put off.

Ryan looked at his watch. "Saturday, my God, where did the days go?" He had been in his office nearly all week.

"I will see you first thing Monday morning," Ryan said as he walked back into his office.

Chapter 35

Serenity passed through the last lock overlooking the white lighthouse on the southeastern shore of Lake Ontario. This area of the large lake was steeped in history. In the distance to their right, Fort Ontario overlooked the lake almost exactly as it had for the past two hundred years. On their left, a large ship bearing a South American flag was unloading a cargo of what looked to Nassir like large generators onto flat bed trucks. The port was bustling with activity as two large cranes worked in unison emptying the cargo out of the ship's hold.

The twin-engine diesels gulped fuel at an incredible rate. Before continuing, they decided to stop and refuel at the International Marina just inside the breaker wall of the lake. The four men were on the fly bridge taking in the sights as they steered away from the lock. The marina was filled with large beautiful sailboats from all over the world. Some were tied to long docks while others were moored out in the water, secured to floating buoys.

As they neared the marina, Sharal radioed ahead to let them know he needed fuel badly.

"International Marina, this is *Serenity*. We are in need of diesel fuel."

"10-4, *Serenity*, pull up to the dock parallel with the sea wall. Someone will meet you there."

"Copy that—out," Sharal said in the handset.

Sharal nudged up to the dock perfectly as the other two made sure the fenders were in the correct position. A young kid walked quickly out onto the floating wooden dock as they finished tying off the lines to the dock cleats, securing the large boat.

"Good afternoon," Nassir said to the kid as he approached.

"That surely is a beautiful boat—what can I help you with?"

"Thank you, we need to top off both tanks," Nassir said as his white teeth became visible through a wide smile.

"Where are you heading today?" the kid asked as he pulled the nozzle and hose from the pumps.

"We are planning on heading out onto the lake to do some fishing," Nassir said, being careful not to provide too much information.

"Yikes! Fishing off this boat? Are you crazy?"

"Actually, we are not fisherman. I just bought this boat, and we are spending time away from the wives. Fishing was a good excuse."

"Well, I have some bad news for you. Do you see those waves crashing over the wall?"

The four men turned, looking out toward the lake. The waves were crashing against the six-foot wall, sending white spray high into the air. "Yes, I see them."

"You won't be going out today unless you are crazy. The Coast Guard issued a small craft advisory this morning in effect until further notice. The lake has been rough for the past two days. Even the professional fishermen have not ventured out."

"Are you sure we can't make it out?" Nassir asked.

"Oh, you can make it out alright, but it will probably be the last trip you make," the kid said, taking his baseball cap off to scratch his head. "The old men liken this lake to an unforgiving lady. She will rip your heart out without thinking twice. I would suggest you anchor here for the night and try tomorrow. "

"I guess we could spend the night here. It is not as if we are in a hurry to catch fish. What do you guys say?"

The three men looked at Nassir and nodded without saying a word.

"That settles it, do you have room for us for the night?" Nassir asked.

"I'll check as soon as I fill the tanks."

"Sounds good."

The pump clicked off as the tanks filled to the top. The kid replaced the nozzle and wrote down the number of gallons on a scratch pad. "That will be $473 even," he yelled up to Nassir.

Nassir came down from the fly bridge and reached into his pocket for his money clip. He counted out five one-hundred-dollar bills and handed them to the kid. "You can keep the change if you could find us a place to fit in for the night. Preferably a place out of the way," Nassir said with a nod.

The kid smiled at Nassir and then ran off to the marina office.

"What are we going to do, Nassir? We can't stay here over night," Kamal said in a whisper.

"You heard the boy. We can't make it today. We don't have a choice. We have enough food to last another two weeks. Once the lake calms, we are two days from our drop off point. Let's just settle in and relax. We need to rest anyway."

Ali shook his head at the exchange of words. He didn't like being stuck on the boat and he knew the longer it took to get to where they were going, the longer he was going to be stuck caring for the infant. "I will go below and check on the boy."

"Very good, Ali," Nassir said.

Just as Nassir turned away from Ali, he saw the kid walking out of the small office with an older gentleman.

"Kamal, go below and let me take care of this."

"Whatever you say. If you need my help just tap on the sliding glass door."

"If I need your help, we will all be in trouble. Just get below and keep quiet."

Nassir climbed over the starboard rail onto the dock. He wanted to meet the two men walking toward him away from the boat just in case the baby started to cry. Four Arab men alone on a boat with an infant would be cause for alarm.

"Hello, sir, my son tells me that you are looking for a place to moor for the evening."

"That is correct. If you have a place that would be excellent."

"Well, the lake advisory has really filled the slips, but I could put you up at a mooring if you won't need to come ashore."

"We are pretty self-sufficient. I don't think we will need anything tonight."

"Very well," the older man said, pointing out into the marina. "Do you see that red and white buoy floating about 50 yards off the last dock?"

"Yes, I believe I do," Nassir said, turning to look out to where the man was pointing.

"Tie a bow line to that buoy and you should be fine for the night. With any luck, the lake will be calm tomorrow. The latest weather forecast is calling for decreasing winds over night."

"That is good news," Nassir said with a sigh of relief.

"How far have you come?" the man asked, noticing the boat name gleaming in large gold lettering with *Geneva, NY* in smaller letters below.

"We spent the last two days coming up from Seneca Lake. It was a beautiful trip. It was actually my first trip through the locks."

"I see. Well, the mooring will be $40 for the night," the marina master said, looking a bit suspicious at the foreigner and his boating crew.

Nassir took his leather wallet out of his pocket again and gave the man $50 and told him to keep the change for his being so accommodating.

"Thank you, sir, and if I can be any help we are on channel 67 on your marine radio. My name is George. Don't hesitate to call in, and my son can come out and pick you up."

"Thank you, but I think we will be fine."

The men shook hands and smiled at each other. Nassir turned and walked away quickly, but the two men stood and watched him untie the dock lines and board the boat.

"I would bet my life that that man is not who he says he is," the older man told his son as he watched the foreigner walk away.

"What are you thinking, Dad?"

"Exactly what I said. They are not here to fish—not in that boat."

"What should we do?"

"Keep an eye on them. I don't trust them," George said, stroking the stubble on his chin.

"You got it," the kid said as he watched the boat cast off from the end of the dock.

The white hull glistened in the dying sunlight as Sharal started the engines and pulled away toward the buoy. The man and his son both watched to make sure the foreigners wouldn't have any problems with the mooring lines.

Nassir grabbed the buoy with the telescoping, hook lifting it out of the water high enough to tie a bow line to it.

After Sharal and Nassir were satisfied everything was secure, Sharal turned the engines off and went below.

"Kamal, I don't want any unnecessary trips on deck. The more we stay below the easier it will be for us. If all goes well, we can head out before day light," Nassir said.

"I think the baby could use some fresh air. Ali is feeding him now, but I really think we should get him out into the air."

"Just tell Ali to stay out of sight. Those men acted awfully suspicious."

"What did you tell them?"

"I told them nothing. Do you think I am a fool?"

"No, Nassir, I was just curious. I meant nothing by it."

"I know, my friend. I am just worried about this setback. I was expecting to have no problems on this trip, and now this minor hold up has me worried for some reason."

*

Nassir had no way of knowing, but his worries were justified. The marina master at the Seneca Harbor Marina back in Geneva had become increasingly suspicious of the van parked in his lot. He didn't like renting his best boat to strangers from out of town, let alone Arabs, but they had the paperwork in order, and he couldn't refuse a cash payment.

After the second day, he decided to call the Geneva Police department to have them check the van out. Sergeant Greg Lawrence had been a member of the Geneva police department for the past thirty-two years. He had seen his share of changes to the town in that time. The small bedroom community had grown considerably with the influx of migrants working for the numerous wineries and apple orchards in the region.

The solid white police cruiser pulled into the marina at a few minutes after four. A polished black boot stepped out touching the dirt parking lot coating it with a fine layer of dust. Sgt. Lawrence liked to look professional wearing his hair shaved close to the skin, his uniforms pressed with heavy starch, and his boots highly polished. Professionalism on the job was more important to him than any other duty.

"Earl, it is good to see you. What has you so concerned?"

"Hi, Greg, thanks for coming. I don't know. It could be nothing, but something is gnawing at me about the four fellows who rented my boat and left out of here a couple days ago. They were Arabs if you get my drift."

The chiseled features on Lawrence's face made no movement as his deeply set eyes scanned the area of the marina stopping on the white van and old Ford pick-up.

"Where were they headed?"

"The paperwork says they were heading north through the canal toward Ontario."

Greg nodded confirmation as he pulled a notepad out of his breast pocket and started scribbling notes. "You said there were four men?"

"I believe so, only one came in to sign the paperwork. The other three stayed behind and loaded the boat with supplies. I think the fourth actually came later in the truck."

"How much did they load?"

"I don't know. It looked like a few suitcases, toolboxes of some sort, and ten or so grocery bags. I didn't pay much attention at the time to be honest."

Lawrence started walking toward the van, still writing the notes. He lifted the door handle of the driver's door, but as he suspected it was locked. He tried the same with the others and all were securely locked. He did peak in the windows, but found nothing out of the ordinary inside. "Why is it that you came to call, Earl?"

"I don't know. Maybe I am feeling a bit anxious to get my boat back."

"When are they due to return?"

"The man said they would be back in five days which gives them another three days I guess."

"I will contact the lock stations to see if the boat has come through. You have the registration numbers and a description of the boat?"

"Yes, if you come into my office I will write them down for you."

"I don't see anything to be alarmed about yet," Lawrence said, adding more to his notes. "I will contact you if something comes up after I contact the lock stations. I will also check the state stolen vehicle reports to see if the van was reported missing."

"Thank you, Greg. You will have to forgive me for bringing you out here."

"It's no problem. I don't like being stuck in that stuffy office on a beautiful afternoon. It isn't very often I get to venture out. You take care of yourself, Earl. Let me know if they check in, will ya?"

"I will do that," Earl said, extending his hand.

Greg finished with his notes, putting the pad back into his shirt pocket. He shook the man's hand and walked back to his cruiser.

Before starting out, he radioed the description and plate numbers of both vehicles back to the office.

Chapter 36

Tony had just finished a short catnap that still left him tired. The boredom of the last three days was nearly unbearable. He had thought through his theory since presenting it to Lassiter and still came to the same conclusions. The kidnappers couldn't be Russian. Too many things didn't make sense, the biggest being the lack of communication. If they were Russians, they would have called immediately with ransom demands. The only snag was the border crossing. If they were foreign terrorists, they would have to cross over the border with Eagle 2. That is unless they didn't have Eagle 2 with them when they crossed.

Ben Lassiter sat in the old chair, looking over the map. He wasn't totally convinced that Tony's idea of the kidnappers not being Russian made sense, but decided to make the call to the White House anyway.

Picking up the STU III encrypted satellite phone, he punched in the numbers to the president.

"Mr. President, sir, this is Ben Lassiter."

"Yes, Ben, how are you and your men holding up?"

"Well, sir, we are quickly getting discouraged waiting for your call. We are dealing with it, but it is difficult."

"Keep your head up, Ben. We are getting close."

"That is good news. I wanted to pass a theory on to you and maybe you could run it by the NSA to see if they could focus their eavesdropping in another location. I don't know if it is anything, but it may prove to be a good start."

"Sure, Ben, what do you have?"

"I can't take credit for this. Tony Hampton came up with the idea, and I have just about convinced myself that he may be right. He feels the terrorists are not Russian, but Georgian or Chechen."

Ben heard nothing but silence on the phone as he continued. "Some things about this attack are not logical. Russians would not have detonated the bomb that killed at least twenty of their own people. Also, I believe they would have called by now with some sort of ransom demands. I just can't imagine that the rioters we saw would be capable of something like this."

Tom sat motionless at his desk thinking heavily on the words just spoken. *Finally someone else thinks the Chechens were behind this.* After the pause he spoke, "I think that is a plausible scenario. Let me run it by the NSA and see what they come up with. I will get back to you when I have something worth passing along."

"Sir, not to press the issue, but what is the latest update on your end?" Ben asked, cringing as he spoke the words.

"We are getting close to a breakthrough. I wouldn't expect it to be more than another day or so."

"What is this breakthrough that you are talking about, if I may ask?"

"I am not at liberty to tell you right now, but I can assure you that when we are finished, you will be the first to know."

Ben was used to the political blow off. He was at the bottom of the ladder when it came to getting information. He was considered only on a "need to know" level when it came to this type of operation and it was obvious he didn't need to know what was going on back there.

"How is your team situated for weapons should the need arise to mount a serious operation?"

"I guess that would depend on how serious the operation is," Lassiter said, showing a little anger at being kept in the dark. He was letting the stress show, and it bothered him.

"Send me an inventory of your weapons as soon as possible. I am working on getting you more firepower. I won't leave you and your men stranded, Ben. I can promise you that."

"I appreciate your concern," Lassiter said in the receiver, turning away from his men, shielding his conversation. "If something doesn't happen soon, I am afraid we won't be making a rescue mission. It will be a recovery mission."

"We are doing everything in our power to see that doesn't happen. I know you are anxious about this. Just hang in there. It won't be long," the president said, hanging up the phone.

Ben replaced the black handset into the drab green STU III and sat motionless for a few seconds. He was running the conversation over in his head to find a shred of optimism he could use to stay positive. He sighed briefly and stood to talk to the men.

"What did he have to say?" Tony asked before Ben could say a word.

"They are close to having something for us. I have no idea what that means or what it could possibly be, but they seem to think it is going to help us find Eagle 2."

"What did he think of our theory?" Tony asked.

"I think he already suspected the Chechen government of foul play. He was going to talk to the NSA and have them take a look into it. They did ask to have an inventory of our weapons. Rodger, I want you to strip the plane of everything you can find. I want you to go through the bags of every man and bring me what you find. I want everything we could possibly use inventoried, including a tire iron if we have one."

"Yes, sir," Rodger said, getting up to walk to the plane. He wasn't enthused about going through the bags of his dead friends, but weapons were weapons.

"What else did he say, sir?"

"Jesus, Tony, enough with the goddamn questions. They are working on something, but wouldn't elaborate on what it was. The president used the word breakthrough, and when I asked him about it, he wouldn't talk. I guess we will find out soon enough. He seemed to think they should have something to us in a day or so."

"What the hell? A breakthrough? We don't have that kind of time. We are confined to this damn hangar at the mercy of everyone, but us, with little hope of getting him back alive, and they are working on some kind of breakthrough. That is perfect," Tony said with as much sarcasm as he could muster.

"That's enough, Hampton," Lassiter said, turning back toward the desk, leaving Tony shaking his head.

Rodger came down thirty minutes later with a solemn look that appeared to Tony that he might have tears in his eyes. Over his shoulder were straps to four bags that belonged to agents who died in the explosion. He set them on the desk with an obvious clunk that meant he had found weapons. "I have been through the entire plane. You will take note that I didn't find a tire iron, but I did find five Glock 9mm's, three Smith and Wesson .38 automatics, and a Colt .45 caliber that is currently in my belt. What we don't have is ammunition. I only found one box of each caliber, aside from what we are all carrying."

"Nice work," Lassiter said as he made a mental note of the inventory. "Listen up, everyone," his voice echoing in the large open space, "I want to know what weapons each of you have and the amount of ammo you are carrying. I want to get the message off to the president in the next half hour, so step it up."

Rodger's facial expression never changed. He walked over to his pack and fell down onto the hard concrete and stared at the floor. None of them said a word as they looked at the bags of their fallen friends laying limp on the desk.

Tony grabbed his bag. He unzipped the front pouch and took the two boxes of ammunition he kept readily available for his two pistols. He also opened the large compartment and unwrapped the .38.

"Ben, this is all I have. They are no match to the AK-47 at long range, but in the right hands, they are deadly accurate in close combat."

"Keep them, Tony. I don't need your weapons. I just want to know what we have."

Tony put them back in the bag for now and walked toward Rodger.

"That was tough duty, man," Tony said to his friend who was still staring at the floor.

"Tell me about it. I have not been through personal things since my Navy days down in Panama. Jesus, Tony, I found pictures of their kids in those bags. Kids who will never again see their father."

"Damn, that sucks. I am sorry, man, but I'm glad he picked you."

"It reminded me of losing two young Petty Officers when we took the airport in Panama. That was dirty work. It was pitch dark and all you could see were lines of tracers flying through the air in all directions. I lost two out of my Seal Squad that night. It was the toughest thing I've ever experienced. We are trained to fight with no emotions, to look at every situation and find the military advantage. But, there is no military advantage in writing letters to wives and mothers."

Tony knelt down and put his hands on Rodger's shoulders. "Look at me, Rodger. This is not Panama. We are going to get through this alive. Trust me."

Rodger looked up and smiled. "I know, but we have many friends who won't be returning with us."

"I know, I've thought about them often the past few days. That's the trick—never forget them."

"I can still see the faces of those two kids that night. At times they haunt my dreams. Their scared faces staring into the sky as they gasped for a breath. You know what is weird?"

"What?" Tony answered, allowing his friend to finish his story.

"You always see this kind of stuff in those old war movies. As they laid there dying, I held their hand as the medic worked frantically trying to save them. They both looked at me with the most serene expressions just before their last breath, and told me to tell their mothers that they loved them," Rodger finished with tears welling up in his eyes.

"You did all you could do, Rodger. Just like we did all we could do today. It was out of our hands."

"I know, but that doesn't make it any easier. I know their families. I had supper at Jim Nelson's house last weekend for Christ's sake. His kids wrestled with me on the floor as he helped his wife clear the table. And now, they have no father."

Tony said nothing, but put his arm around his friend.

Ben Lassiter was frantically typing the weapons inventory into the SIPRNET e-mail program. His typing skills were sorely lacking, taking him twice the time it would have taken anyone else. Everyone could hear his complaining, even whispered under his breath.

Chapter 37

John Bastian stood looking over his notes with bloodshot eyes. He had not slept in the last seventy-two hours and neither had most of his team. Just as they had given up hope, a young scientist had taken the idea of satellite triangulation which most consumer grade Global Positioning Systems use in determining their position on the earth's surface and combined it with a simple scanning device marine researchers use to track underwater sea life. The idea was so basic that everyone had overlooked its simplicity.

However, this was the closest they had come to finding a solution to detection over a long distance. Computer programmers were now frantically writing code into the receiver so the device could pick up the probe's transmissions. This was it. If this didn't work, they had nothing else to fall back on.

John looked around the room at the scientists and they all appeared to be defeated. The only one who actually thought this had a chance to succeed was the one who came up with the idea. John even secretly thought it was not going to work.

"How long before the program code is finished, so we can test it?" John asked one of the programmers with short hair and thick black-rimmed glasses.

"Give us another thirty minutes, and we should have something ready for testing."

"You got it—take your time. I want it right the first time."

John picked up the phone and dialed Ryan's extension.

"Ryan, I think we may have something worth testing in another thirty minutes. We are just finishing the programming."

"Damn, that is the best news I have heard in a long time. I will be down shortly," Ryan said as he hung up the phone.

John walked over to the three engineers working on the box that would hold the receiver unit. It needed to be small enough to fit into a coat pocket, which was proving to be difficult, but not impossible.

"How is it going?" John asked them, not wanting to bother them too much.

"We are almost finished," one of them said dryly, annoyed at the interruption. "As soon as the programmers are finished, we should be able to make the final assembly."

"That is good news. We won't need it for the initial testing, so keep working on it," John said, putting his hands on their shoulders.

"We would have finished it long before now, but we had to design the unit from scratch. Most of the commercial GPS devices are much too small to fit the circuitry this receiver will have. We also have no idea how sensitive the antenna will be once it is completed. The high gain antenna will be collapsible to make its footprint smaller. If needed, the antenna will expand to a full three feet, so we shouldn't have to worry about satellite reception in any part of the world. The main problem with off the shelf GPS units is that the bi-directional antennas don't have enough power to pick up reception in cities with all the interference."

"I have all the faith in the world in you guys. This part of the project is way out of my league."

"Sorry—didn't mean to bore you with too many specifics. I'm getting a little punchy."

"No problem here. We are all getting a little tired. Let me know if you need anything."

"Will do."

John continued to circle the room checking in on each team. The noise in the room was nearly overwhelming to him, but it didn't seem to bother the others. Once in a while, one would get loud as tensions became strained, but for the most part, each team was working diligently on their individual parts of the project with the deadline fast approaching.

He was satisfied on the renewed progress and took the opportunity to sit in his chair and rest his feet. It had been many years since he had worked this long without a break. He couldn't even tell what day it was and only knew the time because he habitually looked at his expensive Rolex on his tanned wrist. The room itself had no external windows, and no one came or left the room since they started working. The only person who had visited was the Director.

The work had picked up in earnest now that the scientists had a purpose. This was the closest they had come in nearly four days and John was actually gaining a level of confidence in the new direction the project was taking.

"Sir, we are ready to test the programming. As soon as the circuitry is finished, we can download it and give it a try," the youngest programmer said with an eager look in his eyes.

"Very good, check with the electrical engineers and find out when they will be ready," John said, not bothering to stand just yet.

The programmer walked off in search of the engineering team working on the internal circuitry boards. John checked his watch one more time and decided it was time to get things moving again. The thirty minutes he had given Ryan were almost up, and he wanted to get the test underway.

He met the programmer walking back.

"What is the ETA from the engineers?" John asked.

"They are finishing up the interface to accept the program as we speak, but they have yet to figure out how to boost the power to the antenna."

"Can initial testing be completed without the antenna?"

"Theoretically it should work. As soon as they are finished, we can upload the tracking software. That should give us a basic idea of how the receiver will perform."

"Excellent, we don't have a lot of time for testing so let's upload the program with or without the antenna."

"I will let you know as soon as it is done."

"Mr. Palmer will be here soon," John said, glancing at his watch again. "Keep your fingers crossed that your program works the first time."

"If what you told us was true about the probe, we should have no problem testing it out without the antenna. We have all been injected with it so it should pick up everyone in the room."

"That's exactly what I am counting on."

The programmer walked off for a final check of his work before the initial test. John walked over to visit with the engineers.

"Hey, guys, how are things coming along?" John asked. One of the engineers had a large magnifying glass attached to a band on his head. He meticulously soldered small wires to the fragile board attaching them permanently in place. The hot smell of the soldering iron hung in the stale air as he expertly attached a pigtail of wiring to the ten-inch board filled with resisters and capacitors. In the middle of the long board was a large square processor fitted with an odd looking fan mounted directly on top of it to help in cooling the silicone based graphite chip. John was amazed at how fast he worked.

The engineer looked up as John looked over his back, the magnifying glass making his eye look five times its normal size. The look actually made John smile a bit, which was the first time in days—and it felt good.

"I think we are finished with the connection piece. Let me clean up the soldering and we can take it over to the computer for the upload," he said, still looking through the large glass.

"The sooner the better. We don't have much time."

"I know. We are working as fast as we can," the man said, returning to work with the hot solder before the iron cooled.

Just as John turned away, he caught sight of Ryan through the long row of windows down the length of hallway wall. His heart immediately started to beat faster, and he felt his mouth go dry as he watched Ryan enter the outer doors. He walked over to the inner doors to meet Ryan as he entered. He wanted to stall Ryan another ten minutes and decided an overview of the progress was the best way to give the engineers time to finish the board and the programmers time to upload the software.

John held out his hand to Ryan as soon as he entered.

"Dr. Bastian, I hope you have good news for me."

"I do, but first let me tell you that this team is, without a doubt, one of the best I have ever worked with."

"That is good to hear. I handpicked them myself from our staff. They are all employed by the CIA."

"So, the platform we came up with works on the same principle as the standard hand-held personal GPS units—a bit more complex mind you, but based loosely on it," John started the explanation. "It uses a complex system of satellite triangulation to determine the location of the unit and also the location of the probe. Our new GPS receiver uses differential control segmenting to narrow down the positioning accuracy from hundreds of meters to less than one meter. The real beauty, however—the specialized receiver is sensitive enough to pick up the transmission of a probe nearly 250 miles away," John said with a smile. "For this, we bastardized a marine tracking device much like the ones used to track whales and dolphins."

"We were hoping for 500 miles," Ryan said with a frown on his face.

"We could never get enough power to the antenna and still have the unit portable. The tricky part was in the programming." John glanced over his shoulder and saw the discreet thumbs up sign from the programmer. "I think we are ready to try the initial testing of the software. If you would like to come with me, we can see how it works," John said, motioning Ryan to the programmer's table.

The programmers were just finishing uploading the software into the new receiver. It still looked very crude without the casing, but it was far enough along to test. The small five-inch LCD screen dangled by wires attached to the circuit board laying flat on the table. The programmers were frantically overseeing the upload in rapt anticipation.

Before the unit was powered up for the first time, John called every member of the team around the small eight-foot table. He wanted this to be a celebration of success for their hard work. As a matter of protocol, the physical act of switching it on fell on Dr. Bastian as more than a couple members of the team stood with fingers crossed behind their backs.

With little fanfare, John pushed the red power button and the five-inch square LCD screen flashed to life. A collective sigh could be heard around the table as the programming initialized. At first, the unit appeared to be dead, but then the triangulation screen displayed attempting to establish a connection to the satellites. Their earlier sighs fell on deaf ears as the LCD screen displayed an error while attempting to establish its location. John felt a flash of embarrassment and nearly had a panic attack as the screen went black. An electrical engineer quickly ran to his table, grabbed the new antenna returning with a soldering iron. Within minutes the new antenna was attached and the unit was powered on again.

After the initialization screen, the attempt at triangulation now picked up four satellites, pinpointed its exact location, displaying it on a color map. The panicky feeling John had moments before was replaced by sheer excitement as the second part of the programming began after a press of another button.

Without specific programming, the receiver would pick up all available probes transmitting within the search radius. The team waited patiently as several lights blinked on the board indicating the software was actually working. The room was deathly quiet, as the screen remained blank for another minute before displaying several probes on the screen as tiny red dots. So many red dots appeared on the small screen; in fact, the small unit could not handle the reception traffic and it blanked out.

Cheers erupted around the table as hands flew up in the air. Everyone was hugging and shaking hands. The exhaustion of the last few days was forgotten as they all focused on the success of the receiver. The engineers immediately went back to work, finishing the casing that would protect the valuable contents during transport.

"Well done, John," Ryan said with the largest smile on his face.

"It was more than me. This team made the project a success."

"As soon as it is ready, I want you to call me. I am going to need you to go with me to the Oval Office. I couldn't even begin to explain the complexity of this project to the president."

"The president of the United States?" John asked. "You want me to brief the president of the United States? Oh, my wife will never believe this."

"Yes, but before we go I want the final piece tested and ready to go. We don't have time to waste. I am sure you can appreciate that."

"Absolutely, I wasn't implying anything. I just didn't expect to be meeting the president today is all. Of course, I didn't expect to be plucked from the bay either."

"I understand. All you need to do is be there to answer the questions I can't. In other words, keep your mouth shut unless we need you. One thing I know he is going ask is how long do you estimate before the receiver will be ready?"

"It should take a couple more hours. The engineers are finalizing the antenna placement and housing to accept the larger circuit board. You will be the first to know when it is finished."

"John, I can't tell you how big this is. I couldn't ask any more from you than what I have already. As soon as we are finished briefing the president you can go home. However, and this is a big however, you must understand that nothing can be said about what you have done here."

"It's not the first time I have heard those words. I will say nothing about it."

"Good. I will be in my office starting plans on how to get this receiver into the hands of those who need it. What are the chances of you coming up with another one in the next two hours?"

"I would think the chances are pretty good. The hard part is over. We just need to duplicate our efforts."

"Do it, then call me," Ryan said as he stepped inside the "dirty" room to remove his white suit. Before he opened the outer door, he flashed the thumbs up sign to John and exited the room.

Chapter 38

Alexander still sat in complete silence in the second floor office unaware of what was transpiring below him. He had not set foot out of the office since arriving over twenty-four hours ago. In his mind, he was avenging his family's death at the hands of the Russians and nothing, not even the pleadings of his friends would persuade him otherwise.

The sun was now setting, but the un-insulated walls of the warehouse still radiated heat like the inside of an oven. His dark hair was soaked and his shirt was stained dark with sweat. The stress of the day had taken its toll. Not just on his mind—his body was exhausted.

He had nothing to eat or drink since the day before and his mind was slowly deteriorating into a state of hunger-induced delirium. The throbbing pain in his hand had lessened considerably, but the swelling in his fingers would still not allow him to make a fist. He could feel the tiny bones in his fingers were fractured, but it was of minor concern at the moment. He would not allow his mind to dwell on the pain or the inconvenience of the temporary handicap of having only one usable hand.

With all the remaining energy he could muster he stood and paced the metal deck surrounding the office. From here he could survey the situation and eavesdrop on the conversation among his men. He could not, and would not, allow them to walk away from this. He wouldn't admit it to anyone, but himself that he needed them now more than ever.

The men were all resting on the floor after getting a quick bite to eat. He glanced at Shevard who was snoring loudly with his head resting on a rolled up blanket he had taken from the trunk of the Lada. He knew they needed the rest and he didn't want to bother them.

The American was still blindfolded sitting with his back on the bare metal wall. Alexander smiled a very crooked smile, seeing the powerful man bound and helpless. He wanted nothing more than to talk to the man. Alexander was positive that if he could make the man understand their cause that the Americans would put pressure on the Russians to move out of his country. It was only at the last minute that he decided that he was being foolish. The Americans would never understand his hardships and tragedies.

Andre heard the pacing of hard plastic soles on the metal grating above him. He slowly opened his eyes to see Alexander standing fifteen feet above them. To Andre he looked like a general looking over his soldiers preparing for battle. Andre did not stir, but continued to eye his friend, appearing from above to be sleeping. He did not want to confront him again just yet. He knew what would happen when Shevard and Leonid woke after getting some badly needed rest. They had eaten a bit, even if it was only a few pieces of hard bread and canned meat and had enough leftover to give their captive. The confrontation would be deadly—that was a foregone conclusion. He just didn't know who would be killed.

Andre was finished with trying to talk with his friend. He meant what he said to him earlier. He was no longer a brother to him. However, he was positive that no matter what happened, he couldn't kill him. No, they had been through too much together for him to do that. He just couldn't let Shevard or Alexander know that.

The hard soled shoes tapped again at the metal grating as Alexander walked back into the office. Andre took the time to recollect his thoughts. He had to come up with a plan. He had to talk to the American. That was the easy part. The tricky part was doing it away from the eyes of the others.

He sat up quickly, feeling a little dizzy and disoriented. The others were sleeping soundly. This was his time. He could talk now without anyone getting suspicious. He didn't know what he was going to ask. He just knew he needed to talk. He quietly made his way over to the American, concealing his movements by hiding between the cars.

He slowly approached the man sitting with his back to the wall and guardedly looked up at the office to make sure he couldn't be seen. With a gentle touch on the American's arm to let him know someone was near, he started to think about what he wanted to say. David flinched slightly at the surprised intrusion, but made no sound.

Andre began in a whisper. "Don't move, I am not going to hurt you."

The vice president did not move except for a slight nod to acknowledge the man talking.

"I am afraid we have made a mistake in taking you. We thought we were taking a Russian politician, not an American."

Still the man made no movement. He was blind, not deaf. He had heard the others talking around him. In the large building it was tough to keep a conversation a secret.

"I am trying to work out a way to let you go, and we walk away from this as if nothing happened. We have nothing against you or your country," Andre continued to whisper.

David listened as best he could. He could tell in the sound and tone of the voice, the man was being genuine.

"Are you crazy?" David asked in a raspy whispered voice. "You will not be able to walk away from this. The American government will come for you. Your only hope is to give up and turn me over to the Russian government. I will do what I can to help save your lives, but mistake or not, you will not be able to just walk away from this," David frantically whispered.

"You have no idea who we are. We can walk away and leave you here to starve. The Americans have no idea where you are," Andre laughed quietly. "You don't even know where you are."

"I know I am not in Russia," David said confidently.

"That's right, you're not, but the world is a big place, and the fact still remains, you are blindfolded and helpless," Andre said, trying not to let his anger show. "I think you will find, sir, we can walk away and disappear."

David's mouth broke into a smile and he placed his head back on the hot metal wall. "You are naïve, you are all naïve. Do you not think we can't find you if you leave. Your fingerprints must be all over this place. All we need is to find one print and the rest will be easy."

Those words smacked Andre square in the face. He had not considered that possibility, but the man was right. They couldn't walk away from this now, not even if they wanted to. He was also surprised how strong the man was. He obviously had not slept in days, had very little to eat and was still defiant in his hopes to live.

"You are wrong. We do have another option. We kill you, drop you in the gutter far away from this building, and then walk," Andre said as he quietly moved back to his sleeping position. He didn't want them to know what he had just done, especially Shevard. Somehow getting the last word in made him feel so much better.

Shevard stirred awake just as Andre returned. He looked over at Andre and back at the man sitting against the wall.

"So, what did he say?" Shevard asked.

"Who, what are you talking about?" Andre said, feigning surprise.

"You know damn well who I am talking about. Don't play stupid with me."

"I just wanted him to understand that we made a mistake."

"You are damn lucky Alexander didn't hear you."

"I was careful. He won't suspect a thing."

"So what did he say?"

Andre didn't want to talk to Shevard here, not in front of the others. Andre motioned for him to walk across the building away from the prying ears.

Andre glanced up at the office careful to keep his back to the office door. He didn't want Alexander to see them talking.

"Shevard, he said we couldn't walk away from here. The Americans will come and even if we are not here they will find us. They can get our fingerprints from anything we touched. It will be impossible to clean this entire building." Shevard looked around at the dust-covered surfaces, keenly aware of everywhere they had been. The dust would be the dead giveaway. Andre was right.

"So, what do you propose we do then?"

"I don't know. I am working on it. I am sure there is something we can do short of killing someone to get out of this alive ourselves."

Shevard fished a cigarette out of his pocket and lit it with his lighter. "While you work, I am going to get something to eat. I am starving," the large man said, walking away, shaking his head in disgust.

The other two men were sitting on the hood of the Lada, opening a can of meat. Shevard grabbed a box of crackers, offered it to the other two, and grabbed a can for himself.

"So, what are we going to do, Shevard?"

"I don't know. Andre is still working out a plan. I am disgusted with this whole thing. I think we should leave Andre and Alexander here to fight it out on their own. It is clear they aren't going to be persuaded to do anything until it is too late."

The two stared at the meat and thought about what Shevard had said. They didn't want to die either and it would be the three of them against two.

"But—But you heard Alexander," Leonid spoke up with a full mouth. "He would kill us before we made it out the door."

"Alexander," Shevard said with disgust, "he is nothing to me."

Chapter 39

Jennifer Cleary had just spent the last two weeks in a sand-infested motel in the middle of Baghdad. She was gathering research for CNN on the treatment of women in the new Iraq. She spent most of her time on the phone setting up interviews, only to be left waiting at the last minute because of the lack of a security detail. She had been around long enough to know that you didn't risk your life on the streets of the broken city without an escort. Western women alone on the streets of Baghdad were more sought after than diamonds.

She did, however, manage to get enough footage to produce a series of three, ten-minute spots exposing the deplorable conditions and treatment women still endured in the new Iraq. The first of which would be airing tonight during the CNN *Primetime* newscast. It wasn't the first time she had this much airtime, but it was the most satisfying.

With her long legs, long flowing brown hair, and sparkling blue eyes, she could have been a model. After her sophomore year at Georgetown, she switched majors from marketing to journalism and found a passion in reporting. With her stunning looks and intimate knowledge of Washington, DC, she was a shoe in for the field reporter position at the local news station, WKDC and she quickly moved up to her current position as lead field reporter for CNN International. At twenty-six, she was destined for great things and with her hard-nosed tactics and penchant for getting the story, she made one hell of a reporter.

With cause for celebration, she was out with some friends at a local hangout in downtown D.C. when her producer called her cell phone.

"Jennifer, I know you just finished up the Iraq expose, but I need you to find out some information on a kidnapping at Johns Hopkins that just came across the wire. The government is being tight lipped about the whole thing. They won't give us any information. See what your sources inside the White House can do. We just need someone to confirm the story before we take it to air. I want to be the first with this, so do what you can and get back to me ASAP," Cal, her producer, said, ending the call.

She pushed the end call button and stared at the small LCD screen on the phone. *Jesus, I haven't had time to celebrate,* she thought as she slowly closed the small phone and looked at her girlfriends laughing around the bar. She didn't even walk back to them before making the call to her source in the White House.

The voice on the other end of the phone sounded out of breath. Jennifer looked at her watch and kicked herself for calling this late at night. She hadn't even considered the time when she dialed the numbers.

"Hello," the voice said.

"Hello, this is Jen. Did I catch you at a bad time?"

"Jesus, Ms. Cleary, you *newsies* have a thing for bad timing. Don't you people ever sleep?"

"I am sorry. I didn't realize what time it was."

"Give me a second," the voice said. Jennifer could hear a muffled whisper as he pressed his phone to his chest. She knew he was banging his wife, but she needed the information badly.

"Okay, Ms. Cleary, what is so urgent that you bothered me at this hour?"

"I have unconfirmed reports that the baby taken from Johns Hopkins was adopted by a high-ranking government official. I also heard that the kidnapping was linked to the terrorist seen in Toronto three days ago," Jennifer said, bluffing her way into a story. She had no clue what she was talking about, but was the quintessential reporter, finding ways to back people into corners to get what she needed.

"Jesus, where did you get that information?"

"Come now, you know I can't reveal my sources."

"It sounds as if your sources are quite well informed even if the story is a bit convoluted."

"Convoluted...I think you will find my facts are right on target."

"I don't know about that."

"Think what you want. That is the story I am going to air unless you can give me something different." Jennifer had done it. She had backed him into a corner so that he either had to confirm it or give her what she wanted.

"You can't strong arm me, Ms. Cleary. I am not a person you want to threaten—air what you like."

She thought she had lost her edge with him, but at the last minute she heard a strong sigh, and she knew she had him against the ropes.

"You listen to me," the voice said. "The baby was to be adopted by a high level official, and that is all I will say about that. You will have to do more dredge work to find out who it is. We don't have a connection to this and the terrorist, but the CIA is working on it as we speak," the voice trailed off.

She had her opening and she decided to open it even more.

"The CIA, why the CIA when this was obviously an FBI investigation?"

"The CIA came in and took the investigation out of the FBI's hands. I don't know why. Why don't you find out and then call me? You know the arrogance of the CIA—they think they have jurisdiction over everything."

She was having luck and decided to press him for just a bit more.

"Who is heading up the investigation?"

"Christ, Ms. Cleary, you really like to lay on the full court press. I don't have a clue. If you want my opinion, this wouldn't have happened if the CIA had done its job. They took over the investigation to cover up their mistakes." He smiled as he spoke the words.

"I see. Well, thank you for your time, and keep in touch. Maybe we can get together for drinks soon. That is if you can get away from that wife of yours."

"Right, that is what you are. A news whore," the man said as he hung up.

Those words hit her like a ton of bricks. A whore, is that what he just called her? She flipped her phone closed and jammed it into her designer purse and walked back to the bar.

She was taken aback at the words and decided to order a scotch on the rocks to settle her down before making another call.

"I am sorry, girls, but I am going to have to make this a short night," she said as she downed the scotch in two swallows. "It seems as if another story is about to break wide open, and I am going to be on top of it. Who knows? This time next year, we may be toasting my promotion to night anchor."

"You go, girl," one of her friends said, lifting a glass of Chardonnay as a send off.

"Wish me luck, and don't forget to watch the news."

On the way out the door of the club, Jennifer pulled her phone out of purse and placed her second call of the night to one of her many contacts in the CIA.

The phone rang five times and then transferred to an answering service. She didn't leave a message preferring instead to hang up and try again in the morning. She wanted the call to be a surprise. Unexpected calls always produced the best results. The final call she made to her producer.

"Hi, this is Jennifer."

"What did you find out?"

"I caught him completely by surprise. He confirmed that the infant was to be adopted by a high-ranking politician, but wouldn't give up the name. He also said the CIA was leading the investigation into the kidnapping. I tried to contact the CIA, but couldn't get anything this late at night. I will try first thing in the morning. Sit tight on the story until you hear from me. I want to get this one right."

"Ok, I will sit on it for twelve hours. That gives you until noon tomorrow to have something on my desk. Oh, nice job on that Iraq piece. The ratings were through the roof tonight."

"Thank you. It was a tough story to get, that is for sure."

"Noon tomorrow, Jennifer. I want to be the first."

"You'll have it! I promise," she said as she flipped the phone closed.

She decided to catch a cab rather than walk the seven blocks to her apartment. Even the time she spent in Baghdad didn't make her hard enough to walk the streets of downtown Washington D.C. alone at midnight. She gave the driver a ten-dollar bill and exited the cab in front of her apartment building. The night security guard was standing on the sidewalk outside the door.

"Good evening, Ms. Cleary," the man said with a slight tip of his cap.

"Good evening, Clarence," she said, smiling up at him. He was her favorite of all the security guards. Only because he was the one she saw coming in most nights well after midnight.

She walked into the lobby and pressed the button to the elevator as her mind ran over her earlier conversation. One thing bothered her. Why would her contact sell out the CIA so easily? He obviously wanted this to take the focus off the White House. The CIA had been the fall organization since the Gulf War. The negative publicity and lack of support they received following those nasty public Senate hearings made them an easy target. But, why the CIA, and why now?

It was dark and deathly hot in her small studio apartment. She wasn't home enough to need anything bigger. She flipped on her kitchen light and decided to make a cup of instant coffee as she thought about approaching her only contact at the CIA. She needed to ask the right questions to get the information she was looking for.

She turned on the television and flipped through the channels. At this time of the morning, the only shows on were those useless info-commercials and old movies that no one liked. She wasn't interested in watching, she just wanted some sound in the quiet room. She sipped the hot coffee as she thought.

The sunlight came through her apartment window as her eyes fluttered open. She hated falling asleep on the couch, but the last thing she remembered was watching some show about penguins on PBS. She quickly got up, gathered her thoughts, and put the tea kettle on for another cup of coffee.

While she waited for the water to heat, she went into the bathroom to brush her teeth. She must have slept with her mouth open all night because her mouth felt pasty. She put the toothpaste on her brush and watered it down with warm water. She didn't even look in the mirror because she wasn't in the mood. She rinsed her mouth with a quick gulp of water and finished just as the teakettle started to whistle.

Two teaspoons of Maxwell House and a full cup of water was just the strength she needed to jolt her senses to life. She looked at the time on the microwave and picked up the phone to make a call.

"Sharon, how are you?" Jennifer said as soon as she heard the voice.

"Hello, who is speaking?" Sharon asked.

"Sharon, this is Jennifer Cleary. It hasn't been that long has it, girl?"

"Jen, how are you? Jesus, it is early. I haven't talked with you since I was in Senator Chamb—"

"Chamberlain's office," Jennifer finished her sentence. "Sorry, I was anxious to see how you liked the new job? I have been meaning to call, but didn't know how to get in touch with you."

"Right, in touch with me," Sharon trailed off her sentence. "I saw you on the news last night. That was one heck of a piece of reporting."

"Oh, you saw that? It was nothing really. I am just happy to be home."

"Well, you did a nice job," Sharon said, trying to both watch carefully what she said and understand the reason for the call.

"So how do you like the new job?"

"It's great. I love it. My boss works like a dog, though. He hasn't left the office in nearly a week."

"I hate bosses like that. They expect you to work as much as they do."

"No, he isn't like that. He is very nice. Just has a lot on his plate right now."

"I see," Jen said, subtly trying to slide in questions. She didn't want to get Sharon in trouble, but she was the only one Jen knew at the CIA. It was a huge opportunity when she read in the paper that Sharon had moved out of Chamberlain's office. Chamberlain was a crook and everyone knew it except for Sharon. She had no idea and was devoted to him until she started to get suspicious herself.

"So what brings you to call?" Sharon asked.

"Nothing, I just got back in town and wondered if you wanted to get together and talk girl-talk about the rich single Senators in town."

"I am really beat, Jen. I have been working hard and just don't have the energy to go out. Sunday is my only day off this week, and I just want to veg."

"Wow, working on a Saturday. That is something."

"Yes, they are trying to finish an emergency project, and I stayed to see if they needed anything done before I left."

"Project huh, sounds boring. What do you have to do with it?"

"Nothing, really. They brought in this doctor from Johns Hopkins to lead it. I just wanted to stay."

Jennifer's ears perked up as she listened. "Well, if you change your mind, give me a call."

"Don't worry, I won't be changing my mind. It was good to talk to you, though."

"You, too. Don't work too hard. We can have that conversation another time," Jennifer said as she hung up the phone.

Sharon looked curiously at the phone before she hung it up. It wasn't every Sunday she got calls from a CNN reporter. She had many conversations with Jennifer at Chamberlain's office when reporters were trying to dig up dirt on him. She was fully aware that she had to watch what she said, but was satisfied that she didn't let out any secrets today.

As Jennifer hung up the phone her mind went into overdrive. The CIA brought in a doctor from Johns Hopkins to work on a secret project, the same hospital the baby was kidnapped from. She dressed quickly as she thought, and she knew she needed to make a trip to the hospital. The puzzle was coming together, but it was coming at a slower pace than she needed it to.

Sunday traffic in D.C. was nonexistent. She eased into the plush leather seats of her red BMW 535 and started out to Baltimore. She loved this car. It was one of her lavish gifts to herself when she received the job at CNN. She didn't even need a car in the city, but couldn't resist when she test-drove it, and the salesman was cute. She turned the radio down and flipped open her cell phone and punched up her producer in the contact list.

"Cal, this is Jennifer, I am going to need a little more time with this. I think we may be on to more than just a simple kidnapping. My source in the White House all but pinned the responsibility on the CIA, and I just found out the CIA has been working all week on a secret project led by a doctor from Johns Hopkins."

"I will give you more time, but if I get any indications the networks are smelling around I am going with it. What you have is enough for us to run with, but I will wait. This may be your big break."

"We'll see. I am on my way to the hospital right now to see what is cooking there."

"Be careful with this. If it is as big as you think it might be some very powerful people will want to keep it quiet."

"Don't worry about me, Cal. I just got back from dodging suicide bombers. I can handle myself."

"Call me as soon as you have something. Don't wait much longer."

"Gotcha," Jen said. She flipped the phone closed, touched the button to open the moon roof, and cranked the radio as she took the ramp onto the beltway.

Chapter 40

It had been the first in a long time the office was quiet. The large leather chair enveloped him as he rested his head back and closed his eyes. Ryan never really rested because his mind wandered over the conversation he had with Gerry two days before. He had his hopes on the project and the progress was unbelievable. The project was the answer, but after so much time he knew it was a long shot.

The ringing phone brought him back as he reached out to answer it.

"Ryan, I think we are ready. I have the second unit together and tested," John said, sounding absolutely exhausted.

"Excellent," Ryan said, looking at his watch. "It is nearly 0900. I will come down and pick you up, so we can get everything ready to brief the president."

"I would like to shower first if we have time."

"Absolutely, you can use the shower in my office. I will be right down."

Ryan and Dr. Bastian sat in the back seat of the black Mercury as it passed through the empty streets of the city. Ryan was asking questions about the project in an attempt to further understand it, so he didn't feel stupid when they briefed the president.

The car pulled through the gates to the White House and into the nearly empty underground parking garage. The always busy garage was devoid of cars this early on a Sunday morning. They both carried a receiver as they took the elevator up to the oval office.

Bill Snyder was sitting at his desk just outside the door as the two men approached.

"Well, Mr. Palmer, to what do we owe this unexpected surprise?" Snyder asked in his usual weak, mocking voice.

"Mr. Snyder, this is Dr. Bastian. We have the receivers ready and would like to see the president," Ryan said very businesslike.

"I am afraid he is at the White House church services," Snyder said, looking at his watch. "He won't be available for another forty-five minutes."

"Do you mind if we wait out here for him?"

"Do you honestly think those things are going to find the vice president?" Snyder said, standing from his desk to look at the pieces of equipment.

"If I didn't, sir, I wouldn't have spent the last five days busting my ass on them," John said, picking up on the sarcasm. He had never met the man and already didn't like him.

"Do you mind if I take a look at one?" Snyder asked, holding out his hand.

"If it's alright with you, I will hold on to them until the president arrives," Ryan said, turning his back on the man.

"Let me make something perfectly clear, Mr. Palmer," Snyder said, raising his voice. "If these don't work, I will personally see the CIA is destroyed forever," Snyder added, returning to his desk.

Ryan just smiled as he walked back down the hallway away from the man. He didn't even want to respond to such a remark. Anything said in response would have put Ryan on the same level and he was too much of a professional to have that happen.

Ryan and John walked back down to the parking garage to wait in the car. They didn't even want to be close to Bill Snyder.

"I sure as hell hope this thing works," Ryan said as he opened the back door of the large car.

"It will work. I stake my reputation on it," John said as he slammed his door closed.

"Don't worry about Bill Snyder. He's just a political ass-kisser."

"He is a real son-of-a-bitch, isn't he?" John asked, regarding his description as fitting if not politically correct.

"That is an understatement. I do have to warn you, though, the president trusts what he says. If you get on Snyder's bad side, you won't make it far in this town."

"I don't think I have much to worry about. I won't be running for office anytime soon."

"Yes, well just watch what you say around him. I will take care of him. You work your magic with those receivers."

"The receivers will work—trust me on that."

Ryan looked at his watch and scratched his head. He felt a tinge of nervousness as the forty-five minutes passed excruciatingly slow and decided to start a conversation to pass the time.

"John, what is your story? How did you end up heading the team on the project?"

"Well, that is a long story."

Ryan looked at his watch again. "Talk on, we have a while yet, and I need something to take my mind off the meeting.

"Well, it all started when I was a senior at Syracuse. I found a notebook in a back room of one of the science labs as I looked for another piece of research. My curiosity got the best of me, and I read the entire thing that evening. I couldn't get my mind off it, and I approached the professor who started the research the very next day."

"Yes, that was Professor Greeley."

"Yes," John said, surprised that Ryan knew about Greeley. "He tried to get me to forget about it, but I couldn't. I joined the Army after graduation to help pay for medical school and during my residency program, I was asked to join a top-secret project. With my background, I became the lead scientist on the project, and we worked for two years in complete secrecy on creating the probe."

"That must have been interesting work," Ryan added.

"Yes, at the time we were making incredible breakthroughs in technology. You must remember this was back in the 1950s. Technology was just starting to come into its own. However, as a medical doctor, I soon became concerned about the ethical issues of the probes if the process of injections became mainstream. I voiced those concerns to my superiors, and soon I found myself on the outside looking in."

"That must have been tough—watching a project you had created being worked on by someone you didn't even know."

"It was at first, but I finally had the time to start a family and I forgot about it until a few days ago."

"John, you should be proud of yourself. What you have accomplished is nothing to be ashamed of," Ryan said in a sincere tone.

"I am not ashamed, not at all. I am worried, though, that my concerns about the project back then are about to be made public. As a medical doctor you must understand that I injected the probes as a matter of public health, nothing more. What the government decides to do with the receiver after this is over is in your hands," John said staring at Ryan.

"I have considered that. Let's hope that this doesn't get out to the press before we have a chance to destroy those receivers." Ryan looked once again at his watch. "It is time to go up. Are you ready?"

"If it means I can get home to my wife, I am ready for anything."

The elevator door closed quickly behind them as they walked down the hallway. Each man had butterflies as they clutched the receivers in their sweaty palms. Bill Snyder's desk was empty, but Sally was sitting at her desk.

"Good morning, Sally. How are you today?" Ryan asked.

"Good morning, Mr. Ryan. I am fine, thanks. He knows you are here—have a seat."

"Thank you. Let me introduce Dr. John Bastian."

"It is nice to meet you, Dr. Bastian," Sally said, standing, holding out her hand.

John took her hand. "It is nice to meet you as well."

"So, let's see if he is ready. I know he is anxious to see you," she said, pressing the intercom button on the phone.

"Yes, sir, Mr. Palmer and a Dr. Bastian are waiting to see you," she said into the phone. "Yes, certainly, sir."

"He is talking with Mr. Snyder right now about the clean-up efforts in Texas. He is almost finished. It shouldn't be much longer."

"Thank you," Ryan said, taking a seat outside the door. "I am surprised to see you here on a Sunday," he said to her, trying to make small talk to calm his stomach.

"It seems as if my job never ends," she said as the door opened, and Bill Snyder emerged.

"Good luck," she whispered to the two of them.

"Okay, gentlemen—show time. The president is waiting to see what you have for him," Snyder said, raising his hands toward the large white door.

The two men stood and gave themselves the once over before walking through the large door. Satisfied they were presentable under the circumstances they followed Snyder into the office.

The president was still in his suit coat and tie talking on the phone as they walked in. They couldn't quite make out what he was talking about, but by his tone he wasn't happy. Neither of the two felt comfortable on the hot seat, and John was more nervous than he could ever remember.

John looked around the room taking in the atmosphere. He never would have believed in a million years he would be standing in the Oval Office. He reveled for a moment in the history, and the many world changing events this office had witnessed. Presidents and world leaders had stood in the very same spot he was standing today. His eye stopped on the red phone made famous during the cold war, sitting on a table next to the president's desk. The sobering thought of nuclear war increased his butterflies, and he continued to look around the office. The large white marble mantle was impressive and the painting of George Washington over it was an original Peale, he was sure of that.

The one item that caught his eye was the massive desk. The ornate carved panels on its front and sides were amazingly intricate, he thought, as he identified the presidential seal on the front center panel.

The president waved them closer as he ended the phone conversation.

"Mr. President, allow me to introduce Dr. Bastian," Ryan said.

Dr. Bastian extended his hand to the president and they shook hands. John was actually in a state of awe as he touched the president of the United States.

"Dr. Bastian, I have heard so much about you over the past couple of days," the president said, using his other hand to grab John's elbow as they continued to shake hands.

"I hope it was all good. That is a beautiful piece of furniture," John said nervously as they concluded the extended handshake.

"You have a good eye for antiques," the president said, smiling. "Actually, Queen Victoria commissioned this desk in 1880 out of timber from the HMS Resolute. It was presented to President Hayes, and it has been called the Resolute desk ever since. So, what do you have for me?"

John took a deep breath and began his explanation of the development of the receiver. He gave the president the one he was holding.

"The receivers look nearly identical to ones that can be purchased at any sporting goods store. However, these are the Porches of the GPS world. They have the tracking ability to receive two different signals to pinpoint the device's location and pick up the transmission of a probe within a radius of two hundred fifty miles. This dual ability allows the unit to accurately pinpoint the location of the probe within three feet," John said in a matter of fact tone.

"Three feet—that is impressive," the president said, whistling. "Can I turn it on?"

"Certainly, we have programmed the infant's number into the unit, so it won't pick up anything, but that specific transmission. If we didn't do that we would pick up a million hits and blow the receiver out of your hands and may even melt the case," John said jokingly.

"Right, melt the case. That is amusing," Snyder said with a leer.

"The two units have each been specially programmed with the individual probe transmitter address. The probe you have now, Mr. President, is the one programmed for the infant taken out of my hospital ward. Mr. Palmer has the one going to Moscow."

"This is excellent work. Mr. Palmer. Now that they are finished, what is your plan to get it to Lassiter?" the president asked.

Ryan looked at the faces of the three men in the room stopping at John.

"Mr. President, I think the best way to ensure the success of this operation is to have John deliver the unit himself. If something should happen, an equipment malfunction or problem with the programming, he will be there to correct it."

The president looked at John to see how he took the news. It was obvious that this was the first time he had heard the plan. "I think that makes perfect sense. Dr. Bastian, how do you feel about it?"

John looked at Ryan before he answered. "I am no spy. I can't conduct your secret games. I have done what you asked, but this is where it ends. I haven't seen my wife in over a week. I have a job at the hospital," John stammered, searching for more excuses.

"I understand perfectly," the president said in response. "We will find someone else. Don't worry about it, Dr. Bastian, you have given us all we have expected and more. Ryan, do you have anyone on the team who would be willing to go?"

"I am sure I can find someone," Ryan said softly, looking at John.

"Ryan, I want the one programmed for the infant in Buffalo by this evening," the president said, returning the receiver to John.

"Yes, sir, I have a helicopter waiting to have it delivered. I will send two agents this afternoon to take control of the investigation. It shouldn't be long now."

"Keep me informed, and remember, don't expose this to the press," the president said. Snyder's ears picked up as he heard those words.

John looked at the hardwood floor, afraid to look up. He knew he was the only person qualified to deliver the receiver, and Ryan was right. If there was a problem, he could fix it. He looked once again into Ryan's eyes before speaking.

"I'll do it."

"Excuse me, Dr. Bastian?" the president asked.

"I'll deliver the receiver to Moscow."

"That is good news," the president said, slapping the older man on the back, thankful that he wouldn't have to order him to deliver it. "Now that we have that settled, let's get to it. How long before we can have him on a plane to Moscow?"

"I will drop John by his house to pick up a change of clothes and see his wife and then have him on a plane by nightfall."

"Hot damn," the president said, slapping his hands together. "I think we are making some positive progress. The sooner you get there, the sooner we will get David back. Don't waste any time. The United States is counting on you and that little piece of technology you are holding in your hand. Ryan, I will call Andrews and have a plane ready for the trip."

"With all due respect, sir, I think it is best if we book him a commercial flight. We have one plane there already. I wouldn't want to risk a second. The situation over there is still not settled, and an American plane on the runway may be just the thing to rattle their chains," Ryan said.

"What about airport security? How will you get him through with that device."

"I will personally put him on the plane. I am not all that worried about Moscow, to be honest. I will have Lassiter's men meet him at the airport and help him through customs if he gets held up."

"I will go with whatever you think is best, Mr. Palmer. Just keep me informed on the status."

John stood, unable to comprehend what he had just got himself into. He couldn't refuse an order from the president.

"Very good," Ryan said as he led John out the door of the Oval Office, leaving the president and Bill Snyder to talk.

"Why the hell didn't you tell me about your plan?" John asked Ryan as the pair walked down the hallway.

"If I told you before, you would have said no immediately."

"That is true, I would have."

"I knew that if I put you on the spot in front of the president you couldn't say no. You scared me for a second though, I must admit."

"Well, I scared myself. I can't believe what I just volunteered to do."

"It will be okay. I will make sure to call Ben Lassiter personally, and tell him take good care of you."

The two men entered the car and started out to Roland Park. John was excited to get home and kiss his wife. This was the longest the two had been apart for a very long time. He had only talked with her once and told her that he was okay.

The car ride was quiet as they made their way onto the 695 beltway. John couldn't quite describe the feeling he was experiencing at this very moment. He thought over the past few days and never would have dreamed he would have been swinging on a rope under a helicopter, finishing a project he started forty years ago, or meeting the president of the United States. Now, he was heading to Russia to help find the vice president. He had to admit that he felt like a twenty-year-old again. He thought about his wife again and wondered if he could perform like a twenty-year-old.

Inside of forty minutes, the car pulled into the driveway of the beautiful Victorian home, and John opened his door. Ryan also exited the Mercury, meeting John on the sidewalk.

"Pack enough clothes for a few days. Make sure you keep the receiver safe. I will have the paperwork ready to get you through customs. I will send a car out for you in," Ryan looked at his watch, "four hours. I need you to brief the two agents I am sending to Buffalo, and then I will escort you to the airport."

"Who should I be meeting when I get there?"

"Don't worry about the specifics. We'll go over all of that at the airport. Tell your wife that I personally thank her for her patience and understanding."

"Yes, I will do that," John said, looking at the ground. "Ryan," John said, looking up briefly.

"Yes?"

"I want to thank you. You have made me feel useful again. I haven't had this much excitement in my life in many years."

"No, it is I who should be thanking you. I could never tell you how much I am indebted to you."

John shook his head and started toward the house, seeing his wife waiting for him on the front porch. Maggie came bounding out the door, running across the porch to meet him on the walk.

He put his knee on the first step of the porch and scratched her ears as she licked his face.

"Oh, I missed you, girl."

"I suppose you missed her more than you did me," Georgia said with a wicked grin.

John stood and embraced his wife with both arms, lifting her off the porch.

"My goodness, John, where did that come from?"

"I don't know, but there is more from wherever it came from," John said with a wink of his eye.

"You dirty man," Georgia said, playfully slapping his chest. "Not out here on the porch—who knows what the neighbors will think."

"Screw the neighbors," John said, slapping her on the ass as they walked through the front door.

*

270

Agents Jackson and Flaherty walked into the director's office just after 4:00 Sunday afternoon. They had no idea why they were called to the office, but they were not going to refuse an order like this. They looked at each other as they waited for the director to finish in the bathroom.

Ryan exited his bathroom and looked at the two young agents. They oddly reminded him of how he used to be when he was a rookie. He was always nicely dressed and eager to take on any project that came along. He knew they must be nervous, so he decided to put them out of their misery and tell them why they were called.

"You two picked up Dr. Bastian in the bay, is that correct?"

"Yes, sir, we did. Did we do something wrong?"

"Sit down and relax. You are not being called on the carpet," Ryan said, smiling, offering them a chair.

The two men let out their breath as they rigidly sat in the chairs. "I don't understand, sir. What was so urgent for a Sunday if we didn't do anything wrong?"

"I need you two to lead an investigation in Buffalo for me."

"Buffalo, sir?" Agent Jackson asked.

"Yes, you heard me correctly, Buffalo. I want you two there ASAP. The FBI is looking into a possible connection between the crossing of PFLP terrorists from Canada and the kidnapping of the infant from Johns Hopkins."

"Excuse me, sir, I don't understand. Isn't that the FBI's job?"

"Yes it is, but like you showing up here on my orders, I was ordered by the president to take over this investigation. You wouldn't want me to get in hot water, now would you?"

"Of course not, sir. We will start out immediately. What is our level of authority?" Agent Flaherty asked.

"As I said, we suspect the terrorists may be responsible for the kidnapping of a baby from Johns Hopkins. That is all I can tell you about it. The FBI Agent in charge in Buffalo is an Agent Metcalf. You are to coordinate all activities with local and state authorities. But do me a favor—don't step on his toes too much. Before you go, I have Dr. John Bastian here to give you some information to take with you," Ryan said.

"Hello, gentlemen," John said.

"Hello, sir," the two young agents said.

John held the receiver in his hands. "This is a customized version of a standard GPS unit," John said, giving them the abridged version of the story. He was sure they wouldn't understand the details, and he didn't have the time anyway. The unit is programmed to receive a transmission I injected into the baby less than an hour after he was born. The range of reception is two hundred fifty miles as long as satellite reception is strong enough. The unit should put you within ten feet of the baby."

"I don't understand," Flaherty said. "Did you know the baby was going to be kidnapped?"

"Absolutely not," John answered.

"Then why inject the baby with a transmitter?"

Ryan intercepted this question before John had a chance to talk.

"Don't worry about that right now. Just concentrate on the function of the GPS receiver."

John glanced at Ryan. Ryan nodded to him to continue.

"As I said, this is a GPS unit. However, over the past few days we added some additional capabilities. To use the device, simply turn it on with this button and the unit will automatically establish a connection with the low orbit satellites to verify your position. That should be familiar to you." The two men nodded in understanding. "The more satellites it connects to, the more accurate the positioning will be. We added a second receiver that will pick up the transmission from the infant."

The two agents looked confused as John finished.

"Have you watched the animal shows on television?" The two men nodded. "Have you seen the marine biologists tag sharks or dolphins and track their movements?" Again the men nodded. "This works on the same idea. The only difference is that we combined the two capabilities together into one unit, so you can track yourself to the target."

"So all we have to do is turn the unit on and then follow the device to the baby?"

"Exactly! It is that easy. If you have any questions or problems when you get there, contact Mr. Palmer. He can put you in touch with one of the scientists on the design team."

Ryan stood up from his desk. "Good luck, gentlemen. We are counting on you."

"We will do what we can."

"I have a helicopter waiting for you outside. You will report back to me only. I don't want anyone else in the loop. Do you understand me?" Ryan asked firmly.

"Yes, sir." They both nodded in agreement. Neither man was happy about getting on another helicopter. They both were still a bit queasy after the trip last week over the bay, but said nothing as they got up to leave.

"Good luck," Ryan said, slapping both men on the back. "Remember—no one in the loop."

The men left the office and took the elevator to the roof. The helicopter was just warming up as they opened the door and slid inside as the long rotor blades started turning.

Chapter 41

The unmistakable ring of the STUIII echoed in the large hangar, startling the five men. They looked at each other almost afraid to answer. Lassiter finally picked it up on the fourth ring.

The smile that erupted on his face lifted their spirits before he even had a chance to talk.

"Yes, sir. We will meet him at the terminal. What is he bringing?"

"He has the special receiver to find Eagle 2. Ben, this guy is not a soldier—he's a doctor. I don't want him in any danger."

"Did I hear you correctly, a doctor?"

"You heard me correctly. His name is John Bastian. He is the scientist in charge of developing the specialized receiver," the president said.

"I will do what I can. How about additional weapons?"

"I couldn't help you with that. You are going to have to make do with what you have."

The men saw Lassiter's face go from jubilation to concern almost immediately.

"Yes, sir, we will do what you ask. With any luck we will have Eagle 2 by tomorrow afternoon."

"Just remember—keep Dr. Bastian out of the operation," the president warned.

"Will do—Lassiter out," he said as he hung up the phone.

The four men gathered around Lassiter before he had a chance to stand.

"So, what did he say?" Tony inquired, placing his hands flat on the desk.

"It appears he is sending us a doctor," Lassiter said, shaking his head in disbelief.

"A doctor? Why?" Tony continued with the questions.

"Well, it seems the doctor has developed some sort of special receiving device."

"A receiving device? What the hell are we going to be receiving?' Rodger joined in with the questions.

"Listen, fellows. I know no more about this whole thing than you do."

"But, what the hell are we going to do with a receiver? Did you know Eagle 2 was carrying a transmitter?" Tony asked in an exasperated tone.

"Mr. Hampton, if I knew he had a transmitter, do you think we would have been sitting here on our asses for the past five days?" Lassiter asked, raising his voice. "Let's all just get focused. The doctor will be arriving on a plane around 0300 tomorrow. I suggest we get some sleep because the next day or so will be quite busy. That includes you, Mr. Hampton," Lassiter said, looking directly at Tony.

"You are right, sir. I am sorry. I am just frustrated, and it is showing."

"We are all frustrated, Tony," Lassiter said, lowering his voice. "Listen, son, no one wants to find Eagle 2 alive more than I. We will just have to wait a few more hours."

"Understood, sir," Tony said, walking away to his spot on the floor. He wasn't sure why he felt so frustrated. They were getting what they had waited endlessly for and finally they would be able to get some answers. But a transmitter—if they had known that Eagle 2 was carrying a transmitter, this thing could be over.

"Rodger, what do you make of the receiver Lassiter was talking about?"

"I have no idea. If the vice president was wearing a transmitter, it is news to me. I suspect Lassiter didn't even know about it by his reaction."

"I agree. I think he is just as surprised as we are. It is just too damn bad we didn't know earlier."

"It doesn't matter. Let it go," Rodger said, beating the dust off his bag to lay his head down.

"I know," Tony looked at his watch, "but still—" he added, putting his head down on his coat.

All five men found it difficult to sleep. The anxiety of the arrival of the visitor weighed heavily on their minds.

Lassiter was up and pacing an hour before the plane was scheduled to land. Now that he had a potential solution to find Eagle 2, he had to come up with the operational aspect. They had no idea how or where to start looking. He thought back to Tony's theory and how the terrorists may not be in Russia and looked again at the map. If he wasn't in Russia, where would be the most obvious choice to start looking? With so much real estate to search, they were literally looking for a needle in a haystack.

He knew that with five people and virtually no firepower, the operation would have to be delicate. They wouldn't have the luxury of overpowering the terrorists with force.

Lassiter couldn't count on support from the Russian military. Regardless of the political situation, Lassiter's men would be doing this on their own, which didn't really concern him. The Russians were not big on being delicate, and going in silent was their only hope. The other big uncertainty was the doctor. What would he do with him during this? He really needed every man he could get and a sixth member would be just the thing the doctor ordered regardless of what the president said. Lassiter chuckled to himself at that thought.

"Okay, fellows, it's time to get moving. Kevin, I want you to go out on the tarmac, and watch for the plane. Tony, Rodger, come over with me to the map. We need to start some planning on our operation, and I want your thoughts. As you know we have a limited number of weapons and we need to keep the element of surprise if we have any hopes of keeping Eagle 2 alive.

"I think it would be a whole lot easier to plan if we knew what we are going to be up against. We don't have any idea of their numbers or what we will be facing as far as terrain when we do find him. If they are hold up in a city building somewhere, the element of surprise will be a lot easier than attacking a barn in the middle of nowhere," Tony said, looking at the map.

"I have thought of that, Tony," Lassiter observed. "However, we have three members of the team, including me, who have never been in a combat situation."

"The plane has arrived," Kevin said, throwing open the door, interrupting the planning session.

"Good, now maybe we will get some answers," Ben said. "His name is Dr. John Bastian. Meet him at the terminal, and escort him directly here."

"How will I know who he is?" Kevin asked.

"I don't know. Improvise for Christ's sake—just get him here. Pick us up some coffee while you are over there."

"OKAY, OKAY," Kevin answered, walking back out the door.

"We are going to need a bigger car to transport all six of us. The small Russian piece of shit that we have been using is just barely big enough for four," Rodger said, looking at the small car.

"That is a good point. Damn, how could I have overlooked that?" Ben asked.

"Looks like we have everything now except for the thing we need the most. Let's wait until we talk to the doctor, and then Rodger and I will go out and see what we can find," Tony said.

"Steve, what are your thoughts on this? You have been quiet the whole time," Ben asked.

"I think Tony is right. We can't do any planning until we pinpoint their location. What about the doctor? Is he going to be capable of helping us in the operation?" Steve asked.

"The president told me to keep him out of harm's way. He is not to be close to the shooting. I say we leave that up to the good doctor. We will take all the help we can get," Ben added.

The door opened slightly as Kevin walked in carrying four large cups of coffee. Behind him was a tall man carrying two large bags. They walked up to Lassiter, and Kevin set the coffee on the desk.

"Dr. Bastian, this is Ben Lassiter, the security chief," Kevin said, introducing the two men.

Ben looked at the man standing in front of him, sizing him up. He would have guessed the man to be in his mid-fifties and in relatively good shape. The dark tan the man sported meant he spent a considerable amount of time outdoors. His designer slacks and button up polo shirt was wrinkled badly after the long plane ride, but he looked rested.

"Dr. Bastian, it is good to meet you. This is Tony Hampton, Rodger Gentry, and Steve Thurmond," Ben said, pointing to each man and John shook each of their hands in turn. "And I believe you have already met Kevin Deal."

"Yes, I have. I am very sorry, but you wouldn't happen to have a bathroom here. I drank a lot of coffee on the plane."

"Steve, show the doctor to the bathroom," Ben ordered.

"Please, call me John," he said as he walked off behind Steve.

When the two were out of earshot, Rodger spoke first.

"What is with this guy? He is older than my father. He must be in his sixties. I think I can say with confidence, he won't be any help to us."

"I am in my sixties, Rodger, what are you saying?" Ben asked. "Would you like to put us both out to pasture?"

"No, I only meant that with his age and profession he will be useless when the lead starts flying," Rodger said, trying to back out of his statement.

"Well, let's see what he has for us before we make any assumptions."

John returned to the small group and opened up one of his bags. He looked at the small group of men looking at him with skepticism. He immediately pulled out a small electronic device and placed in the middle of the desk.

"That gentleman is what you have been waiting for," John said.

"A GPS unit? We have been waiting five days for goddamn GPS?" Tony asked, immediately drawing a glare from Lassiter.

"Ahhh, but this is more than a GPS unit. It is a complex receiving device in GPS clothing," John said with a smile, looking back at the concerned faces of the five men. He could see the hope in their faces turn to complete despair. "Before I go on, I think it is necessary to give you a little background information."

"Was Eagle 2 wearing some sort of transmitting device?" Tony asked, trying to glean something to hope for.

"He does have a transmitting device, but he isn't exactly wearing it."

Every one of their eyebrows went up.

"This story is going to seem far fetched to you all, but what I am going to say is all true," John started. "Let me begin by saying that I wasn't always a private practice doctor. Forty years ago, I was a lieutenant in the Army assigned to a top secret facility conducting research on a tracking device for soldiers on the battlefield. The project I personally led was tasked with developing a specialized probe small enough to be injected into soldiers that constantly transmitted a special signal to receivers that we also developed. Its purpose was to find soldiers who were MIA."

"I don't understand," Ben said as he looked at the doctor and to the unit on the table.

"The specifics of the probe and how it works aren't necessary to understand, so I'll give you the abridged version. I know you are ready and anxious to move out. The probes we invented have been secretly injected into every baby born in the United States since the 1960s. Most of you, with the exception of Mr. Lassiter, have all been injected with the probe. It is a relatively standard procedure and has been kept secret because it has become a way for the government to keep data on the numbers of births. There is no risk to the infant as the probe travels through the blood stream, and it harmlessly regenerates its power as it passes through the blood."

"Let me get something straight. You are saying you invented a probe small enough to be injected into the human body that will transmit secret data until a person dies?" Rodger asked, interrupting the story.

"That is a pretty accurate description. Theoretically, it will even transmit after an individual dies until the power of the probe runs out. You see it gets its power from the red blood cells and after death it can no longer regenerate itself. I estimate, the probe can last for years without being charged. However, we have never tested that."

"Jesus, this must have been the biggest government cover-up in history," Tony said, still unable to believe the man.

"Other than tracking births, the government, for the most part, forgot about it. Without funding, the project was officially disbanded in the mid-sixties. A small company in Ft. Meade, Maryland, NanoSoft, continues to produce and supply the government with the probes."

"I still don't understand how all of this helps us," Ben said.

"I am getting to the best part. As I said, every infant is injected with a probe. However, before it is injected, it is programmed with a unique number that is then transmitted by the probe. Nearly every birth for the past forty years has been recorded and saved on a computer in the NSA. So, gentlemen, with the correct receiver, programmed to read a specific number, we can find any U.S. citizen born after a certain date."

"I think I am beginning to understand," Ben said. "But why did it take so long for us to get our hands on one of those receivers?"

"That's because the original receivers were destroyed twenty years ago. One of the drawbacks of the first generation receivers was their limited reception range. They would have done you no good, trust me. When the CIA found me on my sailboat in the middle of the Chesapeake less than a week ago, a group of CIA scientists and I worked 24 hours a day to come up with what you see on the desk."

"It looks like an ordinary GPS, though. What is so special about it?" Kevin asked.

"We wanted the system to be small enough that it wasn't cumbersome to carry given the circumstances. The unit's real power is in its programming and antenna. The unit has a reception radius of two hundred fifty miles and can pinpoint the probe to within three feet of its true location."

"That is pretty impressive for such a small device," Ben said, sounding skeptical.

"It's true. The real power is in the programming."

"Am I missing something? Are you saying that Eagle 2 has been injected with the probe?" Tony asked.

"I wouldn't be here if he wasn't, now would I?"

"I guess not," Tony added, feeling a bit foolish.

"Ironically, he was the first infant born to be injected in the testing phase," John said.

"If he was the first injected, how can we be sure the probe is still transmitting?"

"We can't be sure of anything. The initial test probes were never positively tested. At that time, the team was still perfecting the self-regenerating properties. I designed the self-regenerating process, but I didn't have a chance to develop it fully. We can only hope it works. However, this is our only hope," John said.

"Okay, boys, now that you have the story, let's get down to planning," Lassiter said.

"I still don't buy it," Tony said, still looking at the small device.

"I don't give a shit what you buy. This is our only hope, and we are going with it. This is not up for debate, Mr. Hampton," Lassiter snapped.

"If we are all injected with the probe, why can't we test it out on us?"

John stepped up to field the question. "As I said, we programmed the device to receive the transmissions of a specific probe. Think about it. If we didn't do that, we could literally pick up millions of hits."

"I can understand that, but only four of us have been injected with it here."

"That is true, but when we tested it, we were in the middle of Washington D.C."

"Any more stupid questions, people?" Lassiter barked.

Tony shrugged his shoulders, but kept his mouth shut.

"Okay, let's get everything arranged. It is nearly 0400, I want to start out at day break. Tony and Rodger, get to work on getting us transportation to carry six. I am going to call the president and let him know Dr. Bastian has arrived safely."

"Yes, sir," they both said as they headed toward the hangar door.

Chapter 42

The large white boat rolled gently on the swells in the relative safety of the inlet. The wind had howled through the night, but the long stone wall had protected them from the worsening conditions on the lake. The sun was now cresting the horizon casting long shadows on the turbulent water while Nassir sipped a cup of steaming coffee on the top deck.

He had not slept much and was watching the white cumulus clouds being pushed across the blue sky by gusts of wind. He also kept an eye on the wall watching the spray rise over it from the endless barrage of waves. He worried that they would be here another day.

The marina was filled with boats mooring for the night, forced off the lake by both the wind and the Coast Guard. Most of them were summer vacationers happy to be stuck in this beautiful place for the day. Nassir, however, was not one of them.

Kamal had smelled the strong coffee and was up pouring himself a cup. He was just about ready to head out on deck to check the weather when he heard the infant rustling in the forward stateroom. He had to wake Ali before the baby started to cry.

"Ali, wake up. The baby is starting to cry. If he is heard, others might get suspicious," Kamal said, nudging his friend sleeping on one of the three fold-out couches.

Ali stirred awake long enough to open his eyes.

"Come on, friend, wake up," Kamal said more forcefully now as the baby started to cry.

Ali rolled over onto his back as his eyes fluttered open.

"I don't feel well, Kamal. My stomach is upset and my head is throbbing," Ali moaned, still more asleep than awake.

"It is the motion of the boat. Let me get you a cup of coffee, and you will feel better."

"I was up all night trying to keep the baby quiet. I am exhausted, Kamal."

"Let me help. What can I do?"

"I have mixed some formula according to the instructions on the can. It's in the bottle on the counter. You can try that. I have not had much luck though.

The baby has not eaten much. I fear that he is getting weak. We must get him to someone soon who knows how to care for him. If we don't, he may die."

"Let's not think about that. We will be on our way today and by tomorrow we will be at our destination. Nassir has given us his promise. Keep your thoughts to yourself until tomorrow. You know what happened to Kahlid," Kamal said softly so as not to be heard outside of the cabin.

"I know. Let's hope tomorrow is not too late. Who is this person Sharal?" Ali asked, taking his first sip of coffee.

"I don't know anything more than he is a member of the PFLP in Canada. His family owns fishing boats around here somewhere. Nassir bought him to get us through the border."

"I don't trust him," Ali said, not feeling any better after the coffee had a chance to settle in his stomach.

"He has gotten us this far. We are close now. Let's just make sure the baby makes it with us."

Kahlid put his coffee down on the Corian counter and picked up the bottle. He opened the forward stateroom door propping it open with a duffle bag for the time being. The crying infant was shaking and Kamal wondered if he would ever be able to get the boy to eat. He gently picked up the tiny infant in his arms and nudged the plastic nipple into his mouth. The baby instinctively began to suckle the nipple, but spit it out immediately crying even more at the intrusion. Kamal tried again only to receive the same results.

"Ali, he doesn't seem to want to eat."

"I don't know what to tell you. I have not had much luck either. We could try to heat the bottle in the microwave. Warming it may make it more like breast milk."

"Good idea, I will try that. How are you feeling now?" Kamal asked, coming back out of the small room to the galley.

"The coffee didn't do much for my stomach, but my head is doing much better."

Kamal placed the bottle inside the microwave and warmed it for one minute. Kamal picked up his coffee, taking a sip before it cooled as the microwave dinged.

"I hope this works," Kamal said.

One more time he picked up the infant and coaxed the nipple into his mouth. The boy clamped down and started to suck very hard. His tiny cheeks were actually concave as the suction increased.

"Ali, I think it's working, the baby is eating," Kamal yelled excitedly.

"Praise Allah, he could not have gone another day without eating."

The baby drained the bottle in ten minutes. Kamal picked the baby up and placed his cheek on his shoulders. He had seen mothers do this when babies finished eating. With gentle taps on his back he tried to coax the air from the infant's stomach that entered while sucking on the bottle. In no time, the baby was dozing off, now that his tiny stomach was filled.

Kamal set the baby back into the makeshift bed, shut the door and quietly refilled his cup with steaming coffee.

"He is sleeping. I am going up on deck to see when we will be leaving. Come up when you get around. Hopefully, it won't be long before we start out again," Kamal said in a whisper.

Kamal picked up the cup and walked the stairs topside. Nassir and Sharal were talking quietly staring out at the large lake. Kamal walked up to them and the talking stopped.

"Ahh, Kamal, my friend, how did you sleep?" Nassir asked.

"Very well. The baby is also now sleeping soundly. Ali is worried about the infant, though. He thinks the baby may not make it."

"What is wrong?" Nassir asked in a concerned voice.

"The baby has not eaten much since we left Baltimore. He is very weak."

"We will have to trust Ali to come through for us. He has done a fine job so far."

"He has, but he looks exhausted," Kamal said, looking at Nassir. "Where are we heading now?"

"Sharal and I have been watching the lake and it does not look like we will be crossing today unless the wind dies down. Do you think he will make it another day?"

"I have no idea. I don't know anything about babies. We will do what we can."

"I know you will, Kamal. That is why you are here. I have all the trust in you."

"What is with the weather?"

"The sun is shining, but the wind is just too much. The waves are crashing over the breaker, and the Coast Guard still has the small-boat lake advisory in effect," Sharal said, looking down from the fly bridge where he was monitoring the marine radio.

Kamal looked out at the long rock wall and saw the spray. From where he stood, it appeared to be shooting high over the small lighthouse at the far end of the wall. He also noticed the number of boats that had taken refuge at the marina over night to get off the lake.

"I want us all to stay out of view of curious eyes. We don't need to appear out of the ordinary," Nassir told them both. "Where is Ali?"

"He is still below. He is not feeling well and is getting some well-deserved rest. He has really become quite attached to the little one," Kamal answered.

"The infant is nothing to us! Do you understand that?" Nassir said, pounding his fist on the fiberglass hull. "I don't want any problems with Ali when the time comes to do what we need to do," Nassir said, continuing his terse tone, letting his frustration of being stuck here another day show.

"I know that, Nassir, and Ali knows that, too. Don't worry about us. We will do what you tell us to do," Kamal said with a nervous tone in his voice.

Nassir had calmed. "Yes, Kamal, I know you know that. I am sorry."

Kamal sipped his coffee as he watched the rolling waves. He couldn't wait for this to be over. "I will go below and see if Ali needs help."

"That is good. Don't say anything about the baby to him," Nassir said, watching his friend walk through the large glass doors.

"Not a word. There is no need to worry him this close to the end," Kamal said.

Inside of an hour, Nassir heard the sound of an outboard engine whining against the waves. He looked toward the marina office and saw a small aluminum boat heading toward them with the bow riding high pushing the water. He grabbed the binoculars off the hook above him and watched the boat move between the moored boats. He clearly saw the marina owner, George and his son making their rounds. They were probably just trying to scare up business. The lake advisory had filled the marina to the limit and they were reaping the benefits.

The boat first pulled up next to a large sailboat flying a Canadian flag and stopped for a few minutes. Nassir was positive the two were going to board her for a quick visit. He wanted nothing more than to untie and leave now before the two men made it to them. He didn't like the intrusion and had a feeling from their first meeting the older man didn't buy his story. He wouldn't be surprised if the man had called the local police.

From the fly bridge, Sharal also watched the two men move from boat to boat. They were leisurely taking their time to talk and get to know the visitors. They even boarded one of the large cruisers for a quick cup of coffee. Nassir had a pit in his stomach as the small skiff pulled up alongside them.

"Hello, Captain," the older man said, yelling from below.

"Good morning," Nassir yelled.

"How did you fare last night?"

"No problems at all. I would sure like to see the wind die down, though, so we could get some action on the lake," Nassir said as he stepped down onto the lower deck.

"Yes, so would everyone here. It seems as if the lake has a mind of its own. The latest weather forecast shows the wind dying down later this afternoon."

"That is perfect. We have to be heading back tomorrow at the latest. The waves get quite high don't they?"

"It is a big lake. This is the worst I have seen it in decades though. You are just lucky enough to have hit it at a bad time," George said sarcastically. "Where are the others?"

"Down below. They are not taking the weather as well as we are," Nassir said, looking up at Sharal.

"I see. So will you be staying another night then?" the man asked.

"No, I don't think so. We will be leaving today. I have to get back to work, and I need to be back in Geneva day after tomorrow."

"Okay, well can I get you anything?"

"No, I think we have everything we need. I must have packed enough food for a month down there."

"Jeez, a month? Where were you boys planning on going, the Atlantic?" he asked, laughing.

Nassir laughed along with the two strangers. He didn't like the man being so curious. Something was wrong, but he couldn't tell what it was. He had a feeling the man was out here getting information, and Nassir wasn't going to give him any.

"Let's hope your weather forecast is right," Nassir said, nodding his head.

"I'll let you in on a little secret," George said, starting the small outboard motor.

"What's that?"

"Do you see that large white Viking forty-five over there?" the man asked, pointing toward the dock next to the marina office.

Both Nassir and Sharal looked at the large white boat with a two-tiered fly bridge and four large outriggers attached to the port and starboard rails. "Yes, I see her. She is a real beauty."

"She sure is. She is a registered fishing charter. Fishermen charter her out on a daily or hourly basis to try their luck at Salmon or large lake trout. She is owned by a local captain who just happens to be a good friend and is losing money with the weather being shitty and all."

Nassir whistled, still looking at the graceful yacht.

"When you see her heading out to the lake, you know it is safe."

"Thanks for the information," Nassir yelled down.

"No problem and good luck," George yelled back, pushing the small aluminum boat away from the Carver.

Chapter 43

A loud grumble echoed in the empty office, but Alexander ignored the warnings of his stomach intently watching the men talk below. He couldn't quite make out what they were talking about, but he didn't need to know. He wasn't as crazed as they made him out to be.

The time he had spent alone in the office the last four days was spent planning. His thoughts were on his father. "If you can't win fair, don't lose," his father's words echoed in his mind, and with Alexander's plan they wouldn't lose.

The time had come. He needed to put his plan into action because he was sure that by now the Americans were coming. Alexander stood and walked toward the door. His thoughts were crystal clear as he walked down the metal stairs toward the dirty concrete floor.

"Alexander, it is good to see you," Andre said as the two met at the bottom of the stairs.

"Andre, the plan is ready, but first I need you to run an errand for me."

"What plan? What are you talking about, Alexander?"

"Just listen to me, and don't tell anyone else what I am about to tell you. I don't trust Shevard or the others with the details."

"Anything, you know I would do anything for you."

"I need you to go back to my flat and get all of the C-4 we have."

"But what if the Americans come while I am out? You will need me."

"They will not come. They have no idea who or where we are yet."

"Why all the explosives?"

"I am spinning my web. We are going to trap the Americans like flies," Alexander said with a smile on his face.

"Like flies, what are you talking about?" Andre asked in a concerned tone.

"I will tell you everything when you return."

"It is good to see you back. I was beginning to worry about you. Hell, we were all worried about you. I haven't seen you smile in the past five days."

Alexander didn't acknowledge Andre's words. "Just get back as soon as you can."

"Right, it shouldn't take more than a few hours," Andre said as he walked to the car.

Shevard heard the talking and walked toward the two just as Andre left the warehouse.

"So, Alexander, you decided to grace us in our hour of need," Shevard said acidly.

"Shevard, it is good to see you too, my friend," Alexander said coldly.

"Friend, shit, you son of a bitch! You are leaving us to die like cowards," Shevard responded bitterly.

"Not true, Shevard. I have just finalized the plan in my head. You are no coward. I am the coward."

Shevard stared at Alexander for a long minute before saying a word. "You are our leader, we trusted you to get us through this alive."

"Do you trust me now?"

Shevard fished another cigarette out of his shirt pocket and lit it. "You have given us no reason to trust you, Alexander," Shevard answered, exhaling the smoke as he spoke. "Andre and I tried to talk to you, but you just ignored our words."

"You didn't answer my question, Shevard. Do you trust me?"

After all the cold words Shevard had said against Alexander in the past few days, he still considered him a friend. He couldn't throw away all the good times they had over the years. "Yes, I trust you, my friend."

Alexander smiled and embraced the large man in a giant bear hug as he did that day following the attack on the tanks.

"I must say, it is good to have you back," Shevard said, taking a drag off the cigarette.

"I was never gone. As you said, I am your leader. I got you into this situation and I am responsible for getting you out."

"Do you honestly think we will get out of this alive?"

"I am positive. We will be victorious against the Americans. If we are not, the Russians will never be forced from our land and we will have failed."

"Okay, so what is your plan?" Shevard asked.

"You will find out in time."

"In time? Why not now? What do you have to hide from us?"

"I am hiding nothing. Andre is going out to pick up some items we will need. When he returns I will describe my plans to you all at one time. I have not even told Andre what my plan is."

"What good is trust if you can't trust me now with your plan?" Shevard pressed.

"Trust has nothing to do with this, Shevard. You will know soon."

Shevard tossed the cigarette on the concrete floor and snubbed it out with the sole of his shoe. The floor was covered with butts, wrappers, and empty cans of meat. "Would you like something to eat?" Shevard asked as he walked away.

"No, thank you. I am fine for now. I will eat when we are victorious."

Shevard stared long and hard at Alexander over his shoulder. He couldn't put his finger on it, but there was still something in Alexander's eyes he didn't trust—and he didn't like it. He had become very distant. The glazed look in his eyes, the cold expressionless face, and the slow purposeful movements almost seemed to be an act. Alexander was just as scared as they all were.

Alexander walked over to their captive. The man had not stood in days. His hand and feet were tightly bound and the sweat soaked bandana covering his eyes had been in place since they left Moscow. The man looked pitiful, but Alexander had no pity to give him.

Alexander strode arrogantly away without looking at anything, but the floor. His thoughts were not on himself, the helpless man, or his friends, but his family huddled in the kitchen of his boyhood home. He had convinced himself that he was not worried about what the future had in store for him.

"Shevard, come get me when Andre returns," Alexander yelled.

Shevard waved to him acknowledging the order. Unlike Alexander, he did feel sorry for the man they had taken. He also felt sorry for the innocent people they had killed. There was no reason for it.

"What did Alexander say to you over there?" Leonid asked.

"He was talking about some plan to get us out of here."

"You have got to be kidding me."

"I am serious! He wouldn't say what it was, only that he would tell us all when Andre returned."

"Did he say where Andre went?"

Shevard glanced up toward the office and noticed Alexander looking down at them from the metal walkway.

"He said nothing," Shevard said, guarding his voice from Alexander.

"Okay, Okay," Leonid said, noticing the sudden change in Shevard.

"Keep an eye out for Andre. He should be returning soon," Shevard said, lighting another cigarette, offering one to Leonid. Leonid took the offered smoke and leaned in to light it. "Don't let Alexander see us talking alone ever again," Shevard whispered as he lit the cigarette. "He does not trust us, and I don't trust him."

The nod was nearly non-perceptible as Leonid took the first long drag. He walked slowly away toward the door with smoke surrounding his head. Shevard walked to the far said of the remaining car and sat on the floor with his back against the tire. He wanted to be out of the eyeshot of Alexander. He didn't like the idea that he was being watched. It made him uncomfortable.

Shevard looked at his watch. It was just after nine in the morning. It was already hot and he wanted nothing more than to go home. He hadn't had a shower in days. Shevard closed his eyes and could almost picture his kids running around him playing while his wife made their Sunday breakfast. He took a deep breath and could smell his wife's cooking. The crackers and meat that he had earlier was just not cutting it.

The only chance he had was to talk to Andre before Alexander. He had to find out what Andre was up to. Was Andre now backing Alexander or was he just stringing him along? He had to find out what Andre's motives were.

Chapter 44

The cab ride to her apartment seemed longer than usual, probably because her head was already starting to throb from the alcohol she consumed earlier. From the rear seat, she watched the people walking on the sidewalk pass by. As the cab stopped at a red light, one couple caught her eye because they were kissing under a streetlight. She stared and sighed out loud as she watched the two lovers. There is nothing like being in love she thought, as the light turned green and the cab left them behind. What she wouldn't give to have a man to go home to and love. But, she was young and married to her work and right now didn't have time to give to anyone.

"Good evening, Clarence," Jennifer said with a large smile. It was well after one in the morning, and she was dead tired. The hospital was no help, and she was running down a lead at the Motel Six on South Street. Her offer for a drink had produced some surprising results.

"Good morning, Ms. Cleary," he said, tipping his hat. "I trust you had a good night."

"Very productive," she said, walking inside.

She had overlooked the earlier whore remark, but still didn't enjoy what she just did. As she pressed the elevator button, she thought it possible that he was right—she really was a whore. With a shrug of her shoulders, she passed off the idea because the information she got tonight was worth the reputation.

Opening her apartment door, she smiled inwardly. She was going to blow the lid off the secret government cover up and that her feel good. This is the kind of reporting veteran journalists had wet dreams about, and she fell into it.

She put the teakettle on the burner of her gas stove and turned the knob slowly until it lit. The flames rose up around the sides and she adjusted it down. She poured some instant coffee into her cup, directly from the glass container, without the aid of a spoon. As she waited for the water to boil, she reached in her purse and pulled out the small tape recorder she secretly used to tape the entire conversation earlier that evening. She couldn't believe that she had actually pulled it off.

It all started with a well-timed phone call late that afternoon. Jennifer was running up against a cement wall with the story and decided to give her White House contact another try. She was sure he wanted to talk. She just had to give him a reason. They made plans to meet at *Jock's*, a regular hangout for the political crowd, at eight. Jock's was convenient because it was around the corner from the Capitol Building and there was an unspoken understanding among the constituents who frequented the place that what went on in the bar, stayed at the bar. More bribe money passed under the table there than Jock, the owner, made in a year, and more importantly, it was also an easy place for politicians to meet secretly with their mistresses.

She purposely wore a mini-skirt and silk camisole that screamed, "Fuck Me." However, it was the stiletto heels that put her outfit over the edge. If he thought she was a whore why not dress for the part, she thought as she looked in the mirror in her bedroom before putting on the finishing touch. She touched the lipstick to her lips and pressed them together to spread it out, grabbed her purse and ran out the door, locking it behind her. She hailed a cab on the street and was off to the bar.

The inside of the bar was decorated like an old English Tavern. The cherry paneling in the walls was stained dark, and the ceilings were low and lined with beams from which hung a collection of brass lanterns that Jock had picked up at antique stores and old ship yards. The curved bar had a long brass foot railing and was topped by planks that Jock swore came from the USS Constitution before it was refitted as a floating museum. The planks were perfectly fitted together and sealed with multiple layers of polyurethane to protect it from the alcohol that was spilled on it nightly. The only lighting came from a few wall sconces, but with the low ceilings it was enough to provide a romantic ambience.

When she walked through the door, every man in the place turned to look at her. She felt momentarily like a piece of meat, but she was pleased with herself and she smiled as she walked confidently toward him. He already had a table in the corner with her favorite drink, scotch on the rocks, waiting.

The teakettle whistled and she quickly removed it from the heat and turned the burner off. She poured the steaming water into the cup and looked at the small recorder for a full minute as she contemplated replaying the evening over in her mind. The thought of it turned her stomach, but still she couldn't resist.

Her fingers pressed the rewind button and the small recorder whined as the tape wound back to the starting point. It seemed to take forever and she glanced at her watch to see exactly how long she had been with him. She depressed the play button, and the conversation began.

He stood as she approached, taking her hands and kissing her on the cheek. "You look stunning," he said as he pulled out her chair.

"Thank you," she said, smiling carefully, placing her small purse strategically on the table. She made sure the clasp was open, but not enough to expose what was hidden inside.

"Well, let me say I was surprised by your call," he said, sitting across from her.

She picked up the glass and took a sip. The scotch was exquisite there, and she loved it. "Oh, well, let me just say I have thought of nothing else all day," she said, lying through her pearl white teeth.

"Is that so? Well, neither have I. The president has been on the phone with the Red Cross all afternoon, trying to get a handle on the hurricane," he said, taking her hands in his.

"Oh, how's it going down there?"

"Let's just say the preparations were not enough. Preliminary reports are coming in as we speak, but it was much worse than anyone thought. Corpus Christi was the worst hit, but it devastated the entire Texas coast. From what we can tell the infrastructure was wiped out. Schools, hospitals, and utilities have all suffered a huge amount of damage. Power is out to nearly 2 million people, including half of Houston."

"Wow, that is pretty bad. It is amazing how fast those storms move," she said, finishing her first scotch. She signaled to the waitress for another as she finished the thought.

"Yes, this one was especially bad. The weather service has deemed it the storm of the decade, but it is too early to tell. The president is planning a trip to tour the damage as soon as it is safe."

"I suppose he feels the need to keep up his image," she said, flashing a smile toward him. She was trying the best she could to flirt with him, but what she really needed was a couple more drinks. Then she would really lay on the charm.

The waitress arrived with their second round and the conversation lulled. She drank this one faster than the first and stopped the waitress on her way back to the bar with another order.

"Wow, you are really putting them away tonight," he said.

"Yes, I needed this. Spending all that time in Iraq took a lot out of me."

"I saw your report on CNN. Very good, I must say. Is it true that women are still treated so poorly?"

"It is true. I honestly don't see any change to that. The entire time I was there, I just thanked God that I was born in the States. The women in Iraq are so repressed."

"I have never been over there, but I have read the thousands of reports that flow through the White House. I know the president will do everything he can to see that we get out of there as soon as possible."

"That will be easier said than done, let me tell you."

"I expect it will be, but it needs to be done," he said.

"Yes, the CIA pulled a real boner on that one didn't they?"

"That is an understatement. They were directly responsible for our involvement."

"It must be tough for the president to support something he didn't start. I mean, he didn't send the troops over and now he is having to give them support without a clear agenda."

"He has a clear agenda. It is to pull the troops out as soon as possible. Give him time. He will do great things during his term."

"Yes, I suspect he will, and he won't have to cover them up like his predecessor."

Jennifer was feeling the effects of the alcohol as the third round arrived. She would take this one slower because she had not yet gotten what she had come for, and she didn't want to get sloppy drunk just yet.

She took a sip while looking into his eyes. "I suspect the president is not too fond of the CIA at this point then," she said, batting her eyes at him.

"That would be sugar coating it. He has been meeting with Mr. Palmer daily, and let's just say, you could cut the tension in the room with a knife."

"Daily? That's unusual."

"Yes, well, the hurricane is not the only thing on the president's plate at the moment," he said lifting the glass to his lips.

"Now there is one job I would just hate. The president deals with nothing, but one crisis after another. With all the time spent away from his wife, I am surprised they remain married."

"Well, the latest crisis is making the hurricane look like nothing more than gentle breeze," he said, feeling the effects of the alcohol overtake him, feeling more intoxicated by the second. Jennifer had no idea, but he had two drinks before she arrived.

"See, that is what I mean. Talk about a high-stress job."

The words were flowing out of his mouth as if a dam just broke free. He didn't care. He was going to be in her pants in a few minutes anyway. He looked at his watch quickly and estimated that they would be naked within the hour. "Let me ask you something," he said, leaning over the table. "Have you seen the vice president lately?"

She thought about the question. "I just saw him coming back from a trip to Mexico. Something about NAFTA, wasn't it?"

"No, I am talking within the past week."

"Hmmm—now that you mention it, I haven't," she said, dragging the topic of the conversation out. She knew she was finally getting somewhere and before he spoke, she ordered another round.

"That is because he is not in the country."

"Jesus, that man knows how to travel."

The drinks arrived and the waitress picked up the four empty glasses on both sides of the table. "This was not a trip he wanted to make. He was supposed to be picking up his baby from the hospital two days ago," he said, slurring his words just a bit.

"His baby? I thought he and his wife couldn't have children."

"They can't. They were adopting one from some runaway."

That was it! She was now getting what she wanted from him. She also realized that the faster she drank, the faster he did and the more he consumed, the looser his lips became. She wasted no time in getting through her fifth of the evening. "That must be tough missing a family moment like that. I bet his wife was pissed."

"She took the news pretty well. She is a very tough lady."

"Yeah, I've met her a few times. She is very down to earth."

"Oh, she is. But the security team got into some trouble over in Moscow, and now he is missing."

"Oh my, missing? The vice president?" she said, seemingly disinterested.

"You heard me—missing," he said sloppily while caressing her hands.

She ordered the sixth round, and he stopped her. "I've had my share," he said. I am drunk enough."

"Yes, well I'm not. Do you mind if I have another?"

"No, by all means go right ahead."

"That is a crisis," she said, trying to get back into the prior conversation.

"Yes, the CIA pulled another boner on this one as you say."

"How so?" she asked, stunned by the information she was getting so easily. It would have taken her days and dozens of phone calls to get this far.

"From what I know, they didn't have the correct background data on the riots ready and the security team literally walked into a trap."

"I can't believe that. Not after all the flak they have taken the past couple of years."

"It's true. That's why Mr. Palmer has been at the White House daily. Did you see the report on CNN when the rioters broke through the gates of the Kremlin?"

"Sure I saw that. Everyone in the Western world saw it."

"Well, did you notice the Mercedes in the street?"

"No, I missed it," she said, looking into his eyes.

"The explosives tore it to pieces. It was actually one of two in the vice president's motorcade. The other one is missing."

"My God! What are they doing to get him back?"

"They have some special project that finds people through a probe injected into his body or something. I don't understand it all. Are you ready to get out of here? I am feeling really horny."

She laughed in a cute way. "Sure, baby, just as soon as I am finished with this one. Did you say a probe? What on earth is that?" she asked calmly.

"You are looking so beautiful tonight," he said, nearly falling over her as he spoke. "I don't know. It has something to do with a project years ago."

"It all sounds rather boring," she said, feigning disinterest.

"It's boring. Come on, let's get out of here."

"You are such a romantic," she said, looking over her glass.

"There is more where that came from," he said with a mischievous grin on his face.

"I'll bet there is. What do you say we get out of here now?" she asked with an ice cube between her teeth.

He walked up to the bartender to pay their tab and glanced over his shoulder to check out her ass in the mini-skirt as she stood by the door waiting for him. He wrapped his arm around her shoulder and the two walked out the door together. The rest of the night she would like to forget.

Chapter 45

The large helicopter landed on the tarmac at the Buffalo airport. Agents Joe Davis and Pete Simpson waited inside the terminal as the two CIA agents exited the aircraft. They didn't like the fact that the CIA was coming in to take over their investigation. They had done the legwork and put in the long hours scanning through hours of security videos for nothing.

Metcalf was so pissed, in fact, he sent his two junior agents to pick them up because he couldn't do it himself. He told them to be professional, but give them nothing they didn't ask for first. He didn't want to make this easy for them. Deep down, he wanted nothing more than to see them fail, but realized the sooner this was solved the CIA would be out of their hair.

After the helicopter had lifted off, Joe and Pete quickly walked out onto the hot blacktop to meet them.

"Agent Flaherty?" Joe asked the one in front.

"I am Agent Jackson," stopping to allow his partner to catch up. "This is Agent Flaherty," he said, pointing to the man behind him, and the four men shook hands, flashing guarded smiles around.

"Yes, well, it is good to meet both of you. We will take you to our office to meet Senior Agent Metcalf. He will update you on our investigation. Do you have any bags?"

"Just this," Flaherty said, holding up a large black suitcase.

"Great, we can get moving," Pete said, pointing toward the automatic glass doors.

The four men got into the Mercury Marquis and sped off toward the city.

Agent Metcalf was waiting in the office. He had no idea what the CIA was doing with his investigation and pleaded with his boss to allow him to continue his work, but it was useless. He only hoped the agents would allow him to take some credit and weren't complete assholes about it. He didn't like riding shotgun, and he would absolutely go ballistic if they were arrogant, as most CIA agents tended to be.

He hated calling his agents on a Sunday, but he didn't have a choice. His boss called him late in the afternoon to tell him that the helicopter was arriving at the Buffalo Airport.

He filled the darkly stained, glass coffee pot with tap water and poured it into the reservoir. The only thing he hated more than having a case taken away from him was working without a cup of coffee in his hand.

Pete had radioed in ten minutes ago to say they were en route to the Federal Building. Metcalf used the time to gather all the reports he had written on the investigation. He reluctantly put them in a folder to save time. To control his bitterness, he kept reminding himself that regardless of who was in charge of the investigation, the infant had to be found before something terrible happened.

The black car pulled into the parking lot, and four men exited. Metcalf met them at the back door to the building, inviting them in.

"Agent Metcalf, this is Agents Jackson and Flaherty," Pete said, introducing the two men.

Metcalf extended his hand to them. "It is good to meet you. Can I get you anything?"

"I just need a bathroom and a bite to eat," Jackson said.

"Double that for me," Flaherty said immediately after.

"Okay, the bathroom is down the hall on the right. We can get something to eat after."

"Sounds good," they echoed in unison as they walked toward the bathroom.

"Did they ask any questions?" Metcalf asked his agents.

"None, they were silent during the entire trip."

"They certainly are young. I wonder if they are part of the CIA Counter Terrorism Unit?"

"I don't know. They flashed us their badges, but we didn't get a good look at them. We were just ready to get back here," Joe said.

"Why don't you two go home? I will go over the investigation with the two agents over supper, and we will get to work first thing in the morning."

"With all due respect, sir, I think we would like to stay and listen to what they have."

"Suit yourselves. I don't ever want to hear you complaining about never giving you time off though," Metcalf said sarcastically.

"My wife complains about it anyway. She is always bitching about how much I am away," Joe said. He had only been married a year, but she knew about his job before they were married.

"I know exactly what you mean," Metcalf said. "My wife left me five years ago. She didn't like playing second seat to my job. But I couldn't give it up. I loved it more than I did her."

"Wow, I didn't know you were married," Pete said.

Metcalf nodded and looked at the floor. "For nearly fifteen years. Actually, the divorce was final a week before our fifteenth anniversary. She is happier now without me. The last I heard she was living in Rochester with an accountant. We don't talk much. I am just glad we never had kids."

The two CIA agents returned now looking a bit less anxious.

"I know of a little diner just down the street that has great food. What do the two of you say?"

"We are your guests."

"Okay then, it's settled. Let's get moving. While we eat, I'll fill you in on what we have so far," Metcalf said, grabbing the folder off the briefing table.

The diner was empty this late on a Sunday. The five men sat around a large table and ordered their food.

"Let's get something straight. I am not happy about the CIA taking over this investigation," Metcalf said, getting it off his chest and in the open.

"We are not here to steal your thunder," Flaherty said defensively.

"So then, why exactly are you here?" Metcalf asked.

"We have something that may help find the baby."

"What are you talking about? What could you have that would make this investigation any easier?"

"We will tell you about it later," Jackson said, looking over his shoulder at the waitress.

"Why can't we talk about it now?" Metcalf asked.

"Not here," Jackson said firmly.

Metcalf tossed the folder in the middle of the table. "If you want to keep secrets from me, I'll be damned if I give you any help. You two are on your own!" Metcalf said, raising his voice.

"Calm down, sir," Jackson said, leaning into Metcalf, lowering his voice to a whisper. "We have a special tracking device that may help."

Metcalf was stunned. He was not told the infant was wearing a transmitter of any type. The FBI agents in Baltimore mentioned nothing about it. "What the hell are you talking about—a tracking device?"

"Lower your voice, sir," Flaherty said, fidgeting in his chair.

Metcalf felt foolish. He was letting his feelings interfere with the investigation already and they hadn't even started. "I am sorry. You must excuse my outbursts."

"Listen, as far as we are concerned, this is still your investigation. We were sent here to assist in any way we can and to bring the device with us," Jackson said.

The food arrived just in time to save Metcalf from any further embarrassment. The two CIA agents ate like they had not eaten in weeks.

"You were right. This food is great," Flaherty said, wiping his mouth with the napkin.

"I very rarely cook for myself anymore. I have most of my meals here. It is just cheaper and easier for me," Metcalf said, swallowing a large piece of roast beef.

When they were finished, Metcalf put a few dollars on the table and paid the bill. Paying for their meal was the least he could do for the way he acted. He looked at his watch.

"First thing, we get you two a room and then we can go back to the office. I am sure you are eager to get moving so you can get back to whatever life you have."

"That sounds good to me," Flaherty said.

The hotel was down another two blocks from the diner and the five of them decided to walk. It was a good way to digest the large meal.

Within an hour, the five men were sitting in the FBI office.

"Can I get either of you a coffee?"

The two politely declined, and Metcalf poured himself a cup. He handed the CIA agents a thick folder with all of the data he had assembled over the past five days.

"I don't expect you to read all of those reports. I will save you the time and give you an overview." Metcalf took a breath and started the briefing. "We received a call from Corporal Schuman, of the Royal Canadian Mounted Police, concerning a body he recovered from the Niagara River. He had identified the body as Kahlid Marqhem, a high-level PFLP terrorist. I am sure you saw the reports of him last week on CNN."

The two men nodded and continued to listen.

"Kahlid was a bad guy. We didn't know why he was poking around the border, but it was obvious from the bullet wounds that he was murdered," Metcalf said, showing the two the pictures of the dead man Schuman had taken. "Based on the condition of the body, Corporal Schuman estimated the body had been dumped less than twenty-four hours before it was found floating tits up in the river. We had two alternatives. The murder was a random act, which almost never happens around here, or another member of his group executed him for being careless. Based on the later assumption, we obtained security videos from Mr. Sam Jefferson, who is in charge of the U.S. border guards. Joe, Pete, and I spent that night watching hours of tape footage, looking for Kahlid's friends. It took a considerable amount of time, but we identified three members on the PFLP terrorist list," Metcalf said, handing them the paper with the names of the three members.

"How did they get the transportation to get across the border?" Flaherty asked.

"We haven't been able to track that down yet. We do know there is a large Palestinian population in Canada. It would make sense that this group would support the PFLP in return for a considerable sum of money. Corporal Schuman and his men are running down a couple leads, but we have nothing concrete yet," Metcalf explained.

"So these three men are the prime suspects in the hospital kidnapping?" Jackson asked.

"To make a long story short, you are correct. We suspect the man in the pictures, Nassir Al-Zarim, to be their leader. The van in the tape crossing the border was also seen leaving the hospital parking garage immediately following the kidnapping. The faxes of the pictures from hospital security cameras are in the folder to back up what I am saying."

The two agents didn't bother looking through the folder. They sat and listened to Metcalf finish the story.

"With this information, we contacted Mr. Jefferson and alerted him with the make and model of the van. He put the alert over the wire to all border crossings in the northeast. We couldn't be sure where they would try to cross back into Canada. That is if they were going to cross at all. We also sent an all points bulletin to every police agency in the state with the same information. If the van is in the state, we will know about it."

"It looks like you have all the bases covered," Jackson said, impressed.

"I hope so, but I have a feeling they are slipping through our fingers."

Agent Flaherty stood and set the black briefcase on the table. He spun the numbers on the combination lock and pressed the buttons on both ends of the top of the case with his thumbs. When the gold clasps clicked, he opened it slowly.

"We told you that we have something that may make finding the infant easier. This is it," Flaherty said, pulling the small GPS unit out of a cloth bag placing it gently on top of the black brief case.

"What the hell is that?" Metcalf asked.

"It is a special receiving unit that is specifically programmed to receive a transmission from the infant," Flaherty said.

"The infant has a transmitter on it?" Metcalf asked.

"The infant was injected with the transmitter an hour after it was born," Flaherty explained.

"Why didn't we know about that? If that is true, we could have found the baby days ago. It may be too late at this point!" Metcalf said, pounding his fist on the table.

"Trust me, sir, we just found out about it this afternoon when we were given the receiver. We were not told how or why the transmitter was injected."

Metcalf couldn't believe this story. "So, turn the thing on and let's see what this miracle of yours can do," Metcalf said with glaring sarcasm.

Flaherty pressed the button and they all watched the screen. They didn't know what to expect to find, but they all had hope. Even Metcalf felt a tinge of optimism as the unit initialized. Their hopes were dashed as the unit failed to pick up a signal.

Metcalf glanced at his watch and noticed it was well after one, Monday morning. "Pardon my lack of support, but this thing is a joke isn't it? Let's pick this up after we have had a chance to get some sleep. It is very late, and I need some time to think more on this."

"Very well, but I assure you that what we say is true. A team of CIA engineers and scientists spent the past week working on this unit."

"Just another secret project by the CIA. It is no wonder the public is so paranoid," Metcalf said, going on the attack. The two men looked at him as he spoke. "I am sorry. I didn't mean to attack you. It is just that if the CIA knew about this supposed transmitter, why did it take so long to get you here?"

"We don't know anything more than what we told you. Don't shoot the messenger," Jackson said in their defense.

"I am sorry! You two are obviously not the ones I need to be having this conversation with. I know you must be exhausted. Let's all rest up. We can plan our search efforts tomorrow morning. By tomorrow night, we should be holding a baby boy in our arms."

The five men all left the office as Metcalf turned off the coffee maker and the lights.

Chapter 46

Sharal stared intently at the large radar screen watching for boat traffic. The illuminated screen cast a green glow over everything within five feet of it. Traveling by boat at dark was extremely dangerous, and at this speed it was nearly suicidal. However, between the GPS unit and the radar, they were making good progress.

The water was calm with large rolling waves allowing the large boat to cruise at nearly ten knots across the lake. The gentle swells caused the boat to rise and fall dramatically as the bow sliced through them.

The feeling inside the cabin was that of a roller coaster. Three of the four men were now feeling a bit sick from the drastic motion. The only one not feeling the effects was Sharal. He spent the majority of his life on the lake and could take anything the old girl could throw at him.

Nassir came up on deck, walking slowly, holding on to the rail tightly as he made his way up to the fly bridge. The motion of the boat was intensified this high up, and his stomach tightened to the point that he thought he was going to vomit.

"How's it going, Sharal?"

"We are making good time. It should take another five hours at this speed to get into the seaway."

Nassir looked out across the lake and could see nothing except water. He glanced at the radar screen noticing three dark blips ahead.

"What are those dark spots?" Nassir asked, pointing at the radar screen.

"Those are ships making their way from the seaway across the lake. They are far enough away that we shouldn't even see them."

"Leaving after dark was pretty risky, but I think it is going to pay off. The only traffic out here will be the large cargo ships heading inland to unload. Most of the pleasure cruisers pull in for the night, not wanting to risk a collision," Sharal commented.

"We didn't have a choice. I think the marina owner and his son were on to us, and we couldn't take the chance—not this close. They were poking around asking too many questions."

Sharal nodded his head. "Well, we are not home free yet. Not by a long stretch. Once we get to the seaway, it will take two of us watching the chart and boat traffic. The channel is narrow and there are some areas that are very shallow. Running aground out there would not be good."

"That's why you are here—to get us through. I don't have to remind you that you could live a year without having to work for what I am paying you."

"I have already put a down payment on a new boat with the money. Don't worry, I will get you where you need to go," Sharal said confidently.

"Do you need anything? Coffee maybe?" Nassir asked.

"Nope, I am fine, thanks."

Nassir looked at the backlit chart plotter next to the radar. The glow of the two units together was enough that a person could read a book. He watched Sharal staring ahead through the windshield at the dark water.

"Have you ever been to Palestine?" Nassir asked inquisitively.

Sharal looked at him, puzzled by the question. "My parents took my brother and I there when we were very little."

"So you have lived in Canada your entire life?"

"I was born in Canada. I am a Canadian citizen."

"Do you ever miss not being with your own people?" Nassir asked, curious about the man he had grown fond of over the past few days.

"These are my people. This is the only life I know. I can remember visiting Israel and feeling like I didn't belong there. It is such a dreadful, poverty stricken place compared to here."

"It has changed. After Rabin Abbas died, the Palestinians started to become stronger. Yassad Al-Bourth will lead us to a resounding victory over the Israeli scum and make life better for everyone. I can feel it."

"How about you? What's your story?" Sharal asked.

"I have no story. I was born in Palestine and will die in Palestine."

"I mean what brings you to do this?"

Nassir pondered over the question. He had never really thought about why he was doing this. He considered not answering, just letting the question hang there in mid air, but he felt safe talking to this man he hardly knew.

"The Americans need to know that in backing the Israelis, they are supporting our enemy. With our new leader, the Palestinian people are becoming stronger, and it will not be long before we unite the region. The money and weapons the Americans provide to the Israeli government kill our people and we must show them once and for all that it has to stop. Before Abbas died, he tried to talk to the American president about the continued support, but before an agreement could be reached, Abbas died. Our new leader, Al-Bourth will not stand for lengthy negotiations. Everyday that goes by that we sit idle, Palestine loses strength. Our people are being killed by the American funded Israeli police and military forces, and we cannot let that happen."

"Do you think we will ever see a day that Palestine will be powerful enough to overtake Israel?"

"Not only do I think I will live to see it, but I think that time is closer than you think. The Hamas party just won the ruling election in Palestine. The groundwork is in place. We just need the Americans to stop the aid to Israel."

"I have to ask then. Why the baby?"

"The baby is the newly adopted son of the vice president," Nassir said with a huge smile on his face.

"You kidnapped the son of the vice president? How did you know about the adoption?"

"It is a long story. The irony is that the boy is Palestinian."

"You must be joking. The vice president is adopting a Palestinian?"

"He doesn't know. The father is an operative of ours working in the city."

"That is quite a story," Sharal said, yawning.

"It is all true. I can assure you."

"I have no reason to doubt you. What are you planning on doing with the infant?"

"Once we cross the border into Canada, we will meet with the rest of my team and take the boy back to Palestine where he belongs. The American government will not get him back until they agree to stop the aid payments. I know governments do not negotiate for the return of adults. I am betting they will bend over backwards when the life of an innocent baby hangs in the balance."

"Do you think getting out of Canada will be any easier than the United States with the infant?"

"Our plan is foolproof. There are more ways to leave a country than by plane."

Sharal's curiosity was now peaked, but he asked no more questions. His job ended with their safe passage through the seaway. He didn't want to make Nassir nervous with too many questions.

Chapter 47

A dirty, brown, rusted out Toyota van pulled up to the doors of the hangar and stopped. The small van wasn't pretty, but it had enough seating for all six of them. Tony honked the weak sounding horn, while inside, Kevin pressed the button to open the large sliding door just enough to let the van through.

The members of the team stared at the ugly vehicle and at Tony who was smiling from ear to ear.

"What the hell is that thing?" Lassiter yelled as Tony and Rodger exited the van.

"That, sir, is our chariot," Tony said, kicking the front tire.

"It looks like an oversized piece of shit," Kevin said, laughing.

"Call it what you like, but it has enough seats for us all to fit," Rodger said.

The blue smoke inside the hangar had just started to dissipate and settle along the floor. "You're right, Tony. It may carry all of us, but it may not move us out of the hangar," Kevin said, waving his hand in front of his face.

"We traded the old car for this beauty even up. It just needs to last a day or two. I think we can get it out of the old girl. It may burn a little oil, but the engine is strong," Tony said trying to build support for his acquisition.

"A little oil? Jesus, man, do you see that blue smoke? It burns more than a little," Kevin said.

"We better take a few quarts with us. It's a long trip," Rodger said.

"Good work, I guess," Lassiter said. "Now let's get to work on where we should begin. Dr. Bastian—sorry—John," Lassiter corrected himself, "activated the receiver while you two were out, and we picked up nothing. So I think it is safe to assume Eagle 2 is not in Moscow. I guess we move now to the outlying areas and continue on until we get a hit. Tony, I think we can use your assumption that the terrorists were not actually Russian and start heading south. This is a big gamble, fellows. What do you think?" Lassiter asked, throwing it out to the men.

"I agree. I don't see any reason to search north of the city," Kevin said, looking at Lassiter.

All the heads nodded in agreement. "Okay with that settled, we can begin to plan the trip. It's too bad we don't have a more detailed map," Lassiter said.

Tony went back to the van and pulled out three folded maps and unfolded them on the table with no fanfare. They were detailed maps of the southern part of Russia, Chechnya, and Georgia.

"Tony, you never cease to amaze me! Where did you get these?"

"Actually, the airport had the maps. We picked these out of the assortment just for starters."

Lassiter took the maps and drew a large circle indicating the reception radius around the hangar. "I think we can effectively rule out this region," he said, pointing to the circle. "If we go on Tony's theory, we can start working our way in overlapping circles directly south to the Chechen border."

"Sounds good to me. When do we get moving?" Tony asked.

"Just as soon as we get everything loaded in the van. Rodger, get the bag of weapons. I will get the satellite phone and the maps. Kevin, scrounge up what food you can fit into a duffle bag from the plan. It is going to be a long trip. Are there any questions before we pull out? Does anyone need to use the bathroom?"

"No, Dad," Tony said with a grin, walking over to get his bag.

"Listen, it is going to take us a good fifteen hours or more, providing the van will even get us there," Lassiter told them as he picked up the STUIII.

"Jeez, how many miles is it down there?" Kevin asked.

"I estimate it at 1,300 miles give or take. Think of it as driving from Washington D.C. to Key West. The only difference is we will not see any girls in bikinis when we get there," Lassiter answered.

"Russian women and bikinis don't mix anyway. Most of them are hairier than I am," Kevin pointed out.

"Come on, guys. Let's get moving."

John picked up his duffel bag and tossed it in the rear of the van. He kept the unit in his hand to keep an eye on it. He wasn't sure how long the batteries would last, and he didn't think about creating a way for them to be recharged. He hoped it was an oversight that wouldn't have drastic repercussions jeopardizing the mission. He couldn't believe he could have been that stupid, and he kept his revelation from the team. He would just have to be careful and keep an eye on the battery level.

"John, is everything ready?" Lassiter asked.

"I think so. I have my things loaded."

"Okay, let's mount up. We have a long way to travel," Lassiter said to his small team. "Tony, you understand more Russian than all of us combined. You drive this heap, and John will ride shotgun. The rest of us will pile in the back.

Kevin flipped the red switch on the wall, opening the door as the van pulled out. As soon as it was clear, Kevin flipped the switch again, and the door started to close slow enough that he could walk out as it moved across the tracks.

For the first time in nearly a week, the men in the van had hope in their eyes. John Bastian's miracle device was finally going to give them the chance to administer a little payback. The atmosphere in the van was electric as they passed the fence skirting the airport.

"Finally," Tony muttered under his breath, as the airport grew smaller in the rearview mirror.

Lassiter was the keeper of the maps. He had the search grid planned out before they reached the highway. The city they were heading for was almost perfectly due south of Moscow. The only problem was that it was so far. The border of Chechnya seemed like a lifetime away, and he still wasn't convinced they were looking in the right place. If this was a mistake, they would be further away from Eagle 2 than they had ever been. But they were moving, and if they were on the road, they were in the game.

Kevin and Rodger drew the short straws and had to sit in the back. The seat was cramped, and the axle ran behind the middle seat, creating a large hump, eliminating any leg room that might have existed.

"Are we there yet?" Kevin yelled out as Rodger playfully backhanded him in the arm.

"Enough!" Lassiter yelled, turning around, but couldn't resist smiling as he said it.

A mile from the city, Tony turned south on E119. The highway would take them to Volgograd, nearly 1,000 miles south. The condition of the road was deplorable. It was more an obstacle course than a highway. The government had not only taken money away from the Russian people, but it had cut money from the infrastructure as well. Some of the holes in the road were big enough to swallow the van, and both Tony and John kept an alert eye.

"It appears that the flow of traffic is heading south. Look at all of the cars," Tony pointed out.

"I haven't seen one car heading north," Steve said.

"Nor have I. Let's hope the traffic dies down. Driving like this is pretty dicey with dodging both potholes and traffic," Tony said, keeping his eyes on the road.

Four quiet hours passed as they moved into the next search grid John turned the receiver on. The reception in this part of the country was not that great and he was having a hard time getting connected to the satellites, even with the antenna extended as far as it would go. The receiver needed four satellites to be effective, and without the triangulation of three satellites, the receiver would not work at all.

"We need to find a high spot," John said, holding the receiver out the window.

"What's wrong?" Lassiter asked.

"We are not getting a strong enough reception from the low orbit satellites to allow the device to figure out where it is."

"If it can't figure out where it is then how the hell will it be able to find where Eagle 2 is?" Lassiter asked skeptically.

"Exactly! We just need a high point on the highway and it should be fine," John said, turning it off. The unit drained power faster searching for a signal than it did in normal operation. He thought it best to turn it off until they could get high enough, to conserve the batteries.

"Tony, if you see a spot, I want you to stop. We should get a reading around here. I don't want to leave an area until we have cleared it," Lassiter said.

"Yes, sir," Tony said, swerving around another large hole.

The southern part of Russia was surprisingly beautiful. The small towns and villages they past by were filled with old homes with some of the most unique architecture Tony had ever seen. Very few homes were located outside of villages. Even farms were located in the villages, and farmers herded their cattle through the streets to pastures on the outskirts as their ancestors had for hundreds of years. It seemed peculiar, but the old practices of the Russian people seemed to be too ingrained for them to ever change.

"I think I see a high spot coming up, sir," Tony said.

"Perfect! Would it help with the reception if we stopped?" Lassiter asked.

"It probably wouldn't hurt," John said, looking at the sky.

"You heard the man—stop right on the very top."

Tony glanced at the gas gauge. It was the first time since leaving.

"We are going to have to stop soon and gas up also. I have been so focused on the road that I overlooked it."

"How much do we have?" Lassiter asked.

"Ummmm, none. We need it badly."

"Good job, Tony!" Rodger yelled from the back seat. "Sure hope you renewed you *Auto Club* bill this year. I wonder if they'll cover this?"

"Shut up, Rodger. If you think you can do any better, you can take over when we stop," Tony said, wrinkling a piece of paper and tossing it over his shoulder, hoping it made it to the back seat.

Chapter 48

Jennifer Cleary had waited as long as she could wait before calling her producer. She had tried dozing off on the couch, but wasted the night watching television. Her body was running on pure adrenaline as she thought about her story.

"Cal, I have got the story of a lifetime," she said into her cell phone.

"I'm listening, what do you have?"

"Let's meet for breakfast, and I will show you," she said, glancing at her watch.

"Okay, how about the American Diner on the corner of 4th and Washington?" Cal asked.

"I know the place. I should be there in thirty minutes."

"Do you have enough to run with?"

"I have enough to run a marathon," she said excitedly into the phone.

"Listen to you. You sound absolutely giddy."

"You are just going to love me when you see what I have," she said as she closed her phone.

The darkness under her eyes was easily concealed by a touch of make-up as she looked in the mirror. She looked presentable enough to go out in public. She grabbed her purse, tape recorder, and car keys, opting to drive rather than take a cab.

The tires of the red BMW screeched onto the street from the underground parking garage as she crossed traffic heading south. The windows were down and she sang to the radio as she wove the sports car through morning traffic. The diner was on the corner and she found a spot across the street. She turned the knob of the old parking meter as her quarters plunked down giving her just over an hour to eat. She walked across the busy street meeting Cal at the door.

"It is good to see you," he said, kissing her cheek. "Shall we?" he said, motioning toward the door.

Jennifer opened the heavy glass and metal door and walked inside opting for a booth out of the way. The diner was decorated in a 50's style motif with large booths around the perimeter and an eating bar running the length of the room. The booths were perfect because they looked out on the sidewalk and were relatively private.

"So, what do you have for me?" Cal asked, looking over the menu.

Jennifer pulled out the tape recorder with a set of small ear bud headphones, handing them to him just as the waitress arrived.

"My name is Birdie. What can I get you folks this morning?"

"I'll have the french toast with a side of bacon and a black coffee," Cal said, placing the menu back between the ketchup and napkins.

"Just coffee and large orange juice for me," Jennifer said.

"They will be ready shortly," the waitress said, pouring the coffee from the pot she carried with her. "Cream and sugar are on the table. If I can get you anything else, let me know."

Cal put the ear buds in his ears and pressed play. He listened, absorbed in the conversation, as Jennifer watched his face. Every time his eyebrows went up she was tempted to ask—"What?" But instead, she sat patiently waiting for the tape to finish.

The french toast arrived just as Cal removed the tiny ear phones, and he gently wrapped the wires around the tape recorder and handed it back to Jennifer.

"I am stunned. When I was thinking of a governmental cover-up, I never thought it would be something this big."

"I know. I couldn't believe it either, and I was sitting right there."

"Judging by the end of the tape, you two had quite an evening."

Jennifer felt her face redden as she heard the words. "It wasn't anything to write home about," she said sheepishly. "So what do you think?"

"I don't know what to think. Do you mind if I take the tape back to the office? I would like to run it by the editors to see where we go with it. Who is your inside person?"

"Cal, you know I can't divulge that information."

"Right. Well, this puts a whole new spin on Deep Throat, now doesn't it?"

"Are you pissed, Cal?"

"Not at all," Cal said, swallowing a large piece of toast.

"Then what is with the attitude?"

"I don't have an attitude. I am just not quite sure how to approach the story seeing as how we got the best lead through one of our reporters sleeping for it."

Jennifer felt as if she just had a door slam in her face. She now truly felt like a whore. "If you don't want the story, I am sure ABC, NBC, or CBS would jump at it. All you have to do is say the word."

"Don't be silly. We just need to proceed carefully with this."

"I am sorry, Cal. I don't mean to be such a bitch. It has been a long week is all."

"Are you crazy? That tape is a smoking gun. Not only will the story expose the government, but it will also have a domino effect on every red-blooded American. My God, Jen, the adopted son of the vice president kidnapped out from under the noses of the doctors—the vice president himself kidnapped—a secret transmitting device injected into every American citizen. It almost sounds like a fantasy story. Think of the consequences this will have when it gets out."

"You're right, of course. What should we do? We can't just sit on the story. What if it's true?"

"Just sit tight, and wait for me to call."

"I want this story, Cal!" she said assertively.

"You'll get it. Just let me do some leg work first."

They both finished their coffee at the same time, and Cal paid the check. Jennifer handed him the tape and walked to her car. She glanced over at the meter displaying two minutes left before starting her car and heading back to her apartment for some well needed and deserved sleep.

She just couldn't help feeling like a piece of trash. What she did put a whole new meaning to the adage, *anything for a story.* She had seduced and slept with a married man to get the information. Suddenly she felt dirty and sickened and couldn't wait to take a shower to wash away whatever of him remained on her.

She parked her car in the garage and took the elevator to her apartment. She unlocked her door and walked inside with tears welling in her eyes. She slowly closed the door and leaned her back on it, sobbing into her hands. She had such high aspirations in college of becoming a network anchor and had lost sight of that dream. She was caught up in the ride and couldn't get off.

She threw the tape recorder against the wall, smashing it into pieces, vowing never to use it again. She regained enough composure to get to her bathroom to undress and turn the shower on. The tears still continued to flow as she tried to wash away the memories of the night before.

Chapter 49

Agent Metcalf patiently waited in front of the hotel for the two CIA agents. Raindrops slapped the windshield as the wipers struggled to keep up. The weather forecast didn't call for rain today, but it was wrong more than they were right.

"*Screaming Jim*" on *WBUF* was in rare form this morning, Metcalf thought watching the drops work their way down the glass. Metcalf listened to him every morning on his way to the office. The topic of the day was weird fetishes, and he laughed out loud when the last caller had admitted that he liked to let cows lick his bare toes.

"What a freak," Metcalf said inside the empty car as the two younger men opened the doors and jumped in.

"Good morning, gentlemen," Metcalf said.

"Good morning, sir," they said to him.

"Listen, before we get back to the office, I just want to apologize about last night. I had no right to say what I said," Metcalf said, looking at both of them.

"Don't think anything of it. Let's just get to work and find that baby."

"You got it," Metcalf said, putting the large car on the street for the short drive to the office. "The radio forecast this morning said the storm is going to end early this afternoon. Do you think the rain will hinder the reception?"

"If this thing works like commercial GPS units, it shouldn't unless the rain becomes heavy. Theoretically, rain could refract the signal enough to degrade the reception. I have personally never seen it, but I've heard of it happening, especially with boats caught in bad weather out in the bay," Agent Flaherty said.

"Are you guys boaters?"

"Yes, sir, last year we won the Baltimore Sailing Club Regatta."

"Really? That is pretty impressive. So you are sailors."

"We have a twenty-five-footer. She is more of a racing-sloop than a day-cruiser, though. We don't have much time to do anything other than take her out for a few hours at a time."

"The agency keeps you boys pretty busy, eh?"

"Yeah, I guess you could say that," Jackson said.

"Well, if you ever want to sail on Lake Erie or Ontario, just give me a call," Metcalf said as they pulled into the back parking lot of the Federal Building, stopping as close to the building as possible to avoid the rain.

"Okay, boys, let's go find that baby," Metcalf said, getting out, shielding his head with his briefcase.

Joe and Pete were already in the office, and the smell of coffee hit Metcalf as soon as he walked in.

"Good morning, gents," Metcalf said in a chipper tone.

"Good morning," they said. "Coffee is fresh, and we are ready to get going."

"Great! Let's see how well this crazy invention really works."

Flaherty pulled it out of the case and placed it on the table, so they all could see it. He depressed the button, and the color screen flickered while it attempted to find the satellites.

No Signal—Unable to establish connection

"What does that mean?" Metcalf asked, staring at the flashing words.

"I don't know. Maybe it is because we are in the basement. Let's go outside," Flaherty said.

"That's a good idea," Metcalf said, grabbing it.

The five piled in the large car. Metcalf placed the GPS on the dash as it attempted once again to find the satellites. Every eye in the car watched the small screen as the rain beat hard on the roof.

After more than a minute, the message still flashed, and all hopes in the car were momentarily dashed.

"So, now what do we do?" Metcalf asked.

"We were told if we had problems with the device to report back to the director," Flaherty said, pulling a cell phone out of his pocket.

"Wait!" Metcalf shouted. "I think we have something. Look at the screen."

"Yes, look at that. The unit is picking something up."

The phone rang twice and was answered.

"Mr. Palmer, sir, this is Agent Flaherty."

"How are things going? Are you having problems?"

"I thought we were, but it appears that the device is working."

"That is good news. Call me when you find something, and good luck!" Ryan said.

"Will do, sir. We are still in Buffalo, but it looks as if we are getting a positive signal."

"Great! Where is it?

"I am not sure, sir. This screen is a bit difficult to read."

"Well, I won't bother you. Call me as soon as you find him," Ryan said, hanging up the phone.

Metcalf picked up the receiver and zoomed in on the signal.

"I don't think this thing is working correctly," Metcalf said.

"Why, it is picking up a signal isn't it?" Flaherty asked.

"Yes, but it shows the signal in the middle of Lake Ontario. I am going in for a map," Metcalf said, going out into the rain.

"I knew we should have brought one of those engineers. I don't understand this thing at all," Flaherty said.

Metcalf returned, shaking off the water before he got in. He unfolded the map and propped it on the dash for them all to see. He took the receiver again and adjusted the screen to show the probe hit.

"Look! I was right. It shows the unit on the northern end of Lake Ontario near the seaway entrance."

"That is impossible," Pete said. "How could it be in the middle of water?"

"Maybe they're on a boat," Jackson said. "It is the only logical answer."

"It is logical—I will give you that. But it just isn't likely. These people are not the boating types."

"What is the distance to the probe's current location?"

"I would estimate it at around 215 miles. It is at least 160 miles to Oswego," Metcalf said, looking at the map.

"We were told the unit has a range of two hundred fifty miles. But with the rain and all, maybe it is giving us a bad reading," Flaherty said, looking at the display for himself.

"It just doesn't make sense," Metcalf said.

"What do we have to lose in going after it?" Jackson asked from the backseat.

"Nothing. Let's get some equipment and get moving," Metcalf said.

The rain had picked up considerably and was pelting the ground with immense force and even moreso—pelting the men as they ran dripping from the rain to the basement door. "I want two twelve-gauge shotguns and whatever other weapons you want to carry. Everyone gets a Kevlar vest on this one. I am not taking any chances. I also want the night vision scope, range finder, and binoculars. If these bastards are on a boat they should be easy to spot," Metcalf said as he stuffed a bag with maps.

"If that thing is right, the bad guys will be in Canadian waters before we get there," Pete said solemnly.

"I know. I have thought of that. Maybe I should get in touch with Corporal Schuman and see what he could do to help."

Metcalf walked into his office as the others gathered the gear. He flipped through his phone directory and dialed the number to the Canadian Mounties.

"This is Agent Metcalf of the FBI. Is Corporal Schuman available?"

"He is in, but is outside on the dock," the receptionist answered.

"I would like to get in touch with him as soon as possible. I have a request."

"Hold one second, I will get him."

"Thank you."

After a momentary pause, Schuman answered the call. "This is Corporal Schuman."

"Corporal Schuman, this is Agent Metcalf."

"Yes, how are you?"

"Fine, just fine. Listen, I am in need of a favor."

"I will do what I can. What do you need?"

"We have found the bad guy who knocked off that body you recovered from the river."

"You did? That's great. So what do you need me for?"

"Well, we think he may be responsible for another crime and we are trying to track him down."

"I still don't understand," Shuman said into the phone.

"What are you doing right now?" Metcalf asked.

"We are going over the water rescue equipment."

"Do you have thirty minutes for me to explain?"

"Sure, come on over," Schuman said.

"Great! I will be there in twenty minutes," Metcalf said, hanging up the phone.

The agents were all sitting around the conference table ready to get moving. They had the bags packed and were talking about the trip.

Just as Metcalf walked up to the men a phone call came in.

"Hello, this is Agent Metcalf."

"Yes, Agent Metcalf of the FBI?" the voice on the other end of the phone asked.

"Yes, how can I help you?"

"My name is Sergeant Greg Lawrence of the Geneva police department. I have called all over searching for information about a white van, and the state police told me to call you."

"A white panel van with no windows and New York plates?"

"Yes, how did you know?"

"It is a long story, Sergeant Lawrence. Do you know where the van is?"

"Yes, it is parked at a marina down here just on the outskirts of town."

"Was anyone in the van?"

"No, it was completely empty. The marina owner said three men cleaned it out and rented one of his boats."

"I see. How long ago was that?"

"Three days ago. He said they were heading north toward Lake Ontario."

Metcalf's eyes lit up immediately. He couldn't believe his fortune.

"That is great news. Do you have a description of the boat?"

"I have a description and registration number. I can fax it to you if you like."

"Yes, I would like that," Metcalf said, sitting down in his chair.

"Oh, one more thing, the marina owner said a fourth man came just before they left. He wasn't sure, but he thought they all left together."

"Good work, Sergeant Lawrence. I am deeply in your debt."

"What did these guys do?" Lawrence finally asked.

"I can't tell you that just yet. But I can say that you have just given us a huge lead," Metcalf said as he hung the phone up.

"Come on, guys, we are crossing the border here. I want to talk to Schuman about getting help. I suspect that receiver thing is correct. The kidnappers are on a boat in Canadian water, and we will need his help. We can't just go barging into Canada with guns blazing."

Everyone except for Metcalf grabbed the bags and headed out the door. Metcalf waited for the fax machine to finish printing the page and then ran up the stairs to the parking lot.

Chapter 50

The large boat was on a northeastern heading and was just ten miles from the entrance to the seaway. The night crossing was rough, but the water had calmed when the storm hit just after midnight. The rain was coming in sheets, cutting visibility to less than one hundred yards. Sharal stood on the fly-bridge protected by a canvas enclosure holding the wheel with both hands as he stared at the radar screen to make sure they didn't run into the ship traffic. This area of the lake was filled with tankers coming from the seaway headed to the other great lakes. Most were bound for either Lake Superior or Michigan using Ontario as a crossing point.

"I think we should pull into the harbor here and wait out the storm," Sharal said, pointing to the radar screen. "The shipping traffic is starting to increase, and it will be very difficult to navigate the seaway in the storm."

"When do you think the storm will end?" Nassir asked in a strained voice.

"The radar shows the storm moving west to east passing over us in another couple of hours. I would expect it to clear just after noon. It will be difficult with good visibility. Now it will be almost impossible."

"We have made good time," Nassir said, looking at his watch. "I will go along with whatever you think is best."

"I think getting a bit closer to shore and then waiting it out is our best bet," Sharal said, relieved that he could take a break for a couple of hours. He was exhausted and needed time to unwind.

"Sounds good. I will go down and tell Ali and Kamal that we are going to stop for a bit. That should make them happy—they are still quite sick. There is no way the Americans will find us here," Nassir said confidently.

Ali and Kamal had not slept at all that night. They were sitting at the table in the galley talking about their homes. They spent the time talking about their families and their dreams. They knew very little about each other before this operation.

Kamal left school at the age of thirteen to train in the camps. He followed in the footsteps of his father and brother and by eighteen found himself in a remote desert camp in the hills of Afghanistan. He learned many things, including a deep hatred for all Americans. Those fighting beside him in the camps were his family. His father and brother were killed one day after a fierce fight with the Israeli Army, leaving only his mother back home in Palestine.

The Israeli Army and police forces crossed the border before dawn to push the Palestinians out of the West Bank The Palestinians were so poorly equipped that they stood little chance of holding back the American backed Israeli's. In fact, the Americans not only equipped them, but also trained them with the weapons.

Kamal was in Afghanistan when it happened, finding out weeks later after a rare phone call home, about the deaths. He had not seen his mother in nearly five years and missed her tremendously. He had spent so much time in Afghanistan that he met a local girl and married her after she became pregnant. He wanted to take her and the baby home to meet his mother terribly. However, within a month of his father's death, he met Nassir and his life was a whirlwind of training.

Ali's background was completely different from Kamal's. He had never spent time in a training camp. His family lived in the West Bank where he saw, first hand, the death and destruction Israeli scum carried out on his countryman. They killed innocent women and children with no remorse, and he wanted nothing more than to stop them.

At nearly 21, and ready to fight, Ali sat in his favorite bar one evening as a couple of Palestinian soldiers talked next to him about joining the PLO. When he turned 25, he joined a more militant group of the PLO and later, the Hamas, where he met Kahlid.

Kahlid and Ali were the same age and quickly became closely attached. Kahlid asked him to come to his house to meet his brother one night after a meeting. Arkhim and Ali hit it off, and before he knew it, he was thrust into the upper echelon of the Hamas where he met Nassir. After that chance meeting, the team was now complete.

"Ali, Kamal, come up. We are stopping for a few hours," Nassir whispered, not wanting to disturb the baby.

"Why are we stopping? Have we made it?" Kamal asked.

"No, the storm is too bad for us to continue. Sharal thinks we should wait it out until after noon."

"We better get to where we are going soon. The baby is not going to make it much longer," Ali said with a frown on his face. "He will not eat, and I think he is getting dehydrated."

"What the hell! Can't you make him eat?" Nassir asked.

"Nassir, I am no doctor! This baby is too little, and I don't know what to do."

"So, if you aren't a doctor, how do you know he is getting dehydrated?" Nassir asked in a raised voice.

"You're right, of course. I don't know for sure," Ali said, looking down at the floor. "But, I do know that he sleeps all the time, has lost weight, and his breathing has become very rough. I am no doctor, but that is not normal. Come on, Nassir, you know me. I wouldn't tell you something not true."

"Just do what you can. We will be there soon," Nassir said, walking back up on deck.

"What does he expect of us?" Ali asked, visibly shaken.

"I don't know. Just do your best. That is all anyone of us can do," Kamal said, putting his hand on Ali's shoulder.

"But you know what happened to Kahlid."

"Kahlid was stupid. You and I both know he would be with us had he not snooped around."

Ali shook his head. "I can remember the first day I went to Kahlid's home. He was so proud of being a fighter for Palestine and of his brother."

"Don't think about that stuff, Ali. We must focus on ourselves and that baby."

"I know, Kamal," Ali said, taking his friend's hand and standing up.

"Come on, let's get some fresh air. We are stopping, and it would do us both good to go outside for a while."

"Okay, I will go with you, but I want to see if the baby will eat something first. You go on. I will be up shortly."

Kamal left to go topside. It was the raining heavily, but it felt good to be in the air. He didn't realize how stale smelling the air below was until he felt the wind in his face.

"Where are we?" Kamal asked, straining his eyes to see through the rain.

"We are heading toward Sacket's Harbor," Sharal stated.

"Sacket's Harbor? Are we in Canada?"

"No, we are going to stop here for a few hours to give the storm a chance to blow over," Nassir told him.

"Sacket's Harbor is a small town in upstate New York. It was a strategic point on the lake during the War of 1812," Sharal said, looking down from above.

"I see," Kamal said, disinterested in the history. "At least the boat has stopped rocking."

"We will get a little closer to land and then drop the anchor. The rocking should just about be over for now," Sharal yelled down.

"That should make Ali feel better," Kamal said, looking up at the two men.

Chapter 51

Tony pulled the van onto the shoulder of the highway as cars sped past. He chose the highest spot he could find, but the road passed directly through the middle of a long valley.

"Anything on that receiver of yours yet?" Lassiter asked.

"No, I am getting reception now, but nothing as far as the probe's location," John said.

"Shit! Alright, Tony, put this heap back on the road and continue south," Lassiter said, looking over the map. "We have another few hours before we should check again."

John turned the receiver off and looked ahead to the road. Just a week ago he was dreading his retirement and now he felt absolutely rejuvenated and alive.

The sun was slowly setting over the hills to their right as the van continued down the highway. The men were cramped, but none of them said a word. Each had plenty of time to think about what happened, but only Tony had thought ahead as the group of men forged on into the unknown.

Somewhere near Volgograd, Tony pulled off at a rest stop to take a break. The last nine hours behind the wheel were anything, but uneventful. Between dodging the pot holes and tractors, every one of his senses was on high alert and the intense concentration had given him a colossal headache.

"Where are we?" Kevin asked.

"We are on the north side of Volgograd" Lassiter said, looking at his map while sitting in the van. He was the only member of the team electing not to get out. "Dr. Bastian, get a reading here. We are close enough to the center of the third circle and 400 miles from Chechnya—maybe we will get lucky."

"I have already checked, and I didn't pick up anything," John said, stretching out his cramped legs.

"Are you sure that thing works?" Tony asked.

John nodded. "I am positive it works. We just need to get closer."

"Wait a second," Kevin spoke up. "What the hell is Volgograd?"

"It is the new and supposedly improved Stalingrad," Tony chimed in. "The Russians changed the name back in the 1960s if I recall correctly," Lassiter added.

"From the looks of it, there is nothing new and improved about it," Kevin surmised.

"Well, we have been riding all day without a break. I need to find a bathroom or I am going to explode," Rodger said.

"There is one in that building, but don't stay too long—it isn't the cleanest," Steve said.

"I don't care, as long as it's not a hole in the floor."

"In that case, I would suggest that tree," Steve said, pointing into the small patch of trees behind the building, smiling.

"What the hell is with this country? Don't they know the entire civilized world has flush toilets?" Rodger asked, raising his hands in astonishment.

"Now you can understand why those poor people were rioting," Tony said, watching Rodger bypass the building, heading toward the trees.

"Steve, was there a place to get something to eat in that building?" Lassiter asked.

"I think I saw a place to get a sandwich and a coffee."

"The food we brought from the plane is good, but I could do with a nice cup of coffee," Lassiter said, finally getting out of the van.

"I'm with him. I could use a sandwich," Rodger said, walking back, zipping his pants.

"Just be careful what you get! You do know they don't just ride the horses over here," Tony yelled to Rodger.

"On second thought, I think I will skip the sandwich and stick with the peanuts we brought."

Tony took the break to lift the hood of the van. He pulled the dipstick out and wiped it on the grass before replacing it and pulling it out again. It was down considerably, and he poured oil directly from the can into the engine. It took nearly one liter, and he was worried they wouldn't make it the rest of the way without stopping again.

"Let's go, fellows. We need to get back on the road," Lassiter said as he swallowed the hot, black coffee.

Tony slammed the hood closed and looked through the windshield at everyone piling in. He opened his door and turned the key. The engine turned over and he drove the old van back out onto the highway.

The traffic became heavy as the highway took them into the heart of the old city. They passed the beautiful Volga dam and saw large ships unloading coal and lumber at the shipping terminal. The eastern section of the city was unbelievably westernized with resort hotels and beaches along the shores of the large river where it turned south to the Caspian Sea.

The Volga channel was created to allow barge traffic from the large Caspian Sea inland during the late nineteenth century. The channel was dredged deeper after World War II to allow for the deeper drafts of ocean-going ships to bring in steel and lumber to help rebuild the devastated city. The port of Volgograd was the northern most terminal supplying nearly all of southern Russia with precious supplies of oil and steel.

Tony almost missed the turn southeast on the M-5 as they stared out the window at the sun bathers getting in the last rays of the day.

"Keep your eyes on the road, Mr. Hampton," Lassiter barked. "We almost missed that turn."

"Sorry, sir," Tony said, keeping an eye out as he merged into the new traffic pattern.

The sky grew dark as the van passed over the long bridge.

"Did the sun go down already?" Kevin asked.

"No, look at those smokestacks," Rodger said, staring out the side window. The large oil refineries and steel mills getting raw materials from shipyards polluted the air and water with tall smokestacks that rose hundreds of feet into the sky. The thick black smoke emanating from them hung heavy in the air creating a blanket of dark clouds for miles.

"My God," Lassiter said as he looked at the ugly sight before him.

"It's a good thing those people are upstream from that mess," Rodger said, looking out the back side window.

"I agree. This place is some kind of ugly. Look at the way the smoke hangs in the air," Lassiter said as he watched the refineries pass by. "I wonder what the people do when the wind changes?"

The air seemed filled with a caustic smell that the five men could almost taste. Tony thought back to a few days ago when his lungs were filled with fresh air and he willed his mind to focus on the highway.

"The EPA would have a heart attack if they saw this," Steve said. "I can't believe the people in the city don't get sick from the pollution."

"Actually, Russia has one of the highest rates of cancer in the world," John said. "I can see now why that is. I just assumed the problems were around their nuclear power plants, but it appears the problems are worse."

"This city has over a million people breathing in that air every day," Lassiter said. "I wonder what the cancer rates are here?"

"I would bet they are higher than normal. It is interesting how truly dirty this country is. I can't believe this country was once a military powerhouse," John stated.

"I agree. It doesn't look as if they possess the technology to get through the day let alone build a nuclear bomb," Tony said, thankful he was watching the smog pass in the rear view mirror.

As the van left the city of nearly one million people, the Caucasus Mountains loomed far in the distance, and they knew they were getting close to the border.

"It won't be long now guys. In another three hours we should be close enough to the Chechan border to check again. If we don't get a reading by then, we need to rethink our options," Lassiter said, looking at his watch.

"He will be there. I can feel it," Tony said.

"Let's hope so. If not, we have made a terrible mistake that we may never recover from," Lassiter said gravely.

"It was the best option," Tony said to the team. "You must trust me. In rock climbing, I look at all of the various paths to the top of the mountain before I start. Many times I study the routes carefully before a path becomes clear. If you look at the evidence, this was the only clear path."

"If I were second guessing you, Mr. Hampton, I would have done it at the airport—not eight hours later. I just hope he is there."

Tony nodded his head in agreement. "I am with Tony," Rodger said from the back seat. "At least we are going somewhere. I was going crazy sitting in that damn hangar."

"Listen, you guys, I want to find him, too. I am just being a realist," Lassiter said, sitting back on the thin foam of the seat.

"Be a realist tomorrow when we find Eagle 2 alive," Rodger said with a renewed hope in his voice.

Chapter 52

The bright morning sunlight slipped through the curtains, but Jennifer wasn't sleeping. In fact, she had not slept a wink all night. Her head was spinning of thoughts of her journalism classes in college and the dreams she had of one day becoming a network anchor. She shamefully wondered what her college professors would think of her behavior the past few days, as she pulled her comforter over her head when the tears came back in full force.

The ring brought her out of her pity as she reached to pick up the phone on the night stand.

"Hello," she stammered through the sobs.

"Jen?" the voice asked.

"Yes, how are you, Cal?"

"I am fine, how are you?" he asked.

"I'm alright, what time is it?"

"It is nearly nine. You sound like shit," Cal said.

"I'm fine, really. I just didn't sleep very well."

"Well, I ran your tape by our editors and they want you to try to get in touch with the White House press secretary for a statement or to see if they want to comment on it before we go to air."

"I will call them now. What if I can't get a comment?"

"Let them know what we have and that if they don't want to give us anything we are going ahead with the story. I'll bet they will give you something once they hear your story. We can't report this without giving them a chance to refute it."

"Give me an hour to get ready, and I'll make the call."

"Let me know what you find out. I want you in here as soon as possible to start taping the intro."

"You still want to give me the story?"

"After a little editing of the tape no one will ever know how you got the information. Listen, Jen, this is not the first time reporters have done something like that to get a story, and mark my words, it will not be the last."

"Thank you, Cal. I will not let you down," Jennifer said, hanging the phone up.

Jennifer threw the covers off and sat up in the bed. She shook the feelings of self-pity out of her head and stood to open the curtains allowing the sun to wash through the small room. She picked through her closet, choosing a conservative outfit and throwing it on the bed before jumping into the shower.

As the warm water cascaded over her bare skin she started to develop a new game plan. First she would call the White House. She knew she would only be able to talk to a junior press agent. Those were the ones tasked with handling the endless stream of questions from reporters, especially young reporters like Jennifer. It made no difference—all she needed was a statement from them anyway.

After drying off, she slid a pair of cotton shorts over her long legs. With just her bra and shorts on, she decided to call before getting dressed.

She opened her cell phone and punched in the number for the press office. The phone rang twice before being answered.

"White House Press Office, can I help you?"

"This is Jennifer Cleary of CNN. I would like to talk to someone in the press office, please."

"One minute please," the receptionist said.

"Hello, this is Jason Adams, Ms. Cleary. How can I help you?" the cheery voice on the phone asked.

"Hello, Jason. I would like to come in and talk with you about a story I am working on."

"What is it relating to? I would just like to know, so I can put you in touch with the right person."

"It is a story concerning the trip the vice president is taking to Russia."

"Hold on just a second. I will put you through to his press office."

"Thank you, Jason."

"Ms. Cleary?" the new voice asked.

"Yes, this is Jennifer Cleary," she answered.

"I am Jack Schwartz. How can I be of help?"

"I am working on a story about the trip the vice president is on."

"I am sorry, Ms. Cleary, but I am not aware of any trip. You must be thinking of the trip he just returned from."

"I don't think so, Mr. Schwartz. I know he is on a goodwill trip to Moscow. I also know that something has gone wrong on that trip. I have information that would lead me to believe he was involved in an incident."

"Hold on a second, Ms. Cleary. Let me verify that."

"This is Duncan Fitzwater, Ms. Cleary."

"Wow, the senior press secretary. How do I rate?" Jennifer blurted out.

"Ms. Cleary, you have information about an alleged trip to Moscow?"

"Yes, that is true. A source has given me information about a trip to Moscow, and I am looking for a statement from the White House before I go to air."

"Ms. Cleary, can I call you back on this number in ten minutes? I would like to see what I can find for you before commenting."

"Sure! Oh, and one more thing, Mr. Fitzwater. The trip is not all I know about. Think about that before blowing me off."

"Ten minutes—I will call you back," and the line went dead.

The phone call was very strange. She was smiling feeling completely back in her groove, and she was playing hardball. Jennifer was taking this nearly unbelievable story to the people, but she wanted to follow the proper channels and give the White House a chance to respond.

Jennifer was suddenly feeling very powerful. She used the time to put on her makeup. The ten minutes she waited had actually come and gone while she quickly put on the cashmere pant suit she had laid on her bed. She curled her long hair and sprayed it lightly with hair spray. She glanced at her watch figuring Mr. Fitzwater had decided to ignore her threats. "Ten minutes," she mumbled under her breath as she walked to the door.

Just as she closed the door behind her, the cell phone rang in her purse.

She looked at the number calling and excitedly flipped it open. "Hello," she said as soon as she had it to her ear.

"Ms. Cleary, this is Duncan Fitzwater."

"I was just about to give up on you."

"Sorry, I had to make a few more calls than I thought. We would like you to come by the White House."

"For what? Don't you people just issue a press statement for things like this?"

"Normally that would be sufficient. However, I would like to talk to you about this in person. Nothing official, you understand."

"I am just heading out now. I can be in your office in 30 minutes or so."

"Very good, I will call the gate and let them know you will be here shortly."

Jennifer flipped her phone closed and slid it back into her purse. "That was easier than I thought it would be," she said to herself as she took the elevator to the parking garage. She dug her keys out and pressed the unlock button as she approached her car.

Traffic was murder getting to the White House. She was thankful that she had told him thirty minutes. The BMW pulled up to the west gate, and the guard carried a clip board as he walked up to the window.

"Name and ID please, ma'am."

"Jennifer Cleary."

"Who are you here to see, Ms. Cleary?" the guard asked, scrutinizing her ID and her car.

"I am a reporter from CNN. I am here to see Mr. Fitzwater."

"I thought you looked familiar. I saw your piece on the Iraqi women last week. It was terrific." The guard flashed a smile.

"Thank you," she said, returning the smile.

He checked her name off the list on his clip board as he raised the gate. "Do you know where to go?" he asked.

"No, not really, this is my first time here."

"Proceed straight ahead. The press offices are between the White House and the west wing. Someone will take your car."

"Thank you, again," she said as she slowly made her way ahead.

Her earlier feelings of power vanished as she passed into the shadow of the White House. Suddenly all of her mental faculties left her, and she felt completely out of her element. Duncan Fitzwater met her at the entrance and walked her into his office.

His office was small with several pictures on the wall of foreign dignitaries shaking Duncan Fitzwater's hand. A large picture of President Lincoln hung on the wall directly behind his desk along with a beautiful painting of General Washington walking through the winter camp at Valley Forge.

"It is nice to finally meet you," Duncan said, offering her a seat in the spacious office.

"And it is nice to meet you, sir," she said nervously.

"Please, call me Duncan," he said, sitting down behind his desk. "So, you have information about a vice presidential trip to Moscow."

"That is correct. I have been in contact with a source close to the White House who has given me the impression that the vice president flew to Moscow where his convoy was attacked by unknown terrorists, and his current location is also unknown."

Duncan's facial expressions did not change as she spoke. He sat completely motionless, as a statue sits on a pedestal, until she was finished. "That is quite a story," he finally said. "Are you sure your source can be trusted?"

"I have no reason to believe it to not be true. You saw the reports by CNN of the massive explosion outside the Kremlin. That explosion coincides at the same time the vice president was visiting. Don't you find it strange?" Jennifer asked, finding her strength return.

"I have no comment on that report. The vice president is currently on a goodwill state visit to Asia. He will be visiting China, Taiwan, and Indonesia. Our political goal in that region is to increase U.S. exports."

"I see. Is that your official statement?"

"It is the truth," Duncan said, wringing his hands as he spoke.

"So, could you tell me why the CIA director has been here daily to meet with the president and why they have developed a secret receiving device to assist in finding the vice president?"

Duncan's face went gravely pale, and he sat back in his chair. "Excuse me? A secret receiving what—?" Duncan stammered.

"Don't toy with me, Mr. Fitzwater. You know exactly what I am talking about."

"Please, Ms. Cleary, I am just relaying what I was told less than an hour ago."

"That's not all," she said with a mischievous grin.

"What else do you have?"

"I know the vice president is adopting a baby."

Duncan grabbed his glass of water and took a long sip. He swallowed hard as the sound of the water passing through his throat seemed to echo in the room.

"Ms. Cleary, would you mind waiting for me outside?"

"This is not a blow off, is it? I have to get down to the station to tape my intro for tonight's broadcast."

"I can assure you it is no blow off. Please, if you don't mind, I need to make a phone call."

"Sure, no problem," she said, walking out the large cherry door.

Before the door closed, he picked up the phone and pressed the top button.

"Mr. President, sir, I am afraid we have a problem," Duncan said, almost unable to get the words out.

"What ever it is Duncan, deal with it," the president said.

"No, sir, this is something you need to hear. We have a leak in the White House—you need to hear what this Jennifer Cleary knows. She knows about the vice president, the project, and the baby."

The line was silent for a long second. "Fine, bring her up," and the line clicked immediately dead.

Duncan stood from behind his large cherry desk and slowly walked to the door. He was not sure how the information got out, but one thing was clear—it was at the highest level. She knew more than he did for goodness' sake.

"Ms. Cleary, would you mind coming with me?"

"That all depends on where you are taking me."

"To meet the President of the United States."

The words "President of the United States" seemed to hit Jennifer with a ton of bricks.

"Do you really think that is necessary?" she asked nervously.

"Not only is it necessary—it is imperative," Duncan said as he looked intently into her face for some indication that she was putting him on, but found none. They walked quickly and deliberately down the hallway without giving Jennifer time enough to actually comprehend what she was getting herself into.

The press corps offices they walked through were the slums of the White House. All major networks had field agents assigned full time here in offices that barely measured ten foot square. The feeling of claustrophobia was evident everywhere they turned. They quickly passed the briefing room which looked much more official on television than in person. The room was very small and dark with lights hanging from the ceiling in each corner. What she didn't know was that the room was actually built over an old swimming pool. There were panels in the floor that could be used to access the old pool which had long since been drained.

"Good morning, Sally. We are here to see the president," Duncan said politely.

"Yes, I know. He just informed me you would be coming up. Go right in," she said with a motherly smile that put Jennifer momentarily at ease.

The door opened and the two walked though. Jennifer looked around the room through her youthful eyes until she focused on Bill Snyder. Her face turned immediately to a bright shade of crimson red as their eyes met.

"Have a seat, both of you," the president said, preferring to stand rather than sit. "Ms. Cleary, Duncan tells me that you came in this morning with quite a story."

Jennifer sat in the chair, willing her mouth to talk, but her brain would not cooperate. "Umm—yes, sir. I guess it is a big story," she said, kicking herself for sounding so stupid.

"Well, would you mind telling me what you just told him?"

Jennifer looked at the floor and then at Bill Snyder before talking. She started with the trip and let the story unfold from there. Before she was finished, the president had taken a seat.

"Mr. Duncan is right. That is quite an interesting story," the president said as he rested his chin on his intertwined fingers.

"I can assure you, sir, that is all my source told me," she said, glancing again and Mr. Snyder who would not look at her.

"Could you possibly tell us who your source is?" the president asked.

"No, sir, I couldn't possibly do that," she said as her voice cracked just a bit from the stress.

"Come now, Jennifer. Is it okay if I call you that?"

"Oh yes, sir,"

"Good. Jennifer, you can't tell us who your source is even as a matter of jeopardizing national security?"

"I can't. I just can't."

The president's eyes narrowed. He was appalled the information she uncovered could have come from anyone in the White House. He thought back to the inner circle of those who knew and decided not to press her. He would find out who it was in due time. Even Duncan didn't know the information she knew. Finding out would be easy. "Don't worry, Jennifer. I am not going to throw you in jail for not revealing your source. This is the United States, not Russia. We are much more civilized here."

Jennifer glanced again at Bill Snyder and then at the president. "I don't understand," she stammered.

"Jennifer, what if I told you that everything you know is true?"

Bill Snyder stood quickly and walked over to the president. He leaned over and whispered something quickly into his ear. The president nodded almost imperceptibly before continuing to talk.

"Mr. Snyder feels that I shouldn't say anything more, but to simply deny everything in your story. I am sorry. I didn't introduce you properly. Jennifer Clearly, this is Mr. Bill Snyder, my Chief of Staff. I don't make a decision without talking it out with Bill first. He is what you could call my right hand and confidant."

Jennifer nervously reached out her hand and shook his with a convincing show of respect.

"Sometimes, as you will see, I don't take his advice. What you have is indeed true. The vice president has been abducted, and we do not currently know who was behind it or where he is at the present time. His newly adopted son was also abducted from the hospital where he was born just days ago. The project you referred to is also true. We are using the probe and a bit of new technology to help us find them."

Jennifer sat perfectly still as the president spoke. She neither acknowledged or showed any sign of surprise in his words.

"Now the question, as I see it, is what are you going to do with your story?" the president asked.

"Jesus Christ!" Mr. Snyder blurted out. "She is nothing more than a two-bit reporter. She probably slept with her source to get the information, and she is coming here to blackmail us," he continued, wildly pointing at Jennifer from across the room.

"Mr. Snyder, that is enough," Tom said sternly. "Ms. Cleary, I must apologize for his outburst."

Although Bill's words stung her soul, Jennifer mocked his anger by allowing a small smile escape her lips. "I must get this information out to the American people. They must know what is going on."

"I can't stress the severity of the situation enough. I alone am responsible for this situation. I sent him to help with the riots. I am sure you can understand how I didn't want this to turn ugly."

"I can understand that, but I have a duty to report this."

The president remained remarkably calm on the outside even though inwardly he was shaken to the core by the revelation.

"Surely, you have a duty to protect the national security of the United States government as well."

"What are you asking of me?"

"I am asking that you give me three more days. We are so close to finding both of them."

Jennifer looked at his kind eyes and the deepening wrinkles on his forehead. She could only imagine what the last week of his life was like. She also looked briefly at Bill Snyder who was seething at her intrusion. Tom also saw her look toward his chief of staff, out of the corner of his eye.

"I can understand the crisis this story would present to you and to the American people. I will agree to hold the story for three days, if you agree to give me an exclusive report detailing the project used to find them."

The president smiled widely. "Ms. Cleary, you drive a hard bargain, but I can live with it."

Duncan Fitzwater led Jennifer out the door of the Oval office and closed the door behind him.

"Jesus, Tom, what were you thinking? You told her everything."

"She already knew everything," Tom said with a bite in his voice.

"But you just confirmed her story," Bill said in a nervous tone.

"If you think for a minute she wasn't going to air the story she had without our statement, you are wrong. I just bought us a few days."

"She was just bluffing. She is nothing but a two-bit reporter."

"Well, that two-bit reporter you are referring to made it into my office with a lot of confidential information."

Bill Snyder chose his words carefully. He knew it wouldn't be difficult for the president to figure out it was him who passed the information to her, and when he found out what he got in return, he would be lucky to keep his job. "Now is our chance to bury the CIA forever. I say we place the blame of the operation failure and the secrecy of the project directly on the CIA."

"Is that what you think?"

"Absolutely! We can destroy their credibility once and for all."

"No, the CIA has given us hope. If Ryan can pull this off, he will have moved up a few notches on my list."

"But don't you see the big picture? If word of this project gets out we will be on the hot seat again."

"Don't you think I have thought about that, Mr. Snyder?" Tom asked as his face reddened.

"So what are you going to do about that?"

"I haven't thought about it. My worry right now is to get David and his son back safely," the president said, looking directly into Bill's eyes.

Bill shook his head in disbelief. He wasn't sure what the political fall out was going to be, but one thing was certain—it was coming soon. He wanted the CIA to pay, and he would stop at nothing to see it happened.

"Bill, I want to be alone for a while. I have some things to think about," Tom said, watching Bill walk toward the door. "I do have one clear thought. When I find out who leaked this to Ms. Cleary, I will have his nuts in a vice."

Bill nodded his head slowly. "It had to have been the CIA. Who knows how many people Ryan has told. I will bet even his secretary knows what's going on over there. At a minimum, he has the two agents in Buffalo, plus Bastian."

"Yes, we will see. I will let you know if I need anything," Tom said, indicating it was time for Bill to leave.

Chapter 53

Agent Metcalf drove the car to meet Corporal Schuman of the Royal Canadian Mounted Police. The fax he just received was on the dashboard, and he ran over the conversation he had with Sergeant Lawrence in his head. He was thankful for the unexpected call because it reinforced the nearly unbelievable finding of the crazy receiver. No, it wasn't that he thought it wouldn't work, it was that he just couldn't believe how it worked. The whole story seemed to be something out of a cheesy science fiction novel. He still couldn't believe the kidnappers were on a boat. It just didn't fit the mold for this type of operation, but it had to be true. He wondered inwardly what their motivation or destination was, but didn't voice his thoughts.

The car entered the paved, half-circle drive of the regional mounted police building. The beautifully landscaped entrance was immaculate. Large boulders delicately placed between strategically planted maple trees gave the drive a majestic look. Two white flags with their red maple leaves fluttered atop large poles on both sides of the entry.

Metcalf stopped the car near the door and the five men exited. They walked in the single-story brick building and waited for Corporal Schuman to meet them.

The mirror shine of granite floor in the lobby brightly reflected the light from the fluorescent fixtures hanging from the ten foot ceilings. It was obvious that Schuman kept his cadets busy cleaning when they weren't training. The receptionist, a rookie cadet, stood behind a chest-high counter in the middle of the open room. Metcalf didn't recall many details from his first visit. He had too many other things on his mind. He did recognize the center hallway directly behind the receptionist they went down to examine the body earlier that week.

"You must be Agent Metcalf," the young cadet said.

"Yes, we are here to see Corporal Schuman," Metcalf said with a nod.

"He will be out momentarily. Can I get you anything to drink, coffee perhaps?"

"We're fine," Metcalf answered for the group.

They didn't wait long before Schuman came walking stiffly down hallway from the briefing room.

"Have you guys been waiting long?" Schuman asked.

"No, actually we just arrived," Metcalf answered.

"Corporal Schuman, this is CIA Agent Flaherty and Agent Jackson," Metcalf said, introducing the new men in his group.

Schuman smiled and shook hands with the two.

"Let's go down to the conference room. We can talk there," Schuman said, leading the group back down the hallway.

The conference room was long and narrow with a thick slab maple table running nearly the entire length of the small room while the walls were completely bare. Schuman took the chair at the head of the table and the others sat on both sides facing each other. CIA Agent Flaherty placed the black briefcase on the table as Metcalf began to speak.

"Corporal Schuman, as I said on the phone, we have been tracking three terrorists after one of them murdered the man you found floating in the river. We have evidence that after they crossed the border, they met in Baltimore and kidnapped an infant from the maternity ward at Johns Hopkins and have made it back into New York State."

"So, if you know where they are, why do you need my help?" Schuman asked.

"Agent Flaherty has something that I think you should see. I must tell you that what you hear and see today must be kept in the highest secrecy."

"You have my word, but I still don't understand."

"Hopefully you will," Metcalf said, nodding at Flaherty to begin explaining the device.

Flaherty pressed the two buttons on the case and it flipped open. He slowly opened the leather top and pulled out the small device, placing it on the table switching it on before removing his hands.

The unit came to life and immediately picked up the probe again.

"It has hasn't moved since we first located it," Flaherty said, looking at the small screen. "That is interesting. What we have here is a reprogrammed GPS that allows us to track a device implanted into the infant taken from the hospital. We have developed a way to both locate the probe and track it within a 250 mile radius," Flaherty explained.

In ten minutes he finished his explanation and Schuman was speechless. He thought it incomprehensible that the Americans had a way of tracking human movements.

"So, even after hearing this, I am still perplexed as to why you need me," Schuman finally said.

"As you can see, we have located the probe in the northeast quadrant of Lake Ontario," Metcalf said, picking up the conversation. "We think the terrorists are on a boat attempting to make it across the border in the seaway. I received a call from a local police sergeant in Geneva just after calling you, indicating four men had rented a large boat heading north for the lake."

"Wait, I thought you said three terrorists crossed the border," Schuman commented.

"Three did cross the border. We are still trying to determine the identity of the fourth. According to the Geneva police, he arrived later in an old Ford pick-up truck."

"Sounds to me as if they brought in a pilot to captain the boat through the canal system," Schuman said as his eyes lit up as if a light had just turned on in his brain. "You need me to help you if they have made their way into Canada."

"Exactly! We also need to keep this out of the news because if it should get out, the American government would be in serious trouble."

"You are in quite a bind," Shuman admitted.

"A bind that I was hoping you could get us out of."

"The area the probe is in is out of my region. I don't know how I could help—the regional commanders are very territorial when it comes to this type of operation."

"We are going regardless. I was hoping you would want to bring your boat and join us," Metcalf said solemnly.

"I can't go with you. I could lose my job," Schuman said to the five men.

"I understand. I wouldn't have you do anything you don't want to do. I don't want to put you in a position where you could lose anything," Metcalf said, trying to lay the guilt on heavy.

Schuman enjoyed the job and his position. The only problem was that it had become very boring, predictable, and safe—three things Schuman despised. He looked at their defeated faces and made the decision.

"I will go with you under one condition," Schuman finally said.

"Anything—you name it."

"If we find them in Canadian waters, you listen to me and follow my orders at all times."

"I wouldn't have it any other way," Metcalf said with a large smile on his face.

"Let me get some gear around, and we can get moving."

"Excellent, we'll get our gear out of the car."

"Move your car around back and transfer your gear to the SUV. It will give us enough room to be comfortable, and it's made to tow the boat," Schuman said, grabbing the keys.

The large white Ford Expedition sat in the rear parking lot of the RCMP office. Schuman used it as his main means of daily transportation. The five agents unloaded their gear from the trunk of the car and tossed it into the back of the Explorer. Agent Flaherty had the receiving unit with him in the black brief case as he sat in the large back seat.

Metcalf sat in the passenger seat as the others filed in. Schuman backed up to the Boston Whaler sitting on the trailer on a concrete slab next to the launching ramp. He hooked up the lights, secured the hitch, and in no time, they were headed toward the highway.

"We will follow highway 401 along the northern shore of Lake Ontario to the seaway. It's a longer trip, but it is the easiest and fastest. It is only twenty miles to Hamilton on the western most tip of the lake, and then we head east to Toronto on the highway," Schuman said with both hands on the wheel.

"We are in your hands," Metcalf said, looking at his watch. "With any hope, the rain will slacken off a bit before too much longer."

"We desperately needed the rain, but it is a nuisance," Schuman said as the wipers whisked the rain away.

"It is nine-thirty. How long do you think it will take us to get to the sea way?" Metcalf asked.

"It is three hours to Ottowa, and the seaway entrance is just south of the city. I would think we should be there sometime around 1:00."

"Flaherty, has the probe moved?"

Flaherty opened the case and turned the unit on. "No, sir, it appears the location has remained the same."

"Why are they not moving?" Metcalf asked out loud.

"Have you ever been out on the lake in a storm? They are close to the seaway entrance which is a dangerous place to be when the visibility is limited by rain. The large ships coming through could easily run a boat of that size over without even knowing it," Schuman commented.

"That's true. They must have pulled into a cove until the storm passes. With any luck, we will catch them there."

"I don't know. Look at the sky—it is clearing to the north and west of us. The weather reports show the storm ending around noon. I am sure they have tuned into the marine weather station and know the same thing," Schuman said, looking at the gray sky.

"Well, they will only have an hour or so head start on us when we do get there."

"We can only hope," Schuman said. "We could put in at Ganonoque and meet them coming north. They have a public marina where we can unload and then head south. There is a map behind the seat, but I think we want route 32 which is off 401. I have been there a few times with my wife."

"That is a great idea."

"I can't cross the border, though. Believe it or not, the border divides the seaway in half. We will have to wait for them on the Canadian side until they decide to cross."

Chapter 54

Shevard heard the Lada pull up in front of the warehouse. He peeked out a hole and motioned for Leonid to open it. Andre pulled the car in slowly as Shevard told Leonid to close the door back up when it was clear. He once again looked out the small hole next to the door to make sure the car wasn't followed and turned to see what Andre returned with.

Alexander also saw the car return and came bounding down the stairs to meet Andre.

"I have everything you asked for," Andre said, getting out of the car.

"Including the remaining explosives?" Alexander asked.

"Everything!"

"Great, now we can start getting ready for the Americans. They are probably just now starting to figure what happened."

"What the hell is the plan?" Shevard asked, walking up to the two men. "You promised me that you would tell us when Andre returned," he added coldly.

"I am not going to back out of my promise, Shevard," Alexander said, looking at him with a hint of disdain in his eyes. I will tell you as soon as I make sure we have everything."

Shevard shook his head as he lit another cigarette. Alexander looked over the items Andre had brought as he laid them out on the dirty concrete floor.

"It looks like everything is here. We are going to take the day when the Americans come," Alexander said, holding the explosives in the air.

"So now that everything is here, what is your plan?" Shevard asked, exhaling smoke through his nostrils.

Alexander looked around at the men staring at him and smiled. "This, my friends, is my plan," he said, holding the C4 explosives in front of him. "We will put these at key points, including inside the large door, and catch the Americans completely off guard. With the explosives and our rifles, we will be able to defeat them and show the world what Russia is doing to our country."

"Explain to me how killing Americans will show the world anything about us," Shevard yelled, his words echoing in the empty building.

"It isn't the Americans at all, Shevard! Can't you see that?" Alexander said acidly. "They are a means to an end. The world will be focused on us and that is the kind of power we need. Only when the people see how we have been pushed around by the Russian government, will we be able to beat it."

"So we kill more innocent people to get what you are searching for?"

"It is not what I am searching for—it is what we are fighting for."

"This is madness, Alexander," Shevard stated. "Absolute madness."

"There is no other way," Alexander said coldly. "Andre, I want one of these placed in the inside of the warehouse door, set the explosive to blow it outward. I also want one taped to the American's chest. If we can't win fair, then we blow the American to hell."

"Wait just a minute. What are you saying?" Shevard asked.

"I am saying that I hate losing," Alexander said with an evil grin on his face.

"I am not taping that thing to the American's chest. You do it," Andre said indignantly.

"I am not doing it either, Alexander," Shevard hissed disgustedly.

"Fine then, I will do it myself. I also want one placed on the ladder going up to the office and one just inside the office door. If they make it that far, they will pay. Leonid, I want you outside as a spotter. Take one of the radios with you, and if you spot anyone in the area, including suspicious cars, I want to know. Take a rifle with you. The rest of us will have rifles with the extra ammunition Andre brought back."

"Will you not even consider our request to just walk away?" Shevard asked, snuffing out the cigarette on the floor with the sole of his shoe.

"No, not only will I not consider it, I don't want to hear it ever again."

Shevard walked away, picking up one of the AK-47s sitting out on the floor. He hated the fact that he had to use it and had a gut-wrenching feeling he would never again see his wife and kids. The only thing he hated more than Alexander at the moment was himself for getting involved in this. He would have never come back after that morning attack if he knew it was going to be this way.

"Let's get moving with those charges—we need to get ready. The Americans are stupid, but even they should know by now where to start looking. It is late, so first thing tomorrow morning I want Leonid outside spotting and the charges in place as I ordered."

"I think we should also set up some defensive positions inside the warehouse so we can protect ourselves," Stephan said, looking at the thin metal walls.

"Good idea, Stephan," Alexander said, slapping him on the back. "That's the kind of thinking we need. Look around for whatever you can find. Just keep your movements outside to a minimum."

"What would you like me to do?" Shevard asked sheepishly.

"I want you to stay close to me," Alexander said.

"Why do you want me to stay close to you? Are you afraid I am going to run away from your madness?"

"That is a possibility I have considered," Alexander nodded as he walked up the metal stairs.

"Bastard," Shevard hissed under his breath.

"Andre, are you going along with this?" Shevard asked.

"I don't see where we have much of a choice. We are all in this together," Andre whispered his answer.

"He is talking about blowing people up."

"I know what he is talking about. I am not stupid, Shevard. But I think we may make it out of this."

"Even if we do make it out of this, do you think you will be able to live with yourself after?"

"Have you considered the possibility that he just might be right?"

"No! And it concerns me that you think this will work," Shevard screamed.

"Keep your voice down. We don't want Alexander to hear," Andre whispered.

"I will not keep my voice down. You are all crazy!" Shevard ranted.

"Listen," Andre said, taking Shevard's arm, leading him away from the others. "This is all we have. It is either this or nothing. The Americans will be here soon. They may be watching the building now. We don't have a choice."

"My God—what has Alexander done to you?"

"He has done nothing. I thought about it when I was out, and I think Alexander is right. We need to fight our way out of this."

"You are fucking nuts. You are all fucking nuts. I can't believe I ever got myself into this," Shevard screamed again, wrapping the pack of cigarettes on the palm of his hand. He pulled one out of the nearly empty pack and put it between his lips. "We are all going to die here."

"Calm down, Shevard, right now," Andre said, raising his voice.

"I don't know how you can remain calm when you are about to murder innocent people. Jesus, Andre, we have already killed innocent people."

"I know that. You don't have to remind me."

"So what are you going to do? You have to make up your mind right now," Shevard said, lowering his voice.

"I have made up my mind. I am staying, and so are you."

"What right do you have in speaking for me, you traitor?"

"Listen to me. Alexander is right. We need all of us if we have any chance at all."

"The five of us against the United States of America is not the kind of odds I would bet on."

"The Americans can't have many left. We killed many of them in the cars. They couldn't have had time to send in replacements. My guess is that they don't have any more than us."

"Your guess? Your guess? What the hell good is your guess?"

"It is all we have. If we do what Alexander has requested, we stand a good chance even if they outnumber us ten to one."

"But that means that we kill fifty innocent Americans, not including the one we have captive."

"If it makes Chechnya free, it will all be worth it."

"Chechnya will never be free after this. The world will never again trust us," Shevard said, finally lighting the cigarette.

"If that is true then it would be a good day for us to die then, my friend."

"I didn't even have a chance to tell my wife and kids goodbye," Shevard said, walking away.

Chapter 55

Sharal watched the storm make its way through the area on the radar screen. The raindrops were small now as it passed while he sat back in the large white captain's chair on the fly-bridge, sipping a hot cup of coffee. And while Nassir had yet to reveal their final destination, Sharal knew they had to be close. In another few days he would be back chartering fishing trips. He told his family he was going to a boat show in Syracuse, New York, so they didn't become suspicious of his absence. He was positive they wouldn't understand what he was doing or why he was doing it. He didn't really understand.

He had met his wife six years ago on a trip to Toronto. She was beautiful, and he loved her from the moment he saw her. He proposed two months after they met and they were married within five months. Her father didn't approve of him, but they didn't care. He knew from the moment he laid eyes on her he was going to marry her with or without her father's blessing.

Their three young children were exactly like him. The oldest was four, and he could spend hours on the boat with his father in what most kids would consider extreme boredom.

A large smile grew on his face as he pictured his family waiting for him at home. He loved it the most when his kids ran to him with their arms as wide as they would go to wrap around his legs. What he loved more than that was the feel of his wife's arms around his body and the taste of her lips. In an instant, the vision was gone, and he was staring at Nassir.

"What are you smiling at, Sharal?"

"Nothing," Sharal said, shaking the thought out of his head. "Nothing at all."

"It looks like the storm will be passing soon," Nassir said, looking up at the sky. "The water is calming now."

"Yes, it is should pass over us in another hour or so."

Nassir looked at his Timex. "It is nearly 11:00. We should be going in another hour—I don't like waiting around."

Sharal looked west and saw the dark sky get lighter. "Yes, I think an hour should do it."

"Excellent, that is good news. We wait an hour, no more."

Kamal heard the talking on deck and decided to join in the conversation. He was getting cabin fever sitting below as he looked at Ali holding the infant against his chest. He stood from the small couch and stretched the ache out of his legs with a moan.

"I will go out and see how much longer we will be here. I need to get off this boat soon, or I am going to go crazy," Kamal said, looking at his exhausted friend holding the sleeping baby.

"I haven't thanked you, Kamal, for helping me. The baby may just make it. His color is getting back to normal, and he is eating like a horse."

"Don't thank me, Ali. It was God's will that the baby is still alive," Kamal said, patting his friend on the shoulder.

"The rain is starting to lighten a bit," Kamal said, stepping into the clean air, closing the sliding door behind him.

"It is clearing to the west," Nassir said from above, upon hearing Kamal emerge. "Sharal and I were just talking about getting underway in another hour, God willing."

"That is great news. Ali and I were just talking below, and he said the infant is doing much better. He is eating and looks healthy."

Nassir smiled at the news. "I knew he could do it. Together we will steal the day right out from under the sleeping Americans."

"We still have to get through the seaway," Sharal said to the two men.

"Yes, but we are so close, I can taste it."

"Speaking of tasting it, I am starving. I will go down and make lunch before we start out," Kamal told them.

"Don't do too much—just a light sandwich would be fine," Nassir told him.

Kamal took another deep breath of the fresh air and went back inside. The air inside the cabin was cool and dry. The generator kept the air conditioning running even when they were stopped. However, it was not all that fresh and the outside air made his lungs feel better.

"Ali, put the baby to sleep and go outside. You need to get some air, you haven't been out since we lift the van."

"I will be okay. The baby needs me."

"Give him to me. You will feel better with new air in your lungs."

"If he stirs, please come and get me."

"Don't worry. He will be fine I promise."

Ali handed the sleeping baby to Kamal. The boy didn't even flinch at the change. His breathing was deep, and his small eyelids were shut so tight that it seemed they would never open. "You promise to get me," Ali said as he stepped through the doors.

The light rain hit his face for the first time in four days. The fog was clearing now, but it was still difficult to make out the shore line. "How far are we from the shore?" Ali asked.

"We are just over a mile from shore," Sharal answered, glancing at the radar screen.

"Wow, that is amazing."

"When it clears, we should have no problem seeing land," Sharal added.

"I don't like not being able to see land. It is disorienting to me."

"It won't be much longer, and we will be in the Seaway. In most areas, you will be able to see both sides with no problem."

"Have you ever been this far, Sharal?" Ali asked.

"Many times. My family and I spent two weeks going up as far as Montreal last year. The seaway is absolutely beautiful."

"How far up are we going?"

"Don't worry about that, Ali," Nassir told him firmly. "I have everything taken care of, my friend."

"I can see blue sky off to the west. It won't be long now."

"Yes, it won't be long. Tell Kamal to get a move on with those sandwiches. As soon as we have eaten, we will be on our way."

Deep down, Nassir knew the Americans had to have put the pieces together. They must have found the van by now. His plan was foolproof—except for the weather delays—he had not counted on that. He would now have to keep a keen eye out for the Coast Guard.

Kamal brought a tray of food up to the fly bridge for Nassir and Sharal. The fiberglass roof of the bridge kept the rain from hitting them from above, while the blue canvas sides kept them dry from the blowing rain. The fly bridge was quite comfortable, and the view was amazing.

"Thank you for the food," Sharal said, taking a sandwich off the tray.

"I left enough below for Ali and me. These are all yours."

"You have outdone yourself, Kamal," Nassir said, swallowing a large bite.

"Thank you both. I'll get things cleaned up below."

"What do you think, Sharal? Is it clear enough to start out?" Nassir asked, looking at his watch. "It is nearly 12:15."

"I think we could. By the time we reach the inlet, it should be past us," Sharal said, turning on the bilge blower to clear out the noxious fumes created by the generator. It was vital to clear the explosive fumes from the enclosed engine compartment. If the engine should spark during startup, it would ignite the fumes and blow the boat out of the water. It was something that novice boaters commonly forgot to do only once in their boating careers. An explosion on the water would easily kill everyone on board.

Sharal decided to run the blower longer than normal just as a precaution. He was a safe boater who didn't take unneeded risks on the water. After five minutes, he turned the key and an alarm sounded until the two engines turned over into a smooth idle.

"Is everything secure?"

Nassir looked over both the port and starboard sides to make sure the fenders were still secure. "All secure," Nassir answered after checking.

Sharal engaged the two inboard props, and the boat slowly made its way out of the protection of the inlet.

The large boat powered into the rolling waves, and Sharal spun the wheel to turn the bow due north. Running parallel to the shore was always the worst because the boat rode the waves like a surfer riding a surfboard. The increased motion was even more pronounced on the fly bridge, and Nassir felt the sandwich start to sour in his stomach.

"It feels good to be moving again, but I think I am going to sit below until we are through this," Nassir admitted to Sharal.

Sharal laughed heartily as he took another bite. "It does indeed, but we made a good decision to wait until the storm passed. The rolling will stop when we turn east in another 45 minutes or so."

"This is more than I can take," Nassir said as he held his stomach.

"It does take some getting used to."

"I agree. Listen, I am afraid we may have visitors before we get to the ship," Nassir said, leaning close to Sharal, whispering in his ear. "We have had too many delays. I don't want to alert Kamal or Ali, but keep an eye out for the Coast Guard."

"What will we do if we are stopped?"

"I don't plan on stopping. The Coast Guard won't go into Canadian waters and we are close. It is probably nothing. I have a tendency to worry too much," Nassir said, slapping Sharal on the back.

"You are scaring me now," Sharal said, staring straight ahead.

"That is exactly why this conversation stays between us. I don't need the other two to get jumpy."

"You still haven't answered my question."

"I want you to push the throttle to the stops and continue straight ahead. Leave the Coast Guard to me."

"What do you mean leave them to you?"

"That is exactly what I mean. Listen, Sharal," Nassir said, looking into the man's eyes. "I am paying you to drive the boat. You will do what I tell you."

"You told me there would be no killing."

"I told you that you would not be involved in any killing," Nassir said, raising his voice slightly. "I am not going to fail this close to the end. Come get me if you see anything suspicious."

Sharal nodded as Nassir made his way down the metal ladder. The conversation was heavy on his mind as he thought about what was going to happen. If anyone was killed, especially an American police officer, they would all sit on death row. Fear swept over him and his palms immediately became sweaty as he contemplated his alternatives. He couldn't leave now. There was nowhere to go. The boat now felt like a jail cell as he watched the radar screen for boat traffic heading toward them.

Chapter 56

John Bastian stared at the small screen growing weary that the batteries of the unit would not last much longer. He had conserved them as much as possible, but with the increased use as they neared the Chechen border, he wasn't sure the special battery they adapted from the GPS back in the lab would hold out. Lassiter wanted to scan more frequently as they neared the border as a precaution. So far the unit was performing as expected, but he couldn't be positive. They had yet to receive anything.

"We are coming up on the Chechen border. Tony, pull over when you can and I will drive," Lassiter said.

"Do you think we will run into any problems?" Tony asked.

"No, but we are not going to take any chances. John, I think it best if you hide that device, too. I don't want the guards to get suspicious of anything they don't understand."

"I have a passport in my bag," John said.

"Don't worry about it right now. You probably won't need it."

"The relationship between the Chechens and Russians has been strained for the past twenty years, and that is putting it lightly. You all know the history. We need to tread lightly after crossing the border—Chechnya does not have the same feelings toward Americans that the Russians do."

"I don't know the history," John admitted.

"The Russians have had their fingers around the neck of Chechnya since the breakup of the USSR. The Russians murdered hundreds of innocent Chechens after a bombing in Moscow that was admittedly planted by a Chechen terrorist," Lassiter recounted.

"If I recall," Tony added, "the Russian army has had a presence in Chechnya ever since."

"That's true, and it has been a source of hostility between the two," Lassiter said, ending the conversation.

"I see a gas station up ahead. I will pull off so we can get some gas, and I will check the oil," Tony said.

"Thank God. I have to piss like a race horse," Kevin yelled from the back seat.

Tony pulled the old van into the gas station. An old man sat watching the traffic go by in a delapidated rocking chair outside of a rundown shack. The dirt parking lot was nearly over-grown with weeds, but they needed gas badly. A single pump stood proudly on a deteriorating concrete pad, but it too was rusted and looked like it might not work.

"Does this thing work?" Tony asked the old man in the chair in perfect Russian.

The man said something barely intelligible and pointed to the pump as the others got out of the van to stretch.

"What did he say?" Lassiter asked.

"I don't know. I think he said pump it yourself," Tony said, pulling the badly cracked hose from the pump.

"Let's get it and get out of here," Lassiter said as he looked around.

"Tony, ask him if there are any bathrooms," Kevin said with an impatient look.

Tony yelled over the van to the man who pointed to the weeds behind the shack. Kevin didn't understand Russian, but he did get the meaning of the conversation. "What the hell is with this country and public toilets?"

Tony flipped the latch and the pumped came to life. He squeezed the handle and gas started to flow. The numbers on the pump rolled as he watched them scroll showing the liters he pumped. When the tank was full, he put the nozzle back on the rusty pump and secured the cap. The smell of hot oil still hung in the air, reminding him to check the level before they left.

Lassiter and Rodger looked over the maps. They had circled all of the search areas from Moscow to their location. "What do you think, sir?" Rodger asked.

"I don't know. I was hoping to find something by now."

"Give me your gut instinct. Do you think he is in Chechnya?" Rodger asked.

"He damn well better be," Lassiter said, tapping the map. "Tony, ask the old man how far it is to Grozny."

Tony was wiping off the dipstick. "It looks like we will be cutting it close on oil," he told Lassiter. He filled the oil one more time, emptying the last container, and closed the hood with a slam. He walked slowly up to the old man who had yet to move from the chair. He pulled out enough money to pay for the gas and asked how far it was to Grozny. The man mumbled as he stuffed the money into his pocket.

Tony walked back to the men. "He said it was around 400 kilometers to Grozny from the border and we are 50 kilometers from the border. That is roughly 270 miles give or take."

"Let's get out of here then. We have been on the road since yesterday and I am anxious to get there," Rodger said.

Lassiter took the driver's seat and the others filled in the back. "John, we have another 30 miles, and we should get a reading on your receiver."

"I will check just after crossing the border. I have it tucked away under the seat out of view for now."

Lassiter turned the key and the engine once again roared to life. "We should get to Grozny in just over four hours," Lassiter announced over his shoulder.

"Thank God. It feels like this trip will never end," Steve said, resting his head on the side window.

"I, for one, hope the ending is better than the beginning," Rodger said.

"Here's to that," Kevin said.

The fields passed by one after another. They had just passed the signs for the border as the traffic started to pick back up again. "The border guards must be swamped by people getting out of Russia. Look at this line of cars. Damn, five hundred yards from the border and we are stuck. It will take us an hour to get through," Tony said, exhaling a deep breath.

"Didn't that old man back at the gas station say Grozny was 240 miles from the border?" John asked.

"Yes, that's what he said." Tony answered.

"Since we are stuck here in traffic, I am going to turn on the receiver before we cross. If we don't pick up anything, I say we wait to cross. We may need to rethink our options."

"That's a good idea," Lassiter said, staring out the windshield.

John reached under his chair and pulled out the receiver, turned it on, and watched the screen flash to life.

"Do you have anything?" Lassiter asked as he inched the van ahead.

"Not yet, but it is still initializing—Wait, I think I am picking up something."

"Where is it?" Lassiter asked excitedly.

"It appears to be located just north of Grozny," John said, scrolling through the screen.

"Damn, Tony was right. Can you tell if he is still alive?" Lassiter asked with a growing frustration of being stuck in traffic.

"Sorry, I can't pick up life signs with this thing. But, the probe would be capable of transmitting them given more time to work on the receiver."

"I'm getting out of this traffic. I can't stand it any longer," Lassiter said impatiently as he turned the steering wheel. If his foot could have pressed the gas pedal through the floor it would have at that moment. The van lurched forward passing the line of cars waiting at the border. At the last minute, he turned back into traffic stopping at the guards carrying AK-47s.

Two guards looked into the van at the six men sitting inside. The guards were obviously overwhelmed at the number of people waiting and motioned to the third guard to raise the long metal gate. Lassiter wasted no time to pass through heading for Grozny.

"Okay, fellows, we know that thing works and we now know where Eagle 2 is. Let's hope we are not too late," Lassiter said.

"How far north from Grozny is the probe?" Tony asked.

"I can't tell for sure, but I would think it is within ten miles of the city," John said, zooming in on the location.

"That means we have just over two hundred miles to go. We should be in position at approximately 1600," Lassiter said, looking at his watch.

Chapter 57

Ganonoque was a quiet town commonly referred to as the gateway to the Thousand Islands. Schuman pulled into the public marina and stopped to disconnect the trailer lights from the Expedition. Metcalf and the others waited on the floating dock next to the ramp as Schuman expertly backed the Whaler down the slippery concrete launch.

"Agent Metcalf, hold on tight to those lines," Schuman yelled as the boat floated free of the trailer. "I am going to park," Schuman yelled out the window.

"How about you guys gather our gear and bring it out to the boat?" Metcalf told the others as he held the boat close to the dock.

Schuman brought his bag with him as he stepped onto the boat. He checked over the gear, making sure he had everything on board. Flaherty stepped onto the boat next carrying the briefcase. The others tossed over the gear and jumped on to the open bow. "Put that stuff under the console. The door is on the port side. If the seaway gets rough, I don't want anything moving around the deck."

"You heard the man—get the stuff stowed away. We need to get moving," Metcalf barked. "Flaherty, keep the receiver in your hands. It should lead us right to them."

"Is everyone ready?" Schuman asked as he started the outboard. The public marina was filled with hundreds of empty boats moored in slips. Large fishing boats with their out riggers sparkling in the sun that just started to emerge from behind the clouds sat quietly beside short runabouts, waiting patiently to pull water skiers again, and beautiful sailboats with their empty masts standing tall like naked trees in a winter forest.

The day was actually turning into one of the most perfect days so far this summer. The humidity was gone, and the water was as flat as a sheet of glass. Schuman pushed the throttle lever in gear and pulled slowly away from the sleeping boats.

Metcalf sat in one of the raised chairs behind the console next to Schuman.

"Okay, boys, I want everyone to put on a Kevlar vest," Metcalf said. "Flaherty, where do you show the probe's location now?" he asked.

Flaherty slid the vest over his shirt and looked at the screen. "The probe is about ten miles southwest of our location."

"Excellent, they have not passed us yet," Metcalf said, slapping his hands together. "Joe, keep an eye out for a large white Carver heading in our direction."

Joe sat in the bow with a pair of binoculars around his neck and the range finder in his right hand nodding back to Metcalf. "Pete, throw me one of those vests. There isn't much to stop bullets up here in the open."

Pete tossed him a vest and sat on the cushion directly in front of the console. "I know what you mean. There isn't much to this boat."

"She may not look like much, but this girl will bring you home every time," Schuman said confidently. "I have seen a Boston Whaler literally split in half and both sections still floated," Schuman added.

"I want to be on the half with the motor then," Pete said with a grin as he moved to one of the seats at the stern.

"I am ready to open her up. Everyone hang on." Schuman jammed the throttle lever forward, and the roar of the motor increased to a point that conversations on board were useless. The bow rose sharply out of the water and then slowly lowered as the boat came up on plane. He pulled back the throttle and raised the outboard motor slightly to adjust for the pitch angle. Joe turned his baseball hat around backward so it didn't fly off in the wind.

The wake behind them dissipated before reaching the shore as the boat cruised easily at 35 miles an hour over the water first heading south to the border then turning west to meet the Carver. The border in this part of the seaway was as fluid as the water that ran through it. It was identified by a dashed line on the marine charts, but it wasn't officially marked on land until further north in the channel. Schuman had a GPS mounted on the console that he watched intently to make sure he didn't inadvertently cross over. He could easily explain his involvement in the operation unless he took his boat into United States water.

Joe periodically scanned the surface with the large binoculars, stopping on each boat carefully looking for a large white Carver. He had never been to this part of Lake Ontario and truth be told, really wasn't all that enthused, he didn't like boating—period.

*

Sharal was still watching the radar screen like a hawk as Nassir came up the ladder. Small islands had started to appear in the channel, indicating they were now in the seaway, and Nassir was smiling confidently. They were so close to the border now—Nassir was positive they were going to make it. His only concern was not meeting up with the ship because of the weather delays. The ship's captain was being paid handsomely, but even that wouldn't hold him there indefinitely.

"Look at the water. It is like a mirror," Nassir commented, looking out the front window.

"The water is always calm here because of the slow currents. Just wait until a ship goes past, the wake could easily swamp a small boat," Sharal stated in a business-like tone, still visibly upset about the earlier conversation.

"I can see you are worried, my friend," Nassir said.

"I don't like doing this," Sharal admitted.

Nassir looked at the compass mounted just above the steering wheel—the heading was northeast.

"Boat traffic is light here," Nassir observed, trying to take Sharal's mind off the conversation.

"Not many boaters come up this way because of the water conditions. It requires a good eye and an even better chart of the area."

"We will be fine," Nassir said softly.

"I've had a bad feeling since you told me about the Coast Guard," Sharal finally admitted.

"I told you I would deal with them."

"But you don't understand. This boat is like a floating target out here. We can't outrun them, and we can't hide. We are dead."

"Don't worry, my friend."

"I will trust you, Nassir, but only because I have no other choice."

*

Metcalf spotted it first before Joe's hand raised up pointing to the west. He leaned over to Schuman and pointed to the white Carver coming directly at them. Schuman eased off the throttle making the wash from behind nearly come over the stern of the boat.

"Sir, I think we have a positive contact," Flaherty stated. "I show the probe coming directly at us.

"Joe, what is the distance of the boat now?" Metcalf asked.

"I have it at just over a thousand yards," Joe yelled back.

"Let's turn the boat around and head back north. I don't want to make anything obvious just yet. Schuman, after the boat passes, fall in behind it so we can confirm the name before we move in. I don't want any chances of making a mistake."

"Understood. Coming about," Schuman relayed the order, turning the boat about on a return course.

Pete watched from the back as the boat moved closer to them. He didn't use the binoculars because at this distance it would have been a dead giveaway. "Sir, the boat is just about to pass our location."

"I see it, Pete. Schuman, when they are well past us, pull in behind, but keep a comfortable distance," Metcalf said. "Everyone, keep your heads down. We have no idea what we are getting into."

Every head nodded as Schuman steered the small boat back on a northeast heading at leisurely pace.

"Bingo, sir. I have a positive on the boat name—*Serenity.*"

"This is it, guys. Joe, Pete, grab the shotguns, but keep them out of sight. I am calling *Serenity* on the radio to see what their intentions are."

"*Serenity,* this is the vessel approaching you from the south," Metcalf said into the radio. "Please stop, so we can board."

"Shit, what are we going to do?" Sharal asked frantically, hearing the message come through on the radio.

"I told you. Push the throttle ahead and drive," Nassir said, sliding down the stairs. Sharal pushed the throttle levers forward and the two large props under the boat churned at over 4,500 revolutions per minute, making the boat shudder with the instant increase in speed.

Metcalf and his men saw the bow of the large boat rise as the stern dug into the water. The wake from the hull was over a foot high as it motored forward. "They are trying to run," Metcalf said.

"I've got it covered," Schuman said, matching the speed.

"*Serenity*, I repeat. This is the FBI. Please stop your engines," Metcalf almost screamed into the radio.

The Whaler quickly overtook the lumbering Carver. Even on a good day, the larger boat was no match in speed and maneuverability to the Whaler. "I see one person on the fly-bridge. The others must be below," Jackson yelled.

Metcalf leaned over to Schuman. "Cut her off at the bow. Let's see if we can't get her to veer off course."

Schuman nodded and increased the throttle. He calculated the speed of the boat and took a heading that would cross her bow at a distance of thirty feet.

The close pass didn't even make the Carver bounce on the wake as it kept a straight line up the seaway at 35 miles an hour. Schuman brought the whaler back around and made another pass this time so close that Pete could reach out and touch the fiberglass bow of the Carver.

"That was close," Metcalf said uneasily.

"It is all we can do," Schuman said, keeping his eye on the prey.

"*Serenity*, this is your final warning. This is the FBI. Please stop your engines, so we can board," Metcalf screamed into the radio.

"Nassir, what are we going to do?" Sharal asked, wiping the sweat off his forehead with the palm of his hand.

Nassir unsnapped the canvas covering the short windshield. He leveled the pistol on the boat veering wildly in front of them, calmly. When the Whaler came in view, thirty feet off the port side, he squeezed the trigger. The bullet went between Schuman and Metcalf hitting the small glass windshield shattering it completely.

"Damn, they are firing on us," Shuman said, the wind now hitting him in the face.

"Slow down. Let's come up behind them," Metcalf said. "Joe, when we get close enough, pump a slug into her stern," Metcalf yelled.

Joe nodded, bringing the 12 gauge to his shoulder. The semi-automatic normally held three cartridges, but with the inner plug removed the shotgun could hold six slug shells. He aimed low and fired into the beautiful boat. The shot just cleared the water line, and as it hit a burst of water and fiberglass sprayed into the air.

"Again! Shoot again!" Metcalf ordered again.

Joe raised the shotgun again and pulled the trigger. The Whaler rose sharply on the Carver's large wake, and the shot went high through the canvas hitting the sliding glass door.

"Be careful. The baby is in there!" Metcalf yelled. Joe looked back at Metcalf, but both knew it was an accident that couldn't be helped. "Fire again at the engines. We can hit the engines and knock them out."

Just as Metcalf ended his order, a spray of bullets hit the Whaler from the bow to the console. Nassir had emptied the 9mm pistol into the small boat. Joe felt the impact before he had a chance to raise the shotgun. The bullet hit him in the middle of the chest and knocked him back off the bow cushion onto the deck. The other shots went wild hitting the smooth fiberglass harmlessly.

Flaherty reached down and helped Joe onto the cushion. The pain in his chest was suffocating and sharp like someone had hit him with a sledgehammer. Afraid to look down, he felt his chest with his hands. The bullet was still lodged in the Kevlar just to the right of his heart. Joe smiled back at Metcalf as his fingers dug the bullet out. He held it up and laughed as Pete came up from the rear and took the shotgun.

"Go to the back, Joe. You probably have a few broken ribs. I will take the shotgun."

"Flaherty and Jackson, keep down!" Metcalf yelled.

Schuman veered off toward the shore on the starboard side after the shots. The Carver was now over a hundred yards in front and pulling away. "Let's give it another run," Schuman said.

"Alright, Pete, get that shotgun ready. We are moving in again," Metcalf yelled.

Schuman increased the speed and steered through the wake. The distance closed quickly as the men on board the smaller boat found what cover they could find.

The boat closed to within 20 yards, and Pete stood and fired two slugs into the stern, and Schuman veered off again this time to the port side into the middle of the seaway. Smoke started to pour out of the back of the Carver, and it slowed in speed.

"I think we got her," Metcalf said.

"Even on one engine, that boat can go a long way," Schuman said.

"Okay, Pete, one more time," Metcalf yelled. "We're going to make another close pass."

Schuman looked onto the fly-bridge of the Carver. "Aim for the fly-bridge. That will stop her for sure," Schuman yelled to Pete.

As the Whaler sped ahead, getting closer, another round of fire hit her on the starboard side. The bullets impacted the fiberglass just below the deck line making six small diameter holes the size of a pinky down the starboard side. "Keep going!" Metcalf yelled.

The wake was larger now as the bow of the Carver rose even higher in the air from the lack of speed. The boat was literally plowing the water sending a white spray from both sides of the hull almost 15 feet as on ech side of the hull, but it still lumbered ahead at close to 25 miles an hour.

Pete raised the shotgun stock to his cheek as he sighted in the fly-bridge. It was almost impossible to pick out people through the dark canvas, so he just aimed to the middle of the cabin and pulled the trigger. The recoil of the gun pressed the butt of the stock deep into his shoulder as the empty shell was ejected and another slid into the chamber. The first shot tore through the canvas opening a large hole. The second shot was to the left of the first and Pete lowered the empty gun. Schuman slowed once again to avoid the return fire, but he constantly eyed the Carver.

"Serenity, shut down your remaining engine before someone gets killed!" Metcalf yelled once again into the radio. "Does this thing work?" he asked Schuman.

"It works, we tested it this morning."

"One more pass. This time I want you to empty that thing. I have had enough of this!" Metcalf yelled over the engines.

"You got it. Here we go—get ready, Pete," Schuman said, cranking the wheel around.

Pete pressed his body into the bow cushions and grabbed the second shotgun, as Schuman brought the boat around. At the last minute, he raised up and fired six shots—three into the stern and three into the fly-bridge.

Schuman pulled back the throttle as he watched the boat start to veer off toward shore. "Look at her," he pointed.

"Well, I be damned. She is stopping."

"She is not stopping, but heading toward shore at full throttle," Metcalf observed.

"Shit, if she runs aground at that speed the boat will be destroyed."

Nassir stared at Sharal with horror in his face. The Canadian born pilot had taken a slug between his shoulder blades that exited just below his throat. Blood splattered all over the controls making them unreadable. Sharal had died immediately—his body slumped over the wheel. Nassir wiped his forehead on his sleeve and he noticed the blood and tissue that he thought was sweat.

Nassir resisted the urge to vomit as he pushed the body off the wheel, away from the controls. Nassir pulled the throttle of the remaining engine back as far as it would go and shifted the gear into reverse, but it was too late. The boat was on a collision course with shore and there was nothing he could do except sit and wait for the grounding. Below, Ali and Kamal were hiding in the bow stateroom away from the shots. They had no idea what was about to happen.

The men on board the Whaler watched with graven faces as the two props dug into the soft river bottom along the shore and then turned no more as the beautiful Carver landed. A thick cloud of mud and seaweed surrounded the rear of the boat as the bow crashed into the rocky shore line. Metcalf was speechless as the boat hit with an unbelievable force. The sound was sickening, and he wondered if the infant was still alive.

The collision made the entire boat shudder. Nassir was thrown forward into the glass windshield knocking him unconscious and those below were thrown harmlessly against the cushioned "vee" of the bow stateroom.

"Ali, are you okay?" Kamal asked, checking himself over.

"I think so, what happened?"

"I don't know."

"Come out with your hands up," Metcalf said into the loudspeaker as Schuman piloted the Whaler directly up to the Carver's aft swim platform. He wasn't sure if anyone was alive on board, but it was better to be safe than sorry. "Bring her in so we can board," Metcalf ordered. "Pete, take the shotgun and board her first. Flaherty and Jackson will be right behind you."

Schuman expertly piloted the boat until the bow touched the swim platform of the grounded Carver. The three men jumped off and quickly cleared the outer cabin. Jackson climbed the ladder to the fly-bridge and found Nassir and Sharal. "Sir, we have one alive up here," Jackson yelled.

"Find something to bind his wrists, and leave him."

Metcalf was now on the deck of the Carver, following behind the two going below. "Keep your eyes alert, but be careful of the infant. We can't risk anything now," Metcalf reminded them.

Pete busted the flimsy wood door to the stateroom open with a strong shoulder and found Ali and Kamal still rubbing their bruises. They immediately raised their hands and surrendered.

"The baby. Where is the baby?" Metcalf yelled, pointing his pistol at their heads.

Ali pointed to the tool box where he had placed the infant just moments after the shooting started, surrounded by pillows and blankets. Flaherty rushed to open it. "Is he alive?" Metcalf asked, frantically holding the pistol to the heads of the two.

Flaherty reached in and picked up the sleeping infant.

"Thank God," Metcalf said. "Tie up these pieces of shit, and get them out of here."

Chapter 58

Lassiter's stomach was in knots as they neared Grozny. He had not eaten in twelve hours, but the feeling was more from nerves than being hungry. John's invention had worked amazingly well up to this point. He felt like a fool for not believing in it.

"How far are we now?" Lassiter asked.

"The probe is ten miles from our location. It is two miles north of the city," John answered.

"Can you tell what is around it?"

"No, I can only see roads, but it doesn't look like there are many roads in that area," John answered. The screen was growing fainter by the minute, and he stared, memorizing the roads just in case it went dead. "Turn right at the next intersection," John said, looking out the windshield.

"I really would like to know what we are getting into before we get there," Tony said.

"Save your breath. We are almost there," Lassiter said gruffly.

Just as the van turned right, the screen went totally dead. "Shit—" John said under his breath.

"What's wrong?" Lassiter asked impatiently.

"The battery went dead."

"So put in more. We are almost there," Lassiter said incredulously.

"You don't understand. These are special batteries. I don't have one to replace it."

"You mean you brought an electronic device with you without a back-up battery?" Lassiter asked.

"I didn't have the time to make another one. We made this practically from scratch. Just be thankful it lasted this long."

"So tell me you know the way to the probe."

"Relax, it is just ahead. One more turn and we will be there."

"One more turn? W are out in the country," Lassiter observed, glancing out the side window.

"I can't help it. This is where the probe is," John said defensively. "Turn left up ahead, and it will be about a mile down that road."

"But there can't be anything out here," Kevin said from the backseat.

Lassiter made the left and all twelve eyes searched the landscape carefully. "Look, is that a parking lot? Ahead of us just off the road, there on the left," Tony asked, pointing over the front seat.

"I think so. I see a large metal building through the trees ahead, also," John said.

"I am going to drive past. I want everyone looking at the area, so we can plan our assault," Lassiter ordered.

Every eye was sizing up the large warehouse that paralleled the road, the front facing them as they passed.

"It looks empty," Tony said. "Are you sure that thing works?"

"I will bet my life on it," John said confidently.

"Your life is not important. Would you bet the vice president's?" Lassiter asked as he drove another mile down the old road and stopped.

"I would bet your life," John said, glancing back at the warehouse as it passed out of sight.

"Okay, fellows, what do you think?" Lassiter asked.

"I think it looks deserted," Tony said.

"The building is big enough. They could have driven their cars inside," Kevin added.

"The building has two front entrances—one large sliding door like garages have and a normal one on the right. They could have easily driven their cars inside to hide them. The parking lot is approximately 30 yards deep, which will leave us vulnerable getting to the building," Steve said. "Plus, if there are people inside, we don't know how many," he added.

"The building looks like it is constructed of sheet metal. I didn't see any windows at all," Tony said.

"Okay, so it's not going to be easy. It's true, the building will not be the easiest to approach. Rodger, can you get to the building and scout it out?" Lassiter asked.

"I see what you are thinking," Rodger stated. "I can get in close, but did anyone see any spotters?"

"I didn't see anyone," Tony said.

"We have another couple hours of daylight," Lassiter said, looking at the sky. Get your ass there as soon as you can. I want to move in before the sun goes down."

"Will do, sir," Rodger said, checking over his gear. "Did you bring the radios?"

"Yes. If you think it is safe, radio back and we will come in right behind you. Oh, and none of the Navy Seal hero shit. Don't do anything stupid to give away your position," Lassiter added, grabbing the radios out of the bag.

Rodger smiled as he put the receiver around his ear. "Testing, testing," he said into the radio.

"I am getting you clear," Lassiter said.

"Give me fifteen minutes to get in place," Rodger said as he stepped into the tall grass alongside the road.

"While we wait, I am open for ideas on getting inside," Lassiter told those remaining.

"We could use the van to bust through the front door," John said.

"That would get us in," Lassiter surmised. "We could probably rig the van to drive into the building. That may surprise them enough to get us through the opening. Does anyone have any better suggestions?"

*

Shevard startled as the thin metal door opened. "Leonid, what is it?"

"A van just drove down the road," Leonid panted, out of breath.

"Did it stop?" Shevard asked, walking over to the man.

"No, it didn't."

"So what is the problem?" Shevard pressed him.

"It was filled with men looking at the building. I think they wanted to stop, but they kept going down the road."

"I think you should alert Alexander," Shevard said, walking over to the door to look out.

Leonid met Alexander coming down the stairs.

"Alexander, I think the Americans have found us," Leonid said frantically.

Alexander smiled. "It took them long enough," he said sarcastically. "How many did you see?"

"I only saw five or six. They were in a small van."

"Excellent! I told you we would take the day. Did they see you?"

"No, I hid in the weeds until they were out of view."

"Stay inside, but keep an eye out. If they know we're here, they will attack," Alexander told him as he walked over to the American. "It looks like your friends have arrived just in time to die."

David said nothing in response to the man. Even though he couldn't see, David knew the voice came from the leader of the terrorists. He was the same one who taped the explosives to his chest. David wouldn't give him the satisfaction of acknowledging what was said.

Alexander glanced over his shoulder at Shevard who was looking out one of the many holes in the wall. Alexander couldn't resist kicking David's foot as he walked away. "It is time to fight," Alexander told his men. "We are as ready as we are going to be. Does anyone have any questions or problems?" Shevard briefly turned disgustedly to look at Alexander and then back around to look out, ignoring the comments. "Stephan, if they come at the front of the building, I want the door blown when they get close. Don't get anxious. I want to catch them off guard." Stephan nodded imperceptibly as he walked over to the front wall. "Andre, I want you at the back of the building just in case they try to surprise us." Alexander ordered him to the rear to hopefully keep him out of the brunt of the attack.

A feeling of helpless despair came over David as he heard the frantic orders. This was his fault. He had approved the trip knowing they didn't have the proper resources, and now his men were walking into a trap, and he couldn't do anything about it. He heard the anxious conversations of the terrorists and his feelings nearly overwhelmed him. He tried to take a deep breath, but the tightly wrapped tape around his chest wouldn't allow his lungs to fill deeply with air. In the darkness, his mind focused on his wife and their new baby.

He had no way of knowing the ordeal that had just ended back home. The image of his wife holding the son he would probably never see brought tears to his eyes as he resigned himself to die. At least it would be quick, he thought, as another deep breath reminded him of his fate.

Alexander walked back up to the office to be alone and keep an eye on the men below. He had the detonator for the C4 on the American and the stairway. He didn't plan on letting any of the Americans live to see another sun rise, even if it meant they all died. The sacrifice the five men of the CLA may ultimately make today, Alexander knew, would carry their cause forward.

*

Rodger had made his way to the edge of the old pavement of the warehouse in the fifteen minutes he told Lassiter. The temperature had dropped considerably, but it was still stifling hot. The mile he just covered was difficult because of the thick underbrush, and he went slowly to avoid being seen. His trained eyes canvassed the building, looking for any hint of movement.

"Sir, I am in place," Rodger whispered into the radio.

"Do you see anything?" Lassiter asked.

"Negative. The building looks abandoned."

"Are there any doors other than the front doors?"

"I see only one door in the back, but it is just a normal sized door. We would have to go in single file and that would be too much of a risk. I'll try to get closer to see if anyone is home."

"Make sure you are not seen," Lassiter ordered.

"Got it, sir," Rodger said, sinking back into the tall weeds. "The only windows I see are near the roof-line. Attacking from the rear is going to be nearly impossible."

"Shit, I guess we knock on the front door then," Lassiter said into the radio. "Rodger, stay put. We are going to plan a little extra special knock."

"What did Rodger find?" Tony asked.

"Nothing good, I'm afraid," Lassiter said, putting the radio down. Do you think we could rig this piece of shit to drive straight into the front door?" Lassiter asked the men.

"From what I saw, the building is pretty standard, like the warehouses back in the States," Tony said. "I think we could do it."

"But what if it doesn't break through?" Kevin asked. "The door will be plugged by the van, and we will be stuck on the outside."

"Do you think you can get this heap going fast enough to break through?" Lassiter asked Tony.

"If we can get a good run at it," Tony said with a nod.

Lassiter picked up the radio. "Rodger, we need the distance the warehouse is from the road."

"What are you thinking?" Rodger asked.

"A little surprise," Lassiter answered.

"I would estimate 25 yards, maybe a little more."

"Is 25 yards enough?" Lassiter asked Tony.

"If we could get something heavy on the accelerator and have someone pop it into gear, it may be enough," Tony speculated.

"Find something. It is our only option," Lassiter ordered.

"Yes, sir, I'm on it," Tony said.

"Sir, I think I see some movement inside," Rodger said excitedly. "There are several holes in the walls, and I swear I saw something."

"Keep an eye out. I would love to know how many we are facing."

Lassiter looked at the sky, and quickly estimated the amount of daylight left. "Mr. Hampton, what did you find?"

"I can wedge this stick between the floorboard and pedal. I also found a rope to tie the steering wheel to the gear shifter to keep the van straight."

"Good, let's get moving. Does everyone have their weapons ready?"

The five checked over their gear closely and nodded. Tony handed John a .45 Blackhawk revolver he had pulled out of one of the bags. "Here, you might need this."

John took the large pistol and checked it quickly to make sure it was loaded. "My wife would kill me right now if she knew what I was doing. She hates guns."

"Just stay behind us. I have orders to keep you out of this," Lassiter said.

"You know I couldn't do that," John said, tucking the pistol between his belt and stomach. "I haven't felt this alive in years."

"Just do me a favor, and be careful," Lassiter ordered, grabbing the radio from the top of the van. "Everyone in—we will use the van to get closer. Rodger, we are on our way. Tony has come up with a way to smash the front door down. Hopefully, it will surprise them enough for us to overpower them."

"I will meet you at the southeast corner," Rodger acknowledged.

"This is it, boys. Time to earn our pay and get Eagle 2 back," Lassiter said, showing no emotion.

*

"Alexander!" Shevard yelled. "I see the van. It is coming back down the road."

"Do you see anyone in it?" Alexander asked, stepping out of the office.

"No, it looks empty. But it is moving very fast."

"Don't be a fool—someone has to be in it."

"Come look for yourself. There is no one driving, and it looks like it is heading right for us."

Alexander ran down the stairs to see for himself. "Someone could be hiding, steering blind. Leonid, I want the door blown on my order."

Leonid nodded, watching the scene from the other side of the door. "It looks like they are trying to use the van to break down the door."

"A good plan," Alexander whispered. "But, if the Americans are really in the van, we will kill them all at once."

The van quickly picked up speed. Tony had the engine revving as high as it could go before putting it into gear. The tires screeched and the van took off in a straight line toward the warehouse. They had managed to find a little more room by angling the approach, using the road to get the van to maximum speed. The plan also allowed the men to hide in the weeds, so they weren't exposed to the terrorists.

"The van is close, Alexander!" Shevard yelled, excitedly grasping the AK47 tightly in his palm.

"Steady—steady—not yet. Wait until it is within five meters of the door." Alexander looked out the small hole incredulously watching the van speed at them. "Now! Blow it now!" he screamed.

Leonid pressed the detonator, and the large door seemed to fold in half before the explosion blew it out toward the van. Small pieces of metal zipped through the air tearing into the grill and hood and steam immediately started to escape from under the hood as the shrapnel sliced through the radiator hoses. A large piece of sheet metal shattered the windshield nearly cutting the drivers seat in half as it passed through like a hot knife through butter.

The concussion of the blast was deafening inside the warehouse. Shevard stood silent, momentarily stunned by the noise as he watched the van slow, but continue forward.

"How is that possible?" he asked. "Look at it!"

"I don't know," Alexander said as the burning van hit the wall just to the right of the door, slamming into the wall, narrowly missing Shevard. "Shevard, check the van. Kill everyone inside."

Shevard quickly ran out the large hole where the door used to be. The sharp, exposed edges of sheet metal caught the arm of his shirt, tearing it, but he still managed to keep the butt of the automatic rifle in the crook of his shoulder tightly. His eyes frantically scanned through the van, convinced with the amount of destruction, the driver must have died. All of the windows were shattered and steam was still rising from the ruptured radiator under the hood. "Alexander, it is empty. The van is empty!" he yelled back anxiously.

Alexander didn't immediately understand what was happening. He was shocked that he had been outsmarted and couldn't comprehend what was coming next. "Everyone to the back! This must be a diversion!" he screamed.

Stephan and Leonid were way ahead of him as they heard the order. They were heading for the rear door.

"Andre, do you see anything?" Stephan asked.

"Nothing," Andre answered.

"They will be coming soon. The van was empty, and Alexander thinks they will be coming this way."

"If they do, we will be ready," Leonid said firmly.

Rodger kneeled with his back against the thin metal wall of the south end of the warehouse. The van speeding across the pavement was the perfect diversion to get to the building. He took a chance that the van would have their attention, and it paid off as he sprinted across the hot pavement. He was almost to the building when the explosion rocked the ground. He ducked, but kept running until he had reached the building.

Beads of sweat dripped slowly down his forehead into his eyes, but he ignored the sting. Rodger held his 9mm in both hands out in front of him as he watched the rest of the team come up behind him. From his location, he couldn't see inside, but if any shooting started, he could react immediately. He couldn't believe there were no shots fired yet. His only guess was that the terrorists, however many there were, couldn't cover all of the building—and that was a good thing.

Tony came up first. "It is good to see you, Rodger," Tony whispered, kneeling down with his knee on the hot pavement.

"That was a good trick with the van. It is a good thing no one was in it. That explosion would have ended this quick," Rodger whispered back.

Tony nodded as the rest of the team filled in beside him.

"The explosives add a whole new twist," Lassiter said, surveying the building. "Our only chance is to go through the front. The hole is big enough to let us all pass through at once. If we use the door in the back, we will be slaughtered."

"Let's get a move on," Tony said as he took out his pistol and crouched with his back tight against the wall.

"Ok, this is it. Watch each other's back, and aim your shots carefully. Eagle 2 is in there," Lassiter ordered.

The six men walked slowly, single file with their backs tight to the metal wall. Tony cautiously looked around the front corner and saw the old van, hood deep inside the building. "The front is clear," Tony whispered over his shoulder. He slipped around the corner and ran to the disabled van, with the others right behind him.

"Do you see anything?" Lassiter asked.

"It looks empty," Kevin said from the rear corner. "I do see an old car parked inside though."

"John, stay right here behind the van. I don't want you to go in with us," Lassiter said, looking into John's eyes.

"If it is alright with you, I want to go in with you. You are going to need every one of us."

"Then stay behind me," Lassiter ordered.

John nodded as they all readied to enter the building. The men all huddled behind the van, each breathing steady but deep. "Okay, on me," Lassiter said, putting one hand on the rear corner. "Let's go," Lassiter said, standing up, sprinting toward the hole.

Leonid spotted them first, but only after they were inside the dark building. He raised his automatic and fired off a burst of shots without aiming, which went wide, hitting the wall, making three holes the size of a dime. "I counted six of them," Leonid screamed. Lassiter saw the rifle firing a split second before he heard the sound. He raised his pistol and squeezed off two rounds at the muzzle flash, but his eyes had not adjusted to the low level of light inside yet before he shot. Tony, Rodger, and Kevin sprawled flat against the concrete floor as Lassiter, John, and Steve made it to the Lada.

"Look, Eagle 2," Steve said, pointing to the rear of the car.

Lassiter looked back toward where Steve was pointing. Eagle 2 was sitting with his back against the wall, still blindfolded. "What is that around his chest?"

"It looks like explosives, sir."

"Shit—Shit."

"See if you can cut it off him," Lassiter said, peeking over the hood of the car. He saw the other three crawling with their stomachs pressed into the floor toward a staircase. A round of shots peppered the hood of the car, punching holes into the thin metal from above. Lassiter lowered his head to avoid the gunfire as the three men crawling looked over toward the car. Lassiter kept his head down and pointed to the office section. Rodger looked up and saw the barrel of the AK-47 sticking out of the window.

"I'll take this one," Rodger said, looking up the flight of metal stairs.

"Watch yourself," Tony said as another round of shots came from the rifle aimed at the Lada. The shots hit low, tearing holes in the tires as they ricocheted off the floor. The tires hissed as they quickly went flat, causing the car to sink while Tony and Kevin crawled past the stairs. Shevard saw the two men coming at them and carefully aimed. His eye narrowed as his finger squeezed the trigger. The recoil of the six round burst caused the barrel to raise just enough to make the last two shots hit the front wall.

Tony looked at Kevin's body shake as it took three rounds and he frantically pulled his injured teammate's body behind the stairway out of the direct line of fire. "Kevin, everything is going to be ok," Tony lied. "I've got you now, you are safe."

"I can't feel my legs," Kevin gasped as blood came out if the corner of his mouth.

"I will get you out of here. Just hold on, do you hear me?"

"No, get those bastards," Kevin said, coughing up more blood. "Do me a favor," he asked as his eyes stared at the roof.

"Anything," Tony said, holding his head in his lap.

"Tell my wife and kids I love them," Kevin said and a long gasp of air escaped his lungs just as his body went limp.

Tony gently laid Kevin's head back on the floor. He looked up the stairs at Rodger who had made his way to the door. Tony's eyes searched the back of the building crazily from around the edge of the stairway, but the sun had set and without lights, the building was growing dark. Another burst of firing came from the rear of the building. The bright muzzle flash split the darkness, and Tony finally had a target. The clink of the rounds hitting the back of the metal stairs sobered him for a second. He shot twice at the flash unable to see if he hit his quarry.

Rodger kneeled at the entrance to the door slowly, quietly twisting the door handle. He was just about to bust in when another explosion tore through the stairway, hurtling shrapnel at Rodger and Tony. Tony felt the blast overpower him as his body was thrown into the air. When he hit the ground, his body was numb from the pain. He landed on his back, fifteen feet from the stairway with a loud groan. He opened his eyes and couldn't see the ceiling through the smoke and blood that was flowing from a large gash on his forehead. The bulletproof vest he wore had taken most of the flying shrapnel, but the backs of his legs were a mess. He wiped the blood from his eyes and turned over on his stomach, still flat to the ground. The numbness had worn off, and the pain that immersed his body made him nauseous to the point that he was sure he was going to vomit.

Rodger had instinctively raised his arms to shield his face and had escaped the blast with only minor cuts on both arms. The explosives were set under the middle of the stairs and he was high enough to avoid the worst of it. He saw Tony's body hurtling through the air like a rag doll. He feared the worst, but when he saw Tony move, he breathed a sigh of relief. Just as he turned to enter, six bullets ripped through the middle of the wooden door where he had been moments earlier.

Steve had crawled his way to Eagle 2 when the explosive went off. He shielded his head with his hands fearing the worst—Eagle 2 was gone. But when he looked up, Eagle 2 was still there. He quickly crawled the last ten feet and with the pocket knife he always carried, cut the thick tape securing the explosives to Eagle 2's chest. He tossed the C4 up onto the metal walkway just underneath the window of the second floor office and dragged Eagle 2 behind the Lada.

Lassiter ripped the blindfold off and untied his hands and feet. "It is good to see you, sir," Lassiter said, relieved.

"It is good to see you again, too," David said, rubbing his wrists.

"How many are in here?" Lassiter asked him.

"I don't know for sure. I have been blindfolded since we left Moscow. I would guess there are five or six."

"We are down to two," Lassiter said slowly. "I don't know how many of them are left. I think I hit one of them when we came through the door, and Tony may have winged one. We are pinned down with automatic fire from that window."

"That one up there is the leader," David said, motioning with his head to the office. "If we take him out, I am sure the others will give up."

"Rodger is at the door, but I think the one inside is onto him. Steve, can you make out anyone in that back corner?"

"It is too dark," Steve admitted.

"We have three or four bad guys still out there. Let's end this now." Lassiter fished the radio out of his pocket. "Rodger, can you read me?"

"Yes, loud and clear," Rodger whispered.

"Eagle 2 is safe."

"Thank God. What would you like me to do?"

"We will draw his fire while you gain access to the office."

"Copy that," Rodger said, holding his thumb up to Lassiter who was peeking above the hood of the car.

"John, are you ready? I want all the firepower you can muster to be directed at that window."

"I'm ready. Just tell me when."

"Now," Lassiter said, pointing the pistol toward the window and firing.

Steve and John both raised up to their knees and started firing in unison sending a hail of lead into the office. Rodger rushed through the door as the gun fire stopped. He saw the scraggly man holding a detonator in his hand as Rodger leveled the pistol on the man's head.

"It took you long enough to find us," Alexander said with a grin on his face.

"Better late than never," Rodger said. "Drop the detonator, and you will live to see another day."

"I don't think so. This detonator is set to blow your precious vice president to hell," Alexander said with the same shit-eating grin. "You can shoot me, but I will still press the button and we both lose."

"Sir, the office is secure, but the bad guy has a detonator," Rodger said into the radio. "He says it is set to blow Eagle 2." He heard the response in his ear. "I said drop the detonator," Rodger ordered the man again, this time with a smile.

"Your indifference to the situation puzzles me," Alexander said with a puzzled look.

"Let's just say your time on this earth is indeed short."

"Didn't you hear me? I said I will kill the man you are here to save."

"I heard you, shit head. Tell me something before you die, why did you do this?"

Before he had a chance to get an answer, the unmistakable sound of gunfire rang out from below startling them both. The .38 caliber Tony always carried was the last four shots they heard. The pair were at a standoff for what seemed like hours, but was only a little over a minute.

"Rodger, the building is secure. I repeat, the building is secure," Lassiter said into the radio.

"Copy," Rodger said.

"What did you say?" Alexander asked.

"I was just acknowledging to the person on the other end of the radio that I received his last message."

"What was the message?" Alexander asked, looking out the window and then back at Rodger.

"He just said that your friends have all been killed."

Alexander stared at him for a split second, trying to determine if the man was bluffing. He had been outsmarted once by the Americans. He would not be that stupid again.

"You are it. Now, put the detonator down, and come with us."

"Never," Alexander fumed, holding the detonator out in front of him. "I will spend eternity with my friends and your vice president."

Rodger knew the explosives were right outside the window. He decided against shooting the man opting instead get out and save himself. He jumped back through the door and off the second story balcony just as Alexander pressed the button. The loud explosion rocked the entire building, hitting Rodger in mid-air, sending him to the hard concrete in a heap, but he was not hurt.

The explosion demolished the office section. The supports securing the balcony to the ceiling were snapped off the metal beams like a twig. The heavy metal crashed to the floor, bringing the entire office section with it. Lassiter and Steve rushed toward the wreckage to make sure the man was dead. They saw Alexander lying twisted and broken across a shattered desk that sat just underneath the window. There was no need to check for life signs—the body was ripped in half.

Lassiter ran over to Tony who was limping toward him from the rear of the building.

"Are you ok?" Lassiter asked.

"I will be fine. Kevin didn't make it, though," Tony said, looking down at the floor.

"I know, I saw it happen," Lassiter said solemly.

"How is Eagle 2?" Tony asked.

"He is a bit sore, but not hurt."

Tony didn't look up as he turned around and walked out into the fresh air.

Chapter 59

Jennifer had waited as long as she promised. It was very early in the morning for her; she wasn't a morning person, and she was already sitting at her office desk. The meeting with the president was still fresh in her mind as she looked over a few notes from her previous visit. The phone rang, startling her, and she answered it quickly, so it didn't ring any more than once.

"Hello, this is Jennifer Cleary," she said into the speaker.

"Ms. Cleary, Duncan Fitzwater here."

"Yes, Mr. Fitzwater," she said, picking up the handset.

"The president would like to talk to you as soon as possible."

"I can come right over," she told him.

"I will send a driver for you."

"Great, that would save time."

"See you in thirty minutes," he said and hung up.

Jennifer grabbed her tape recorder and notebook as she walked out of her office, elated that she was finally going to get the exclusive that may get her a position with a major network. Before going down to the lobby to wait for the car, she stopped by Cal's office to let him know where she was going—just in case would be looking for her.

"Cal, they actually called me!" she blurted out.

"Wait a sec," he said, looking up from his desk. "Who called you?"

"The White House! They just called and are sending a car for me."

"What are you going to do?"

"I'm going, of course, and listen to what they have to say. This is my chance, Cal, I can feel it."

"What if they press you for your source?"

"You know I wouldn't give up the source. Wish me luck," she said with a giant smile and walked out the door.

"Good luck," he yelled as she rushed out to the elevator.

The car had not yet made it when she reached the lobby so she waited outside on the street. Physically she was ready, but mentally she was a hysterical mess. Her thoughts jumbled together as she fought the demons in her head. She wondered if Bill would be there. She knew he was pissed—but he also got what he wanted. She thought about the story as she paced the sidewalk, but her mind couldn't focus.

A large black sedan pulled up to the curb.

"You Ms. Cleary?" a large man asked, rolling down the passenger window.

"Yes."

"The name is Scott, ma'am. I am your driver."

Jennifer opened the rear door and settled into the large seat.

"I saw the piece you did on Iraq," the driver said over his shoulder as he entered traffic. "That took a lot of guts."

"Thanks," she said, flashing him a smile. "I can say that I am more nervous about meeting with the president than I was on the streets of Baghdad."

Scott chuckled a bit at the comment. "It will all work out, whatever it is. Things always do."

"Let me ask you a question, Scott. Have you ever faced one of the most defining points in your life and not had a clue how to handle it?"

"That's what makes life interesting. If we knew exactly how to deal with every situation with certainty, life would be very boring."

"I suppose that's true."

The gate guard stopped the car and checked Jennifer's ID. He reviewed the visitors list and motioned the guard in the shack to raise the gate. As the car pulled up to the White House, Jennifer scribbled some notes onto a piece of paper.

"Thanks for listening, Scott," she said as she opened the door.

"It was my pleasure. Good luck," he said as the door slammed closed.

Duncan met her outside, and the two walked in together. They didn't speak as they walked the long hallway toward the Oval Office.

"Good morning, Sally," Duncan said, stopping at her desk.

"Good morning, Mr. Fitzwater. Go on in, they are waiting."

"They are waiting?" Jennifer asked him before they entered.

"Yes, you heard correctly."

Duncan opened the door and Jennifer walked in ahead of Duncan. The president was sitting behind his large desk, and she saw Bill Snyder standing behind him, staring out the large window. As she approached the two, David Arthur stood from one of the large wing-back chairs, and her mouth dropped to the floor. He was holding a baby, smiling at Jennifer and Duncan.

"I can see you are surprised, Ms. Cleary," the president said.

"I am a bit, sir. I can see a lot has happened over the past few days."

"I don't know what you are talking about. Have you met David?" the president asked.

"I don't believe I have," she said with a dry mouth.

"Well, let me do the honors. Ms. Jennifer Cleary, this is Mr. David Arthur."

She reached out to take his hand, and he carefully extended his arm so as not to disrupt the sleeping baby.

"It is a pleasure to meet you, sir," she said, averting her eyes.

"The pleasure is all mine," he offered with a large smile. "This is my son, Tyler."

"He is just beautiful, sir."

"Thank you. My wife and I adopted him just a few days ago."

"I am afraid I am a bit confused," she admitted.

"Oh, about what?" the president asked, feigning surprise.

"Well, to be honest, sir, about everything."

"Let me clear things up for you then," the president said, folding his hands in front of him. "But first, Mr. Snyder, do me a favor and come have a seat."

"Of course, sir," Bill said sheepishly, taking one of the chairs next to the vice president.

"Now, as you can see, Ms. Cleary, the vice president is safe and sound along with his baby. I think I can say with the utmost certainty that he has been here since his return from Mexico."

"But, I don't understand," she blurted, feeling like the rug was just pulled out from under her.

"What's not to understand?" the president said with a grin. "I am telling you that David has been here—end of story."

"With all due respect, sir, you told me that he was in Moscow. You—You lied to me."

"Not at all. I told you that you would have a story in three days and a story you will have."

"But, the vice president is here. What is the story?"

"Ahhh, the story. I am going to give you an exclusive, a story that has yet to unfold, but an exclusive nonetheless."

"But it has nothing to do with the trip to Moscow?"

"What trip to Moscow?" the president asked. "No, the story I am going to give you is the forced resignation of my Chief of Staff."

Jennifer immediately looked at Bill who was now standing.

"My resignation?" Bill asked with a rage in his voice.

"You heard me, Mr. Snyder. Your resignation. I have taken the liberty of writing the letter myself. All you need to do is sign it."

"But why?"

"I cannot tolerate traitors in my cabinet, and you, sir, are the highest order of a traitor."

"I am no traitor," Bill screamed, as the veins in his neck started to show.

"You, sir, have divulged information of the highest secrecy to a reporter, in direct violation of my orders."

"I did no such thing," Bill said forcefully.

"Wrong, Mr. Snyder, you did," the president said, tossing an envelope across his desk. "Are you curious as to what is in the envelope?"

Bill snatched the large white envelope from the desk and opened it. Inside were five photographs of him with Jennifer at *Jock's*. He glared at Jennifer as he thumbed through the pictures, his face growing red with embarrassment. The tension in the office was thicker than pea soup. Bill's hands shook with anger as he closed the envelope. At that moment, he stared daggers at Jennifer who was in turn staring back at him.

"Jennifer, would you care to look at those?" the president asked.

"No, I don't care what they are," she said with tears welling in her eyes.

"Why the tears? This is your exclusive story, a chance to be a star."

Embarrassed and beaten, Jennifer turned and walked out of the office in tears. Duncan followed behind her.

"I will call the car for you to take you back," he said.

"No, I don't want to go back. I would like to be taken to my apartment."

"As you wish."

Bill threw the envelope back on the desk. "I was just doing what I thought was best. I wanted to cover all the bases should this get out. My plan would have placed all the blame on the CIA, shielding you from the press."

"Mr. Snyder, thanks to the CIA, we have both David and Tyler back. Now, sign the damn letter and get your ass out of here. Oh, and one more thing. If I catch you talking to the press about this, I will finish you for good."

Snyder picked up the pen on the desk, and with an unsteady hand signed the letter. He said nothing as he turned and left the Oval Office for good.

*

John sat in the back seat of the blue Mercury, looking at the tall oak trees on his street. The car had not even stopped in the driveway as his wife came running out of the house toward him.

"I have been worried sick about you," she said, giving him a kiss.

"I am fine. Actually, I am better than fine," he told her, giving her a bear hug, lifting her off the ground. He closed the car door, and it backed out into the street and sped away.

"What have you been doing?" she asked inquisitively.

"I can't tell you exactly what I was doing, but I have had the time of my life. I have done more in the past few days than I have in years. I feel so alive," he said with a smile.

He put his arm around her shoulder as they walked up to the front porch. Maggie was just inside the door crying to get out—to tell him hello. Georgia opened the door, and Maggie jumped into his arms.

"Hi, sweetie," John said, scratching behind her ears. "Yes, I've missed you, too," he said as he put her down. "Oh, baby, someday I will tell you about it," he said, taking her hands in his and looking deep into her eyes. "I love you, Georgia. I have missed you dearly."

"I love you, too," she said, looking back into his eyes. "You know, you missed your retirement party."

"Oh, that is too bad," he said sarcastically. "Actually, we need to talk about something."

"Oh no, this doesn't sound good at all," she said, squeezing his hands.

"I have spent the last few hours talking with the Director of the CIA, and he wants me to work for him. Baby, I have been offered a job. I can start next week if I want."

"But you need to take some time off for you. You are not as young as you used to be."

"But, Georgia, I feel like I am useful again. I feel like I am making a difference again."

"But, the CIA? What could you possibly do at the CIA?"

"I am going to be working on the project that I started fifty years ago."

"But I thought the project was destroyed decades ago."

"It was, but I am going to bring it back to life," John said as he opened the door and they walked inside.

Printed in the United States
78522LV00005B/1-75